PRAISE FOR

the storyteller

"*The Storyteller* is a fantastic, spellbinding thriller . . . It's about the somewhat anguished love between two young people from worlds that couldn't be more different, and about staying true to someone. It's also about a murder foretold in a fairy tale. The author has written a captivating story, told without sensationalism. This is a book you won't want to put down."
—*Berliner Morgenpost*

"The book is an effective mix of thriller, fairy tale, and love story. At times, a real shocker and unbelievably brutal. At other times, very poetic and romantic. The end is almost unbearable . . . The book is so compellingly written, you can't put it down." —www.lizzynet.de

"*The Storyteller* has the reader hooked from the first line, casting a spell over you, its thrilling plot unfolding bit by bit. To the very end, a gruesome and convincing story of first love, violence, and desperation. In a gripping, emotional, and authentic voice, Antonia Michaelis presents a book that is a love story, teen novel, and thriller all in one. The would-be happy ending has a bitter aftertaste."
—*Bulletin Jugend & Literatur*

the storyteller

ANTONIA MICHAELIS

Translated by Miriam Debbage

AMULET BOOKS · LONDON

Cataloging-in-Publication Data has been applied for and may be obtained from the Library of Congress.

ISBN for this edition: 978-1-4197-0122-1

ABRAMS

THE ART OF BOOKS SINCE 1949
The Market Building
72-82 Rosebery Avenue
London, UK
EC1R 4RW
www.abramsbooks.co.uk

To Anna *K.* and the lighthouse keeper,
whose names I borrowed
To Charlotte R., Bea W., and Fine M.,
who will turn eighteen sooner or later
To Kerstin B., Beate R., and Eva W.,
who were eighteen once
And to all those who never will be

BALLAD FOR THE YOUNG

My child, I know you're not a child
But I still see you running wild
Between those flowering trees.
Your sparkling dreams, your silver laugh
Your wishes to the stars above
Are just my memories.

And in your eyes the ocean
And in your eyes the sea
The waters frozen over
With your longing to be free.

Yesterday you'd awoken
To a world incredibly old.
This is the age you are broken
Or turned into gold.

You had to kill this child, I know,
To break the arrows and the bow
To shed your skin and change.
The trees are flowering no more
There's blood upon the tiled floor
This place is dark and strange.

I see you standing in the storm
Holding the curse of youth
Each of you with your story
Each of you with your truth.

Some words will never be spoken
Some stories never be told.
This is the age you are broken
Or turned into gold.

I didn't say the world was good.
I hoped by now you understood
Why I could never lie.
I didn't promise you a thing.
Don't ask my wintervoice for spring
Just spread your wings and fly.

Though in the hidden garden
Down by the green green lane
The plant of love grows next to
The tree of hate and pain.

So take my tears as a token.
They'll keep you warm in the cold.
This is the age you are broken
Or turned into gold

You've lived too long among us
To leave without a trace
You've lived too short to understand
A thing about this place.

Some of you just sit there smoking
And some are already sold.
This is the age you are broken
Or turned into gold.
This is the age you are broken or turned into gold.

At first
༄

BLOOD.

There is blood everywhere. On his hands, on her hands, on his shirt, on his face, on the tiles, on the small round carpet. The carpet used to be blue; it never will be blue again.

The blood is red. He is kneeling in it. He hadn't realized it was so bright . . . big, burst droplets, the color of poppies. They are beautiful, as beautiful as a spring day in a sunny meadow . . . But the tiles are cold and white as snow, and it is winter.

It will be winter forever.

Strange thought: Why should it be winter forever?

He's got to do something. Something about the blood. A sea—a red, endless sea: crimson waves, carmine froth, splashing color. All these words in his head!

How long has he been kneeling here, with these words in his head? The red is starting to dry, it is forming edges, losing a little of its beauty; the poppies are wilting, yellowing, like words on paper . . .

He closes his eyes. Get a hold of yourself. One thought at a time. What must be done? What first? What is most important?

It's most important that nobody finds out.

Towels. He needs towels. And water. A rag. The splatters on the wall are hard to remove . . . the grout between the tiles will be stained forever. Will anybody find out? Soap. There's dried blood under his fingernails, too. A brush. He scrubs his hands until the skin is red—a different red, a warm, living red flushed with pain.

She's not looking at him. She's turned her eyes away, but she always turned away, didn't she? That's how she lived—with her eyes turned away. He throws the dirty towels into the dark, greedy mouth of the washing machine.

She's just sitting there, leaning against the wall, refusing to speak to him.

He kneels down in front of her, on the clean floor, takes her hands in his. He whispers a question, a single word, "Where?"

And he reads the answer in her cold hands.

Do you remember? The woods? It was spring, and under the beeches, small white flowers were blooming . . . we were walking hand in hand and you asked me the name of the flowers . . . I didn't know . . . the woods. The woods were the only place we had to ourselves, a place just for us . . . back in the only time we had together, just the two of us . . . do you remember, do you remember, do you remember?

"I do," he whispers. "I remember. The woods. Anemones. I know what they're called now. Anemones . . ."

He lifts her up in his arms like a child. She is heavy and light at the same time. His heart is beating in the rhythm of fear as he carries her outside, into the night. Hold onto me so I don't drop you. Hold on, will you? Why won't you help me? Help me! Please . . . just this once!

The cold envelops him like an icy robe; he smells the frost in the air. The ground hasn't frozen yet. He's lucky. A strange thought . . . that he's lucky on this February night. The woods aren't far. They are too far. He looks around. There is no one. No one knows . . . no one will remember what happened tonight.

There aren't any small white flowers blooming in the woods. The ground is muddy and brown, and the gray beeches are bare, leafless. He can't make out the details . . . it is too dark. Just dark enough. There aren't streetlights here. The earth gives way, reluctantly, to the blunt spade. He swears under his breath. She still won't look at him. Propped against a tree, she seems far away in her thoughts. And suddenly, anger wells up in him.

He kneels in front of her for the third time. He shakes her, tries to pull her up, make her stand on her feet; he wants to shout at her, and he does, but only in his head, silently, with his mouth open wide.

You're the most selfish, thoughtless person I've ever known! What you've done is unforgivable. You know what's going to happen, don't you? You knew it all along. But you didn't care. Of course not. All you thought about was yourself and your small, pitiful world. You found a solution for yourself, though not a solution for me . . . for us. You didn't think about us for a second . . . and then he's crying, crying like a child, with his head on her shoulder.

He feels her stroke his hair, her touch light as the breeze. No . . . it is only a branch.

1

Anna
꙰

THE DAY THAT ANNA FOUND THE DOLL WAS THE
first really cold day of winter. A blue day.

The sky was big and clear, like a glass dome over the town. On
her bike, on her way to school, she decided she would ride to the
beach at noon to see if the ocean was frozen at the edges. It would
ice over—if not today, then in a few days.

The ice always came in February.

And she breathed in the winter air with childish anticipation,
pushing her scarf away from her face, slipping her woolen hat off her
dark hair, inhaling the cold until she felt drunk and dizzy.

She wondered which of the many boxes in the attic held her
skates, and if it would snow, and if her skis were sitting in the
basement. And if she could persuade Gitta to get out her heavy old
sled, the one with the red stripe. Gitta would probably say they were
too old, she thought.

My God, Gitta would say, *do you want to make a complete fool of yourself? You're graduating this summer, little lamb.* Anna smiled as she parked her bike at school. Gitta, who was only six months older, always called her "little lamb." But then Gitta behaved like a grown-up—or like someone who believed herself to be grown-up—unlike Anna. Gitta went out dancing on Friday nights. She'd been driving a scooter to school for two years and would trade it in for a car as soon as she had the money.

She wore black; she wore thongs; she slept with boys. *Little lamb, we're almost eighteen . . . we've been old enough for a long, long time . . . shouldn't you think about growing up?*

Gitta was leaning against the school wall now, talking to Hennes and smoking.

Anna joined them, still breathing hard from the ride, her breath forming clouds in the cold air.

"So," Hennes said, smiling, "it looks like you've started smoking after all."

Anna laughed and shook her head, "No. I don't have time to smoke."

"Good for you," Gitta said and put her arm around her friend's slender shoulders. "You start, you can't stop. It's hell, little lamb, remember that."

"No, seriously." Anna laughed. "I don't know when I'd find the time to smoke. There are so many other things to do."

Hennes nodded. "Like school, right?"

"Well," said Anna, "that too." And she knew Hennes didn't get what she meant, but that didn't matter. She couldn't explain to him that she needed to go to the beach to see if the sea had started to freeze. And that she'd been dreaming about Gitta's sled with the red stripe. He wouldn't have understood anyway. Gitta would make a show of not wanting to get the sled out, but then she would, finally. Gitta did understand. And as long as no one was watching, she'd go sledding with Anna and act like a five-year-old. She'd done it last winter . . . and every winter before that. While Hennes and the other kids at school were sitting at home studying.

"Time's up," said Hennes, glancing at his watch. "We should get going." He put out his cigarette, tilted his head back, and blew his red hair off his forehead. Golden, Anna decided. Red-gold. And she thought that Hennes probably practiced blowing hair from his forehead every morning, in front of the mirror. Hennes was perfect. He was tall, slender, athletic, smart; he'd spent his Christmas vacation snowboarding somewhere in Greenland . . . no, probably Norway. He had a "von" of nobility in his last name, a distinction he left out of his signature. That made him even more perfect. There were definitely good reasons for Gitta to hang out smoking with him. Gitta was always falling in love with somebody—and every third time, it was with Hennes.

Anna, however, could not stand the slightly ironic smile that he gave the world. Like the one he was giving now. Right now.

"Should we tell our Polish peddler?" he asked, nodding in the direction of the bike stands, where a figure in a green military jacket was hunched over, a black knit cap pulled low over his face, the plugs of an old Walkman in his ears. The cigarette in his bare hand had almost burned down. Anna wondered if he even noticed. Why hadn't he come over here to share a smoke with Gitta and Hennes?

"Tannatek!" Hennes called out. "Eight o'clock. You coming in with us?"

"Forget about it," said Gitta. "He can't hear you. He's in his own world. Let's go."

She turned to hurry after Hennes as he strode up the stairs to the glass front doors of the school, but Anna held her friend back.

"Listen . . . it's probably a silly question," she began, "but . . ."

"There are only silly questions," Gitta interrupted good-naturedly.

"Please," Anna said seriously, "explain the 'Polish peddler' to me."

Gitta glanced at the figure with the black knit cap. "Him? Nobody can explain him," she said. "Half the school's wondering why he came here in the eleventh grade. Isn't he in your literature class?"

"Explain his *nickname* to me," Anna insisted. "The Polish peddler? Why does everyone call him that?"

"Little lamb." Gitta sighed. "I've really gotta go. Mrs. Siederstädt doesn't like people being late for class. And if you strain that clever little head of yours, you'll guess what our Polish friend sells. I'll give you a hint: it's not roses."

"Dope," Anna said and realized how ridiculous the word sounded when *she* said it. "Are you sure?"

"The whole school knows," Gitta replied. "Of course I'm sure." At the entrance she turned and winked. "His prices have gone up." Then she waved and disappeared through the glass doors.

Anna stayed outside. She felt stupid. She wanted to think about the old sled with the red stripe, but instead she thought "soap bubble." I live in a soap bubble. The whole school knows things I don't. But maybe I don't want to know them. And fine, I'll ride out to the beach by myself, without Gitta. I'm sick of being called "little lamb," because compared to her, I know what I want. It's much more childish to walk around in black clothes believing that they make you look smarter.

✦ ✦ ✦

And then, after sixth period, and a deadly boring biology class, she found the doll.

Later she often wondered what would have happened if she hadn't found it. Nothing, probably. Everything would have stayed as it was. Forever. Anna living inside her soap bubble, a beautiful and stubborn soap bubble. But does anything stay the same when you're almost eighteen? Of course it doesn't.

The older students had their own lounge, a small room cluttered with two old tables, too-small wooden chairs, old sofas, and an even older coffee maker that usually didn't work. Anna was the first to arrive at lunch break. She'd promised to wait there for Bertil, who wanted to copy her notes from their literature class. Bertil was an absentminded-professor type. Too busy thinking great thoughts behind his thick nerdy glasses to pay attention in class. Anna suspected that he lived inside his own soap bubble and that his was fogged up from the inside, like his glasses.

She'd never have found the doll if she hadn't been waiting for Bertil.

She'd never have found the doll if she hadn't taken all her stuff out of her backpack to search for the worksheet . . . and if a pencil hadn't rolled under the sofa in the process . . . and if . . .

She bent down to retrieve the pencil.

And there was the doll.

Lodged in the dust beneath the sofa, it lay among gum wrappers and paperclips. Anna tried to push the sofa away from the wall, but it was too heavy. Beneath its old cushions, it must be made of stone, a marble sofa, a sofa made of black holes of infinite weight. She lay down on the floor, reached out, gripped the doll, pulled it out. And for a moment, she was alone with her prize.

She sat on the floor in front of the sofa, holding the doll in her lap. As Anna looked at her, she seemed to look back. The doll was about as big as Anna's hand, lightweight, made of fabric. Her face, framed by two dark braids, was embroidered with a red mouth, a tiny nose, and two blue eyes. She was wearing a short dress with a faint pattern of blue flowers on a field of white, so pale that the flowers had nearly vanished, like a fading garden eaten up by time. The hem was ragged, as if someone had shortened it or torn a piece from it to use for some other purpose. The hand-stitched eyes were worn. As if they'd seen too much. They looked tired and a little afraid. Anna brushed the dust from the doll's hair with her fingers.

"Where did you come from?" she whispered. "What are you doing in this room? Who lost you here?"

She was still sitting on the floor when a group of students came rushing in, and, for a moment, she had the odd sensation that she should protect the doll from their eyes. Of course it was nonsense. As she stood, she held the doll up. "Does anybody know whose this is?" she asked, so loudly that the doll seemed to start at the sound. "I found it under the sofa. Has anybody lost it there?"

"Hey," Tim said. "That's my favorite doll. Man, I've been searching for her for days!"

"No, stupid, it's mine!" Hennes laughed. "I take her to bed with me every night! Can't sleep without her!"

"Hmm," Nicole said, nodding, "well, there are people who do it with dogs, why not with children's dolls?"

"Lemme see, maybe it's mine," Jörg said, taking the doll from

Anna. "Ah, no, mine had pink panties. And look, this one doesn't have any panties at all . . . very unseemly."

"Give it to me!" someone shouted, and suddenly the doll was flying through the air. As Anna watched them toss the toy around, she laughed about it. Though something inside hurt. She clenched her fists. It was like she was six and this was her doll. Once more, she sensed fear in the worn blue eyes.

"Stop it!" she yelled. "Stop it! Now! She belongs to some little kid and you can't . . . what if she falls apart . . . she belongs to someone! You're behaving like you're in first grade!"

"It's the stress of finals," Tim said apologetically. But he didn't let go of the toy. "See if you can catch her," he challenged, and then he really sounded like he was six. Anna didn't catch the doll when he threw it again. Bertil did.

Bertil with his too-thick glasses. He gave her back to Anna, without saying a word. In silence, she gave him the worksheet he'd wanted to copy. And the others forgot about the doll.

"The janitor," Bertil said gently, before he left. "Maybe the janitor has a child . . . it's possible, isn't it?"

"It's possible," Anna said, smiling. "Thanks."

But as soon as he turned to go, she knew she shouldn't have smiled at him. Behind his glasses, he had pleading puppy-dog eyes, and she knew exactly what their expression meant.

When the others had gone—to their afternoon classes, to the coffeeshop, into town—when the student lounge was empty and quiet, Anna remained, sitting on the sofa, alone, with the doll perched on her knee. Outside, the day was still blue. The frost in the trees glittered like silver. Surely by now the ocean was freezing over.

She looked at the row of trees outside the window. She saw the branches, heavy with ice crystals, wave in the breeze—and then she caught sight of the figure perched on the radiator by the window. She jumped. Had he been there the whole time, sitting motionless?

It was Tannatek, the Polish peddler, and he was staring at her. Anna swallowed. He was still wearing the black knit cap, even indoors. Under his open military parka she could see the logo of Böhse Onkelz, the skinhead rock group, on his black sweatshirt. His eyes were blue.

At the moment, she couldn't remember his Christian name. She was all alone with him. And she was afraid. Her hands gripped the doll.

He cleared his throat. And then he said something surprising. "Be careful with her."

"What?" Anna asked, taken aback.

"You're holding her too tightly. Be careful with her," Tannatek repeated.

Anna let go of the doll, which fell to the floor. Tannatek shook his head. Then he got up, came over to Anna—she froze—and he bent over to retrieve the doll.

"It was me," he said. "I lost her. Understand?"

"No," Anna said honestly.

"Of course not." He looked at the doll for a moment; he was holding it—her—like a living being. He tucked her into his backpack and returned to the radiator. He pulled out a single cigarette, then, obviously remembering that he was not allowed to smoke in the lounge, shrugged and put it back in his bag.

Anna got up from the sofa. "Well," said Anna, her voice still sounding much too timid. "Well, if the doll is really yours . . . then I guess everything's fine. Then I can go now, can't I? No more classes for me anyway, not today."

Tannatek nodded. But Anna didn't go. She stood in the middle of the room as if something kept her there, some invisible bond . . . and this was one of the moments she couldn't explain later on—not to herself or to anyone else. What happened just happened.

She stood there until he had to say something.

"Thank you."

"Thank you for what?" she asked. She wanted an explanation. Any kind of explanation.

"Thank you for finding her," he said and nodded to his backpack, from which the hand of the doll seemed to be waving.

"Well, hmm, oh," said Anna. "I . . ." she tried to produce a laugh, the small, insignificant kind of laugh necessary to rescue a conversation in danger of drying up before it even starts.

"You look as if you were planning to rob a bank," she said, and when he looked puzzled, she continued, "with that hat, I mean."

"It's cold."

"In here?" Anna asked, and managed a smile in place of the insignificant laugh, although she wasn't sure it was convincing.

He was still looking at her. And then he peeled off the hat, very slowly, like a ritual. His hair was blond and tousled. Anna had forgotten it was blond. He'd been wearing the hat for a while—a month? Two? And before that he'd had a thug's buzz cut, but now his hair almost covered his ears.

"The doll, I figured . . . I figured she belonged to a little girl . . . ," Anna began.

He nodded. "She does belong to a little girl." And suddenly he was the one to smile. "What did you think? That she's mine?"

The moment he smiled, Anna remembered his first name. Abel. Abel Tannatek. She'd seen it last year on some list.

"Well, whose is she?" Anna inquired. The great interrogator, Anna Leemann, she thought, who's asking too many questions, who's persistent and nosy.

"I've got a sister," said Abel. "She's six."

"And why . . ." Why are you carrying her doll around with you? And how did you manage to lose her under a sofa in the student lounge, the great interrogator Anna Leemann longed to ask. But then she let it be. Great interrogators aren't especially polite.

"Micha," said Abel. "Her name is Micha. She'll be glad to have her dolly back."

He glanced at his watch, stood up, and slung the backpack over his shoulder.

"I should get going."

"Yeah . . . me too," Anna said quickly.

Side by side, they stepped out into the blue, cold day, and Abel said, "I suppose you don't mind if I put my hat back on again?"

The frost on the trees glittered so brightly now one had to squint, and the puddles in the schoolyard reflected the sun—gleaming, glaring.

Everything had become brighter, almost dangerously bright.

A chatting, giggling group of ninth graders was gathered next to the bike rack. Anna watched as Abel unlocked his bike. She still had so many questions. She had to ask them now, quickly, before this conversation ended. Before Abel Tannatek turned back into the anonymous, hunched figure with the Walkman, back into the Polish peddler, whose nickname others had supplied and that he wore like a protective cover.

"Why didn't you say it was your sister's doll . . . when they were throwing it around?" she asked. "Why did you wait until everyone had left?"

He pulled his bike out backward, from the tangle of other bicycles. He was almost gone, almost somewhere else. Almost back in his own world. "They wouldn't have understood," he said. "And besides, it's nobody's business." Me included, Anna thought. Abel took the ancient Walkman out of the pocket of his old military jacket and untangled the wires. Wait! Anna longed to call.

"Do you really listen to the Onkelz?" she asked, looking at his sweatshirt.

He smiled again. "How old do you think I am? Twelve?"

"But the . . . the sweatshirt . . ."

"Inherited," he said. "It's warm. That's what matters."

He handed her an earplug. "White noise."

Anna heard nothing but a loud rustle. White noise, the sound emitted by a radio without reception.

"It helps keep people away," said Abel as he gently pulled the earplug from her ear and got on his bike. "In case I want to think."

And then he rode away. Anna stood there.

Everything had changed.

White noise.

She didn't ask Gitta for the old sled with the red stripe. She rode out to the beach by herself later, as it was getting dark. The beach at twilight was the best place to get her thoughts in order, to spread them out over the sand like pieces of cloth, to unfold and refold them, again and again.

It wasn't even a proper ocean. It was only a shallow bay, no more than several meters deep, nestled between the shore and the isle of Rügen. Once the water was frozen over, you could reach the island on foot.

Anna stood on the empty beach for a long time, gazing out over the water, which was beginning to get a skin of ice. The surface was so smooth now, it looked like the wooden floor at home, waxed and polished by time.

She thought about her "soap bubble" life. The house Anna and her parents lived in was old, its high-ceilinged rooms from another, more elegant, time. It was in a nice part of town, between other old houses that had been gray and derelict in times of socialism and were now restored and redecorated. Earlier today, when she'd arrived home from school, she had found herself looking at the house differently. It felt as if she were standing beneath its high ceilings with Abel Tannatek by her side. She looked at the huge bookshelves through his eyes, at the comfortable armchairs, the ancient exposed-wood beams in the kitchen, the artwork on the walls—black-and-white, modern. The fireplace in the living room, the winter branches in the elegant vase on the coffee table. Everything was beautiful, beautiful like a picture, untouchable and unreal in its beauty.

With Abel still next to her, she had climbed the wide, wooden staircase in the middle of the living room, up to her room, where a music stand was waiting for her next to the window. She tried to shake Abel Tannatek out of her head: his wool cap, his old military parka, his inherited sweatshirt, the ragged doll. She felt the weight of her flute in her hand. Even her flute was beautiful.

She caught herself trying to blow a different kind of sound from her instrument, a tuneless, atonal sound, something more scratchy and unruly: a white noise.

Outside her window, a single rose was in full winter bloom on the rosebush. It was so alone that it looked unbearably out of place, and Anna had to suppress the desire to pluck it . . .

Now, as she stood on the beach, the air above the sea had turned midnight blue. A fishing boat hung between ocean and sky. Anna smashed the thin layer of ice with the tip of her boot and heard the little cracks and the gurgling of the brine beneath. "He doesn't live in a house like mine," she whispered. "I know that for sure. I don't know how somebody like that lives. Differently."

And then she walked into the water until it seeped into her boot, until the wetness and the cold reached her skin. "I don't know anything!" she shouted at the sea. "Nothing at all!"

About what? asked the sea.

"About the world outside my soap bubble!" Anna cried. "I want to . . . I want . . ." She raised her hands, woolen, red-blue–patterned gloved hands, a gesture of helplessness, and let them drop again.

And the sea laughed, but it wasn't a friendly laugh. It was making fun of her. Do you think *you* could get to know somebody like Tannatek? it asked. Think of the sweatshirt. Are you sure you're not getting involved with a Nazi? Not everyone with a little sister is a nice guy. What is a nice guy, by the way? How do you define that? And does he even have a little sister? Maybe . . .

"Oh, be quiet, will you," Anna said, turning to walk back over the cold sand.

To her left, behind the beach, there was a big forest, deep and black. In spring there would be anemones blooming underneath the tall leafy-green beeches, but it would be a long, long time till then.

2

Abel
෨

"DO YOU THINK YOU COULD ACTUALLY GET TO know somebody like Tannatek?" Gitta asked. "Think of the buzz cut . . ." She pulled up her legs onto the couch; Anna suddenly remembered the times they had used this couch as a trampoline, when they were little. The couch sat in front of a wall made entirely of glass, beyond which lay the beach. Though from here, you couldn't see the sand, you couldn't see the water; half the housing development lay between the house and the sea. Gitta's house, a geometric cube, was modern but of a failed kind of modernity.

Everything about it was too tidy, even the garden. Gitta was almost positive her mother disinfected the leaves of the box hedge when no one was looking.

Gitta didn't get along well with her mother, who worked as a surgeon at the hospital where Anna's father used to work; but he hadn't gotten along with Gitta's mother either and had run away to the less orderly, more comfortable rooms of a private practice.

"Anna?" Gitta said. "What are you thinking about?"

"I was thinking . . . about our parents," Anna said. "And that they are all doctors or whatever."

"Whatever . . ." Gitta snorted as she put out a forbidden cigarette on a saucer. "Exactly. What's that gotta do with Tannatek?"

"Nothing." Anna sighed. "Everything. I was just wondering what his parents do. Where he comes from. Where he lives."

"In one of those concrete tower blocks between here and the city. The Seaside District. I've always thought it was such an ironic name . . . I see him riding there every day." She leaned forward and peered at Anna. Gitta's eyes were blue. Like Abel's, Anna thought, but still different. How many shades of blue are there in this world? In theory, it must be an infinite number . . . "Why d'you wanna know all this stuff?" Gitta asked suspiciously.

"Just . . . so." Anna shrugged.

"Oh, just so. I see," Gitta said. "I'll tell you something, little lamb. You're in love. No need to turn red like that; it happens to everyone. But you've chosen the wrong guy. Don't make yourself crazy. With someone like Tannatek, all you'll get is a relationship based on fucking, and besides, you'll probably catch something nasty. There's nothing in it for you."

"Shut up!" Anna said. There was an edge of anger to her voice that surprised her. "We're not talking about a relationship, or about . . . about *that* . . . Did you ever consider that maybe my worldview is not as limited as yours? That maybe I think about other things besides sex and the next time I'm going to get laid?"

"The next time?" Gitta asked, grinning. "Was there a first? Did I miss something?"

"You're impossible," Anna said, getting up, but Gitta pulled her back down onto the white leather couch, which looked as if it was easy to disinfect. Probably came in handy, Anna thought, considering her daughter's lifestyle.

"Anna," Gitta said. "Calm down. I didn't mean to upset you. I just don't want to see you unhappy. Can't you fall in love with someone else?"

"I am *not* in love," Anna said, "and stop trying to persuade me that I am." She looked out the huge window, across the development and its too-modern houses. If she squinted, she might be able to render the houses invisible and see the ocean beyond. It was a question of sheer determination. And maybe, if she tried really hard, she could discover something about Abel Tannatek. Without Gitta. Why hadn't she just kept her mouth shut? Why did she have to tell Gitta that she'd talked to Abel? Maybe because it had been two days and they hadn't exchanged a single word since then. The soap bubble had closed around Anna again, and the cold wall of silence had closed around Abel. Inside the soap bubble, though, something had changed. There was a sparkle of light. Curiosity.

"Listen, little lamb," Gitta said as she lit a fresh cigarette. Did her life consist of cigarettes? She made Anna nervous fiddling with them, lighting them, putting them out all the time. "I know that you're smarter than I am. All those good grades you get, the music . . . you're thinking about things other people don't think about. And of course it's stupid that I call you little lamb. I know that. But this one time, you really should listen to me. Forget Tannatek. That doll . . . why does he run around with a child's doll? A little sister? Well, I dunno. But maybe you should have looked at that doll more closely. Didn't he say you should be careful with it? Don't you ever read crime novels? I know you're always reading books! I mean, it's none of my business where he gets the stuff he sells, but once he said something about knowing people in Poland. He's gotta bring the stuff over somehow . . ."

"You're saying he's using this doll . . ."

Gitta shrugged. "I'm not saying anything. I'm just thinking aloud. I mean, we're all glad he's there, our Polish peddler. He still has the best products . . . don't look at me like that. I'm no junkie. Not everybody who likes beer is an alcoholic, is she? I just wouldn't believe everything our dry-goods merchant tells you. He's just looking out for himself. But aren't we all?"

"What do you mean?"

Gitta laughed. "I'm not sure. It sounded good though, didn't it? Kind of like philosophy. Anyway, that story about the doll and the little sister is really touching. And the white noise . . . maybe he's a little weird, our Polish friend. But maybe he just invented all that stuff to get your attention. You're good at school. And he definitely needs help if he's going to pass exams. So maybe he invented something to get you interested."

"Right," Anna said. "He's trying to get me interested. By not talking to me. Congratulations on your logic, Gitta."

"But . . . it does make sense!" Gitta lit up the umpteenth cigarette and gestured with it. "He plays hard to get, lets you suffer for a while, and then . . ."

"Stop waving that cigarette around," Anna said, getting up, this time not giving Gitta the chance to pull her back down. "You're going to set your living room on fire."

"I'd love to," Gitta replied. "Unfortunately, it doesn't burn very well."

◆ ◆ ◆

She had to try. She would try. If Abel talked only to the people he sold stuff to, she'd buy something. The thought was daring and new, and she needed another day to pluck up the courage.

A day of watching Abel, first in lit class, in which he never said a word. He was also in her biology class and math. Silent. He fell asleep during the lectures. She wondered what he did at night. She wondered if she really wanted to know.

It was Friday when she finally decided to take the next step. Tannatek was hanging out near the bike rack, near the end, where only a few bicycles were stashed. His hands were deep in his pockets, the earplugs of his Walkman in his ears, the zipper of his military parka closed right up to his chin. Everything about him looked frozen, his whole figure like an ice sculpture in the February cold. He didn't smoke; he just stood there staring at nothing.

The schoolyard was nearly empty. On Fridays most people hurried home. Two guys from eleventh grade came over and spoke to Tannatek. Anna stopped dead in her tracks—standing in the middle of the yard, stupidly, she waited. She felt herself losing heart. She thought she saw Tannatek give something to one of the boys, but she wasn't sure; there were too many jacket sleeves and backpacks in the way to see clearly. She hoped he would say, "Me? You think I'm selling dope? That's a lot of crap!" And the whole thing would turn out to be just another Gitta story.

The boys left, Tannatek turned and watched them go, and somehow Anna's feet carried her over to him.

"Abel," she said.

He started and then looked at her, surprise in his eyes. It was clear no one called him by his first name. The surprise retreated behind the blueness of his gaze, a blue that narrowed as it waited, as if asking: what do you want? He was a lot taller than she was, and his broad, hunched shoulders made her think of the dogs that people kept in the Seaside District. Some of them had old German runes burned into the leather of their collars . . . suddenly, she was afraid of Tannatek again, and the name "Abel" slipped out of her head, made itself small, and crept into a hidden crevice of her brain, out of sight. Ridiculous. Gitta had been right. From a distance, Anna had dreamed up a different Tannatek than the one standing in front of her.

"Anna?" he said.

"Yes," she said. "I . . . I wanted . . . I wanted to ask you . . . ask . . ." Now she had to go through with it. Damn. All the words in her head had been obliterated—by a broad-shouldered, threatening figure. She took a deep breath. "There's gonna be a party at Gitta's place," she said—a white lie. "And we need something to help us . . . celebrate. What exactly do you have?"

"When?" he asked. "When do you need something?"

It didn't work like this. Stupid child, she thought, of course he wasn't carrying around kilos of the stuff; it would have to be delivered later. He was reading her thoughts. "Actually . . . ," he began, "wait. Maybe I've got something for you. Now."

He looked around, reached into the pocket of his parka, and took out a small plastic bag. She leaned forward, expecting some sort of powder; she didn't know much about these things. She had tried Google, but Google Drugs hadn't been invented, a problem that Google would certainly rectify soon . . . He took something out of the milky-white plastic bag with his thumb and forefinger. A blister pack. Anna saw that there were still a couple of blisters left in the bag . . . and they were full of pills. The ones he held out to her now were round and white.

"You said it's for celebrating?" he asked, his voice low. "Like . . . staying awake, dancing, having a good time?"

Anna nodded.

Tannatek nodded, too. "Twenty," he said.

She took a twenty-euro note out of her purse and put away the blister pack quickly. There were ten tablets. The price didn't seem high to her.

"You know how to use that stuff?" Tannatek asked, and it was obvious that he figured she didn't.

"I don't," Anna answered. "But Gitta does."

He nodded again, put the money away, and grabbed the earplugs of his old Walkman.

"White noise?" Anna asked, but by now she didn't really want to continue the conversation; she only asked so that she could tell herself later that she hadn't been too scared to ask. Her heart was racing inside her chest. All she wanted to do was run away—far away from the schoolyard, from Tannatek, the fighting dog, from the white tablets in her purse, far, far away. She longed for the cool silver of her flute in her hands. For a melody. Not for white noise, for a real melody.

She didn't expect Tannatek to hand her one of his hopelessly ancient earplugs again. But he did just that. The whole I'll-try-to-understand-the-Polish-peddler-thereby-turning-into-a-more-interesting-person project suddenly made her nauseous.

What floated through the earplug into her head was not white noise. It was a melody. As if someone had heard Anna's wish. "It's not always white noise," Tannatek said. The melody was as old as the Walkman. No, a lot older. "Suzanne." Anna had known the words by heart since she was small.

She gave the earplug back, perplexed.

"Cohen? You're listening to Leonard Cohen? My mother listens to him."

"Yeah," he said, "so did mine. I don't even know how she got into him. There's no way she understood a word. She didn't speak English. And she was too young for this kind of music."

"Was?" Anna asked. The air had grown colder, just now, about five degrees. "Has she . . . died?"

"Died?" His voice turned hard. "No. Just disappeared. She's been gone for two weeks now. It doesn't make much of a difference anyway. I don't think she'll come back. Micha . . . Micha thinks she will. My sister, she . . ." He stopped, looked up from the ground, and leveled his gaze at her.

"Have I lost my mind? Why am I telling you this?"

"Because I asked?"

"It's too cold," he said as he pulled up the collar of his parka. She stood there while he unlocked his bike. It was just like when they had first spoken—words in the ice-cold air, stolen words, homeless-seeming, between worlds. Later, one could imagine that one hadn't said anything.

"Doesn't anybody else ask?" Anna said.

He shook his head, freed his bike. "Who? There is no one."

"There are a lot of people," Anna said. "Everywhere." She made a wide sweep with her arm, gesturing to the empty schoolyard, the concrete block that was their school, the trees, the world beyond. But there was no one. Abel was right. It was only the two of them,

Anna and him, only they two under the endless, icy sky. It was strangely unsettling. The world would end in five minutes.

Nonsense.

He managed to free his bike. He pulled the black woolen hat down over his ears, nodded—a good-bye nod, maybe, or just a nod to himself, saying, yes, see, there is no one. Then he rode away.

Ridiculous—to follow someone through the outskirts of town on a bicycle on a Friday afternoon. Not inconspicuous either. But Abel didn't glance back, not once. The February wind was too biting. She rode along behind, down Wolgaster Street, a big, straight street leading into and out of town to the southeast, connecting the city with Gitta's sterile housing development; with the beach; with the winter woods full of tall, bare beeches; with the fields behind them; with the world. Wolgaster Street passed by the ugly concrete blocks of the Seaside District and the district of "beautiful woods." The German Democratic Republic had been quite ironic when it came to naming city districts.

Leaving the endless stream of cars behind, Abel crossed the Netto supermarket parking lot and turned through a small chain-link gate, painted dark green and framed by dead winter shrubbery. Once inside, he got off his bike. A chain-link fence surrounded a light-colored building and a playground with a castle made of red, blue, and yellow plastic. On the NO TRESPASSING sign on the gate, the ghost of a black spray-painted swastika skulked. Someone had crossed the nasty image out, but you could still see it.

A school. It was a school, an elementary school. Now, long after the bell had rung to announce the weekend, it was bereft of life and human breath. Anna pushed her bike into the dense shrubbery near the gate, stood beside it, and tried to make herself invisible.

At first, she thought Abel was here on business: Ding-dong—
the Polish peddler calling! The frame of the big modern front door
was made of red plastic; someone had taped a paper snowflake to the
window. An attempt to make things nicer, friendlier: it felt strained
somehow; like forced cheerfulness, it belied the desolation Anna
saw. It made the cold February wind seem harsher.

Anna watched as Abel walked across the empty schoolyard;
she wondered whether there was a limit to desolation or whether
it grew endlessly, infinitely. Desolation with a hundred faces and
more, desolation of a hundred different kinds and more, like the
color blue.

And then something strange happened. The desolation broke.

Abel started running. Somebody was running toward him,
somebody who had been waiting in the shadows. Somebody small
in a worn, pink down jacket. They flew toward each other, the small
and tall figures, with arms outstretched—their feet didn't seem to
touch the ground—they met in the middle. The tall figure lifted up
the small one, spun her around through the winter air, once, twice,
three times in a whirl of light, childish laughter.

"It's true," Anna whispered behind the bush. "Gitta, it is true. He
does have a sister. Micha."

Abel put down the pink child as Anna ducked. He didn't see
her lurking. Talking to Micha, he turned and walked back to his
bicycle. He was laughing. He lifted the little girl up again and
placed her on his bike carrier, said something else, and got on the
bike himself. Anna didn't understand any of his words, but his voice
sounded different than it did at school. Somebody had lit a flame
between the sentences, warmed them with a bright, crackling fire.
Maybe, she thought, he was speaking a different language. Polish.

If Polish burned so brightly, she would learn it. Don't fool yourself, Anna, Gitta said from inside her head. You'd probably learn Serbo-Croatian if it helped you talk to Tannatek. Anna replied angrily: his name is Abel! But then she remembered that Gitta wasn't there and that she'd better hunker down if she didn't want to be spotted by Abel and Micha.

They didn't see her. Abel rode by without looking left or right, and Anna heard him say, "They've got Königsberg-style meatballs today; it's on the menu. You know, the ones in the white sauce with capers."

"Meatballs Königsberg," a high child's voice repeated. "I like meatballs. We could take a trip to Königsberg one day, couldn't we?"

"One day," Abel replied. "But now we're on a trip to the students' dining hall and . . ."

And then they were gone, and Anna couldn't hear any more of what they said. But she understood that it was not a different language that illuminated Abel's sentences, neither Polish nor Serbo-Croatian. It was a child in a pink down jacket, a child with a turquoise schoolbag and two wispy, blond braids, a child who clung to her brother's back with gloveless little hands, red from the cold.

To the commons. We're on a trip to the student dining hall.

The university dining hall was in the city, near the entrance to the pedestrian area. Anna went there from time to time with Gitta. The dining hall was open to the public, had inexpensive cakes, and Gitta was often in love with one of the students.

Anna didn't follow behind Abel. Instead, she took the path along the Ryck, a little river running parallel to Wolgaster Street. There was a broad strip of houses and gardens between the street and the river so you couldn't see from one to the other. She rode as fast as she could, for the route along the Ryck, with all its bends and turns, was longer. The gravel here clung together in small, mean, icy chunks. The thin tires of her bicycle slipped on the frozen puddles, the wind blew in her face, her nose hurt with the cold—yet something inside her was singing. Never had the sky been so high and blue, never had the branches of the trees along the river's edge been so golden. Never had the growing layer of ice on the water sparkled so brightly. She didn't know if this excitement was fueled by her ambition to find out something that nobody else knew. Or by the anticipation of finding out.

The entrance to the dining hall was a chaos of people and bicycles, conversations and phone calls, weekend plans and dates. For a moment Anna was afraid she wouldn't spot Abel in the chaos. But then she saw something pink in the crowd, a small figure spinning through a revolving door. Anna followed. Once inside, she climbed the broad staircase to the first floor, where the food was served. Halfway up she stopped, took her scarf from her backpack, tied it around her head, and felt absolutely ridiculous. *What am I? A stalker?* She took one of the orange plastic trays from the stack and stood in the line of university students waiting for food. It was odd to realize that she'd soon be one of them. After a year off working as an au pair in England, that is. Not that she'd study here—the world was too big to stay in your hometown. A world of unlimited possibility was waiting out there for Anna.

Abel and Micha had already reached the checkout. Anna squeezed past the other students, put something unidentifiable on her plate—something that could be potatoes or could be run-over dog—and hurried to the checkout counter.

She saw Abel tuck a plastic card in his backpack, a white rectangle with light blue print on it. All the students seemed to have them. "Excuse me," she said to the girl behind her, "do I need one of those cards, too?"

"If you pay cash, they'll charge you more," the girl replied. "Are you new? They sell those cards downstairs. You've gotta show them your student ID. It's a five-euro deposit for the card, and you can load it with money in the machine near the stairs and . . ."

"Wait," Anna said. "What if I don't have a student ID?"

The girl shrugged. "Then you'll have to pay full price. You'd better find your ID."

Anna nodded. She wondered where Abel had found his.

Even at full price, the cost of run-over dog wasn't especially high. And so soon Anna was standing at the checkout with her tray, scanning the room for a little girl in a pink down jacket.

She wasn't the only one craning her neck in search of someone; a lot of people seemed to be similarly occupied. The pink jacket had disappeared, and there wasn't a child with thin blond braids anywhere. Anna panicked; she'd lost them forever and she'd never find them . . . she'd never talk to Abel Tannatek again. She couldn't pretend to buy more pills she'd never use. She'd go to England as an au pair and never find out why he was the way he was and who that other Abel was, the one who had tenderly lifted his sister up into the air; she would never . . .

"There are some free tables in the other room," someone next to her said to someone else as two trays moved past her, out the door. Anna followed. There was a second dining room, across the corridor and down the stairs to the right. And on the left, behind a glass wall, right in the middle of the second room, was a pink jacket.

The floor was wet with the traces of winter boots. Anna carefully balanced her tray as she wove through the tables—it wasn't that she was worried for the run-over dog, that was beyond saving—but if she slipped and fell, dog and all, it would definitely draw everybody's attention. The pink jacket was hanging over a chair, and there, at a small table, were Abel and Micha. Anna was lucky; Abel was sitting with his back to her. She sat down at the next table, her back to Abel's.

"What is that?" a student next to her asked as he contemplated her plate with suspicion.

"Dead dog," Anna said, and he laughed and tried to spark a conversation—where was she from, somewhere abroad? Because of the head scarf? Was it her first semester, and did she live on Fleischmann Street, where most students lived, and . . .

"But you said you'd tell me a story today," said a child's voice behind her. "You promised. You haven't told me any stories for . . . for a hundred years. Since Mama went away."

"I had to think," Abel said.

"Hey, are you dreaming? I just asked you something," the student said. Anna looked at him. He was handsome; Gitta would have been interested. But Anna wasn't. She didn't want to talk to him, not now. She didn't want Abel to hear her voice. "I'm . . . I'm not feeling good," she whispered. "I . . . can't talk much. My throat . . . why don't you just go ahead and tell me something about you?"

He was only too happy to oblige. "I haven't been here for long. I was hoping you could tell me something about this town. I'm from Munich; my parents sent me here because I wasn't accepted anywhere else. As soon as I am, I'll transfer . . ."

Anna started eating the dead dog, which was indeed potatoes (dead potatoes), nodded from time to time, and did her best to block out the student and switch to another channel, the Abel-and-Micha channel. For a while there was nothing but white noise in her head, the white noise between channels, and then—then it worked. She stopped hearing the student. She didn't hear the noise in the room, the people eating, laughing, chatting. She heard Abel. Only Abel.

And this was the moment when everything turned inside out. When the story that Anna would take part in truly began. Of course, it had begun earlier, with the doll, with the Walkman, with the little girl waiting in that grim, gray schoolyard. With the wish to understand how many different people Abel Tannatek was.

Anna closed her eyes for a second and fell out of the real world. She fell into the beginning of a fairy tale. Because the Abel sitting here, in the students' dining hall, only a few inches away, amid orange plastic trays and the hum of first-semester conversation, in front of a small girl with blond braids . . . this Abel was a storyteller.

The fairy tale into which Anna fell was as bright and magical as the moment in which he'd spun Micha in his arms. But beneath his words, Anna sensed the darkness that lurked in the shadows, the ancient darkness of fairy tales.

Only later, much later, and too late, would Anna understand that this fairy tale was a deadly one.

They hadn't seen him. None of them. He had disappeared, dissolved in the crowd of students; he had turned invisible behind his orange tray with the white plate and unidentifiable contents.

He smiled at his own invisibility. He smiled at the two of them sitting over there, so close and yet at different tables, back-to-back.

They were here together and didn't know it. How young they were!
He'd been young once, too. Maybe that was the reason he still went
to the dining hall from time to time. It wasn't like back then of
course; it was a different dining hall in a different town, and yet
here he could visit his own memories.

He watched the two at their separate tables as if he were studying
a painting. No, not two. Three. There was a child with Abel, a little
girl. So here he wasn't the school drug dealer; here he was someone
else. And Anna Leemann, with her head scarf, which she thought
would keep people from recognizing her; Anna, too, was a different
Anna. Not the nice, well-bred girl. They were actors performing
roles in a school play. And him? He had a role, too . . .

Some roles were more dangerous than others.

Anna lifted her head and looked in his direction; he hid his face
behind a newspaper like an amateur detective. He'd stay invisible for
a little while longer . . .

3

Micha
☙

"TELL ME ABOUT THE ISLAND," MICHA SAID. "TELL me what it looks like."

"I've told you a hundred times." Abel laughed. "You know exactly what the island looks like."

"I forgot. The last story was so long ago! A thousand years ago! You told me about the island when Mama was still here. Where's she now?"

"I don't know, and I've told you that a hundred times, too. The note she left only said that she had to go away. Suddenly. And that she loves you."

"And you? Didn't she love you, too?"

"The island," Abel said, "is made of nothing but rocks. Or should I say, it *was*? The island *was* made of nothing but rocks. It was the tiniest island anyone can imagine, and it lay far, far out at sea. On the island, there lived a single person, a very small person—and because her favorite place was the cliffs, the very top of the cliffs, where she could look out over the sea—because of that, they called her the cliff queen. Or, actually, it was only she who called herself that, for there was no one else.

"The birds had told her about other islands. They had also told her about the mainland. The mainland, the birds said, was an unimaginably huge island, over which you could wander for weeks on end without ever reaching the shore on the other side. That was something the little cliff queen couldn't picture. To walk around her own island took only three hours, after which you'd be where you started. And so, for the little queen, the mainland remained a faraway, unreal dream. In the evening, she told herself stories about it, about the houses that had a thousand rooms each, and about the stores in which you could get everything you longed for—you had only to lift things down from the shelves. But actually the cliff queen didn't need a thousand rooms, nor did she need stores full of shelves. She was happy on her tiny island. The castle in which she lived had exactly one room, and in this room, there was nothing but a bed. For the little queen's playroom was the island's green meadows and her bathroom was the sea.

"Every morning, she braided her pale blond hair into two thin braids, put on her pink down jacket, and ran out into the wind. Mrs. Margaret, her doll with the flower-patterned dress to whom she could tell everything, lived in the pocket of the down jacket. And in the middle of the island, in a garden of apple and pear trees, a white mare grazed all day long. When she felt like it, the little queen raced across the island on the horse's back, quicker than a storm, and she laughed out loud when the mane of the white mare fluttered in the breeze and her scarf was carried away by the wind. The mare's scarf, of course. The cliff queen didn't need a scarf;

she had a collar made of artificial fur on her pink jacket, but she had knitted a scarf for the white mare. She had learned to knit at school."

"But there isn't anyone living on the island! Did you forget? How can I go to school?"

"Surely there must have been a school," Abel said. "There was exactly one teacher. She was the cliff queen herself, and one headmistress, who was also the cliff queen, and one pupil, who was the cliff queen, too. She had taught herself how to knit, and for the mare's scarf—it was green—she had given herself the best grade possible. And . . ."

"That's silly!" Micha giggled.

"Well, who is the cliff queen, you or me?" Abel asked. "It isn't my fault if you're giving yourself grades! By the way, it was always summer on the island. The little queen was never cold. When she was hungry, the cliff queen plucked apples and pears from the trees, or she fetched her butterfly net and climbed to the top of one of the cliffs to catch a flying fish, which she fried over a fire. She made flour from her field of wheat, and sometimes she baked apple cake for herself and Mrs. Margaret. The cake was decorated with the island's flowers—blue forget-me-nots, violet bellflowers, and red and yellow snapdragons . . ."

"And the tiny white flowers that grow in the woods?" Micha asked. "What's their name—anemones? Were they there, too?"

"No," Abel said. "And now it's time for the story. But, Micha? Do you remember all those other stories I've told you about the little cliff queen? The story about the empress made of froth and the one about the melancholy dragon? The story about the sunken east wind and the giggling whirlpool?"

"Of course, I remember. The cliff queen makes everything turn out okay, doesn't she? She always does."

"Yes," Abel answered. "She does. But this story is different. I don't know if she'll manage this time. I don't know what will happen to her. This story is . . . dangerous. Do you still want to hear it?"

"Of course," Micha said. "I'm brave. You know that. I wasn't scared of the dragon. Even though it wanted to eat me. I solved all its problems, and then it was happy and flew away and . . ."

"Okay . . . if you are sure you're ready to listen, I will tell you the story. It will take some time."

"How long? As long as a movie? As long as reading a book?"

"To be exact . . . till Wednesday, the thirteenth of March. If everything turns out all right, that is." He cleared his throat, because all storytellers clear their throats when their stories are about to get interesting, and began: "One night, the little queen awoke and felt that something was happening outside. Something big and meaningful. She lay motionless in her bed—it was a canopy bed, the canopy being the night sky itself, for there was a big hole in the ceiling above. Usually the little queen saw the stars when she awoke at night. This night, however, the sky was empty. The stars had run away, and she felt a pang of fear in her heart. She felt a different kind of fear than she had with the melancholy dragon or the empress made of froth. And all of a sudden, she understood that her adventures up to now had been nothing but games. But this— whatever it was—was serious.

"She owned two dresses—one nightdress and one day dress— and that being so, she was the person with the most dresses on the island. Now she put the red day dress over the blue nightdress, because if something important happens it's better to wear warm clothes. In the end, she put the down jacket on, too, with Mrs. Margaret sleeping in one of its pockets. Then she pulled up the collar of artificial fur and stepped out into the night. It was very quiet. Not a single bird was singing. Not a single cricket chirping. Not a single branch rustling its leaves. Even the wind had died down. The little queen walked to her pasture, and there the white mare stood, looking as if she had been expecting her. Later, the little queen did not know how she could see the white mare in the starless darkness, but see her she did. If you have known someone your whole life, you can see her in the dark.

"The mare laid her head against the little queen's neck as if trying to console herself. 'Do you feel what's going on?' she asked. 'Do you feel how afraid the trees are? They're going to die. Tonight. And I'm going to die with them. I will never see you again.'

"'But why?' the little queen cried. 'Why should that be so?'

"In that moment, a tremble rolled through the island, and the little queen grabbed onto the white mare so as not to lose her balance. The ground trembled a second time, a dark gurgling noise came from the depths of the earth, a dangerous rumble . . .

"'Take good care of yourself,' the mare said. 'Should you meet a man with a blond mustache, a man who is wearing your name, turn around and run. Have you got that?'

"The little queen shook her head. 'How can a man be wearing my name?'

"A third earthquake made the ground shake, and the first trees fell.

"'It is the island,' the mare said. 'Run, my little queen. Run to the highest cliff. Run quick. The island is sinking.'

"'The island is . . . sinking?' asked the little queen. 'How can an island sink?'

"But the mare just inclined her head, silently.

"'I . . . I will run to the highest cliff,' the little queen said. 'But what about you? Aren't you coming with me?'

"'Run, my little queen,' the mare repeated. 'Run quick.'

"So the little queen ran. She ran as quick as her bare feet would carry her; she ran like the wind, like the storm, like a hurricane. Mrs. Margaret woke up and peeked out of her pocket fearfully. As the little queen reached the bottom of the highest cliff and started climbing up it, the night was torn open and a light came crashing through. The light swept the little queen off her feet, but she kept climbing on her hands and knees, higher and higher on the bare, rocky cliff, and when she arrived at the top, she turned and saw that the light was coming from the island. It rose from the middle like a column of fire, and she covered her face with her hands. All around her, the other cliffs broke; one after the other, she heard the pieces fall into the sea. Her heart was paralyzed with fear. Finally, after an eternity, the earth stopped quivering and the little queen dared to look up again.

"The island had disappeared. Only a few cliffs were left, sticking out of the sea. In the sky, though, there hung the memory of the light that had risen from the middle of the island like a flame. In that nightmare light the little queen saw the sea. And the sea was red with blood.

"It was made of crimson waves, carmine froth, splashing color. It was beautiful, like a field of poppies on a day in spring, though spring was far away. The little queen realized that she was shivering. And in that instant, she understood that winter had come."

♦ ♦ ♦

Anna heard a chair scraping the floor, being drawn back. She blinked. The dining room was nearly empty. Two women in striped coats were wiping down the tables with wet rags and throwing angry looks at those who hadn't yet left. The handsome student was no longer sitting at Anna's table. When had he left? Had she said good-bye to him?

"And then?" she heard Micha ask. "What happened then?"

"Then it was time to go," Abel replied. "You can see they want to close. Is there any space left in your tummy for chocolate milk or an ice cream?"

"Oh yes," Micha said. "I can feel an empty space right here, see . . . there's actually space for ice cream *and* chocolate milk."

"You've got to choose," Abel said, and Anna heard him smile. "Let's go back to the kitchen, shall we?"

Anna got up in a hurry. She wanted to leave the room before Abel saw her face. She put the orange tray with the barely touched potato-dog onto the conveyor belt, where it was sucked into a hole in the wall on two moving rubber strips. Gitta's mother would have liked the tray and the rubber strips—they were probably easy to sterilize.

Anna pulled the head scarf tighter. Then she remembered that she wasn't the one sitting on the edge of a cliff in soaking-wet clothes; it was somebody else, and for the millionth time that day, she felt extremely stupid.

She reached the kitchen without being seen or recognized. Abel and Micha took their time—the kitchen was crowded with people. Anna felt herself becoming almost invisible in the crowd; she dissolved into the anonymous mass of students and pretended to study the party flyers lying on the windowsill. And then she heard Micha's high, childish voice behind her. She let the voice pass and then turned and followed it between glass shelves laden with cake and sandwiches. Suddenly too close to the voice and its owner, she busied herself with the complicated procedure of getting coffee from a machine without flooding the whole place. But somehow she ended up standing at the counter behind Micha and the pink down jacket. Micha stood on tiptoes, pushed a slightly sauce-smeared strand of hair out of her face, and said, "I think I'd like to have hot chocolate. But if you have vanilla ice cream with hot chocolate, I'd take that."

The woman behind the counter straightened her white-and-blue-striped apron and stared at the child blankly. "Excuse me?"

"Um, maybe you have something like vanilla ice cream plus hot chocolate for less money? Like they have at McDonald's. You can buy coffee and a hot dog there for just one euro fifty."

"We're not McDonald's," the aproned woman said. "And we definitely don't sell hot dogs here. So you need to decide what you want, young lady. You're not the only one waiting in line." The tone of her voice was at least as cold as ice cream, but it didn't taste of vanilla. It tasted of scrubbing powder and a white-and-blue-aproned disappointment in life. Around the woman's mouth were wrinkles, carved by bitterness, in which Anna read: You! All of you! You don't know nothing about nothing. You're eating and drinking and wasting your parents' money. Upper-class brats, you haven't worked a day in your educated little lives. Bah. Nobody's ever given *me* anything for free.

But it isn't our fault, Anna wanted to reply. Whose fault is it? Can you explain that to me? I want to understand, to understand so many things . . .

The aproned woman put a white cafeteria cup with pale hot chocolate onto Micha's tray. Obviously the little girl had decided on hot chocolate. Micha nodded, reached out her hand for the straws on the side of the counter, straws surely not meant for hot chocolate—they were the grass thin, brightly colored kind—and took two, a green one and a blue one. "Well, young lady, I'd say one is enough," the aproned woman said, as if those straws were her own personal ones and she had to take special care of them. In reality, there were thousands of straws; Micha could have taken a dozen and nobody would have noticed. The aproned woman now tried to retrieve one of the straws from Micha's grip, but Micha held onto both of them. The struggle took place just above the counter, just above the tray with the cocoa. Anna shut her eyes and heard the cup fall. She opened her eyes again. The floor was covered with hot chocolate and broken pieces of cup.

Micha just stood there, both straws in her hand, looking at the aproned woman with big blue eyes filled with terror. The people in line were shuffling their feet.

The aproned woman lifted her hands. "I don't believe it!" she exclaimed. "How clumsy can you be? Young lady, that cup . . . you're going to have to pay for that cup. Now look what you've done. What a mess! And I'm the one who has to clean it up. You hurry up and pay for that cup now and leave. The hot chocolate and the cup, that's two euro fifty; the cup is one fifty."

When she said that, light rain began to fall from the sweet blue eyes. A small fist—the one without the straws—was held out, and in it, lay a single euro coin. "I only have this," Micha's voice said through the rain.

"Don't tell me you're here by yourself!" Now the aproned woman was nearly shouting. "There must be an adult somewhere who can pay for this!"

"No," Micha said, bravely, fighting against her tears. "Nobody has to pay for me. I'm all alone. On the cliff. All alone."

"Oh my God, would you leave her alone! She's a kid! Just a kid! Don't you have kids?"

Anna looked around for the person who'd said this and realized that it was her. Damn. She'd sworn she wouldn't interfere, wouldn't draw attention to herself, wouldn't give up her invisibility . . .

"I do have children, as a matter of fact," the aproned woman said. "Two, if you must know. But *they* know how to behave."

"Oh sure," Anna said, bitterly; now that she had started she couldn't stop. "And they've never broken a single cup in their lives, and they've never wanted two straws. And you, you're perfect, of course. You never drop anything, right? And this cup, lady, is worth twenty cents at most."

Now it wasn't just the aproned woman who was staring at Anna, mouth open wide, but Micha as well. Anna was swimming on a wave of anger, and, though it felt good, she had an inkling that she'd be sorry in about three seconds. "I'll pay for that hot chocolate and my coffee and another fresh hot chocolate," she said. "And if you'd be kind enough to hand me a dustpan and broom, I'll clean up the mess on the floor. And when you have a chance, you should see if adult ed offers evening classes in friendliness."

"You don't have to shout at me like that," the aproned woman said as she took Anna's money. "I didn't do anything . . ."

Now Anna noticed the other students in line, impatient students with coffee trays and tired eyes, and suddenly felt embarrassed by her outburst. But then two guys behind her started laughing and both reached for the broom at the same time, trying to help her. "You're absolutely right," one of them said. "These people are impossible . . . there's another piece of the cup over there . . ."

"What are you studying?" the other one asked. "I haven't seen you before."

"Gardening, third semester," Anna murmured, and a strange thought popped up in her head. I'm collecting male students. Gitta'd be surprised.

When she finished cleaning up and went to put the pieces of the cup into the trash, someone took the dustpan from her. But it wasn't one of the students she'd been talking to—it was someone in a green military parka.

"Abel?" she asked, sounding as surprised as possible. She looked from Abel to Micha, who stood next to him with her fresh cup of hot chocolate and a broad grin—and back to Abel. "What a small world. Are you . . . is this . . . your sister?"

One of the guys who'd been helping her placed a coffee tray in her hands. "You better take this and go now," he said. "Otherwise, our friend at the counter will totally lose it." Anna smiled a thank-you. Now I'm stuck with one of these students, she thought, and Abel will leave. Maybe that's better anyway . . . but Abel didn't leave.

"You'll get the money back," he said. "Thank you. I didn't see what happened exactly . . ."

"Oh, some stupid thing with the straws," Anna answered. "Forget about the money. You must be . . . Micha?"

Micha nodded.

"Is your doll okay?" Anna asked politely. "She was lost at our school. Underneath a sofa. I found her, accidentally."

"Mrs. Margaret," Micha said. "Yes, I think she's fine. She's at

home now. We're not allowed to bring dolls to school, and anyway
she always wants too much dessert when we come to the dining hall.
Can I keep my euro then, for ice cream?"

"Sure," Anna said.

"No way," Abel shook his head. "You'll give that euro to Anna.
Now." And to Anna he said, "Take it. We're against antiauthoritarian
education here."

"What?" Anna asked, confused, and then they both followed
Micha, who'd worked the small wonder of discovering an empty
table. And Abel asked, "Why are you wearing a head scarf?"

"Oh, this, well, um," Anna said and took it off. "It's . . . uh, kind
of a replacement for a hat I lost and . . . um, it's a long story. So,
um, have you seen Gitta? We were supposed to meet here and she's
fifteen minutes late . . ."

Abel looked around, but of course there was no Gitta. "Hmm,
I guess I'll have to keep waiting," Anna said. "Does Micha have
enough straws for her hot chocolate now?"

"Five. I'll tell her that she shouldn't—"

"Tell her that she can bend them when they're warm," Anna said
quickly. "You can curl them like hair. And make people, too. But I
guess she knows that already." With those words, she sat down at
the next table—even though there was room for her at the table that
Micha had found.

She took a yellow paperback from her backpack: *Faust II*, one
of the books they had to read before finals. As she opened the thin
pages with the tiny letters on them, she thought about a small island
in a blood-red sea. She didn't read *Faust II*. She hadn't really planned
to. Instead, she listened to the conversation at the table behind her,
just as she'd done before. Eventually, Anna thought, her ears would

turn around and slowly migrate to the back of her head. And what would that look like?

"Go on," Micha said. "I will make a cliff with this straw. The island reappeared the next day, didn't it? And the mare was still there and everything, right?"

"No. The little cliff queen sat on her cliff for a long time, shivering in the cold. When dawn broke, the sea was blue once more. But the sun that rose over the sea that day was a cold winter sun, and it didn't warm the little queen.

"'Mrs. Margaret,' the little queen said. 'Maybe we'll die.' Mrs. Margaret said nothing. She always listened but never spoke. 'I don't know what it feels like to die,' the little queen went on. 'Nobody ever explained death to me. Not the birds and not the white mare, either. I think they were afraid to talk about it . . .' At that moment the water next to the cliff stirred. The little cliff queen grew frightened. A dark round head emerged from the waves, a head with whiskers and glittering sea eyes.

"'Who are you?' the little queen asked. 'Are you death?'

"'No,' the something in the sea said, and then he laughed a deep, bass laugh. 'Death is much bigger than I am. I am a sea lion. Or let's say: I am the sea lion. The others swam away so long ago that I don't remember if there were others.'

"'What is a sea lion?' the little cliff queen asked and leaned forward to see the creature better.

"'A sea lion is something that knows the depths,' the sea lion answered. 'Something that can swim for miles on end without getting tired. Something that comes from the sea and always returns to the sea. But these descriptions are useless, for there are many creatures who can swim miles on end without getting tired. What a sea lion really is, a sea lion can never know. The others—they can learn it, but he cannot. You can learn it, maybe, if you stay with me.'

"'But I can't swim miles on end!' the little queen sighed. 'I will drown.'

"'You don't have to swim,' said the sea lion. 'You own a ship. It's been lying in the water waiting for you since you were born; it lies hidden in a secret cove, and I have been watching over it. I saved it last night. I pushed it away from the edge of the cliff with my nose so that it wouldn't be destroyed by the falling rocks. But even I couldn't do anything to save the island or the apple trees or the poor white mare. I will bring you your ship now and show you how to catch the breeze in its white sails. You must trust me, though. We have to reach the mainland before winter comes. On the mainland, you will be safe.'

"'Safe from what?' asked the little queen.

"The sea lion didn't answer. He swam out a little and disappeared around the next cliff and then returned, pushing the little ship with his flippers. It was green like the summer meadows on the sunken island had been; its three white sails were white like the bed covers of the sunken canopy bed; and the rudder was yellow like the pears on the sunken pear trees.

"'Come aboard,' the sea lion said.

"So the little queen jumped onto the ship's deck. Its planks were golden brown like the floor planks of the sunken castle. From the water, the sea lion told her how to raise the sails and steer the ship, and, as the white sails gathered the wind, the ship moved out to sea.

"The little queen stood at the stern with Mrs. Margaret in her arms and watched the last cliffs of the island disappear.

"'I'll never see my island again,' she whispered. 'I'll never lie in the canopy bed and watch the stars again. I'll never ride through a field of summer flowers on the white mare again . . .'

"'There will be other summer flowers on the mainland,' said the sea lion. 'Flowers more beautiful than the ones on your island. There will be other white mares.'

"'But none of them will be my white mare,' the little queen said.

"She wanted to cry, but then she spied another ship just over the horizon. A ship a lot bigger than hers. And suddenly, she shivered, even though her down jacket had dried by now. The big ship was all black, as if it had been cut from construction paper. It had black sails and a black hull, black lines and a black cabin.

"'Those are the hunters,' the sea lion said. 'They hunt by day and by night, in the rain and the wind. Don't turn to look at them too often, little queen.'

"'What is it they want?' the little queen whispered. 'What are they after?'

"'They are after you,' the sea lion replied. 'There is something you should know. Your heart, little queen . . . it's not like other hearts. It's a diamond. Pure and white and big and valuable like no other diamond in the world. Should someone pluck this diamond from your breast, it would shine as brightly as the sun.'

"'But it's not possible to pluck it from my breast, is it?' the little queen asked.

"'No,' the sea lion said. 'Not as long as you are alive.'"

4

In between
ॐ

IT WAS QUIET THEN. OF COURSE, IT WASN'T REALLY
quiet. Dozens of people were talking and laughing, and because they
were young people, they were talking loudly. Plates clinked against
each other; the door of the ladies' room slammed shut; the pages of
books, of notepads, of newspapers were turned. Jackets were put on
or off with a rustle; here someone sneezed; there someone blew his
nose noisily; two people were kissing; and someone had turned up
the volume of his MP3 player too loud.

But still it was quiet. The silence at the table behind Anna
muffled every other noise in this whole lively, chaotic, bustling
student universe. It was the silence of a story ending. It wouldn't
go on here; the period at the end of that last sentence had been
definitive—a well-thought-out cliff-hanger.

Then Micha broke the silence. "She won't die, will she?" she
asked. "She will reach the mainland, right? Do you think she will?
Before it's too late?"

Anna waited for an answer from Abel, but none came. "Tell me!" Micha said with fearful impatience. "What do you think? You listened, too, didn't you!"

Only then did Anna understand that it wasn't Abel Micha had asked. It was her. She thought about acting like she hadn't listened at all and that she didn't know what the little girl was talking about. She thought about it for a split second but realized it was no good. Micha's question was too direct, too innocent, too loud. She turned to look, but not into Micha's face—into Abel's. He'd been sitting with his back to her. Now he turned and he was too close, much too close. The blues of their eyes, his and Micha's, were not the same. His eyes were colder. Their cold was the cold of a deep freezer, an artificial and necessary cold—necessary to keep something functioning. Cold that needed energy. He didn't smile.

"Tell me!" Micha repeated from the other side of the little round table.

"I admit, I was listening," Anna said and tried to smile. "What I'm reading is not especially . . . comprehensible. Besides, Gitta doesn't seem to be coming," she added. "That is why I listened. Was it . . . was it a secret story?"

Micha looked from Anna to Abel, suddenly worried. "Is it a secret story?" she wanted to know.

Abel didn't say anything.

And because something had to be said, Anna said, "No. I don't think she will die, no way. She's going to make it. The sea lion will help her."

"But what can a sea lion do against a huge black ship full of diamond hunters?" Micha asked, not without logic.

"Well, it's a fairy tale, isn't it? Maybe the sea lion can . . . change."

"Change? Into what?"

Anna shook her head. "It's not *my* fairy tale. I can't tell you how it will end. I'm not in it."

She put *Faust II* back in her bag and stood up. "I don't think Gitta's going to make it, and I can't spend all day waiting for her. I need to get going."

Abel got up from his chair as well. "We're also leaving. Micha? Take the empty cup back."

"But not the straws," Micha said and held them up, five brightly colored straws, bent in the heat, twisted into knots, into . . . something.

"I made a sea lion," she said.

Anna nodded. "I see."

They left the cafeteria together, then passed through the revolving door and out into the cold. And Anna kept thinking, he hates the fact that I listened. He hates it. He hates me, maybe. He knows I'm spying on him.

Outside, Abel stood at the top of the steps in front of the dining hall while Micha ran sliding over the frozen puddles—back and forth, back and forth . . .

Anna stood there, too, not knowing what to do. Abel took a pouch of tobacco and some papers out of his pocket and started rolling a cigarette, but he stared at her the whole time, and she couldn't leave with him watching her. It was like leaving in the middle of a conversation.

"You don't smoke, do you?" Abel asked. She shook her head and he lit up.

Micha kept sliding.

"Abel," Anna said, finally. "Abel Saint-Exupéry."

"Yeah, it was a bit too much like Saint-Ex," Abel said, as if he knew Saint-Exupéry personally.

Anna nodded. "Literally. Nearly. 'None of them will be my white mare . . . '"

"The rose in Saint-Exupéry. Of course. I couldn't predict that you'd be listening."

"I didn't come to listen," Anna said and thought, Well, that's the lie of the day. "I . . . had to listen. It . . . is a wonderful story. Where do you get all those words from? All those pictures?"

"From reality," Abel said. "That's all we got."

She realized he wasn't wearing the black hat. The sunlight caught his thick blond hair. He stood straighter than he did in the schoolyard. And suddenly he was near, not physically but mentally. "Literature," Anna began. "Lit class. Not that it's important . . ."

"It is important," he said. "That is why I am in literature class. That is what I want to do. Tell stories. Not only to Micha. Later—I want to . . ." He stopped. "That . . . about Micha . . . it's no one's business. And the stories aren't either."

"Yes," she said. "No. What about Micha?"

Abel contemplated the glowing tip of his cigarette. "That isn't your business either."

"Okay," she said. But she didn't leave.

Abel tossed the half-smoked cigarette to the ground and stomped it out. "What if I tell you that I'm not her brother but her father?" He laughed suddenly. "You can stop calculating . . . Not in the biological sense. I'm taking care of her. There are too many bad things out there. Somebody has to take care of her. You know I miss a lot of classes. Now you know why."

"But . . . your real father . . . ?" Anna asked.

He shook his head. "Haven't seen mine for fifteen years. Micha's got a different father. I don't know where that guy is, but it's possible he'll turn up sooner or later, when he learns that Michelle has disappeared. Our mother. He'll come looking for Micha then. And I know two people who won't be at home."

Anna looked at him, questioningly. "Don't ask," he said. "There are some things you don't want to know." And suddenly he grabbed Anna's arm, hard. "Don't tell anyone at school about Micha," he said. "Not even Gitta. None of those friends of yours. If you tell anyone . . ."

"You don't know me," Anna said. She didn't try to pull her arm free because she knew that that was what he expected. She held still. Her fear of him had drowned in the sea he had invented, with the island and the white mare and the castle with one single room. Strange.

"You have no clue," she repeated. "I don't hang out with those people much. They're not my friends. And . . . Abel? Put the hat back on. You look much more frightening when you're wearing your black hat."

Later, she lay on her bed and looked out the window, down into the backyard garden. The rose was still in bloom.

She had just walked out. She had made the comment about the hat and walked out. She hadn't even said good-bye to Micha; she had behaved like some stupid girl in a chick flick.

But she had been so angry that he thought she was like the others. Of course, she was like the others—a little. Surely everybody was, at eighteen. But how could she avoid telling Gitta . . .

She grabbed the phone off the antique nightstand she had once, on a too-gray day, painted green. She dialed Gitta's number—to get it over with.

"Gitta?" she said. "Remember we were talking about Abel?"

"Who?"

"Tannatek. Abel is his first name . . . whatever. And you said maybe it's not true that he has a little sister and everything was a lie . . ."

Gitta, stuck in the middle of a formula she was trying to understand or at least learn by heart for a physics test, was slow to react. "Yeah . . . I remember," she said finally. "Your fuck buddy."

Anna wasn't going to let Gitta annoy her, not this time. Gitta was ridiculous. She had something to tell Gitta, and she was going to tell it. "You were right," she said. "He doesn't have a sister. It was a lie."

"Excuse me, what? How do you know?"

"Never mind," said Anna. "You were right about something else. You said I was in love with him . . . it's true. Was true. But now I am in love with someone else."

"That's good," Gitta said. "Little lamb, you know I'd love to talk longer, but physics is calling . . ."

"Sure." Anna cut her off and hung up. She covered her face with her hands and sat like that for a while, in self-made darkness. She would have to invent a crush now, for Gitta. But on whom? Bertil, Anna thought. But if Gitta told Bertil, he would be happy about it, and it wouldn't be fair to him. One of the university students maybe. She got up and took her flute from the music stand. When she held it to her ear, just to check, she heard the white noise, like the sound of a radio between channels. She lifted the flute to her lips and played the first notes of "Suzanne" into the white noise, or from the white noise, or entwined with the white noise: "Suzanne takes you down—to her place near the river—you can hear the boats go by—you can spend the night beside her . . ."

What an old song. Where did someone like Abel's mother get a cassette of Leonard Cohen? *Michelle*—he'd called her Michelle. How had Michelle, who didn't speak a word of English, who at most learned Russian at school—like they did back then—how had she come by that particular cassette? And where, Anna wondered all of a sudden, was Michelle?

Anna was standing in front of the glass door leading out to the fading light of the garden when her mother came home. She'd been staring at her own figure reflected in the glass: the outline of her narrow shoulders, her long dark hair—a see-through person full of winter shrubs. People told her she was pretty; grown-ups said it with the approving tone they seemed to reserve for young girls whom they also considered "nice" and "well-bred." Adults were always quick to tell her how much she looked like her mother, and how little like her father. Though Anna thought that on the inside she was much more like him . . . there was this strong, unbreakable will in her to fight for something . . . somewhere . . . but where? For what? And against whom?

She knew that her mother was home only because she heard the key being turned in the lock, very gently. Linda was a gentle person, a quiet person; you could easily overlook her, and she was often overlooked. She was an assistant professor at the university, where she taught literature. She was neither very popular with her students nor very unpopular; they hardly noticed her. They went to her lectures and later only remembered her words, not who had spoken them. Maybe that was the best and purest kind of a lecture. Or the worst.

Linda walked up behind Anna without a sound. But Anna felt her silent, unobtrusive presence. She thought of Abel's words: "If you have known someone your whole life, you can see them in the dark." She smiled involuntarily.

"You're thinking about something," Linda said.

Anna nodded. "I'm always thinking about something."

For a while, they just stood there looking out into the small world of the garden, where a robin was hopping around under the rosebush and pecking at the seeds Anna's father put there for the birds. Magnus loved the birds. Maybe as much as he loved his daughter and his gentle, quiet wife. It was easier for him, Anna thought, to talk to the birds, though. They didn't think about things too much or try to be invisible . . . He would stay in the garden all day if he could. Just to watch the birds.

"Lately I seem to be thinking about everything at the same time," Anna said. "Just now, I thought about Papa and his robins. And about you . . . and me . . . it sounds silly, but it isn't. We . . . we live in a world in which only we exist and . . . other people live in a different world . . . but ours . . . it's so . . . I don't know . . . pretty? Maybe too pretty."

"Too . . . pretty," Linda repeated, confused.

"Do you realize that the light inside this house is always blue?" Anna asked. "It's as if there's a filter—maybe the garden—and when the light passes through the filter, it turns soft and blue before it gets into the house. Or maybe the filter is you . . . or Papa . . ." She turned and looked at her mother and saw that Linda didn't understand. "Have you ever been to the elementary school in the

Seaside District, behind the pasture, near the Netto market? Next to all those concrete tower blocks?"

Linda shook her head. "No, never. Why? I know which school you're talking about, though. I've seen it many times; I've driven past it on Wolgaster Street . . ."

"Exactly." Anna nodded. "That's what I mean. You drive past it. You look at it and think: my, what an ugly block; it should be torn down, like all these blocks should, and then you drive on and forget all about it because in our pretty blue world with the robins and the rosebush that school doesn't exist. But it does. All the concrete blocks do, as do the people living in them and . . ." She fell silent. She couldn't find the right words. Abel had more words in his head, better words—how astonishing that it was Abel Tannatek who had the right words.

"When you got to know Papa," she said, "what was the first thing you thought? The very first thing?"

Linda thought about it for a moment. "It was at a dance for the medical students," she said. "At the end of college. You know the story. Someone had dragged me along; I had even bought a new dress. The dance was horrible. It was noisy; it was full of cigarette smoke—those were the days when you were allowed to smoke just about everywhere . . . you couldn't see anything, really, because of all the smoke. The first thing I thought about your father was that he noticed me. Even with all those people and all that smoke, even though nobody ever notices me . . . he came toward me, a big, slightly too-broad-shouldered man whom I had never seen before . . . and he said he didn't know how to dance and asked if I would like to 'not dance' with him." Her gaze slipped into the past, her gray eyes sliding behind a golden veil, and Anna nodded. But inside, she shook her head. All of this was of little use. A new dress. A dance for the medical students. Linda and Magnus had been living in the same world from the very start.

All weekend long, Anna's thoughts circled back to the blood-red sea and the ship with black sails. The frost on the trees outside looked like a gown made from the feathers of the birds that talked to little girls about the mainland, and the shadows of the bushes in the evening resembled the waves of an endless sea. To distract herself, Anna practiced her flute more than usual, but the flute had a strange new sound to it. She couldn't say if she liked it or if it made her afraid.

On Monday morning, she suffered through two long hours of history class in a suffocating, lightless room in the school's basement, in which Abel Tannatek should have been sitting, too, at the very back of the room, where he would have been asleep . . . had he been there. But he wasn't there. Anna wondered if something was wrong with Micha. She whispered an invented story to Gitta about a student she had met in the dining hall, and Gitta seemed to believe her. "There's just one thing," she said, "that I don't quite get. Why were you at the dining hall all by yourself?"

Anna nearly lied. "I was waiting for you." But then she put her fingers to her lips and gestured toward their indignant history teacher, who treated her students like little kids who would not get cookies at break if they kept whispering.

Abel turned up later, during lit class, looking like he hadn't slept much the night before. He put his head on his arms and fell asleep instantly; Mr. Knaake noticed but didn't say anything. In fact, he never said anything to Abel, as if they had an unspoken agreement not to disturb each other. They hadn't exchanged a word for a year and a half. Anna wondered why Abel showed up for this class just to sleep, but maybe he craved the words, maybe the readings and discussion found their way into his head while he slept . . . Only toward the end of class did it occur to her that he was safe here, without anyone to bother him or anyone to look after. When the bell rang, Abel woke. He didn't once look at Anna.

He stayed back after class, as if waiting for something. Anna took her time in the hallway outside the room, pretending to look for something in her backpack and then untangling a jacket sleeve that hadn't been tangled in the first place. But Abel didn't come out. Then she heard his voice inside the classroom, talking to Knaake. So did their mutually agreed silence apply only in class?

"No," Abel said. "No way."

"You could pay me back later," the deeper voice of Knaake said.

"I don't wanna be like that," Abel replied. "My mother did . . . does things like that, and I'm not going to. Do you understand? I just want your help, not your money. If you could help me find a job . . . anything. You know people . . . people at the university . . . maybe . . . I can do something there . . . in the evenings . . . anything that starts after seven."

"After seven?" Knaake asked. "What's that about?"

"That's my business," Abel answered, and Anna thought, at seven little girls go to bed.

"You're working nights already," Knaake said. "That's why you're sleeping in class. It's okay with me; you can go ahead and sleep. It's fine. But it won't work with the other teachers. And somehow, you've got to get the grades you need in your other classes. You can't make up for everything by doing well in literature."

"I know," Abel replied. "That's why I want to stop working nights and in the evenings instead. At the university . . . aren't there assistant jobs a student can do? Like . . . paperwork . . . copying things . . . you can do that in the evening . . ."

"For those kinds of job, you have to be enrolled."

"I do have a student ID."

"I didn't hear that," Knaake said. "All right, I'll ask around. I promise. But I can't do more than ask. You need to be more flexible. It would be a lot easier to find something in the afternoons." The voices were moving toward the door now, so Anna bent over her backpack again. "I know," she heard Abel say. "If it was possible to work afternoons, I'd have . . ." He fell silent.

"Anna!" Knaake stroked his graying beard in surprise. He looked a bit like an aging walrus in a knitted sweater. "What are you still doing here?"

"I wanted to . . . to discuss the reading list with you," Anna lied. "I . . ." She talked about the reading list for almost fifteen minutes, about which books she might not need to read for the final exams and those she absolutely had to read. As she spoke, she didn't even listen to herself; she didn't care which books she'd read or not before the final exams. There was only one story that really interested her. And it was a fairy tale.

And it wasn't on any list.

During lunch break, it began to snow. It snowed in soft, heavy flakes that fell for a while before anybody noticed them. The sky was full of white snow clouds that pushed cold air down onto the city. Anna sat on the radiator in the student lounge, her hands wrapped around a paper cup full of coffee, trying to warm up. Behind her, the majority of the French class was desperately cramming for a test at two thirty—one of the last before the end of the semester, and before final exams. An oppressive silence filled the room.

Life seemed to consist of collecting points, points that were tallied into your final grade, like dollar bills in a strange game of Monopoly. Anna imagined the points, like snowflakes, falling gently, slowly—yet still so hard to catch.

Out the window, she caught sight of someone padding through the new snow, someone in a military parka and a black knit cap. It was Abel walking over to his bike. Abel took French, just like Gitta. Anna took music instead.. She glanced at her watch. It was two minutes past two. Abel unlocked his bicycle. She put the paper cup down, grabbed her backpack, and slid into her jacket. In seconds she was outside. The snow was slippery under her feet. Nevertheless, she started running.

When she reached him, he was already sitting on his bike and shaking the earplugs of his old Walkman out to untangle the wires—she wanted to snatch those damn earplugs out of his hands. "Where . . ." She had to catch her breath after running. "Where . . . are you planning to go?"

Abel looked at her. "That's my business."

"Sure, right," Anna said, angry. "Everything is your business. But you're supposed to be taking a French test in fifteen minutes." She narrowed her eyes. "Are you running away? From the test?"

"Crap," he said, putting the earplugs into his ears, laying his hands on the handlebars of his bike.

"If you don't take this test, you'll get a zero, and you know it."

"Have you ever thought that maybe there are more important things in life than a checkmark next to your name?"

"Yes," Anna said. "A smiley face. But . . ."

He grinned, though she saw he didn't mean to. "A smiley face, huh."

"What's the matter?"

He took his hands from the handlebars. "I'm not running away from the test. I'll be back. I'll be late, but I'll come back. I'll take half of it."

"What's the matter?"

"Micha," Abel said. "She forgot her key. I just realized it. I found it in my backpack. She put it in there or it just found its way in somehow. She usually walks home from school by herself. I don't want her to wait outside all afternoon . . . people have seen her father around lately, and I don't want . . . do you understand? And now just forget about it. Tell that friend of yours that I'm sick."

Anna put out her hand. "I'm not telling 'that friend of mine' anything. Give me the key."

"Excuse me?"

"Give me the key. I'll go. I'll only miss a regular music class. No test."

He laughed, shaking his head. "Anna Leemann, do you really think I would give you the key to our place?"

"I believe," she said, "that you've got seven minutes before the French test starts. And that you need all the time you can get to pass it. I don't eat little children. Or at least, not often. Give me the key."

It wouldn't work. He'd just tell her that she was completely crazy. Of course, he would. She knew it. He said, "You're completely crazy." Then he got off his bike.

"Six minutes until the test," Anna said. "Run."

Abel gave her the ring with the key. She closed her fingers around it.

"Take my bike. Do you know the Aldi supermarket in the Seaside District? We live on Amundsen Street. It's just behind it. Number 18. The entrance is in a huge backyard; you have to walk between the concrete blocks, behind the parking lot."

"I think I can manage to read the numbers on the doors." Anna smiled. "Which school does she go to?" she asked slyly. "I mean . . . what if she realized she hasn't got the key and is waiting at school, because she thinks maybe you'll come get her or . . ."

He frowned. "Maybe you're right. You know that school near the old stadium? Behind the Netto market? You have to make the turn across from the gas station on Wolgaster Street. She'll be somewhere between her school and number 18 Amundsen Street. Just give her the key; she'll manage the rest by herself."

"Hurry up," Anna said. She saw him walk across the white layer of snow that had fallen on the schoolyard. When she was already perched on the too-high seat of his bike, he turned. He shouted something she didn't understand. Maybe it was "Thank you."

Neither Anna nor Abel saw Bertil. He was standing at the window of the student lounge, watching them.

Anna went to Micha's school first. She wondered how she'd explain her absence from music class. Magnus would write something for her. I mean, he was a doctor, wasn't he? But how would she explain to Magnus why she had to miss class?

The supermarket parking lot and the elementary school looked different in the snow—cleaner, friendlier, and more peaceful somehow. A lot of small children were running around in the schoolyard, throwing snowballs at each other. Nobody was in a hurry to go home. Anna looked around, searching for a pink down jacket with an artificial fur collar, but she didn't see one. She spotted a young woman with curly blond hair, who looked as if she might be a teacher, and made her way toward her, through the screaming, laughing, snowball-throwing children in their bright-colored winter clothes.

"Excuse me," she began. "I'm looking for Micha . . . Micha Tannatek. Her brother sent me to pick her up. She forgot her key."

"Oh, Micha," the young woman said. "Yeah, Micha's in my class. Does she have to walk home alone?"

That's none of your business, Anna wanted to say. Abel would have said that. She didn't.

"Most days," she answered. "Except Fridays."

The young woman nodded. "Are you her sister?"

"No," said Anna. "Her cousin. Has she left already?"

"Yeah. Yeah, she has," the woman said thoughtfully, and Anna felt that the teacher had as many questions as she did. "She said she has to go out to the village of Wieck," the teacher said. "To where the Ryck flows into the sea and all the ships are moored. *Has to.* So serious. She told me that she has to look at the ships. Today she was going on and on about ships in class . . . there was a green ship with yellow sails that she talked about."

"Rudder," Anna corrected. "With a yellow rudder. Thank you. Then I'd better go and see if I can find her in Wieck."

"Well, you might meet her uncle out there," the teacher said. Uncle, Anna thought. "He was hoping to find her today, too."

Without bothering to reply, Anna ran back to Abel's bike and pedaled away as fast as she could.

◆ ◆ ◆

Gitta was swearing between clenched teeth. She wasn't doing well on this test. The French sentences formed knots in her head, knots she couldn't untangle, as the deeper meanings behind the words escaped her. She'd screw up this test, she knew it. She hadn't the foggiest idea what she was doing—and, come to think of it, why she was even bothering.

She looked up, looked for a crown of red hair among the other heads, bent over their tests. When she found it, she smiled. God, she really had better things to think about than French essays. These fucking tests. She needed a cigarette. Hennes was writing; he didn't lift his head. If she kept staring at him long enough, she thought, staring at him in a certain way, he'd notice, he'd feel his body getting warmer. All she had to do was concentrate . . . But it wasn't Hennes who looked up a little later. It was someone sitting at the table next to him. Tannatek. He'd almost come too late to take the test; he'd sat down at the very last minute and been scribbling away frantically ever since. But now he stopped writing. He looked at her. His eyes were extremely blue. It wasn't a pleasant kind of blue. Too icy.

Gitta narrowed her eyes and held his gaze. She thought of Anna, of Anna's words: tell me about the Polish peddler . . .

It was as if they were having a conversation with their eyes, in the middle of a French test, in complete silence.

I'm not blind, you know, Gitta said. I mean, I don't know exactly what is going on between you two . . . Anna and you . . . I don't know what you hope to get out of it. But you do expect something, don't you? You're using her; you need her to accomplish something or you would never have talked to her.

Leave me alone, Abel said.

You leave Anna alone. She lives in her own world. Sometimes I envy her . . . she's not like us; she's different. So . . . so fragile, so easy to hurt. Keep your hands off her.

Excuse me? Have you lost it completely now? I don't even know her.

And *she* doesn't know *you*. That's the point.

What do you mean?

Gitta sighed. I told you. I'm not blind. I know a few things I'm definitely not gonna tell Anna.

He lowered his head again, looked at his test; he'd ended the conversation. Had he really read what her eyes had said to him?

After the test, she stood in the schoolyard with Hennes and the others, smoking. Hennes's red hair tickled her neck when he bent forward and reached past her to lend his lighter to someone. Oh, come on, why did she keep worrying about Anna? Hadn't Anna told her that she had a crush on a university student? Everything was all right.

"Hey," Hennes said in a low voice, "whose bike is our Polish peddler getting onto?"

"That's Anna's bike," Gitta replied in the same low voice. And, in a whisper, just to herself, added, "A student? You don't say, little lamb." She crushed the half-smoked cigarette in a sudden burst of anger. "Shit," she said, a little too loudly. "This isn't going to end well."

"Excuse me?" Hennes asked.

"Oh, nothing," Gitta said lightly and laughed. "The test. The final exams. Anything. What ends well in life? You got another smoke for me?"

5

Rainer

❧

IN SUMMERTIME, SHIPS WERE PACKED TIGHTLY IN
Wieck, where the Ryck met the sea, and the harbor was crowded
with sailors and tourists. Now, in February, the village and harbor
were nearly empty. Only fishing boats were left. The fish caught
here were sold in Hamburg or Denmark, and the fish sold in the
store a block behind the harbor came mainly from the Netherlands,
delivered by trucks in the night: there seemed to be a global fish
exchange.

Little red flags on poles, markers for the fishing nets, were leaning
against the boats in stacks now, the flags waving tiredly behind the
falling snow. The railing of the old drawbridge was freshly painted
with the white of the snow. On the bank of the river where Anna
stood there was a path leading to the village of Eldena. It wound
past the housing development where Gitta lived, in the house with
the glass wall through which she couldn't see the sea.

Anna leaned Abel's bike against the fence outside a sleepy-looking restaurant, a place caught in a limbo between open and closed. She followed the river, past fishing boats, looking for a pink down jacket. And then she saw it. Micha appeared from behind a pile of plastic boxes used to ship fish, stood there for a moment, apparently not sure what to do. It took Anna a while to figure out what the little girl was looking at: a sailboat, a single leftover pleasure craft still docked among the fishing boats. It was big and a bit clumsy looking. And dark green. Micha shook the braids so they fell down her back, and seemed to be talking to someone on board, to be calling out to someone . . . she was too far away for Anna to hear what she said. When the little girl stepped onto the rickety gangplank that connected the boat to the dock, Anna started running. She skidded and fell—snow on fish scales is a slippery combination, snow on dirt is, too, and there was snow in her eyes as well—got up, and ran on.

Something was wrong. Abel hadn't mentioned anything about Micha boarding a dark green ship. The dark green ship belonged to the fairy tale, not to the harbor of Wieck. For several seconds, Anna feared the mysterious craft would cast off and sail down the broad part of the river, right before her eyes—out to the slowly freezing sea, into a wall of snow—and that she would never see Micha again.

The ship didn't go anywhere, though. Anna stopped next to it. There was nobody to be seen on deck now, but she heard voices from inside the cabin. Micha's voice and the voice of an adult. The cold carried the voices to Anna, the words clearly distinguishable now, as clear as if they'd been written on paper.

"It doesn't have a yellow rudder?" Micha asked.

"No," said the adult voice—a man's voice. "Should it have a yellow rudder?"

"I think so. Abel said it would. Is the ship yours? All yours?"

"Yes, it is," the man answered. "But if you want, it can also be yours. We could take a sailing trip on it together. This summer . . . if you like ships, that is."

"Oh, I absolutely like ships," Micha replied. "I just don't know if Abel will let me. In my fairy tale, I have a ship, you know, and it nearly looks like this one. But only nearly. You don't have a . . . a sea lion here?"

"A sea lion? No. None that I know of . . ."

"Abel said, on the green ship, there is a sea lion. Or swimming next to it. He fetched it. The ship. Or did he build it? I don't remember."

"Abel seems to say a lot," the man said.

"Yes," said Micha, and she sounded proud. "He's my brother."

"I know, Micha." The man sighed. "I know."

"You know?" Micha asked. "Who told you? And how come you know my name?"

"I've been waiting for you," the man replied. "I've been waiting for a long, long time. I knew you would find me one day. Maybe you really can come sailing with me this summer. I have been very lonely without you."

In his voice, there was the sadness of all the lonely men of the earth. Anna didn't like the taste of this sadness. There was too much cunning in it. She walked a few steps farther. The man was sitting at the stern. Micha stood beside him in her pink jacket, looking at him with big eyes, not really understanding what he meant. Anna could see that Micha felt sorry for a stranger. She was the kind of little girl who would take pity on a lonely man. She was the cliff queen, after all. She had healed the melancholy dragon.

"You don't know who I am, do you?" The sadness in the man's

voice moved back and forth, deep and low, like a swing hung from a very high branch of a beech tree. Or—a rope. The sadness was faked, Anna thought. Definitely.

"No," Micha said. "Who are you?"

"Oh, Micha," the man said. "My little Micha." He pulled up the sleeve of his jacket, and Anna could see that there was a tattoo on his bicep.

"But . . . that's my name!"

The man pulled her gently, onto his knees, onto the swing of sadness. "Of course that is your name," he said. "I am Rainer. Do you know who Rainer is? Rainer Lierski?"

"I've heard that name before," Micha answered. "Who is that again?"

"Your father, Micha. I am your father. I wasn't allowed to see you for a very, very long time. They forbid me to. Your mother and . . . Abel. He hates me. I don't know why. Your mother . . . she's gone, isn't she?"

Micha nodded her head. "She's on a trip. But she'll be back soon."

"Until she comes back you could live with me," the man said. "I have a nice, big apartment. You'd have your own room there, a nice, big room with tall windows that let in lots of light . . . The apartment seems very empty at the moment. It's sad to live in an empty place all by yourself, you know."

Micha stood up. "No thank you," she said politely. "I'd rather stay with Abel. Abel hasn't gone away, you see, and he won't, not ever, not without me. Promise not to tell my mother, but I love Abel best. Can I . . . can I go on a sailing trip with you, without having to move?"

"Sure," the man said. "I'd be happy to have you along. But you still have to think about the nice, big apartment. I happen to know your apartment. It's really tiny. I lived there once, you know. Only for two years. But you wouldn't remember that. You're going there now? Home? Do you want me to come with you?"

"I can find the way myself, thank you," Micha said. "But . . . could I have a look at your ship before I go? Like . . . could I see what the cabin looks like from the inside? I've never been in the cabin of a ship."

"Certainly," the man said, getting up and putting an arm around Micha. That was enough. Maybe Anna had misjudged him; after all, it wasn't his fault that he had a name like Rainer. Maybe she was sticking her nose into something that had nothing to do with her— but just the same, she didn't like this guy. Everything about him seemed artificial, fake, creepy: his badly tailored jeans, his sneakers, his sweater beneath his thickly padded winter vest, even his hat. Through and through, Rainer Lierski seemed to be from a sale at Aldi. Anna doubted he owned the boat. Anybody can board a ship, especially in winter when no one's around.

He was a liar.

"Micha!" she called out. "Micha!"

Micha looked up, and Rainer looked up, too. In his eyes, there was something like anger at being caught. His arm was still around Micha's shoulders. "Who is this?" he asked.

"Oh, that is Anna." Micha sounded as if it was the most natural thing in the world that Anna was here, as if she'd known Anna for years, which made Anna hurt with a strange pain from deep inside.

"You forgot your key!" she said. "I've got it with me! I'll explain it to you later. Come on! It's cold!"

"I just wanna look at the cabin!" Micha said. "I'll come after that!"

"No!" Anna almost shouted. "You're coming now. Right now." She put as much authority into her voice as she could muster. It wasn't enough.

"In a minute!" Micha said.

"Now!"

"It won't take long, I promise!"

Rainer Lierski looked around as if someone might be watching them. Then he stepped forward to the dark green railing. "Anna," he said. "So you are Anna. And who is this Anna who thinks she can tell my daughter what to do? Who are you?"

Anna cleared her throat. Who was she? A girl inside a bubble. The daughter of Magnus and Linda Leemann, from a nice district of Greifswald, from a house of blue air. High school student in her last year, musician, English au pair to be. Gitta's squeaky-clean little lamb. No. She was someone who didn't know yet who she was or would be. She cleared her throat again. Rainer in his cheap, ugly sweater from the Aldi sale frightened her more than Abel did. Micha had slipped away from him, but he pulled her back with his long arm and pressed her against his side. "She is my daughter," he repeated.

"No," Anna said. "No, she isn't. Maybe . . . maybe in a biological sense."

Rainer snorted. Micha looked from Anna to him and back again, uncertain. "And I don't believe," Anna challenged, "that this is your ship."

"Of course it is," Rainer said in a low, sharp voice, and his tone confirmed Anna's suspicions. "Abel sent you, didn't he? You can tell him that I know about Michelle. She isn't coming back, that one. Gone for good. Run away. I'll take care of my daughter like every father should. And if he wants to hear that from me in person, he can come himself."

His arm was still bared, and Anna saw him flex his muscles under his tattoo. And then she knew. She knew what it was she had to say. She found the ace up her sleeve.

"Micha," she said, "do you remember what the white mare told you? Before the island sank?"

She saw Rainer's expression glide into incomprehension. "What the fuck are you talking about?" he asked angrily. "What is this? Some kind of stupid code?"

"The white mare?" Micha asked. "She said I'd die . . . oh, that part was horrible . . . and that I must run fast, to the highest cliff . . . and if I meet a man who's wearing my name . . ."

Anna pointed to Rainer's bicep. The word "Micha" was tattooed across it in big, dark blue letters. Micha understood. For someone who was only six years old, she understood quickly.

"I . . . gotta go now," she said and pulled free from Rainer a second time, this time for good. "I'll look at the cabin another day. Good-bye."

"Wait!" Rainer shouted, but Micha was racing along the deck, quick as a weasel; she bounded out of the ship like a small rubber ball, and took the hand Anna held out to her.

"Let's run together," Anna said. "Whoever gets to the bridge first wins. One, two . . ."

And then they ran. Anna let Micha win. She didn't turned around until they had reached the drawbridge. Rainer wasn't following them.

"Anna?" Micha asked, trying to catch her breath. "Is it true? Did Abel send you?"

"Yes," Anna said. "He lent me his bike. And you shouldn't believe a word of what that man said, do you hear me? Michelle . . . your mother . . . she will be back soon, I'm sure of it. I know it, because . . . because Abel told me. I'll take you home."

"But the ship," Micha said, already perched on the carrier of the bike. "Anna, the ship . . . it was nice, wasn't it? And, actually, he was nice, too. Maybe he would have given me candy, down there in the cabin. He looked like someone who would have candy."

"Exactly," Anna said, shivering. "That's what he looked like."

Secretly she wondered if Michelle would come back. Abel didn't think so. Rainer didn't think so. Did they know more about Michelle's whereabouts than they cared to admit?

Anna could have just dropped off Micha at the right tower block. Given her the key. Waved good-bye. Gone back to school for the second half of music class. Or gone home. She could have said, "Don't let anybody in" and "Abel will be here in a moment," or a thousand other things.

Instead, she said, "Is it okay if I come up with you and make lunch?"

The blocks with entrances 18, 19, and 20 were on one side of a huge courtyard, where dead grass had turned to winter mud. Anna felt hundreds of pairs of eyes watching her through hundreds of curtained windows around the courtyard as she waited for Micha to answer. Hundreds of pairs of eyes and hundreds of minds wondering what she was doing here, where she so obviously didn't belong.

"Can you do that?" Micha asked. "Make lunch?"

Anna laughed. "I am guessing you have something I can make lunch with, right? It can't be too hard."

Micha frowned as she unlocked the main door of tower number 18. "Mama couldn't . . . she couldn't make lunch. She always forgot, anyway; or she had other things to do or other places to go." Then she added hastily, "But she was nice. She should come back."

"She'll come back," Anna said softly. "Definitely. Just not today."

The staircase was dark and narrow, the concrete steps old and gray and full of muddy footprints. The banister didn't look like anything anyone should touch. Micha didn't touch it. There was no elevator—seven floors without an elevator! Good exercise, Anna thought sarcastically, cheaper than a gym.

Micha and Abel lived on the fourth floor. There were windows in the staircase; on the second floor, the window had broken—or been broken by somebody. On the fourth floor, there was a dead potted palm on the windowsill, the kind of houseplant that doesn't belong to anybody in particular, a stray plant, so to speak, dead of thirst in the end without anybody noticing. When Anna passed the plant, a door downstairs opened, and someone called up, "Micha? Is that you?"

"Yeah, it's me!" Micha called back, and to Anna, in a low voice, she said, "That's Mrs. Ketow. I don't like her. She has three little kids . . . they're not really her kids. They're always crying and screaming, and then she starts screaming, too, and it's very loud in her place."

"Your mother come back?" Mrs. Ketow bellowed.

A fat arm in a striped tracksuit top, draped across the banister on the ground floor, was all that Anna saw of Mrs. Ketow.

"No," Micha said. "This is Anna."

"And who is Anna?" Mrs. Ketow shouted. "Is she taking care of you now?"

Micha didn't answer. She hurried and unlocked the door of the apartment. Anna followed behind her and stepped into the odor of old damp carpets and ancient gas heating.

"You have to put your shoes here," Micha said. "See that picture? I made that. That one, too." The wall was covered with her artwork. Micha could draw apple trees but not horses. She could draw houses with only one room but not canopy beds. She could do sea lions but not men. "This one here in the kitchen, I just drew it yesterday," she said proudly, pulling Anna into a room that wasn't much bigger than a bathroom. Above the gas stove, there was a picture of some kind of round thing with a lot of confusing pencil lines inside, lines that didn't seem to know where they wanted to go.

"That's the diamond," Micha explained. "The heart, remember? The heart of the little cliff queen."

The kitchen was tidy, yet it made Anna sad. There was the same desolateness she felt in Micha's schoolyard on Friday, after everyone had gone home. The pictures, obvious attempts to overcome the bleakness, only served to emphasize it. The thin veneer of the cupboards on the wall was peeling at the edges, exposing the bare chipboard beneath. A handful of faded photos were stuck to the door of the wheezing fridge. They couldn't possibly be as old as they looked. Anna glanced at a picture of a boy, probably about twelve years old, holding a small girl in his arms, stubbornly looking away from the camera. There were more pictures of the girl, on a playground, as a pink-clad baby in a carrier, standing in line with some other kids from a kindergarten group. There were no photos of their mother. Anna turned away. She located flour and eggs and a pan; she found sugar and oil. She ended up making pancakes on the gas stove while Micha sat on top of the counter watching her. Legs pulled up and back bent, she was perfectly formed to fit under the overhanging cupboard.

"Abel," she said, "always flips them in the air."

"And today," Anna said, "he nearly missed a test. But I didn't let him."

"Those will get burned," Micha cautioned, leaning forward. "Doesn't matter, though. When I'm alone, I eat bread and butter. Anna, I'm still thinking about Rainer. Is he really my father or isn't he? 'Biological,' you said. What's that mean?"

"That means . . ." Anna scraped the blackened pancake off the pan, "that your mother and he . . ."

"I see," Micha said. "That he fucked her?" Then she quickly put her finger to her lips. "Don't tell Abel I said that word," she whispered. "He pretends that I don't know it."

"Do you know what it means?" Anna asked.

"Well . . . not really."

"You'll learn eventually," Anna said. "Someday. When I learn how to make proper pancakes. If I ever do. Do you have jam?"

"Strawberry," Micha offered.

They sat in the living room, which was as tidy and dreary as the kitchen, at a tiny, dark table, on a gray corduroy couch leftover from the sixties or seventies, probably scavenged. Next to the couch there was a huge old TV. The wallpaper was bubbling. The pattern of mustard-colored flowers was typical of the German Democratic Republic. Probably worth something by now, Anna thought, if you could get it down in one piece.

The strawberry jam was 110 percent chemicals and 2 percent

artificial sweetener. Micha ate three pancakes, black edges and all, and, in the process, managed to distribute the jam over most of her grinning face. "You can make those more often," she said approvingly.

Anna smiled. "If you want me to." And she thought of Linda's pancakes at home, in the blue air, beneath the old wooden beams: pancakes served with salmon and crème fraîche and a flowering branch from the garden on the table and Mahler's symphonies on the old record player, which stood on the antique chest with its colored knobs. She balled up the blue universe and its flowering branches and Mahler symphonies and swallowed it with the last bite of burned Anna pancake. And suddenly, there was a lump in her throat so big she barely could breathe.

"You look so sad," Micha said. "Is something wrong?"

"N-n-no. I just thought of something sad, that's all."

"Oh," Micha said. "I sometimes think of something sad, too. I know something to bistract you."

"Do you mean . . . *dis*tract me?"

"I think that's what I mean." Micha leaned forward and whispered secretively, "Do you want to know what happens in the fairy tale with the little cliff queen?"

"I do," Anna answered.

Micha nodded. "Me, too. He didn't tell me anything last night. He told me he's got to think it up first. But I know he wrote something down. I think I know where he keeps the paper. We could take a peek, what do you think?"

"Maybe," Anna whispered.

So Micha got up and ran to the back of the apartment. Anna washed the plates while Micha searched for the secret pages. She also did the dishes stacked next to the sink. The water wasn't draining properly—the sink was blocked. Anna recognized the pattern on the light, cheap cutlery, another relic, like the wallpaper, from DDR times. She wondered how old Michelle had been then. *Had been?* Had she really thought that?

"Got them!" Micha exclaimed in triumph from the hallway, where she stood like Joan of Arc, holding a few white sheets triumphantly above her head—her own tricolor. Anna smiled. "Come to my room with me," Joan of Arc commanded. Anna felt honored. Micha led her into a small room almost completely filled by a loft bed. Under the bed was a makeshift desk: a piece of chipboard over two sawhorses. There was no window.

"Abel built the bed," Micha explained. "Come on. There's room for the two of us; there's room for Abel and me, too. Be careful . . . the third step is a little loose . . ." She handed Anna two sheets of paper, both of which were covered with tiny handwriting. "You read. Mrs. Margaret and me, we'll listen. She's in the story, too, remember? That's why she wants to know what happens . . ."

"Of course," Anna said. "I remember."

"The green ship with the yellow rudder sailed northwest for three days. The wind pushed it steadily forward; the little cliff queen stood at the bow, holding Mrs. Margaret, whose blue dress with the white flowers on it fluttered in the wind. Sometimes the sea was clear for hours, like blue glass, and then they could see far into the deep, where there were violet jellyfish with silver patterns and long ruby-red tentacles more beautiful than all the summer flowers in the world.

"'Yes, they are beautiful,' the sea lion said, 'but they are also dangerous. They can burn you with their beauty.'

"The sea lion swam beside the ship; from time to time he disappeared, but when the little cliff queen started thinking that the sea was too big and that she was too small and lost, he would reappear all of a sudden. At night, the little queen and Mrs. Margaret slept in the cabin of their ship. There was a broad bed there, covered in polar bear fur. Where the polar bears used to live, the sea lion explained, the ice was melting. So they had come ashore and become politicians, but before that they were forced to get rid of their coats so as not to be recognized. The sea lion collected their fur from the waves . . .

"One night, the little queen went up on deck to see the stars. She spotted the Big Dipper, but she also saw the outline of an apple tree and a mare and a canopy bed, all made of stars. 'So this is where you have gotten to!' she exclaimed in surprise. 'How beautiful you are! The nights out here are so beautiful . . .'

"'Yes, they are beautiful,' the sea lion whispered from the black night sea. 'But they are also cold. They can freeze you with their beauty if you look at them for too long.'

And the little queen crawled back under the polar bear coats as quickly as she could. In the morning, the early sun was dancing on the water in red and orange sparkles, and the little cliff queen looked at the waves. 'Maybe,' she said to her doll, 'it would be nice to swim next to the ship for a while like the sea lion does. The waves are so beautiful . . .'

"'Yes, they are beautiful,' the sea lion said, popping his head out of one of the froth-covered swells. 'But they are also greedy. They can devour you if you're not careful.'

"'Oh!' the little queen said. 'Isn't there anything that is just beautiful and not also dangerous?'

"'Maybe we'll find something on our journey,' the sea lion replied. 'But we can't waste too much time searching. Look behind you, little queen. There is something very dangerous and not at all beautiful.'

"The little queen turned, and she saw that the black ship had come closer.

"'Last night I swam to it,' the sea lion told her. 'When I reached the ship's bow, a hunter with a robe as red as blood was standing at the wheel. He had a blond mustache and eyes the same color as yours, little queen. And on the right sleeve of his gown, a diamond was stitched—the aim of his search: your heart.'

"'But what does he want my heart for?' the little queen asked.

"'He just wants to own it,' replied the sea lion. 'That is enough. He wants to look on its beauty and know that his hands alone can touch it.'

"'How can you be sure of that?' the little queen wanted to know. 'You're making that up, aren't you?'

"'I wish I was,' the sea lion sighed. 'But the red hunter is not unknown in these waters. He has stolen many jewels. He keeps them on his own island, far from here, for a while. One day, however, they lose their sparkle, and he grows tired of owning and touching them. So he throws them back into the sea. Your heart, little queen, is the biggest jewel in all the world. And he's been searching for it for a long time.'

"'What is the name of the hunter with the red robe?' the little cliff queen asked with a shiver. 'What shall I call him when I dream of him?'

"'When you meet him,' the sea lion said, 'he will ask you to call him father.'

"On the morning of their first day at sea, they saw a light gliding over the water, flashing back and forth again and again. 'That's a lighthouse,' the sea lion remarked.

"'Oh, let's go there!' the little queen cried. 'Maybe the lighthouse keeper has a cup of hot chocolate for us!'

"The sea lion turned his head toward the black ship. It had fallen back a bit. Two of its black sails seemed to be loose and not working properly, as if someone had bitten through the ropes at night. Someone who had swum near without making a sound, someone who had climbed the deck using the claws on his flippers . . .

"'Very well,' the sea lion said. 'Our advantage should allow for a cup of hot chocolate.'

"Shortly after, they moored the ship at the lighthouse keeper's island, and the little cliff queen went ashore with Mrs. Margaret. She took a few steps and had to laugh because she was walking with a rolling gait like a real sailor.

"'Sea lion!' she called out, for she wanted to show him, but when she turned back, there was a big silver-gray dog with golden eyes sitting behind her. 'It is me,' the silver dog said. 'Ashore, I am something else.'

"The little queen found this strange, and she began to wonder which was the animal's real form and if it had another.

"She knocked on the red door of the lighthouse, and the keeper opened it.

"'Come in,' he said. 'I have been watching your ship through my binoculars. And I lighted your way so that you wouldn't run onto one of the rocks that lie hidden beneath the water . . .' He stroked his graying beard contentedly and adjusted his round glasses. 'Would you like to come up for a cup of hot chocolate?'

"They followed the lighthouse keeper to the top of his lighthouse, from where you could see far, far out over the sea. The water looked so smooth from here, you couldn't pick out the waves; it was as if there were none.

"The lighthouse keeper tied an apron over his dark blue woolen sweater and stirred the hot chocolate on his little stove.

"The silver-gray dog lay under the table.

"'There is another ship out there,' the little queen said, as she was blowing into her cup. 'A black one, on the horizon. Do you show that ship the way, too?'

"'Of course,' the lighthouse keeper replied. 'I show all ships the way.'

"'But how can you know which of them are bad ships and which of them are good?' the little queen asked. 'That black one, you see, it's a bad ship. I know that, but maybe you do not, which is why you show it the way.'

"'It's true,' the lighthouse keeper answered in great earnestness, 'I don't know the bad ships from the good ships.' In his nearly gray beard, there were drops of milk.

"'The black ship belongs to the hunters,' the little queen continued. 'They want to steal my heart, and if they are successful, I will die. We have to reach the mainland before they catch us. We have just enough of a lead for one cup of hot chocolate.'

"'Oh,' the lighthouse keeper said. 'But that's horrible! I might have shown many bad ships the way.' He took off his glasses and scratched his head. 'What am I here for then?'

"He turned to face the little queen, putting the glasses on again.

'If I show the way to bad and good people alike, it amounts to the same as if I show the way to no one,' he said. 'Isn't that so? Maybe . . . maybe I should just stop showing the way. Maybe I should go to the mainland with you.'

"The silver-gray dog came out from under the table and sniffed the lighthouse keeper's shoes; then he watched him intently with his golden eyes. And in the end, he wagged his tail.

"'See,' the little queen said happily. 'He's saying you're allowed to come with us.'

"'That's great,' the lighthouse keeper said. 'I'll just pack my toothbrush. I might be of some help on that ship of yours. What's her name, by the way?'

"'I don't know,' the little queen replied honestly. 'Maybe one day we'll find out.'

So the lighthouse keeper turned out the light, making the lighthouse just a house. There wouldn't be any light to show the black ship the way. But the day was still bright; the night was yet to come.

"The lighthouse keeper unfastened the line that held the green ship, and they sailed away with a bold breeze in their three white sails. Next to the ship, the round head of the sea lion popped up among the waves. The lighthouse keeper nodded his head in recognition.

"Meanwhile, behind them, the black ship came closer and closer still. The little queen felt the red hunter's greed, and her diamond heart beat faster than ever before."

Anna and Micha were silent for a while. Then Micha asked, "That's all?"

"That's all."

"Are you sure? Did you turn the page over?"

"I did. That was the second side. There isn't any more. Not yet at least."

"A heart made of diamond," Micha whispered. "Do you think I've really got something like that? If they put me in one of those X-ray machines at the hospital, they could see it, couldn't they?"

Anna laughed. "You've got a perfectly normal heart made of flesh and blood. This is just a fairy tale."

"Yes, but . . ." Micha said.

At that moment, they heard the front door open and footsteps in the hallway. Anna sat absolutely still, and she saw that Micha, too, was trying not to breathe. It was as if they were standing aboard the green ship together, between the beautiful, dangerous waves of a blue winter sea. Rainer Lierski, Anna thought. He doesn't have a key, does he? Did we leave the door open? How long have we been here? Surely more than enough time to walk here on foot from Wieck . . .

The door to Micha's room opened. It was Abel. Of course it was Abel. Anna breathed a sigh of relief and climbed down, behind Micha, from the bed. But when she was standing in front of him, Abel's eyes were colder than ever. They were as cold as the winter night on a ship in a fairy tale.

"What are you doing here?" he asked.

"I . . . I made pancakes . . . for lunch . . ."

And then she remembered that she was still holding the pages. Abel followed her gaze and snatched them from her hand.

"Micha is perfectly capable of buttering a slice of bread for lunch," he said. "That's what she usually does. I didn't ask you to come here."

"I . . . no . . . I didn't intend to . . . ," Anna began. "How was the French test?"

"The story is my fault," Micha said. "I told Anna to read it to me. I found the pages. It was very nice, you know, having her read to me, and maybe you could show her how to make pancakes so that they aren't burned around the edges . . ."

"Anna has to go now," Abel said. "She's got her own home and a lot to do there." He didn't touch Anna. He didn't push her out of the room. He just looked at her. She held up her hands, helplessly, and walked toward the apartment door. Abel didn't take his eyes off her as she put on her jacket and shoes. "Your bicycle is outside," he said. "I rode it here."

"My . . . bicycle? It was . . . locked?"

"With a combination lock," Abel said, "the kind that anybody can open. I guess you've got the money to buy a better lock when you find the time."

She made one last try. "Abel, I just brought Micha home! You asked me to do that."

"I asked you for nothing," he said in a hard voice. She had been wrong. He could be scary without the black hat. "It was your idea. And, now, leave us alone. Thank you for bringing her the key."

Never had the words *Thank you* stung like that, like a blow. She ran down the stairs without stopping. On the ground floor Mrs. Ketow had opened her door just a little, to listen. Anna slammed the outer door shut behind her. She was crying. Shit, she was really crying. Searching for a tissue, she found the blister pack with the white pills in her pocket. Maybe, she thought, she should take one, just so . . . She pressed one of the pills out of the foil and put it in her mouth. It tasted bitter. She spit it out, a white pill in white snow—

like white paper waiting for letters, for words, for the next part of a fairy tale. He had locked her bicycle with the useless combination lock. She unlocked it and rode home, her head empty . . . white paper, white snow, white ice on a white street, white sails, white noise.

When she closed her eyes, she saw a diamond embroidered in white, embroidered onto the sleeve of a blood-red coat. Or was it tattooed onto Rainer Lierski's bicep?

6

Rose Girl
꩜

THAT NIGHT, ANNA COULDN'T SLEEP. SHE PUT HER clothes back on and went downstairs to the living room, where Magnus was still sitting in his old armchair reading the newspaper, another sleepless person, but one of the steadier sort. She looked at his big, broad figure in the big, broad armchair; they were at one, he and his chair, a rock, unshiftable, unyielding, strong. When she'd been small, she had thought her father could protect her from everything. Everything in the whole world. Children are stupid.

Next to Magnus, on the small parquet table, a relic of some trip to the Middle East, there was a bottle of red wine and a glass. Anna took another glass from the cupboard and poured herself some wine. Then she sat down on the second armchair. For a while they drank and shared the silence, Magnus focused on his newspaper and Anna on her thoughts. Finally, he folded the paper.

"What's on your mind?" he asked.

"Nothing," she replied. He looked at her. She shrugged her

narrow shoulders. She was so much narrower than him, a slender branch in the wind. "The world," she said.

"Yes. That's what you look like. As if you have the world on your mind."

"Why are people so different? Why are some happy and others unhappy? Why do some people have money and others . . . I know," she sighed, "this sounds childish."

"You could study the answers," Magnus said, wineglass in hand. "Philosophy. Or, no . . . economics."

"I need a sick note," Anna said. "For my music class today. Two to four o'clock . . . about."

Magnus raised an eyebrow. He didn't say anything.

"When I was your age," he started, "I also . . ." Then he stopped.

"Thank you," Anna said, getting up. "And, Magnus." She was already standing in the door.

"Yes?"

"The wine's turned."

The next day the white snow turned into brown mud. Anna asked Bertil if he had time to study math with her that afternoon. Gitta had a study date with Hennes.

"Unfortunately not just Hennes," she complained, "but some other people too . . . rats . . ."

Abel came to school late and slept through geography class— they didn't have literature that day. During break, Anna sat in the student lounge by herself. Through the window, she saw Abel talking to Knaake outside, but she couldn't make out what they were saying. All day she'd felt like she was swimming . . . her feet weren't touching the ground and her head wasn't in whatever she was doing.

Somewhere on the steps of the old concrete tower block, she had lost her grip on reality, as if a veil of tears was streaming over everything she saw. Knaake took off his round glasses and scratched his head with them. A single snowflake fell onto his nearly gray beard. And suddenly, Anna sat up.

The lighthouse keeper. The lighthouse keeper looked exactly like Knaake. The glasses, the dark blue woolen sweater, the beard—everything was right. Abel had written the literature teacher into his fairy tale. He'd come aboard to help the little queen. Knaake had promised to look for a job for Abel. Knaake was one of the good guys. She nearly smiled—but only a little. The world of fairy tales was easy: good and bad, cold and warm, summer and winter, black ship and white sails.

At lunchtime, she left Gitta and wandered alone to the bakery, the one farther away from school. When she got there, she wondered why she had come. The gleeful signs for colorfully wrapped treats with Ikea-like names made her nauseous. She wasn't even hungry. Next to the bakery, there was a kebab stand with several tall white plastic tables in front, empty despite the lunch hour. Anna felt drawn to its loneliness, compelled by the kebab seller shivering in his thin jacket. She bought a cup of lukewarm coffee from him and stood at one of the tables to drink it. His coffee was even worse than the coffee from the machine in the student lounge. She started sketching patterns into a coffee stain left on the table.

"Anna," somebody said. "Anna, I'm sorry."

She started and knocked over her cup, and when she looked up, she felt coffee trickling down her sleeve. It was Abel. "Ex-excuse me?" she said.

He took a paper napkin from a plastic holder and handed it to her. "I'm sorry I made you leave," he continued. "I didn't know that Rainer . . . Micha told me. You didn't want to leave her alone. I . . . I didn't want . . . see, it's not anyone's business how we live and . . . I'm sorry, really."

She had never heard him search for words before. She smiled and fell back into reality with a bang, the veil of tears ripped; her sleeve felt very wet indeed.

"It's okay," she said. "You're right. It's not my business how you live. But, for the record, my room isn't half as tidy."

"Did Micha take you on a tour of the 'villa'?"

She shook her head. "Don't worry, I didn't see the decaying dead bodies under the bed."

His face broke into a grin. "What about the suitcase full of stolen money or the smuggled uranium in the closet?"

"No," she said. "Though I did wonder what the gold ingots and the machine gun were doing in the drawer with the forks and knives." It felt good to talk nonsense. It felt good to laugh about meaningless things with Abel, like uranium in the closet.

"About the story . . . I'm sorry about that," she said quickly. "We shouldn't have read it by ourselves."

"No, you shouldn't have," Abel said, but he was smiling. "Rainer . . . ," he went on, and stopped smiling. "Micha's father. He . . . he was gone for a while . . . out of town . . . at least I haven't seen him for a long time. And now . . . you met him. You understand why I don't want him to turn up, don't you?"

"I think so."

"Think a little more and then take the square of the result and you'll have the truth. He's known around here . . . in the cheap bars . . .

Michelle was a departure for him. Usually his girlfriends are more like fifteen, sixteen. If they are even that old."

"Micha is six. That's something different."

"Exactly." He picked the used napkin up off the table and scrunched it up in his fist.

"Do you really think he would . . . That's a horrible accusation. If there was proof he did something like that, he would go to prison . . ."

Abel looked up from the napkin. His eyes glowed with a blue fire. "If there was proof," he repeated, " he would go to prison. People are talking. I know some things. I know very well. When I . . ." He stopped. "Would you take the chance?"

Anna shook her head. "But there are agencies that could help, judges, court orders . . . custody rights . . . if he isn't allowed to see her, he isn't allowed to see her, and that's that . . . there are institutions set up to protect children!"

"Anna," he said in a very quiet voice. "You didn't understand a thing I said."

"No?"

"I'm not eighteen. I don't have custody rights. If Michelle really doesn't come back, Micha is his. Like a piece of . . . flotsam. Like a stray dog. Like . . ."

"Like a lost diamond," Anna said.

"And that's why it is important that you keep your mouth shut," Abel whispered. "Do you get that? We're living with our mother in that apartment, everything's fine, we don't have any problems. Do you get that? *Do you get that?*" He grabbed her wrist, sounding as desperate as a helpless child. And somewhere in Anna, there was, for an instant, the sense that this was what he had once been, living in the same small apartment with Rainer, and she pushed the thought far, far away—to the dark side of the moon.

"I get it," she whispered. "I've never been in the apartment. And if I was . . . then I had a really nice talk with your mother. She and my mother listen to the same music, so that was what we talked about . . ."

He let go of her wrist. Suddenly he seemed embarrassed about having touched her. He looked around, but there was no one who had seen. The lonely, cold kebab seller was leaning against his stand, playing with his cell phone, lost in a world of SMS emoticons.

"I'm going to walk her home from school now," Abel said.

"You're not going to math class?"

"I'm going to pick up Micha," he repeated. "This afternoon . . . around five . . . we'll be in Wieck. Sometimes we sit in that café, out by the water, and have hot chocolate. When we have extra cash. We've got to do *something* with that stuff, don't we?" The grin returned to his face. "And there is a green ship there that has to sail on . . . another island has appeared on the horizon . . ."

"Around five," Anna said.

She didn't remember Bertil's existence till after math.

"Anna," he said with a smile in his too-narrow, earnest face. "You're not looking as if you understood much."

"I did," Anna murmured. "A few things . . . what?"

"We could go over the rest at my place," Bertil said. "I'll try to explain a few more things to you, if you can explain that last formula . . . you're looking at me like I'm a ghost."

"Yes," Anna said. "Oh no. Shit. Bertil, I can't come over today."

He hunched his shoulders, which were as narrow as hers. He was too tall for those shoulders. Anna liked Bertil with his dark, unruly hair and thoughtful expressions, but today she had no time for him. Or math formulas.

"This was your idea," he said. "You wanted to go over the formulas, not me."

"I know, and I still do." Math was one of the things she really didn't understand, and she was too Anna Leemann to accept getting a bad grade on a big test without putting up a fight. "But, Bertil, not today. It's just not going to work today. Something's come up."

Bertil pushed his glasses back up his nose. "Something or someone, Anna?" He looked so dead serious. As if he could read every single thought in her head, every sorrow.

"Somebody," she said. Nonsense. He didn't know her thoughts. She smiled at him. "My flute teacher. She called me during lunch to tell me that we have to move this week's lesson to today. I forgot all about it till now."

Bertil nodded. "Don't forget to lower the saddle of your flute teacher's bike," he murmured. "It's a quick release. Looked dangerous last time."

Anna shook her head. "Bertil Hagemann," she said. "Take a break from studying. You're mixed up." She knew she'd turned red. Red like a child caught doing something she shouldn't. Of course, she knew whose bike Bertil was talking about.

Anna rode home first. She had the vague feeling that Bertil was somewhere nearby, watching her, even though she didn't see him. She looked back a few times and told herself that she was getting paranoid. Why would Bertil follow her? Still, she'd put her backpack down in the hall at home and gone upstairs to get her flute and her notes. Paranoid. Absolutely. She rode in the direction of her flute teacher's house for about two streets, though she wasn't sure that Bertil even knew where her teacher lived. Paranoid. Stop it, will you! It was five minutes past five. She turned her bike onto Wolgaster Street and headed toward the water.

When she reached the turn to Wieck, it began to snow again. The café lay on the other side of the drawbridge, where the breakwater led out to sea. It was just at the end of the . . . no, not the cliff but the harbor arm, she thought. It looked a bit like a ship made of glass, that café, a ship full of chairs and tables and little lights on curious, bendable long necks. Anna hadn't known it was even open in February, but the café was like a living being; it seemed to change its habits at any given time and without any reason. By the time Anna shook the snow from her hat, the big clock on the wall read five thirty. She had the sense that she was too late for the most important date of her life.

The fairy tale had started without her; the little queen had sailed on, aboard her green ship, without waiting for Anna. Maybe she had sailed away for good . . . There they were, sitting at the back of the café, or at the front, depending on your perspective; they sat at the stern of the glass ship, where only a glass wall and a little terrace outside separated the tables from the water. Micha's pink jacket hung over her chair in an untidy heap, and she had put her hands around her cup as if to warm them. Abel and she were sitting opposite each other, leaning forward like conspirators, whispering. There were a lot of small tables with two chairs, but they had chosen one with a third chair, and the chair was empty. When Anna saw that, something began to sing inside her, and she forgot her worries and her guilty conscience over Bertil and math—she walked over to the empty chair, walked through the crowd of winter tourists, her feet barely touching the floor.

Abel and Micha looked up.

"See," Micha said. "I told you she'd come."

Abel nodded. "Anna," he said, as if to make sure it was her and not somebody else.

"I . . . I hurried," she said, "but I couldn't get here earlier. Hi, Micha. Good afternoon, Mrs. Margaret."

Mrs. Margaret was leaning against the sugar bowl, and Micha made her nod graciously.

"Mrs. Margaret has been very impatient," Micha explained. "Can we start now?"

Anna sat down. They had been waiting for her. They had really been waiting for her.

"Abel said, if you're not here by six, we start without you," Micha said. "And he said that you weren't coming anyway and that . . ."

"Micha," Abel interrupted her, "do you want me to begin or not?"

And then Micha said, "begin," and Anna said, "yes," and somehow she managed to order a cup of tea by signaling the waitress—and Abel, the fairy-tale teller, opened the door to a wide blue sea and a green ship whose name was as yet unknown.

"The black ship with its black sails darkened the sky behind them. More and more, its darkness seemed to leak out into the blue.

"'One day, the sun will disappear,' the little queen said, and at that moment the lighthouse keeper called out from the crow's nest high up on the mast, 'I can see an island! Can't properly see it, mind you—my glasses are fogged up . . .'

"Shortly after that, the little queen and Mrs. Margaret saw the island, too. And then—and then, they smelled it. All of a sudden, a smell from a thousand flowers in full bloom enveloped the ship. And the little queen's diamond heart became light and happy. The black ship seemed to recede in the distance.

"When they were very close to the island, it started snowing. The lighthouse keeper had lit a pipe, but now the pipe wasn't working anymore.

"'It's clogged with snowflakes . . .' he said. 'No, wait a second! It's clogged with rose petals! It's snowing rose petals!'

"He was right. They weren't snowflakes falling onto the planks of the green ship but the fragile petals of a thousand roses—white, red, and pink. Soon they covered the whole deck, and the little queen walked over a soft carpet of them to clear the ropes.

"'Little queen,' the sea lion said, emerging from a wave, on which floated white petals instead of white foam. 'Are you sure you want to go ashore here?'

"'Of course!' the little queen exclaimed. 'Look how beautiful the island is! It's full of rosebushes, and they are all in bloom! This island is much more beautiful than my small island!'

"The sea lion sighed. The little queen put Mrs. Margaret into her pocket, and she and the lighthouse keeper walked down the pier—a pier made of rosewood that led to a white beach. Behind them, the silver-gray dog with the golden eyes came out of the sea and shook the water from its fur. Then it sniffed the ground, gave three loud and angry barks, and returned to the sea.

"'Seems he doesn't like it here,' the lighthouse keeper said.

"'But I like it a lot!' said the little queen, walking up the path on the other side of the beach with her bare feet. She passed under an arch of red roses, and the lighthouse keeper followed, smoking his unclogged pipe thoughtfully. Behind the arch made of roses, a group of people waited for them.

"'Welcome to Rose Island,' one of them said.

"'We don't get many visitors,' another one added. 'Who are you?'

"'I am the little cliff queen,' the little cliff queen said, 'but my kingdom—or was it a queendom?—has sunk into the sea. This here, in my pocket, is Mrs. Margaret, but there isn't a Mr. Margaret, and this is the lighthouse keeper, but his lighthouse no longer has light. And who are you?'

"'We are the rose people,' the rose people replied, and, actually, that was quite obvious. For all of them—men, women, and children—were clad in nothing but blossoming roses. Their skin was fair and their cheeks were a little rosy, too, and their hair was dark like the branches of the rosebushes. Their eyes were friendly, and they had dreamy expressions.

"'Come on, you must be hungry,' a rose girl said, and the rose people led the little queen farther inland, till they reached a small pavilion filled with rosebushes. Inside, there was a big table, and on the table the rose people had laid out butter and bread, rose-petal jam, and tea made from rose hips.

"'Oh, how very, very nice!' the little queen exclaimed, pressing Mrs. Margaret so hard to her chest that the doll's face became wrinkled. The lighthouse keeper sat down at one of the chairs but quickly jumped up again. 'They're prickly!'

"The rose people were very sorry about that. They themselves didn't feel the thorns. They covered the chairs with white cushions filled with petals, which worked well. But after she had eaten enough bread with rose-petal jam and drunk enough tea, the little queen suddenly realized that her feet were hurting. The lighthouse keeper was wearing shoes, but she had walked to the pavilion barefoot. Now that she looked at the soles of her feet, she saw that they were covered with little red, burning dots.

"'Oh no,' said the rose girl who had spoken to them before. 'Those are from the thorns on the path! Sometimes the bushes stretch out their arms over the ground and onto the paths . . . one doesn't see them under the fallen petals . . .'

"And the rose people fetched a pair of wonderful white boots made of many layers of white silk for the little queen. 'That's silk from the rose caterpillar,' the rose girl explained.

"'Such beautiful boots,' the little queen said. 'I've never seen such beautiful boots.' Which was true, for she hadn't seen any boots until then, not in her whole life.

"After a while, the rose people left to get on with their work, cutting bushes, binding up branches, watering. Only the rose girl stayed with the little queen and the lighthouse keeper. She showed them around the whole island—showed them the rosewood houses and the lake, in which you bathed in rose petals instead of water.

"'It's a little boring, you see,' she said. 'Roses everywhere and nothing else. I'm happy you have come. Some change at last!'

"'I wish I could stay,' the little queen said, 'but I can't. The hunters on their black ship will come, and they will find me here between the rosebushes, no matter how deep I burrow in the leaves.'

"'But they can't,' the rose girl said. 'Just climb up that ladder to the lookout, little queen, and you'll see the black ship. It's anchored out there, far offshore. It can't come any closer. The scent of the roses keeps it away.'

"So the little queen climbed the ladder—the lighthouse keeper helped her up the wooden rungs—and she saw the black ship anchored far away. But she also saw something else. She saw a dark, narrow rowboat approaching the white beach, a boat in which a man with dark clothes was sitting, all alone. He gazed at the rose island with longing in his eyes, but he couldn't manage to get his boat any closer than it already was.

"'There is somebody,' the little queen said, 'who needs my help.'

"And she climbed down the ladder and ran over the island, down to the beach, as fast as she could. For she had a good heart, a heart made of diamond. When she stood on the white beach, she saw that the rowboat was delicately decorated: there were flowers carved into the dark wood, and the stern had a golden tip. Strange, the little queen thought, how the beautiful boat didn't fit with the old sweater and fleece-lined vest of the man who was rowing it.

"'Can I help you?' the little queen shouted. 'Surely the two of us can pull the boat ashore!'

"'I don't think so,' the man replied sadly. 'This island holds something against me and my rowboat. It's as if the current wants to keep us from getting any closer . . . I guess I have to be content just to sit here and look at the island.' Suddenly, he sighed. 'It would be much nicer, though, if I had someone to sit with me.'

"'I'll sit with you for a little while!' the little queen said and started wading out into the water. 'Take me with you, as you row along the shore!'

"'Oh yes, come with me!' the man said happily. And he helped the little queen into the boat.

"'Sit here on this bench . . .' He stroked his blond mustache and rolled up his sleeves, and then he started rowing. The boat shot forward like an arrow, but it also seemed to move away from the shore. 'That's the current,' the man said. 'It wants to push us away . . .'

"'Little queen!' someone shouted from the beach. 'Little cliff queen!' It was the lighthouse keeper—and the rose girl. They were standing on the beach, waving.

"'Wait!' the little queen said. 'Maybe they want to come with us.'

"The man shook his head. 'No,' he said in a quiet voice, 'I think it's much nicer with just the two of us. They'd only disturb us.'

"'Jump out, little queen!' the rose girl shouted, and the lighthouse keeper shouted, 'Come back!'

"'She's my passenger now!' the man shouted back. 'You don't have any say in the matter!'

"The little queen saw the rose girl take a deep breath before the girl shouted, even louder than she had shouted before, 'Do you remember what the white mare told you?'

"'The white mare?' The little queen thought about that. 'She said that I must run . . . as fast as I can . . . to the highest cliff . . . and if I meet a man wearing my name . . .' The man still had his sleeves rolled up and, suddenly, the little queen saw the tattoo on his right bicep. When he saw where she was looking, he quickly pulled the sleeve down, but she had already read the letters there. And her heart turned ice-cold from fear. 'Who are you?' she asked the man.

"'You can call me father,' the man said.

"'I've got to go now,' the little queen said, and then she jumped overboard and started swimming toward the shore. But the water was as ice-cold as her heart. Even colder. The waves, she thought, are beautiful, but they are dangerous . . . They will devour me . . . Then she felt somebody lift her out of the water and carry her to the beach. It was the rose girl. The roses that she wore seemed to fend off the cold and protect her slender body. She put the little queen down on the beach, and the lighthouse keeper shook his head and pointed at the rowboat. The man in it was removing his fleece-lined vest and his old sweater; underneath he wore a red gown. A diamond was embroidered onto the sleeve of the blood-red material in exactly the same place the man had his tattoo—a tattoo of the little queen's name.

"He turned his boat and slid away, without a sound, toward a dark shadow in the water beyond, back to where he'd come from. Toward the black ship with its black sails.

"'Oh, let's stay here!' the little queen cried. 'This is the only place where I am safe from him and the other hunters on the ship!'

"'If you really want to stay,' the rose girl said, 'take this necklace.' And she put a garland of fresh, blooming roses over the little queen's head. When the little queen turned her head, the thorns of the stems cut into her skin, and a trickle of blood ran down her neck and dyed the artificial fur collar of her jacket red. And the little queen was afraid.

"'I worried this would happen,' the rose girl sighed as she took the necklace away. 'Go back to your own ship, little queen. Only the rose people can live on Rose Island.'

"She accompanied the little queen and the lighthouse keeper back to the pier, and the lighthouse keeper, from sheer nervousness, was already smoking his third pipe.

"'Rose girl . . . how did you know what the white mare said to me?' the little queen asked.

"'When your island sank, the wind carried her words over the sea,' the rose girl answered. 'The others didn't hear them, but I did.

I heard the breaking of the trees, the bursting of the rocks, and the last words of your white mare. And I knew you were in danger, and I was worried about you even then, though I didn't know you. But now I know you. And now, I'm even more worried.'

"The rose girl laid her pale hands on the little queen's shoulders, and the two looked at each other for a long time. On the rose girl's nose there were five tiny freckles, which distinguished her from the other rose people.

"'I am fed up with seeing nothing but roses, day after day,' she whispered. 'Can't I sail with you and take care of you, little queen?'

"'You can,' the little queen said, 'but I don't know what will happen to us. Maybe we will die out there on the blue sea.'

"'Maybe,' the rose girl said, smiling.

"The lighthouse keeper helped the rose girl aboard. The little queen helped Mrs. Margaret, who was a little vain and had donned a rose petal for a hat. But all of a sudden, the silver-gray dog was standing on the pier barking. He jumped over the green railing of the ship, bared his teeth, and ripped the branches from the rose girl's arm, and the roses covering that arm withered instantly.

"'What are you doing?' the little queen shouted angrily. 'She has just saved me! The hunter with the red gown wanted to take me away in his rowboat, but she took me back to the shore! You just didn't see it because you were here, on this side of the island . . .'

"The silver-gray dog dove back into the water with an angry snarl and disappeared. The green ship sailed on, though, and the little queen worried that maybe she would never see the sea lion or the dog again. And she felt a prick of pain in her diamond heart.

"But in the morning, there was a bouquet of white sea roses next to the bed in the cabin, where the rose girl had slept. They were the kind of sea roses that grow only far out in the sea and only in winter. Somebody must have plucked them from the froth on the waves. Possibly a sea lion. The rose girl smiled. But there, behind the green ship, were black sails, very close, much too close, and the little queen was cold in spite of her down jacket."

Abel looked down into his cup. He drank the last bit of hot chocolate, which was long cold. He gazed out at the sea in the February dusk. Silently. Maybe he had used up all his words. Micha tore a little corner from the paper napkin and put it on Mrs. Margaret's head, like a white rose petal.

"I think I . . . I'll be back," Anna said and got up. "Too much tea. Rose-hip tea . . ."

Anna was alone in the tiny room that led to the ladies' room. She stood in front of the mirror, combed her dark hair behind her ears with her fingers, and leaned forward, over the marble counter with the two built-in sinks, so far that the tip of her nose nearly touched the tip of her reflection's nose.

It was true. She had five tiny freckles there. You couldn't see them unless you were really close. She took a deep breath and splashed her face with cold water. "Thank you," she finally whispered. "Thank you for the sea roses. It doesn't matter that you destroyed the roses on my arm with your teeth. They were unnecessary anyway." And then she smiled at her mirror image. It seemed beautiful all of a sudden.

Abel and Micha weren't talking about the story when Anna returned to the table. They were talking about school, Micha's school, and about a picture she had painted there. And about Micha's teacher with the blond curls: Mrs. Milowicz, whose name

Micha never managed to spell correctly and who'd been wanting to talk to Micha's mother for a long time now.

"She can talk to you instead, can't she?" Micha said, shrugging. "I told her that. Like she did on the first day of school, back then."

"Yes," Abel answered, but he looked away, out at the sea.

"Didn't your mother come on that first day?" Anna asked, and then was immediately sorry that she'd asked.

"Mama doesn't like school," Micha said to Anna. "She always has other things to do. And sometimes she has to sleep in really late in the morning, if she's been out the night before. Abel, what I wanted to tell you before was we had to draw a fish, and I made one with a whole lot of colorful scales, and you know what I can write now? X. Even though you never need it. It's strange what you learn in school, isn't it?"

"Yeah, strange." Abel laughed. "Why don't you tell Anna about the time you had to learn about the inner parts of the eye, and nobody understood a thing . . ."

He didn't want to talk about Michelle. Anna was getting the impression, more and more, that Michelle just happened to live in the same flat as Abel and Micha, who also just happened to be her children. It sounded like Abel had been taking care of Micha for a long time, even before Michelle had disappeared. Maybe since Micha was born.

How old had he been then? Eleven? When Rainer was living in that small apartment, too . . . and then they had thrown Rainer out.

Anna tried to pay the bill, but Abel's eyes turned cold once more, and she let it be. "We don't need charity, but thanks," he said quietly. She nodded.

Outside, in front of the café, it was difficult to say good-bye. Anna couldn't find the right words. She wanted to say "see you tomorrow," but she didn't know whether Abel would talk to her tomorrow or whether he would go back to behaving as if he didn't know her. Abel stood beside her smoking. Micha jumped up and down in the snow, her pink down jacket with the artificial fur collar bouncing, her boots making as many weird footprints as they could.

"The problem is, we don't get full social services," Abel said all of a sudden. "Not without Michelle. She has to go in and sign for it herself. We get the children's allowance. That's something, at least."

"How many bank accounts do you have?" Anna asked.

"Just one."

"And you said you're getting the children's allowance, so I take it you're drawing from that account, right? Michelle's not the only one who can, right?"

"Of course. I'm the one taking care of the fucking household." He laughed. "I've been doing that for a long time now. Michelle, she . . . well, she had problems. Drinking, for example. Not only that, though."

Anna nodded. "If that's the only account, you can check to see if anybody else is withdrawing money. And from which ATM. Maybe that's the way to find out where she is. I mean, she has to live on something. She'll need money."

Abel didn't say anything for a moment. "She hasn't taken out any money," he murmured finally.

"You're sure? Did you check?"

He nodded. "Nothing's been taken out." But Anna wasn't sure

he was telling the truth. She wanted to say, You know where she is! Why don't you tell someone? Don't you want her to come back . . . even a little bit? Or are you protecting her? From what? From whom?

"If I can do anything," she began, and then she realized how stupid she sounded. "I mean, I could lend you something . . . it wouldn't be charity then . . ." He shook his head, smoking in silence. Micha made baby footprints in the snow, using the sides of her fists, and Anna remembered doing the same thing when she was a child. Linda had showed her how.

"Where I live everything is so different," she said. And suddenly she heard herself telling him things. About the blue light; about Magnus; about Linda, who was nearly invisible; about the single rose in the garden; the robins; England; Gitta's glass wall, through which you couldn't see anything worth seeing; and the easy-to-clean furniture—and when she mentioned Gitta's mother disinfecting the white sofa, Abel started laughing.

He ground out his cigarette in the snow with his foot and looked at her. "Thanks," he said. "It's . . . it's good to not always be doing the talking." He unlocked his bike, helped Micha onto the carrier, and pulled the black woolen cap down over his ears. "About charity," he said, before he rode away. "You know . . . you could donate the eighteen euros. The ones I owe you."

"Excuse me?"

Abel turned around to look at Micha, who was busy stuffing Mrs. Margaret deeper into her pocket and whispering to her that she'd be cold otherwise. Micha wasn't listening.

"You gave me twenty," Abel said quietly. "Two is what that blister pack was worth."

"I . . . I don't understand . . ."

"I was afraid you'd really take some of that stuff. You looked so determined." And he smiled, his smile gliding past her, out to sea. "Lucky nothing was written on the back of the package. Tylenol. I sold you Tylenol. Children's Tylenol."

Then he rode away, and Anna stood there alone, in the snow. She felt an absurd, sparkling laugh creep up her throat and shake her whole body.

"Young lady," said an elderly gentleman, who had just come down the staircase of the café with his wife on his arm, "young lady, can I offer you my handkerchief? You're crying."

"Oh," Anna said. "Really? I thought I was laughing. Stupid mistake."

It didn't matter that she had canceled their date.

He told himself that it didn't matter. Why should it? He stood on the beach alone and looked out over the ice. It was nearly thick enough to walk on. No. He wasn't alone. There was the dog—the dog that probably wondered why, over the past few days, Bertil had taken it out so often.

Bertil made a snowball and threw it as far as he could, out onto the ice, by now surely thick enough to bear the weight of the dog. He watched the silver-gray flash run over the frozen sea.

He was lucky they let him have the car so often. It had surprised him in the beginning, but with the car, he was less conspicuous; he became a part of the traffic, and she didn't realize that he was following her, didn't have the slightest idea how close he was. He knew even now where she was. He could have thrown a snowball over the Ryck and hit the window of the café, where she was sitting at the table. She couldn't escape him. She would come to understand how much she needed him. His presence. His care. She didn't understand it now, but in time she would.

He wrote her name in the snow and knew he was being childish, ridiculous. But hers was such a beautiful name, a name that sometimes filled his whole head—and nearly burst it. A N N A.

7

Gold Eye
❧

THE STUDY DATE WITH BERTIL GOT POSTPONED TO
Saturday, and Gitta said that she would come, too. Couldn't they
work on math and physics? She could definitely use a little help with
physics before the test next week, and Frauke, from Anna's literature
class, said that she could use some help as well—and in the end, they
met at Anna's house, which was in town and easier for most of them
to get to.

"So, Bertil, it looks like you're the rooster in the henhouse," Gitta
said, and Bertil grinned.

"I guess the hens aren't clever enough to help each other out
with math and physics," he said good-naturedly, and he patiently
answered their questions for three full hours. Anna watched him get
absolutely lost in his role as professor (and rooster), and she tried to
listen and to understand what he was saying. But that turned out to
be difficult. Her mind was elsewhere.

Abel hadn't spoken to her all week. On Wednesday, she had

tried to catch his eye in literature class because he wasn't sleeping for a change, but she didn't have any luck. Had the rose girl left the ship again, disembarking on an unknown, bare, and rocky island, where she could do nothing but watch the white sails disappear behind the horizon?

"My God, Anna." Bertil shook his head, and his glasses slid down his nose. "You really don't get this, do you? Musicians shouldn't have trouble with math—they say the parts of the brain that process math and music are next to each other! Where's your head today?"

Anna saw the friendly, indulgent professorial look in his dark eyes. But his look wasn't just friendly, it was also curious; and she wondered if he really had followed her on Tuesday after all.

"I don't think I'll ever understand things like integrals," she replied. "And to be honest, I don't believe anyone in our class really does; they just act like they do. Let's take a break."

"Oh yes, please," Gitta said. "Freaks like Bertil can go for three hours without oxygen, but I can't. Who wants to join me in Anna's perfect garden for a smoke?"

On the rosebush, in front of the wall with the winter-brown honeysuckle, a second rosebud had opened. The flowerbeds were covered in snow. Gitta's voice was too loud for the robins, which fled deeper into the entangled branches. Anna, freezing in her sweater, thought, "If I were standing here with Abel, the robins would stay. Maybe even more of them would come. Robins from all over town. They would perch on the branches quietly, their little heads inclined thoughtfully, listening to his fairy-tale words . . ."

Magnus joined them and bummed a cigarette from Gitta. "Bertil," he remarked, "you're the rooster in the henhouse, today." And everybody laughed, because this time, Bertil rolled his eyes.

"So what are all of you doing after graduation?" Magnus asked.

"I've got no idea," Gitta replied. "My mother wants me to go to university, of course, but I'm not going to go just because she wants me to."

"Well, it's too bad, isn't it, if you can't do things that you might enjoy simply because you've got to be rebellious," Magnus said, grinning.

"I'm going to stay here and study business administration," Frauke said. Frauke's parents had rebelled against their parents when they were young. Frauke had grown up in the chaos of a communal farm, and the most rebellious thing that she had ever done was to *not* be rebellious and to iron her shirts instead. Anna sighed.

"What about you, Bertil?" Anna asked, just to be friendly and also because she realized that she had never bothered to ask him before. "What are you going to do?"

"Army," Bertil said as he blew a smoke ring into the winter air. All these people and all their strange reasons for doing things, Anna thought. Bertil, for example, probably smokes only because nobody expects him to.

"Come on, Bertil," Gitta said. "The army? That's not the place for you! You'll be trampled to death there, poor lamb."

"And have fun in Afghanistan," Frauke added. "What was it someone said? All soldiers are murderers . . ."

"Tucholsky," Bertil nodded. "He was right. Back then. In Germany. But you can't compare now to then, Frauke. German soldiers are in Afghanistan to protect the civilians and to bring order to the chaos."

"Oh, are they . . . ," Frauke said.

Magnus put out his cigarette in the ashtray that Anna had made of clay when she was a little girl and given to him for his birthday. It was supposed to be a bird, but it looked more like a hippopotamus. She loved her father for still using it. "You go ahead and solve the world's problems without me," he said, smiling on his way to the door. "I'm too old for discussions like this."

"Seriously, Bertil," Gitta said when Magnus had gone. "Do you really want to join the army? You wouldn't hurt a fly, let alone aim a weapon at someone."

"Just because he's in the army doesn't mean he'll be running around shooting people," Anna said.

But Bertil ignored her. "Could *you?*" he asked Gitta, with a strange tone in his voice. "Could you ever aim a weapon at someone, Gitta?"

"Of course she couldn't," Frauke replied. "And you couldn't either."

"Oh, I'm not sure about that," Bertil said, staring into the distance beyond the garden. "If it were someone I really loathed . . . someone who made me so angry I couldn't breathe anymore . . . if I had good reason to hate that someone . . . it would probably give me some kind of kick to pull the trigger. To watch them fall."

"But that doesn't have anything to do with the army," Anna said, getting uncomfortable.

Bertil looked at her. His glasses weren't sliding down his nose anymore. "I know how to aim properly," he said, "even if you don't believe it. I'm not a bad shot."

"You're crazy," Gitta said, "where would *you* have learned to fire a gun?"

"My father hunts," Bertil replied. "He's got a hunting lodge in the woods behind the village of Eldena, not far from your house,

Gitta. Right after finals, I'm getting my hunting license. Hunting isn't as bad as you think. The animals you shoot . . . they don't feel anything, nothing at all. They don't even know, don't understand; they suddenly just don't exist anymore, and never had to be afraid. It's much better than the slaughterhouse, where an animal hears other animals screaming and dying before it's killed."

"Bertil," Gitta said. "Stop it. That's horrible. I don't even want to think about things like that. How come we're even talking about slaughterhouses and death?"

The air in the garden wasn't as blue anymore; something reddish had seeped into it. Anna thought that Bertil was trying to look taller and had ended up looking smaller instead—without realizing it.

"Death is definitely something you should think about from time to time," he said. "Most people don't, you know. And then they die, and it's too late. Then there's no time left to think . . . have you ever seen someone die?"

"No," Anna said. The other two shook their heads. "What about you?" asked Frauke.

Bertil nodded. "Our dog. If you watch your dog die, it's like watching a family member. Him and me, we kind of grew up together. In the beginning, he was friendly, but then he became aggressive. It wasn't his fault—it was in his blood; the breed is just like that, no matter how you train them, but my father learned too late. The dog thought it was his job to protect us . . . he attacked a jogger when we were out on a walk. If my father hadn't stopped him, he'd have killed the guy. Unforgivable. A child would have been killed instantly . . . my father shot the dog in our yard."

For a while no one spoke. They were so quiet, the robins came back.

"I saw his eyes," Bertil said. "When he died, they were golden. He knew that he was dying. In the end, he knew."

"Golden," Anna murmured. "A dog with golden eyes."

"A Weimaraner," Bertil said. "He had a silver coat and golden eyes. A beautiful dog. Some have blue eyes, though . . ."

"Let's go back inside," Frauke said. "It's frickin' cold out here."

"And next cigarette break, we're not discussing death . . . ," Gitta added on the stairs, with forced cheerfulness. "Instead, let's talk about the very beginning of life."

"Why, Gitta," said Frauke, "are you going to become a midwife after all?"

"I'm not talking about midwifery," Gitta replied. "I'm talking about sex."

Later, in the growing darkness, they stood in front of the house, talking about meaningless things. Bertil was the first to leave. He had borrowed his parents' car. He had turned eighteen quite a while ago and, unlike Gitta, had convinced his parents to pay for his driver's license.

"Gitta's right, what a freak," Frauke repeated. "What was it he said about shooting people? Is Bertil Hagemann not who we think he is?" She lowered her voice. "Like, is he secretly a serial killer?"

"Bertil Hagemann just doesn't like being Bertil Hagemann," Gitta said matter-of-factly. "He was just acting. And he's looking for a girlfriend. Desperately." She looked at Anna. "Face it, little lamb. You won't be getting rid of him anytime soon. But Anna's got a university guy, you know."

"I don't *have* a university guy," Anna said and congratulated herself for her angry tone—it sounded very convincing. "I only had a cup of coffee with him. In the student dining hall."

That wasn't really a lie after all.

"How sweet," Frauke said. "He invited you for a coffee?" She sighed. "We shouldn't be thinking about math and physics and death. We should think about love instead. I've been wondering who to fall in love with for sometime now . . . there's Hennes von Biederitz, but somehow that seems unimaginative. I mean, everybody's in love with Hennes von Biederitz."

Gitta cleared her throat.

"Just recently, I considered falling in love with someone, experimentally," Frauke went on dreamily. "Somebody absolutely absurd. André."

"Who is André?" Gitta and Anna asked at the same time.

"The Pole," Frauke answered. "Our peddler with the pretty little pills. Isn't his first name André?"

Anna bit her tongue.

"I'm a little afraid of him." Frauke gave a little shudder, like a child on an amusement park ride. "But maybe he's one of those guys with, you know, a rough exterior that conceals a heart of gold . . . if he wasn't running around in those cheap clothes from the Polish market . . . actually, he's quite a hot guy." Anna felt nauseated. She was thankful when Gitta put on her helmet and got on her scooter. But Gitta didn't leave.

"Don't do that, Frauke," she said. "Don't fall in love with that one. I already dissuaded someone else. I know a few things about our Polish friend that you don't."

"Things? What kind of things?" Frauke asked, wide-eyed.

Gitta shrugged. "Not G-rated," she said, winking, and Anna knew that she was making something up, like she'd done when they were children.

"A man with a secret," Frauke whispered. "And such *beautiful* blue eyes. Dahling."

"Gee, don't forget to invite me to your thirteenth birthday party," Anna said, teasing.

And that was the moment the call came.

Before heading inside with her cell phone, Anna saw Gitta ride away on her scooter and Frauke get onto her bike. At first, she didn't understand who was talking to her. The connection was bad. It was a woman—or maybe a child. The woman or child was afraid of something.

"Anna?" she asked. "Anna, is that you?" A child. It was Micha. Anna didn't know where Micha'd gotten her number, but that wasn't important. She sat down on one of the old carved wooden chairs in the hall and put her finger in her other ear to hear better. "Micha?" she said. "Micha, is that you?"

"Yes," Micha answered. "I . . ." She seemed not to be holding the telephone properly; there was a lot of noise in the background. Something seemed to fall and possibly break. The island, Anna thought. The island is sinking; the rocks are bursting.

"Micha, I don't understand you!" she shouted. "Say it again! Louder!"

". . . not, what should I do?" Micha's voice said, and now it was clearer. "I locked the bathroom door with the key. They're fighting, Anna. I can hear them. Mrs. Margaret is in the living room, but I guess she can't do anything either . . ."

"Who is fighting?" Anna asked. "Micha . . . Slowly . . . Where are you?"

"In the bathroom," Micha repeated. "I have to help him, but I'm afraid. I can't. Anna, I don't dare open the door . . . There's a note stuck to the mirror . . . It says 'Anna' and 'Emergency' with your number on it, so . . ."

"*What?*" Anna asked and thought, this isn't the moment to feel happy, but she couldn't help it. Micha was crying now; she could hear her. She also heard more things breaking or being thrown or falling into the winter sea. She tried one last time. "Micha, *who is there in the apartment with you? Has your mother come back?*"

"No," Micha sobbed. "She hasn't, and she never will. She's gone for good. He said that. He said that I have to live with him now; he doesn't have a red gown, but still . . . Anna . . ."

"I'm on my way," Anna said.

For a moment, she considered calling the police. But the note on the bathroom mirror didn't say *Emergency* and the number of the police, it said *Emergency* and *Anna*—and surely not because Abel thought Anna would put the police on his trail. The police would ask questions: questions about Michelle Tannatek, questions about who was looking after Micha, questions about custody. And even if Rainer Lierski didn't get custody of Micha, even if they locked him up, which didn't seem likely . . . even then, Anna thought while struggling to get her coat on, even then they'd take Micha from Abel. And there wouldn't be fairy tales anymore or hot chocolate at the pier or meals in the student dining hall . . . gotten with a fake ID.

And no pink down jacket flying across the schoolyard on Friday afternoons, eager to be caught in someone's arms and whirled about.

By the time she had arrived at this thought, she was riding down Wolgaster Street, which seemed endless today, like a steadily growing plant. No matter how fast Anna rode, the street, with its bike lane and its cars and its traffic signs, just got longer and longer. The wind was blowing single icy snowflakes into her face. She had forgotten to put on gloves, and the cold bit into her fingers, the pain causing tears to well up in her eyes until finally she didn't feel it anymore—neither the pain nor her frozen fingers.

The whole way she tried to convince herself that nothing had happened, that everything was fine, that Micha had been exaggerating, that the whole thing was a misunderstanding, that you couldn't believe everything a six-year-old child said— Amundsen Street was deserted in the halfhearted snow flurry. The door of block number eighteen was wide open. Anna didn't lock her bicycle—why bother, if anybody could pick the lock. The staircase smelled of a mixture of beer, times past, and vomit. On the ground floor, an overweight woman with greasy hair stood inside her door with a small child in her arms, shaking her head. Her eyes were tired and without a spark of life; they reminded Anna of a fish's. She scrutinized Anna, obviously curious who she was. But Anna didn't have time for explanations. In the apartment behind the woman, two children screamed at each other. Mrs. Ketow, Anna thought, she's got three small children, but they are not her children . . . Anna was running up the stairs now. Her heart pounded. What are you planning to do? You don't have anything to defend yourself with, yourself or anybody else . . . on the fourth floor she stopped, listening. From an apartment down the hall, she heard the voice of a radio; from another one, shots sounded. She started, but the shots were accompanied by loud, dramatic music, and Anna nearly laughed: TV. Maybe a western. She went on, slowly now. Behind the door with a white nameplate that said "Tannatek," it was very quiet. Micha had called from home, hadn't she? Or . . . had she called from Rainer Lierski's house? From somewhere else?

Anna took a deep breath. Then she pressed the bell.

And then Abel opened the door.

His fist was raised, and she ducked instinctively.

"Anna," he said, as if she was the last person he had expected to see. "I . . ."

"Yeah, me too," Anna said, incoherently and very relieved. "Has he gone?"

Abel nodded. "Can I come in?" He nodded again. Anna shut the door behind her. She turned on the light in the hall and saw that Micha was hugging Abel's leg like a small creeper.

"You can let go of me now," Abel said. "Micha, hey! It's all right! It's just Anna; he hasn't come back! I can't walk with you hanging onto me like that! Let go, will you?"

"If I absolutely have to," Micha said, and Abel laughed.

Anna looked at him. She almost wished that she hadn't turned on the light. "Shit," she said. "Abel."

The hall looked as if a search or a bombing or possibly both had taken place there. Jackets had been pulled down from their hooks, and, on one side, the coatrack had been ripped out of the wall entirely. The floor was covered with toys, shattered plates, pieces of a broken glass bottle. Abel stepped over all of this and led Anna to the kitchen. "I'm making hot chocolate," he said. "Do you want to have a cup, too?"

"Hot chocolate?" Anna repeated, her voice strangely dull.

The kitchen looked like the hall. One door of the wall cupboard above the sink had been pulled from its hinges; a pot of basil was lying on the floor in front of the window, the plant crushed, the soil scattered; and, in one corner, there were the pieces of what had once been the contents of a whole cupboard. The word *rage* had new meaning here, Anna thought. And in the middle of the chaos, Abel stood at the stove stirring milk in a pot, completely calm. No, *calm* was the wrong word. His hand was shaking.

Abel didn't look much better than the apartment. His left eye was starting to swell, and his right temple was covered with blood, as if he had fallen from his bike—or maybe from an accelerating car—onto a gravel path. "What . . . ?" Anna began, finally.

Abel nodded toward the heap of broken plates and cups in the corner. "I took a fall."

"I hope you didn't fall alone?"

"Oh no," Abel said, not without pride, adding chocolate powder to the milk. "Believe me, there's someone else who looks just as bad as I do."

She realized that he was stirring with his left hand. When he had opened the door, he had raised his left fist. He held the right one awkwardly.

"Micha," he said, "you two could clean up the living room a bit, what do you think?"

Micha grabbed Anna's sleeve and pulled her into the living room, where the two ragged old armchairs and the couch had been turned over and books had been thrown onto the floor. They righted the armchairs and put the books back on the shelves in silence. Anna found several packages of pills scattered in the floor. Not Children's Tylenol. In any case, the pills weren't what the person who'd been

raging here had wanted. Anna and Micha put the jackets back on
the hooks as best they could, and Micha whispered, "He just came
in. The hunter with the red coat. I was nice to him because I thought
that maybe then he'd go away. And somehow, I felt sorry for him,
too . . . he seemed so lonely. Abel had gone down to get some things
at the store . . . we just talked, on the couch, and he said again that
I could come live with him, but then Abel came home and told him
that he should leave . . . and he didn't want to leave, and they started
shouting at each other, and then they were fighting . . . and the red
hunter started breaking things; he just opened the cupboards and
pulled stuff out . . . and he said that everything in this apartment is
old and broken anyway, that we don't own anything but garbage . . .
it's my fault, isn't it? It's all my fault. Abel is angry with me. I should
never have opened the door and let the red hunter in . . ."

Anna held Micha in her arms, in the middle of the chaos in the
ravaged living room. "Don't cry," she said. "Oh, hell, just go ahead
and cry. It's not your fault, Micha. And Abel isn't angry with you.
I'm sure of it. He's angry with your father. Abel just wants to protect
you."

"He doesn't have to," Micha said, sniffling.

"Yes he does," Anna said.

"And from what, anyway?" Micha asked, wiping her nose on
Anna's sleeve.

"You know what," Anna replied. "The red hunter wants your
diamond heart."

Five minutes later, the three of them were sitting at the living
room table. The table was missing a leg now. They were drinking
their chocolate from water glasses because there weren't any un-
broken mugs left.

"Abel," Anna began, "we've got to do something about that wound of yours. Your face. I can see at least three glass splinters in there. We've got to . . ."

"Later," said Abel.

"But getting that treated is more important than hot chocolate."

"No," he said, and Anna nodded; his eyes allowed for no disagreement. "Now it's important that everything goes back to normal and everybody calms down," he said. "And that is why I'm going to tell you a three-minute piece of the fairy tale."

Micha lay down on the sofa, exhausted from fear and crying and relief, her head on Abel's knee; and Anna remembered how she herself used to lie like that when she was a small girl, her head on her mother's knee, her mother reading a book to her.

"You remember that white cat we saw yesterday?" Abel asked. "When we were walking at the harbor in Wieck? The white cat you wanted to take home with you?"

"I remember," Micha whispered and yawned, "she was all dirty and disheveled, but she didn't want to be petted by me . . . I remember."

"That's good. The green ship sailed through the waves for a long time, and day by day, the little queen and the rose girl became colder. The wind was bringing snow now, real snow.

"'Your roses are already starting to wilt,' the sea lion said to the rose girl. 'Not only where I tore them but everywhere else on your body, too. They will wither. And you will freeze in the cold wind.'

"But the rose girl wasn't the only one to feel the cold. Mrs. Margaret and the little queen were shivering, too, now that they were standing on deck.

"'Maybe it's the black ship,' the little queen said. 'It brings the cold with it! It comes closer and closer without ever reaching us. Isn't that weird? I almost wish it were here and something would happen at last!'

"'Something is happening,' the sea lion said, lifting his head out of the waves as far as he could. 'Look there! There's the next island.'

"'It's all covered in snow,' the rose girl said. But she was mistaken.

"A little later, they anchored the ship, and there on the shore of the island stood an information board.

"'Island of the Blind White Cats,' read the lighthouse keeper, and he scratched his head with his glasses. 'It is forbidden for strangers to hum ashore.'

"'That's a spelling mistake,' the rose girl said. 'They must have meant that strangers are forbidden to *come* ashore.'

"The little queen began to hum a tune, the first one that came into her head, just to test things out. And, instantly, a white cat appeared and came racing toward her like a living snowball, shouting, 'Quiet! It's forbidden to hum ashore! Can't you read? You're startling our weavers and spinstresses, and that leads to the most awful mistakes in the fabrics they're producing.'

"The little queen and her friends followed the white cat inland, where many white cats were sitting at spinning wheels and handlooms, or, in their case, paw looms. They seemed to have been spinning threads and weaving fabric all day long. The threads were made out of their own white fur, which clearly grew rapidly. But because the white cats were blind, they couldn't see where their pieces of fabric began and where they should have ended. They just spun and wove, on and on. The white layers covered the whole island, poured into the sea, and floated on the waves in huge white drifts.

"'Oh, could you spare some of that lovely white material?' the little queen asked excitedly. 'Just a little bit, so that we can make a few warm clothes?'

"'Well, you'll have to pay for it, of course,' one of the cats said.

"'Our fabric is the best and most durable,' another of them added.

"'It protects against the rain, snow, and fire,' a third one remarked.

"'Everything has its price,' all three said.

"'Oh, but we don't have anything we could give to you,' the little queen sighed. 'You see, our clothes aren't made for the icy winter here. Don't you see how urgently we need your fabric?'

"'How could we see that?' an elderly cat asked crankily. 'We are blind. Visitors tell us our fabric is beautiful, though. They say that if you look at it for a long time, rainbows spring from its folds. But we have never seen that ourselves.'

"'Oh, you poor creatures!' the little queen exclaimed.

"They sat down to take a closer look at the fabric that covered the island; and, indeed, after a while, a rainbow shot up in front of them, gleaming and sparkling in all the colors of the world. A second one followed, and then a third. The rainbows began to swirl into each other, as if they were threads themselves. They danced and spun around; they formed spirals and knots up there, in the clear, cold winter air—blue, green, yellow, orange, pink, red, violet—and everyone got a bit dizzy looking at them.

"'How beautiful!' the little queen said finally. 'Isn't it so sad the cats are blind?'

"'Glasses,' the lighthouse keeper murmured. 'Maybe they aren't blind after all; maybe glasses are all they need. I left my own glasses on the ship . . .'

"'I'll go and get them!' the little queen said. She picked up one of the white cats to carry it with her, for the cats looked so soft and nice, but the cat complained. 'Come on, you can warm my hands till we reach the ship,' the little queen said. 'Like a muff made of white fur.'

"'If you insist,' the cat said begrudgingly.

"On the beach, the silver-gray dog with the golden eyes was pacing to and fro nervously.

"'Just imagine . . . this fabric can create rainbows!' the little queen shouted, out of breath. 'Oh, if only we had clothes made of such fabric!'

"The silver-gray dog just growled. 'Don't put that fabric on,' he said. 'Little queen, don't do it! Ever! Whoever wears that cloth sees nothing but rainbows and forgets about danger!'

"'Oh, you! You just don't like *anything*!' the little queen said. 'Think of the rose girl . . . you wanted to bite her when she first joined us!'

"'I will go and see what the others are doing,' the silver-gray dog snarled. 'So we don't lose them to rainbows.'

"The little queen climbed aboard the ship and put the cat down on the deck, where it curled into a ball on the planks and fell asleep instantly. She looked for the lighthouse keeper's glasses everywhere, but she couldn't find them. At last, when she was on her knees searching under one of the benches, someone knocked on the rail very politely. The little queen looked up, and there was a man there, clad from head to toe in glittering white fabric.

"'Come aboard,' the little queen said. 'Is it true that one sees only rainbows when one is wearing that fabric?'

"The man didn't answer. He plopped down on the bench. 'Oh,

little queen,' he said. 'I am so tired! I have come far, far across the water, just to see you.'

"'To see *me?*' the little queen repeated, surprised.

"At that moment, the man reached out and grabbed her, pulling her closer. His grip was strong. The little queen gave a cry of fear and pain. Only now did she see that the man had a blond mustache.

"'Your diamond heart is more beautiful than all the rainbows in the world,' he whispered. 'And it is mine, rightfully mine. For you owe your very existence to me. I am your father.' His white gown slid to the floor; the little queen saw the blood-red coat he was wearing beneath. And the next second, the red hunter lifted her up, as if she weighed no more than a sheet of paper. But then he stepped on a rose branch the rose girl had lost, and thorns pricked through the sole of his boot. He lost his balance and fell, swearing loudly.

"When he sat up, the little queen saw the silver-gray dog racing toward the ship. The rose girl and the lighthouse keeper were behind him. The red hunter stood up. He had let go of the little queen as he fell, and now she fled into the cabin and slammed the door. Then, there was a terrible noise from outside, on the ship's deck. Some things fell down, and wood splintered; she heard the heavy breathing of two people and pressed Mrs. Margaret to her breast.

"Finally, she glanced through a crack in the wood of the cabin door. Outside, two bodies were rolling over the planks between toppled-over benches and torn sails. It wasn't a dog that was fighting with the red hunter. It was a wolf. A big gray wolf. The red hunter sprang to his feet and swung his rapier, from which he cast dangerous, glowing sparkles.

"'Oh, my sea lion, my dog, my wolf!' the little queen whispered. 'He will kill you!'

"But she couldn't do anything; she was too frightened. And she felt very ashamed of herself.

"She saw that the wolf's fur was dark with blood in some places. Then the wolf collapsed and lay on the floor very still. The red hunter put his rapier away. He kicked the wolf with his boot one last time, stepped over it, and walked to the rail. Caressing the wood, he smiled contentedly. 'This could be my ship,' he said. 'I will not sail her, though. She is too green. I will take nothing from here but the little queen's heart. I will cut it from her body with my rapier . . .'

"The little queen wanted to cry. Now, she thought, I'll die after all, and I still don't know anything about death. But then something unexpected happened. The big gray wolf moved. It stood up very slowly, very silently, and approached the red hunter from behind. When it was directly behind him, it stood on its hind legs and laid its paws on the railing, on either side of the red hunter; the red hunter turned his head. In his eyes there was nothing but surprise; there was no time for fear. The wolf sank its teeth into the hunter's neck.

"The little queen covered her face with her hands. She sat like that, all alone, in the darkness of the cabin, until the rose girl opened the door and took the little queen into her arms.

"'The red hunter is dead,' she whispered. 'You don't have to be afraid any longer. We were hiding in the folds of the white fabric and didn't see what happened. Did you?'

"'I don't know,' the little queen replied. 'I didn't see anything.'

"Outside on the deck, the white cat blinked at them lazily. She had been asleep until now. The lighthouse keeper raised the sails that hadn't been torn, and they sailed on. A little while later, the sea lion poked his head out of a wave.

"'Little queen!' he said. 'The black ship still hovers on the horizon! There are more hunters there, more greedy hands. Don't ever forget that.' With those words, he dove down, back into the deep water. He left a red trace of blood behind.'"

Abel ran his fingers through Micha's hair. She was sleeping. "I didn't realize she had fallen asleep," he whispered. "How long has she been sleeping?"

"About since the rainbows," Anna replied.

He sighed. "I'll have to tell the story again."

"Yes," Anna said quietly. "Do that. Maybe a different version, though. Without blood and teeth and the cutting out of hearts. Tell her . . . tell her a version in which she doesn't look through the door."

Abel nodded. "But the rose girl was wrong," he whispered. "It's wrong not to be afraid."

"Abel . . ." Anna began. "You . . . you didn't kill him, did you? Rainer?"

He looked up. His eyes were so dark they weren't blue anymore. Unless it was a shade of blue at night. "No," he said. "I wish I had."

He stood and lifted Micha up to carry her to her bed. She looked almost dead, lying in his arms like that. As if someone had cut out her heart with a rapier and left only her body. But her heart was still there . . . still there dreaming, Anna thought, dreaming of rainbows.

Anna swept up the pieces of broken dishes in the kitchen while Abel undressed the sleeping Micha and got her into her pajamas. She heard him struggle with a sleeve and curse, the way a father curses a frustrating chore—lovingly and without anger in his voice. She shook her head. None of the pieces fit together.

"And now we'll do something about that wound," she said when Abel closed the door to Micha's room. "Do you have tweezers? Disinfectant?"

"Wait for me in the living room," Abel said. But she followed him and stood at the doorway of the tiny bathroom, watching him pull a cardboard box from the top of a cupboard and search around inside it.

"We could use alcohol," she began, and Abel gave a start.

"Didn't I say to wait in the living room?" He hadn't realized that she'd followed him. Suddenly, he sounded angry, and she didn't understand why.

She took a step back, out of the bathroom and into the hall. "In case you don't want me to see my phone number on the mirror," she said with a smile. "I know it's there; Micha told me. She couldn't have called me otherwise."

He gently pushed her toward the living room and followed, closing the bathroom door behind him.

"Yeah, that," he said. "That's a little embarrassing. It's just that the apartment is such a horrible mess at the moment. Here." He gave her a pair of tweezers and a small bottle of old disinfectant. "What will you do?"

"I thought I'd drink the disinfectant and stuff the tweezers up my nose," Anna said. "What do you think I am going to do? Sit down. Those splinters can't stay in the wound." She could hear that she sounded like Magnus when he was talking to his patients, who usually replied, "Yes, Doctor Leemann." And, "Do what you think is right, Doctor Leemann."

Abel took the tweezers and said, "I can do that myself. We do own a mirror, though that might surprise you. You should go now.

Sorry about the number on the mirror . . . she shouldn't have called you."

"Abel." Anna tried to toughen the Magnus part inside her. "Sit down. There, on the sofa."

"It's late, Anna . . . they'll be waiting for you at home . . . in that house where the air is always blue . . . they'll be worried."

"It's not late. I'll call them later. Sit down on the sofa."

Helplessly, he held up his hands and sat down. Anna sat next to him, adjusted a floor lamp that had miraculously survived the fight, and looked at the wound on Abel's temple. She didn't understand how cups and plates could break into so many tiny pieces. Maybe if you were pushed into them. Maybe if you were pushed into them again and again. She fished the splinters, one by one, out of his skin and flesh, her mind with thoughts about the past, with the history of the apartment, with Abel and Micha's story. He was gritting his teeth, swearing under his breath. "Hold still," Anna said. "You know how lucky you are that nothing happened to that eye?"

"I know somebody else who was damn lucky," Abel said. "Rainer Lierski. He was damn lucky to walk out of here on his own two feet."

Then he fell silent. As Anna retrieved splinters, a seemingly never-ending task, like working on an assembly line, she suddenly noticed how close she was to Abel. Unbelievably close, daringly close.

She smiled. "Why do you have a buzz cut?" she asked, just to ask something matter-of-factly.

"The trimmer only does buzz cuts," Abel replied. "It's old. I don't want to waste money on a barber."

"That's the only reason?"

"That's all. Plus, people here leave you alone if you have a buzz cut. And if you're wearing a Böhse Onkelz sweatshirt. I don't want any trouble."

"But . . . politically . . . you're not . . . you're not like skinheads?"

"A Nazi?" Abel asked and started to laugh. "I'm not dumb."

"And . . . the white cats . . . the fabric of the white cats . . . the rainbows . . ."

"Today is question day," Abel said. "But with Anna Leemann, it's always question day, isn't it? You want to know everything."

"Yes," she said. "Everything. About the world." She sounded like a child again. So what.

"It's just that it's not always answering day," Abel murmured. And, after a while, "The white fabric is exactly what you think, of course. But that's not what you want to know. You want to know why I'm selling." He turned his head, and she pulled away the tweezers, which had almost touched his eye. "I don't take the stuff I sell, Anna."

"And I'm the queen of Sheba." Anna laughed.

Abel didn't laugh. "It's true. I'm dealing it, that's all. It brings in cash. Michelle has . . . I got my contacts through her, a long time ago. It's always good to have contacts. I can't afford to take anything. I need a clear head. Because of Micha. You understand? And because of school. I want to pass. It's hard enough, when I miss so many classes . . ."

"And when you sleep so much," Anna said. He picked up their hot chocolate glasses and carried them to the kitchen. When he came back, the glasses were clean and he was carrying a bottle of vodka. He put the glasses on the table in silence and poured. Then he sat down again, taking one of the glasses in both hands, the way

Micha had held her hot chocolate. He was sitting farther away from her than he had before. Not that much, though. He didn't say anything more about a clear head.

"Why do you think I sleep at school? What do you think I do at night that I'm so tired?" he asked seriously. "Tell me what you think. I'm sure everybody thinks something."

"Well, I . . . I don't know," Anna said, picking up the other glass. "Maybe you're selling white cat's fur in the clubs?"

He laughed. "Yeah," he said, relieved. She didn't understand his relief. "Well, yeah. But I have legal work, too. If you have contacts . . . I'm helping out in two bars out here. Sometimes in town, too."

"You asked Knaake for a job. Our lighthouse keeper."

Abel nodded. "The lighthouse keeper. Yes. Sometimes it gets to me, and I think I should do something totally different to earn money. Something that doesn't have anything to do with bars and clubs and . . . something that's got to do with thinking. Thinking is something you can do at home, too. I dunno . . . like maybe I could be a research assistant for someone at the university . . . that kind of thing . . . Micha shouldn't be by herself so much. She doesn't realize because she's sleeping, but after what happened today . . . I don't know if Lierski'll come back." He downed the rest of the vodka in one swig and set the glass back onto the table with a thud. "If he touches Micha, I'll kill him."

Anna emptied her glass. She didn't like vodka. "Could I have another one?" she asked.

While pouring, Abel moved closer, and she wondered whether it happened accidentally. Probably. He seemed too lost in his own thoughts to even notice. "Back then . . . back then, I couldn't defend myself against Lierski," he said. "But now I can. I'm as strong as he is. I . . ."

Anna reached over to take his right hand, and he pulled it away. "Defend. Yeah, I understand," she said. "You hurt your wrist. Maybe it's broken."

"Oh, come on," Abel said. "It just got too close to a chair's leg."

"Can you move it?"

"The chair's leg?" Abel tried to laugh. He tried to move the hand. "Sure, I can. Shit. No."

"You should see a doctor," Anna said.

"Crap."

Anna took his hand to gauge the swelling. "Let's at least put something cold around it. Frozen peas work pretty well."

"Do I have to eat them?"

"No, you just have to inject them into a vein," Anna said. How good it felt to laugh! How good it felt to sit on the sofa, to be close to each other, just for a little while, and to laugh. He hadn't pulled his hand away, not this time. The moment stretched into an eternity, a moment in which nothing happened; their laughs died down, dried out. They just sat there, and that was enough; nobody had to do or say anything . . .

Anna's cell phone rang, and Abel started, jumping up as if he'd just remembered something urgent he had to do. It was home. A blue number, full of roses. Anna sighed.

"Not that it's any of my business," Linda said, "but where *are* you?"

"I got kidnapped by a serial killer," Anna answered. "You can transfer the ransom to Gitta's account."

"I see." Linda was trying hard to sound casual. "When does she plan to release you?"

"Gitta," Anna said to Abel, "when do you plan to release me? Right now, I think," she said into the phone. "I'm on my way."

"Okay . . ." Linda said, hanging up.

Abel shook his head. "So now I'm Gitta . . ."

"Should I have told the truth?"

"No. I don't think at the house of blue air they'd like the fact that Anna Leemann is hanging out with the Polish peddler. By the way, I know exactly three words of Polish."

"That's two more than I know," Anna said. "But that's not the reason I lied. I thought . . . I thought you wouldn't want them to know . . . but for the record, in the house of blue air, they really wouldn't mind. They're not like you think."

Abel turned to collect the glasses.

"You should go."

8

Damocles
ॐ

ANNA SPENT ALL OF SUNDAY WONDERING WHETHER
she should drive out to Abel's. To make sure that everything was all
right. She would have called, but she didn't have his number. She
finally figured out how Abel had gotten her number—the lighthouse
keeper must have given it to him. He had the cell phone number
of everybody in his intensive class, just in case of an emergency.
Emergency and *Anna* were the two words Abel had written on the
note that Micha had found stuck to the mirror . . . she almost called
Knaake to ask him for Abel's number.

"Excuse me, I'm sorry to bother you on a Sunday, but Abel
Tannatek left his ecstasy in my backpack . . ."

She put the phone back on the bookshelf. She didn't call.

Later, she would think, what if she had called, if she had talked
to him on that Sunday, if she had . . . but who cares about *later*? Later
is always too late.

Anna studied for her math exam. She did her homework for

literature class, lying on the sofa in the living room, reading some random book, not taking any of it in. She practiced her flute as an afterthought. Music had been her passion, her purpose in life; she shouldn't neglect it, like a lover she no longer wanted. The flute didn't seem to take it personally . . . it lay in her hands, calm and cool as always, seeming to understand why, on that particular Sunday, she played so many wrong notes.

Only Magnus and Linda were surprised.

"Is there something on your mind, bunny?" Magnus asked. "Is it life again? Or something different?"

Anna shook her head and smiled. "It's life," she said.

Monday morning, Magnus opened the local newspaper and said, "Chicago."

"Chicago?" Linda asked with a laugh, pouring more tea. "Are we going on vacation?"

Magnus laid the paper down on the table as Linda instinctively put her hand on the light-blue ceramic butter dish to keep him from knocking it to the floor.

"We don't need to go to Chicago," Magnus said. He whistled through his teeth, impressed. "Chicago has come here. Listen to this: 'Deadly bar brawl. On Sunday morning, after a heated argument at the Admiral, a bar in the woods District of Wieck, Rainer Lierski, forty-one, was found dead between two parked cars. A resident of the area discovered the snow-covered body as he headed to his own car . . .' Imagine going out to your car after breakfast and finding a dead body next to it. Jesus Christ!"

"You usually bike to your office," Linda said.

"Yes, and thank God I do," Magnus said cheerfully, "with dead bodies popping up in parking lots . . . 'Mirko Studier, fifty-two, the owner of the bar, stated that Lierski was a frequent customer. "Lierski liked to pick fights," says Studier, "always wanted to argue, but I never thought it would end like this. When things started to get violent, I threw him and his three friends out. By the time I closed up for the night, I figured they'd all gone home." The police are still searching for Lierski's companions, ages twenty-five to fifty, according to Studier. They are also looking for possible witnesses to the crime and/or anyone in the vicinity of the Admiral between ten o'clock and midnight on Saturday night . . .' Hey, they don't give the ages of the witnesses they're looking for. What a surprise!"

"Magnus," Linda said. "This isn't funny."

"No . . . I'm sorry. Of course it isn't. It's just this local paper is so ridiculous . . . Anna? Anna, are you okay?"

Anna nodded. She held her teacup in both hands and pictured Micha's hands around a cup of hot chocolate and Abel's hands around a glass of vodka. Abel's injured wrist. The tiny cuts in his face. The splinters. She closed her eyes for a moment. If he touches Micha, I'll kill him. Had he really meant it? Had he been at the Admiral? Or had he been close by, at just the right place and time to get hold of Rainer Lierski? She opened her eyes. She felt dizzy. For a second she wished her parents would dissolve into fog, that she was sitting at the table alone. She'd take the newspaper and read the article herself, leave her breakfast untouched, and make a cup of really strong coffee. No. She'd take the whiskey bottle down from the shelf, pour a drink, pace back and forth, get her thoughts in order . . .

"I'm fine," she replied and forced herself to finish her yogurt. "That article . . . I was just thinking . . . It reminds me of something we've been talking about at school . . . Can I have the paper?"

Magnus refolded the pages and passed them to her, almost knocking over a jar of jam in the process. "Don't get into 'a heated argument,'" he joked. "You don't want it to end up 'deadly.'"

"Ha-ha," Anna answered shortly. "I gotta go."

She couldn't focus in her literature class that day. She watched Knaake opening and closing his mouth, but she didn't hear what he was saying; it didn't get through. It was in this class that she had studied Abel Tannatek, hoping to learn more about him. That seemed like ages ago.

Abel didn't sleep in class this time. Anna saw how the others were looking at his face, at the black eye and thousand tiny cuts on his temple—a thousand small, single wounds, a field of dark, dried blood. He took his time gathering his things after class; he let the others go first, like he always did. Anna waited for him. She told Frauke that she had to talk to Knaake.

Knaake knew that she didn't have to talk to him.

He looked from Abel to Anna and back, saw that they needed to talk, shrugged, and said that he was desperate for a cup of coffee; he'd leave the room open, come back later to lock it up.

Anna spread the newspaper on the table and pointed to the article: "Deadly Bar Brawl . . . Rainer Lierski (41)" . . . Abel put his hands on the table on either side of the newspaper and leaned over it, reading without looking at Anna. A big gray wolf, she thought, that had its paws to the left and right of its victim, on a ship's railing—an instant before it kills that victim by breaking his neck with its long teeth.

"Shit," he finally said, stepping back and covering his face with his hands, taking a deep breath. "Shit."

When he moved his hands away from his face, she saw that he'd grown pale. "He's dead," he said.

Anna nodded.

"And I said I'd kill him."

She nodded again.

"I would have done it," Abel whispered. "I would have done it if he'd come back."

"Did he come back?"

"No." Abel shook his head. He went over to the window and looked down at the schoolyard on which more snow silently fell. Anna stood next to him. Fifth graders in colorful coats were making a sled run; a small group of smokers was standing near the bike stands—Anna saw Gitta. The lights in the classroom weren't on. To the people outside, they were invisible, high in their tower.

"I wasn't there," Abel said. "I wish I could feel relief . . . he's never gonna bother us again. But I wasn't there."

"At the Admiral?"

He nodded. He didn't ask the question that needed to be asked. He didn't ask, Do you believe me?

"You need an alibi," Anna said. "I left your apartment on Saturday night, a little after midnight."

"No," Abel whispered and turned to her. "You didn't. It was much earlier."

"No, it was past midnight," Anna insisted. "I remember how I looked at my watch and thought, it's already twelve thirty . . . and if my parents imagined that I was home earlier, then I guess they were mistaken."

He shook his head, slowly. "No," he repeated. "No. My alibi is my business."

And then he did something absolutely unexpected. He pulled her close and held her for a moment, so tight she thought she could feel every single bone in his body. And somewhere between them, she felt his heart beating, fast and nervous. Hunted. He let go of her before the hug became a real hug, left her standing there, and fled from the tower. Anna balled up the paper and threw it in the wastebasket.

When Linda came home that afternoon, Anna was sitting on a folding chair in the snow-covered garden, listening to the birds. She was wearing her winter coat but no hat, and white snow crystals, which the wind had brought down from the roof, were blooming in her dark hair. The snow had stopped falling at midday; the world was very quiet, apart from the twitter of the birds in the rosebushes.

Linda stood in the doorway for a moment, watching her daughter. Anna was sitting as motionless as a statue, a work of art someone had installed in the garden, like a birdbath maybe, a birdbath in the shape of a seated girl. Linda stepped forward and put a hand on the statue's shoulder, and the statue jumped and turned back into a girl. And all the robins flew away.

"Have you been sitting here for a long time?" Linda asked.

"I don't know," Anna said, looking up. Her lips were blue from the cold. Even her eyebrows were laced with snow crystals.

"Come inside?" Linda asked. She didn't command; she asked. "Have a cup of coffee with me. Tell me . . . if you want to . . . tell me, what happened."

"Nothing," Anna said. "Nothing has happened. I'm just thinking . . . I'm still thinking about that article . . . Chicago . . . the man who was beaten to death. I wonder . . . I wonder how furious you would have to be to kill someone and if you can do it with your fists or . . . or if one fist is enough, because you can't use the other one . . . I wonder how somebody dies then . . . I mean, even if he's deserved it . . ." She got up and followed Linda inside, and Linda took Anna's coat off with gentle hands.

"You're ice-cold," she said. "Anna, this man . . . he didn't die from a fistfight. It wasn't in the paper but . . . well, I shouldn't be telling you this, I guess."

"What—what did he die from then? How come you . . . ?"

Linda turned away and put the kettle on.

"The husband of a colleague of mine works in the forensics department. She told me. I don't know why they didn't give this information in the newspaper . . . maybe the police have their reasons for not saying . . . but I'll tell you. He died instantly. He was shot."

Anna grabbed her mother's arm and saw the surprise in Linda's eyes. "Shot? Are you sure?"

Linda nodded. "From behind, she said. A shot in the neck. He didn't suffer. I just want you to know that."

Anna looked at her watch. "Oh no. I almost forgot that I promised Gitta to . . . I have to go, I'm sorry," she said. "Thanks for the coffee."

Linda shook her head while Anna put her coat back on. "I haven't even made the coffee."

"Then go ahead and make it now," Anna said. "I won't be gone long."

She knew Linda was standing at the window, watching her ride away, watching her teeter as her bike wheels slid in the snow that was turning to ice on the road. Linda had always wanted another child, but it hadn't worked out. After Anna, all her pregnancies had dissolved into nothingness, each and every one of the possible children shifting from nearly being to not being—too soon for Linda to get used to a presence, but late enough to feel its loss. She feared for Anna, always had—from her first step—and Anna knew it. This made life difficult. Linda tried to conceal her fear, by not controlling Anna, by not asking her where she went, by not ordering her around, by saying she thought it was a great idea to go to England for a year, that it was great she wanted to study in a different city. Though if it had been up to Linda, she would have tucked Anna into a small pocket, lined with soft fabric, next to her heart, where she would be safe and warm and nothing would ever happen to her. Like Abel would have done with Micha, if he could have, Anna thought, surprised by this thought: Abel. You're just like Linda.

She rang the doorbell three times before he opened. He was wearing a faded T-shirt and his hair was messy—messier than usual—as if he had just gotten out of bed or toweled himself off after showering. Two of the tiny cuts next to his eye had opened and were glistening, wet and red.

"Do you know how to shoot a gun?" Anna asked without any introduction.

"What? No," Abel said. "Do you need to find someone who does?"

"No. You're sure you don't know?" she asked. "And that you don't have a weapon, either?"

"No!" he repeated. She thought he would step back to let her in. He didn't. He stepped forward and almost pulled the door closed behind him. He was shivering in his thin T-shirt, she could see. "Why are you asking me this?" he said.

"If you're telling the truth, you're safe," Anna said. "He was shot. Rainer was shot. My mother knows someone in the forensics department. He was shot in the neck; he wasn't beaten to death."

Slowly, very slowly, a smile started to broaden on his face.

"Thank God," he said. "I've never been so glad that somebody was shot."

For a while they were standing there in the cold staircase. Then his smile disappeared. "But I can't really prove that I don't know how to shoot a gun," he said. "Can I? I mean, it's hard to prove that you *can't* do something."

"Why would you have to prove that?" She nearly started to laugh.

"They will think it was me," he said in a low voice. "Despite everything." He glanced back at the apartment.

"Micha?" she asked. "Is she not supposed to hear what we're talking about? Haven't you told her . . . ?"

"Micha's on a field trip with her school." He folded his arms across his chest, as if this would protect him from the cold. Or possibly, from something else. On his upper-left arm she saw a shiny round red spot, like a burn. It looked new. It looked like a cigarette burn. He saw what she was looking at and put his hand over the wound.

"Abel . . ." she began, "do we have to stay out here on the landing?"

He shook his head. "No. You have to go home. You don't belong here. You'll catch cold."

"It's warmer in your apartment."

"Anna," he said, his voice even lower than before, and very

insistent. "I don't have time now." He seemed to be listening for something, straining his ears in the direction of the apartment.

"You've got a visitor," she said.

"Someone I owe money to."

"I could lend you . . ."

"Please," he said. "Go."

For a moment, he hesitated. As if he would prefer to stay on the landing, forever. But finally, he smoothed back his hair and turned to go. He closed the door behind him, with a click.

Anna kicked the tires of her bike because there wasn't anything else to kick. The voices of children shouting abuse at one another came from the first floor. Anna was pretty sure Mrs. Ketow was watching her again, but she didn't care. Who was with Abel? It's none of my business, she told herself. It definitely isn't. I'm interfering, and he was right. I don't belong here.

But why, when they were alone in the classroom, had he hugged her? She walked back to Wolgaster Street, dragging her bike, in the event she found anything suitable for kicking. Only at the traffic lights, where she had to cross Wolgaster Street to reach the path on the other side, did she get on her bike. She was sitting there, holding onto a lamppost with one hand, waiting for the light to turn green, staring at the cars with hostility, when a hand landed on top of her own. She started.

"Bertil!" He was next to her, sitting on his own bike, his feet on the pedals, keeping his balance by resting his hand over hers. She smiled. His glasses were halfway down his nose again. "What a small world," he said. "Have you been at your flute lesson?"

She narrowed her eyes. "And where are you coming from?"

He didn't give her any more of an answer than she had given him.

"If I asked you something that's none of my business . . . ," he began.

"I wouldn't reply," Anna said, pulling away her hand so that he nearly lost his balance. The light turned green, and they crossed together.

"You're spying on me," Anna said. "Aren't you?"

"Is there anything worth spying on? Maybe I'm just making sure you don't do anything stupid."

"Bertil Hagemann, leave me alone," Anna said. "I don't need a babysitter."

"Oh yes, you do," Bertil said. "More than you realize." Then he pedaled away, leaving her behind. He was more athletic than she had realized.

The sword of Damocles hovered. Anna tried to stay angry, to sustain the anger that had compelled her to kick the wheel of her bike. It didn't work. Abel's fear was too palpable. She felt the sword hanging over him from a thin, fragile thread; he looked at her now in class—that was new—and in his eyes she saw fear. *They will think it was me. It's impossible to prove that you cannot do something.* He no longer slept in class. Maybe he wasn't working nights anymore. Or, maybe he just couldn't sleep, not even in class, because he was no longer safe—anywhere. When the classroom door opened because someone was late, he started as if he expected the police. The sword was lowering. Its tip was the bullet that had pierced Rainer Lierski's neck like the long teeth of a wolf.

On Wednesday, Anna stood at the window of the student lounge, which was humming with excitement before the physics exam. She didn't have to take it—she'd completed physics last semester. She realized that Abel was standing beside her.

"I'd be relieved if they'd come for me," he said in a low voice. "If they'd show up at our front door and demand an explanation. Where I was that Saturday night . . . so I could tell them . . . So I could tell them that I wasn't there, I don't own a gun, I don't know how to use one, I didn't kill him . . . But they don't come; they don't give me a chance to defend myself . . ."

She felt his hand on hers as he gave her something. A piece of paper.

"Good luck with physics," she said.

"I'm not taking the exam."

She looked at him. He looked away. No one could take an exam with a sword hanging over his head. Anna felt rage build inside her. Lierski had really managed to mess life up for Abel. Now he was keeping him from passing the classes he needed to graduate.

She looked at the paper during her next class. It was folded to form an envelope and closed with pieces of scotch tape. It was even decorated with a not-really-round red circle, which might have been meant to be a seal. In one corner, someone had written "ANNA" in pencil. She opened the envelope, carefully smoothed the paper, and saw little hearts drawn with an orange magic marker. The letter was from Micha; Abel hadn't opened it.

Deer ANNA,
You hav to com agan soon so the farytal can go on.
Love MiCHA.

Deer ANNA 2
kwestions that I do not no:
1 were dus a persun go when he dies?
2 is the red hunter gon now or will he com bak?
3 kan you help Abel not be afrad any moor deer anna
Love micha.

Anna took a pen to write an answer on the paper. "Dear Micha," she wrote. But she didn't know what to say after that. She couldn't answer a single one of Micha's questions.

On Friday after school, Anna rode her bike into town and wandered aimlessly down the main shopping street. Her legs wanted to carry her to the student dining hall, but she didn't let them; instead, she forced them to walk in the opposite direction, to take her window shopping . . . as if she wanted to buy something, as if she had a reason for being there. She didn't. She just didn't want to go home. At the beach in Eldena, where she usually went if she felt this way, there were too many thoughts strewn in the sand near the frozen sea; it was too lonely there. And besides, maybe her stupid legs would win and carry her to the dining hall, where she'd find Abel and Micha, sitting at one of the tables, eating dead dog and drinking hot chocolate with five straws each.

She wandered over to the old snow-covered fish market behind the town hall, where they hadn't sold fish for a long time. Children were ice-skating on the shallow pond in front. She could, she thought, walk over to the fair trade shop on the other side of the square and buy a bar of chocolate, to at least do something that made sense. As she climbed the steps to the store, the winter scene at the pond swam in her head, a picture of children, in colorful snowsuits, laughing—and all of a sudden, she remembered a small pink down jacket. She turned around. Of course, there wouldn't be a pink down jacket, and if there was one, it would belong to another child, one that Anna didn't know and . . . somebody was running toward her from the pond. It wasn't a child. It was someone in an open green military parka and a gray scarf, which was trailing behind. Someone without a hat, someone with snow in his blond hair. She thought of the scene in the schoolyard; she thought: he's flying, flying like he did then; then he was there, sweeping her up the stairs with him, into the store, between the boxes of half-frozen leeks and bright orange pumpkins. Somewhere behind him, she saw the pink jacket now, playing on the ice with the other children.

"They . . . they got him," Abel gasped. He had snow on his jacket, snow on his sweater, snow in the folds of his gray scarf, as if he'd been playing on the ice with the children and fallen on his nose. He was out of breath and his eyes sparkled with laughter.

The sword . . . the sword was gone.

"Who?" Anna asked. "Who did they get? Who?"

"The guy who shot Micha's father." He seemed to realize that he was still holding her arm and let go as he tried to catch his breath. "It's . . . it's almost certain it was him. I've been asking around a bit . . . maybe it will be in the papers tomorrow. Rainer shouldn't have picked a fight with at least one of those three guys last Saturday. The police didn't find just one gun in his apartment—they found a whole arsenal. It looks like he was trading in weapons. In any case, they're holding him now for illegal possession; he had run away after they found Rainer's body, but then he seems to have come back to his apartment to get something; the guy from the bar saw him, and now they've got him. And . . ." He stopped, panting.

"That . . . that's . . . great," Anna said, smiling. "Did he confess?"

"I don't know," Abel said. "But even if he doesn't . . . it's got to be him, don't you think?"

She nodded, slowly. "Yeah. It's got to be him."

Micha came toward them now, swinging her turquoise backpack. And she was carrying something else, too, a bag that looked as if it was from a bookshop. She tried to wave with the bag and the backpack, dropped both, and picked them up again. "What are you doing in the vegetables?" she asked, grinning, as she entered the store. Her face was red from cold and excitement, and she was beaming.

"You didn't see us," she said to Anna. "I was skating on my shoes! You just walked past me . . . I waved to you, but I was so out of breath, I couldn't call your name right away . . . why didn't you see us?"

"I was . . . lost in thought," Anna replied.

"What were you thinking about?"

"You," Anna said. "Isn't that strange? I was thinking of you two so hard that I didn't see you." The leeks were astonishingly green. The pumpkins were unbelievably orange. The tomatoes had never been so red and the lettuce never so lettuce-colored. Never before had Anna realized how beautiful vegetables could be.

"Are we gonna buy something here?" Micha wanted to know. "We already bought something at the bookshop. A book, see! To celebrate. Because there won't be any policemen coming now."

"We won't buy anything here," Anna said. "But next door, we can get something, in that café. What's it called? Gleam of Hope?

Gosh. Whatever . . . they do have hot chocolate. Do you have time for a cup of hot chocolate? Am I allowed to . . . I mean . . . just today . . . to treat?"

Micha looked at Abel, and Abel seemed to be thinking. Finally he nodded. "Just today," he said.

The "gleam of hope" didn't sell just hot chocolate; it also carried clothes made of felt as well as wooden toys. Half the people working there were mentally handicapped, though there was probably a more correct word for it. When Anna was in town with Linda, they always stopped by. The air there seemed blue, like the air at home, but maybe that was just because of all the handmade blue dishes.

"We've never been here," Micha said. "I like it. We could come every day."

"Down the road," Abel said. "When I've finished school and am working more . . . *then* we can come here every day."

"Are you going to stay here?" Anna asked when they were standing in line at the counter while Micha admired the cakes. "For university?"

"We'll see," Abel said. "Maybe we'll go away. I don't know yet."

And Anna imagined him moving, with Micha. It was always "we" and never "I," but how would Abel take care of Micha when he was going to school and working at the same time? And what about custody—would he get custody rights when he turned eighteen?

"This cake is very pretty," Micha remarked.

Anna pushed away her doubts about the future and paid for the hot chocolate and a piece of the very pretty cake, and they carried the blue plate and the blue cups over to a table. Outside the window, the sun was shining and turning the snow into silver. And Anna wished everything could stay like this—wished that she could sit at this table forever, with Abel and Micha, with the sun shining outside . . .

"In the sky above the green ship," Abel said as he drank a little of his chocolate, "the sun was shining brighter than before. The black ship had fallen behind. But it never vanished completely. And despite the sun, the air didn't get any warmer. The rose girl's leaves withered, one after the other, and one night as she stood on deck all by herself, the last one fell. She was completely naked.

"'Oh, if only I could spin a thread of moonlight! If only I could spin a thread of the froth on the waves to make clothes!'

"Single snowflakes fell from the night sky and snuggled in her dark hair, and she sighed and said, 'Oh, if only I could spin a thread of snow to make clothes!'

"Then she sat down on the deck and waited to freeze to death.

"At that moment something dark emerged from a corner— something very big—and the rose girl was frightened. It was the wolf. The big gray wolf who had killed the red hunter. She had seen it, even though she hadn't told the little queen. Now the wolf approached her slowly; she saw that he was limping, dragging his right front paw. And she saw his teeth. When the wolf was very close, she realized he was still bleeding from a wound on his flank. 'From the rapier of the red hunter,' the wolf said, looking at her with his golden eyes.

"'But how is it possible that you're still bleeding?' she asked. 'It's been a long time since we threw the red hunter's body into the sea. And the sea lion that swims along next to the ship in daytime doesn't have any wounds.'

"The wolf didn't reply. 'You're shivering,' he said. 'Do you believe that you could spin a thread of my blood? To make clothes from?'

"The rose girl tried hard to believe. And the moment she did, the wolf's blood turned into a red thread that started weaving itself into a soft, red fabric. The thread was pouring out of the wound, yard up yard, and the fabric's folds covered the rose girl, covered her and warmed her until she didn't feel the cold of the winter night anymore. A piece of fabric draped itself around her face, and when she swept it aside, she saw that the wolf had gone.

"The rest of the night the rose girl spent sewing. Her needle was a rose thorn she had taken from one of the dried branches. There was enough fabric to make warm clothes for all of them—for the rose girl and the little queen and the lighthouse keeper and Mrs. Margaret. Only the white cat, who constantly slept, didn't need warm clothes. She was much too disinterested in the world to feel the cold.

"When the morning came, they stood on the deck of the ship, clad in red velvet, and the lighthouse keeper looked through his glasses and called out: 'There! I can see two islands, very close! We can go ashore on one of them and stretch our legs a little!'

"The little queen wondered where he had found his glasses. Hadn't she gone back to the ship alone, to get those glasses? And hadn't she almost been caught by the red hunter because of it? She pushed the thought away and watched as the lighthouse keeper and the rose girl secured the ship's lines to a pole on one of the islands. The island was full of people, waving and shouting questions: 'Where does the moon come from?' 'What's the meaning of life?' 'Why is it impossible to turn a yogurt container inside out to eat the last bits?'

"'This,' the sea lion explained, 'is the island of questions, little queen.'

"The little queen jumped ashore, and the asking people caught her in their arms. But they didn't set her down. They lifted her up, above their heads, and carried her away, all the while shouting more questions. In the end, they started shaking her impatiently in hopes she would answer.

"'Where does someone go when he dies?' 'When does fear end?' 'Where are all the single socks that disappeared in the washing machine?'

"The little queen didn't know the answers to any of their questions.

"'Help me!' the little queen cried fearfully. 'They will tear me to pieces!'

"Then the silver-gray dog appeared between the asking people. He snapped left and right with his teeth, and the asking people stepped back. 'Why is he doing that?' they asked. 'Where does he come from? Is he good or bad?'

"The silver-gray dog plucked the little queen from their arms, like a bird from the air. Suddenly, she was sitting on his back, and he was running toward the ship, running through the passage the asking people had opened for fear of his teeth. Soon, the little queen was back on board. On the island, there was a crowd of asking people, who were still stretching out their dozens of arms and shouting hundreds of questions.

"'Cast off!' the sea lion called from the waves. 'Quick! Too many questions can be dangerous!'

"So they pulled away from shore and headed over to the second island. But one of the asking people had managed to jump aboard and climb over the rail. 'Can I come with you?' he asked. 'Are you sailing toward the mainland? What does the mainland look like?'

"'Shut up,' the white cat said. 'How is anyone supposed to sleep when you're asking so many questions!'

"They now approached another island, where there was also a crowd of people waiting and waving. The travelers could see that they were shouting something, but their words didn't reach the island of questions.

"'I wouldn't be too surprised,' the lighthouse keeper said, 'if that was the island of answers.'

"When they were halfway between the two islands, a whirlpool took hold of the ship, turning it around and around in a circle, and they all lost their balance and fell down onto the deck. Finally, the lighthouse keeper managed to steer the ship out of the whirlpool and back on course toward the second island. The sea lion stuck his head out of a wave. 'That was the place,' he said, 'where all the shouted words fall into the water. They're too weak to make it from shore to shore. I saw the words underwater, millions of them; they're lying there on the bottom of the sea, a whole load of wrecked sentences, sentences that never reached their destination, questions from one side and answers from the other . . .'

"'How sad!' the little queen exclaimed. 'A cemetery of words!'

"'Some are swallowed by the fish,' the sea lion said, 'and they start sprouting the strangest things. Sunfish and electric eels and even crossopterygians . . .'

"'I do hope the answering people allow us to go ashore for a bit,' the little queen sighed. 'I'd really like to walk on solid ground again, just to feel that something exists.'

"But the shore of the island of answers was packed with too many people, too, all of them wanting to get rid of their answers.

"'Seven o'clock!' someone called out.

"'That adds up to 529.7!' another one shouted.

"The rose girl pushed the asking man gently to the rail. 'Here, you will find answers to your questions!' she said.

"'But how will I know the correct questions if there are so many answers in my head?' the asking man asked, his eyes full of tears. And he ran into the cabin and hid between the polar bear skins.

"'To do good!' one of the answering people shouted without being asked.

"'Boil it for three minutes, then let it simmer in the hot water for ten more minutes,' another one answered.

"'I don't think we want to go ashore here,' the sea lion said. 'We'll go ashore when we reach the mainland.'

"Before they sailed away from the island of answers, one of the answering people jumped aboard the ship. He went straight to the cabin, where the asking man was hiding, and for a while all you could hear were questions and answers shooting back and forth: 'Is he telling the truth?' 'On the thirteenth of March.' 'Is he good or bad?' 'Beneath the beeches, where the anemones grow in spring.' And then the cabin door flew open and both the asking man and the answering man came running out, in a state of confusion. One of them fled to the stern and the other to the bow, and they climbed over the rail and clung to the ship's hull from the outside, like two figureheads. Obviously they hoped never to meet again.

"In the meantime, the green ship set course once more for the mainland. The shipmates laughed for a good while about the asking man and the answering man. Then they turned and noticed that the black ship was very close now. So close that they could clearly see the four dark figures aboard. And they stopped laughing."

❖ ❖ ❖

Abel looked into his cup, stirred the cold chocolate, and then looked out the window, as if his thoughts were still lost inside the story.

"Those glasses," Micha said. "I guess the lighthouse keeper just had them in his pocket. That happens to a lot of people. It happens to my teacher. She isn't even really old or anything, just kind of old—thirty or something—but she always forgets where she puts her glasses. By the way, she asked me again when she can talk to Mama. I wonder why. But, Abel . . . when the red hunter came aboard the ship . . . I let him in, didn't I? I mean, in reality?"

Abel nodded. "You did."

"And now . . . now I shouldn't let anyone in, right?"

"That's right."

Micha nodded. "I didn't let that man in," she announced in triumph. "Yesterday. I forgot to tell you."

Abel sat up straight. "Who didn't you let in, Micha?" he asked.

"I don't know," Micha replied, "since I didn't let him in. He'd already come up the stairs, he was on the landing, talking to me through the door."

"What did he say?" Anna asked.

Micha thought for a while. "That he's from some kind of office. Something with a shell and a sister. He said it several times, real clear, as if he thought I was half-deaf. Wait . . . it started with *so* . . . shell . . . a sister office? I think he was from an office for shells and sisters. And he wanted to talk to Mama, too. I didn't say anything; I was perfectly quiet, as if I wasn't there at all."

"That's good, Micha," Abel said.

"Possibly . . . possibly I did say hello, very quickly, at the beginning," Micha murmured, and Anna laughed, although she really didn't feel like laughing.

"So-shell-a-sister-office," she said. "Social assistance office—that's it!" Micha exclaimed. "That's where he came from."

Abel lifted his cup and downed the rest of the chocolate like vodka. Then he covered his face with his hands, like he had done in the tower made of newspaper, in the literature classroom. As if he'd gone to a private room to calm down. When he took his hands away, he wore something resembling a smile on his face. It was a very strained smile.

"The black ship is still there," he said. "But today . . . today, we wanted to celebrate, didn't we, Micha?"

He got up and put on his jacket. "So let's celebrate. We'll . . . we'll do something special, we'll . . ." Behind his smile, the silhouette of a black ship loomed. She had to distract him, Anna thought. She had to make the black ship vanish before it came too close . . .

"I know what we'll do," she said. "We'll have ice cream. Do you still have room for ice cream?"

"I think so." Micha nodded. "We haven't had lunch yet. But can you eat ice cream in winter?"

"Ice cream isn't lunch," Abel said. "We should eat something sensible."

"Oh, come on." Anna laughed. "Stop being sensible for a while, will you? Ice cream is the best lunch imaginable. When I was your age, Micha, we always went for ice cream when we had a reason to celebrate. Especially in winter. My father used to say that anybody can eat ice cream in summer—that's no challenge—but we can do it in winter; then we'd go to the Italian restaurant at the market and get our ice cream cones and window shop and laugh at all the people who gave us strange looks. We still have a picture my mother took with an outstretched arm, of the three of us in the snow holding ice cream cones. And if we felt cold after eating them, we went home and sat in front of the fireplace . . ." She stopped.

"Rose girl," Abel said softly, "you must be awfully happy on your island."

"No," Anna replied. "There are too many thorns. I started feeling them. Like the little queen . . ."

The man at the Italian restaurant was surprised, of course, that they wanted ice cream cones to take away. But only a little. Maybe he remembered a little girl and her parents, who had come from time to time, to do the same thing—a father with broad shoulders, who could save you from every danger in the world, and a very gentle mother, who was almost invisible. Had he seen the rose branches beneath their clothes? Anna wondered. The petals? Maybe even the thorns?

Micha tried to order four scoops of ice cream, but Abel said "two," and then, "okay . . . okay, three," and Anna paid without his saying a word about it. And finally, they all stood outside in the snow-covered market square, in the icy wind, with their cones. Abel pulled his gray scarf tighter and shook his head. Then he started grinning. And then he headed down the street, walking without any particular aim or direction, as Anna had earlier. But now it was totally different. They walked next to each other, in silence, while Micha ran ahead, stopping at this or that window, saying what she would buy when she was rich; between the shops, she decorated the snow with brightly colored drips of her turquoise, Smurf-colored ice cream.

The street was full of people: people pushing strollers, people on bicycles, people with heavy bags or dogs on leashes, people who blended into an anonymous mass. Unimportant and, somehow, almost invisible. The ice cream was long gone, but they just kept walking, walking slowly, without hurrying; Anna wondered whether they would walk to the end of the street, and on and on, to the end of the world, and whether there would be a blue ocean there and a green ship waiting for them. She thought about the very first time she had talked to Abel. How he had been sitting on the radiator in the student lounge, looking threatening. Back then, she never would have considered it possible to walk down the street next to him, in silence—and to think that for the moment, everything was all right.

When she had arrived at this point in her thoughts, she realized that her hand was in his. She was not sure how long it had been there, and she was afraid to move it even a millimeter, in case he shied away. Micha had run ahead; now she came back, looked at Abel and Anna, glanced at their hands and grinned. Anna thought he would pull his hand back then. But he didn't. He squeezed her hand very quickly and very hard, and she squeezed back. Who had painted the snow golden?

Micha ran ahead again. They watched her draw something with her finger in the dirt on a shop window, then giggle and bounce away . . . a rubber ball with a fake fur collar and flying blond braids.

They stopped in front of the window; it was the window of a Chinese restaurant, and there was a red dragon painted on it. Next to that dragon Micha had written: "K IS EacH Oth ER."

Abel looked at Anna. Anna looked at Abel.

"She is the little queen," said Abel, "in our fairy tale, at least."

"One must obey the queen," said Anna.

Abel nodded seriously.

But, of course, we will walk farther now, Anna thought. And we will forget what was written on the window . . . It's almost forgotten already. Then, very suddenly, Abel pulled her into the doorway beside the shop window, into the smell of hot vegetable oil and MSG, next to a glass door with another red dragon on it, and kissed her.

Damn, thought Anna. I'm nearly eighteen years old, and I've never been kissed. Not properly, anyway. His lips were as cold as snow, but beyond the lips lay the warmth of a fairy-tale sun. She felt his tongue search for hers, and she thought of the wolf. And if it is true, she thought . . . if the fairy tale is true? A shot in the neck and a deadly bite in the neck. It all fits. And if I am kissing a murderer?

And if so? Then what?

A murderer, a wolf, a brother, an innocent, a fairy-tale teller. She rested her hands on the rough, cold material of his military parka and kissed him back. She closed her eyes; she no longer saw the red Chinese dragon on the door; she was aboard a ship, far out on the ocean. She heard the waves beat against the rail; she felt the rolling of the ship beneath her feet. If only one could spin a thread of the froth of the waves to make clothes . . . She tasted the fairy tale's words on his tongue, not vanilla ice cream or chocolate or cigarettes. No. She tasted the words themselves, the ocean's salt water and the wolf's blood . . . and behind the words, winter. But behind the winter, there was another taste, a taste she only recognized after a while: the taste of fear. He was afraid, and he was not holding her— he was holding onto her. She was suddenly and completely aware of that. Fairy-tale teller, she thought, where is the ship in your fairy tale sailing to? Where does the fairy tale lead? Will there be more blood, flowing into the cracks between the deck planks? I don't need anyone to protect me, she had said.

Oh yes, you do, Bertil had said. More than you think.

✦ ✦ ✦

They wandered back on the broad street that had once been the city's rampart. It was lined with tall old chestnuts, which in summer were covered in white and red blossoms. Now, there was only snow. They were holding hands again. For a while, Micha had walked between them, and they had swung her in the air as if she were a much smaller child. But then she had run ahead again, and they took each other's hands. When they reached Anna's bicycle, back at the market, somebody in a dark blue woolen sweater came out of the bank next door. Knaake. Again, Anna expected Abel to pull his hand away, and again he didn't. He just nodded in greeting; Knaake nodded back, and Micha asked a little too loudly, "Who's that?"

"The lighthouse keeper," Anna answered. And suddenly, she remembered something. The white cat.

"Michelle," she whispered. "Is it possible that Michelle had come aboard, too?"

"Who knows," Abel said.

"The white cat who sleeps all the time and blocks out the world . . . Has she come back, Abel? Have you spoken to her?"

Abel shook his head. "No. She just slipped into the fairy tale."

Anna wasn't sure she believed him. Something about the Michelle story was strange. That day, when he hadn't let her in . . . who had been in the apartment with him? Was Abel hiding his own mother? Protecting her? But from whom?

He let go of her hand. "Time to go home," he said. "Take care of yourself, rose girl. They say it's going to get even colder."

He watched them ride away on their bikes, ride away in separate directions. And he remembered the day he had seen them together for the first time, in the student dining hall. He smiled. Their outlines seemed to radiate light, seemed to sparkle. Like something dipped into liquid gold. How long had it been since he'd been part of a story outlined in gold? Except when he read literature? Too long. He remembered one golden story, the last one. He remembered the smell of her hair, the intoxicating smell of cheap shampoo; he'd bought her nice, expensive shampoo and later missed the smell of the cheap one . . . he remembered talking about things she hadn't understood, things that had meant too much to him . . . he remembered the music from the old, scratched LPs. Dancing in a tiny living room. An old sofa and dreams that had broken into pieces, later.

Dance me to the children who are asking to be born
Dance me through the curtains that our kisses have outworn
Raise a tent of shelter now, though every thread is torn
Dance me to the end of love

Dance me to your beauty with a burning violin
Dance me through the panic till I'm gathered safely in
Touch me with your naked hand or touch me with your glove
Dance me to the end of love . . .

And for a moment, he wished he were back there, young again, or younger—a little—so he could do everything over again and make different decisions . . . Faust. But no, no . . . no Gretchen questions . . . please, no.

And then, as they left the market square, Abel and Micha taking one street and Anna taking another, he saw their shadows. He

hadn't noticed them before; he'd only seen the bright shining gold . . .
their shadows were long and black. Of course, that was because of
the setting sun; it didn't mean anything. But suddenly he felt afraid.
Afraid for these two young people.

He didn't have children. But if he had, he thought, they'd be
Anna and Abel's age now. And he'd worry about them. He wouldn't
sleep at night; he'd lie in bed, sleepless, worrying. He'd yell at them
when they came home late, or maybe he wouldn't; maybe he'd be
silent and lose them in silence. It just wasn't possible, he thought, to
do right by your children.

Better to be alone.

Abel and Anna weren't his children. They were only his students.
Damn. Yet he still carried his fear for them home with him.

Who's that? That's the lighthouse keeper.

The lighthouse keeper? Why was he a lighthouse keeper? Which
lighthouse did he keep, and what was it that kept him there?

9

Bertil

THAT NIGHT, ANNA SLEPT WITH THE FAIRY-TALE TELLER.

Not in reality. In her dreams. She lay in her bed, in the house of blue air, and dreamed a pocket of time into Abel's fairy tale, a time pocket that would never be told. It was night on the deck of the green ship. The little queen was dreaming, too, between her polar bear skins in the cabin below, Mrs. Margaret in her arms, the asking man and the answering man, who had finally come in to get some sleep, beside her. And the lighthouse keeper. The lighthouse keeper slept in his boots and his glasses, which were pushed up into the graying hair on his head. The little queen was smiling in her sleep. Maybe she dreamed of the reality beyond her fairy tale, of turquoise ice cream on a snow-covered market square, of letters in the dirt on a window.

Anna was standing on the deck all alone, watching the stars. She found the Big Dipper and Ursa Major and Minor, but Ursa Minor looked like a dog, Ursa Major, like a wolf. She found Perseus, but he looked like a hunter with a long robe, and he wasn't alone; there were five hunters altogether—four of them, she thought, are still on the black ship. Four of them are still following us. Four of them want to catch us before we reach the mainland. She stepped to the rail and saw the moonlight on the waves. Small pieces of ice danced within it. The sea would freeze. Maybe soon. From one of the waves, a head appeared, the head of the sea lion. She wanted to reach out her arms to pull him on board. And suddenly the sea lion lifted himself out of the water and flew across the waves in a spray of small drops; in the next instant, the wolf was standing next to Anna. But no, she was mistaken. It was the silver dog with the golden eyes—but no, no, it wasn't the silver dog either. It was a human being. It was Abel, and yet, not Abel. His eyes were the wrong color; they were golden. He wore black, but not the black Böhse Onkelz sweatshirt she hated so much. He wore an ironed black shirt that looked strange on him; it was the kind of black shirt you wear to a funeral. She wanted to ask him whose funeral it was, and if he'd just come from it or was he headed to it later, but before she could ask, he had pulled her into his arms. It was like a weird ballet.

The white sails that the red hunter had torn to pieces with his rapier were still heaped on deck. Anna saw that someone had started to mend them, probably she herself, the rose girl, who had also made clothes for everyone. She felt the red velvet on her skin. She felt the red velvet slide down. She was naked. For a moment she stood like that, in the moonlight, but she wasn't cold. She undid the buttons of his black shirt—it was easy, like removing one's own clothes—and the black material slid down, too, and got entangled with the red velvet; black and red like night and blood. She looked at Abel. She tried to smile. She was a little afraid.

The round burn on his upper arm was shining like a second moon, or an eye.

"Don't look at it," he whispered, as he pulled her down onto the deck, between the white sails that closed around them like a tent. It was completely dark in that tent; there was nothing to be seen, only to be heard and to be felt and to be tasted.

"It's a dream," Anna whispered.

"It's a time pocket in the fairy tale," Abel whispered. "That is what you wished for, isn't it?"

In a dream, in a fairy tale, nothing has to be explained, everything happens of its own accord. That night, Anna knew everything and understood everything and was familiar with everything; she thought of Gitta and had to laugh because Gitta didn't understand anything—she only talked like she did. The tent made of sails became a cocoon and moved over the deck, rolling to and fro in the rhythm of the waves, an artwork by Christo and Jeanne-Claude, a package whose contents were no one's business. Anna felt blood on her fingers; she wasn't sure whose blood it was . . . maybe her own, maybe blood from the wound on Abel's temple, or maybe just a memory—or the blood of a third person? No, she thought, there is nobody here. Just the two of us.

And the cocoon, the artwork, the tent rolled over the deck, rolled over the rail, and sank into the icy waters of the night ocean, with Anna and Abel inside it. The white cat, who was lying on deck, silently shook her head at the sight.

When Anna awoke, it was five o'clock in the morning, and she was out of breath. The white cat, she suddenly thought—wasn't the white cat blind? She sat up in her bed and realized that she was shivering. Her bed seemed vast, and she was very alone in it.

◆ ◆ ◆

"Check out our Polish peddler," Gitta said on Monday, looking out the window. "If he keeps standing there, he'll be covered in snow like a statue. I don't get it. He's been standing there since early morning; he wasn't in French class—he's just been standing out there with plugs in his ears."

"White noise," Anna said.

Gitta looked at her. "Excuse me?"

"Maybe he hasn't earned his daily wage." Hennes laughed. He pushed his red hair back and nudged Gitta in a friendly way. "Hey, physics is over, and the math test tomorrow is the last one before finals . . . shouldn't we celebrate? Tomorrow night . . . we could ask him if he's got some weed. Or does he only sell pills?"

"He's a peddler." Gitta put a suggestive hand on Hennes's arm. "I'm guessing he can get almost anything. But if you ask him for weed, he'll laugh. Weed's easy—it's for children. I'm sure he makes more selling other stuff."

"Today, I'm feeling generous," Hennes said, grinning. "I actually feel like tipping. What do you think, does our Polish peddler take tips?"

He slipped into his ski jacket, and a moment later was walking across the yard, through the gently falling snowflakes. Gitta sighed and said, "Those snowflakes really look good in his hair. You could put that guy in a frame, hang him up on the wall . . ."

"If he really wants to party . . . maybe he'll let you hang him on the wall. You never know," Frauke said and laughed.

"Depends on what he arranges with the Pole," Gitta said, ". . . and what he plans to smoke. Anna, do you want to come tomorrow?"

"I'll think about it," Anna said.

She saw Hennes standing at the bike rack next to Abel. She saw
Hennes's bright-colored ski jacket, his glowing red hair, his upright
posture; she saw Abel beside him, hands dug deep into the pockets
of his old parka, hat pulled down low, back bent—a dark lump of a
human being, almost totally holed up in himself, nearly invisible, an
ugly blotch in the immaculate white snow. She saw Hennes talking
to Abel, who didn't take the plugs out of his ears.

"You know, it's possible to party without weed," Bertil said. Anna
jumped. She hadn't seen him there. He looked at her.

"What do you think?"

"I'm thinking," Anna replied in a low voice, "that I don't like
Hennes von Biederitz."

The math test went well. At first, Anna thought she would be too
distracted. All the words Abel hadn't said to her since Monday
were filling her head. She saw him sitting at his desk, his test in
front of him. Halfway through, he pulled off his black sweatshirt
and sat there in his T-shirt; she forced herself not to look at him
too closely, not to search for the round scar, not to think of her
dream. In the end, she managed to solve most of the test problems.
She remembered Bertil's patient explanations, the look behind his
glasses, and his voice—the voice of an indulgent professor—and it
was like Bertil was there, taking the test for her. She didn't want to
think that; she didn't want to think of Bertil; she hated the way he
kept sneaking up on her, seeming to appear out of nowhere, without
a sound.

But during lunch, there he was, all by himself, as usual. He hadn't
had to take the math test since he wasn't in the basic class—he was
in the intensive—and suddenly, Anna felt sorry for him. Bertil,

who understood all numbers and integrals and statistics, and whose glasses were always sliding down his nose, and whose soap bubble was fogged up from inside. She went over to him and thanked him again for his help, and he smiled.

"We're all getting together tonight to celebrate before finals," she said. "Why don't you come too?"

"Me?" Bertil asked.

Anna nodded. "Yes, you," she said. "Just do me a favor. Don't appear out of nowhere."

"I'll try and walk like an elephant," Bertil promised, grinning. She'd never seen him look so happy.

Linda didn't ask where Anna was going to celebrate with the others. All she said was, "Be careful on your bike; the streets are slippery."

"Just imagine! Your last test!" Magnus said.

"Only for Hennes," Anna replied. "We've still got our last history test on Friday. And then finals."

Magnus shook his head. "God, it seems like only yesterday you were in kindergarten."

Before she left to meet the others, he bent down—he was still so much taller than she was—and said in a low voice, "What of the world has been on your mind lately? Has it passed? Or . . . is it possible . . . that you'll meet whatever it is tonight, when you're out celebrating with the others?"

"No," Anna said. "The others are absolutely unworldly."

Magnus watched her smile. "One day you'll tell us, won't you? Linda's worried, you know. Because lately, you've been . . . she says you've been acting so different."

"One day I'll explain," Anna said. "But tonight is just a perfectly

normal night at the bar, with Gitta and the others. It's got nothing
to do with anything."

But Anna was wrong.

They met at the Mittendrin, opposite the dome. The Mittendrin
was one of the few bars where you could still smoke. In the tiny side
room, separated from the bar by a heavy black curtain that extended
from ceiling to floor, a cigarette machine blinked.

Anna always felt like she'd stepped onto a stage when she passed
through the curtain. Magnus had told her that in his day there had
been a table made of an old door, complete with the handle and
everything, and that the armchairs had been more comfortable.
The Mittendrin had been renovated a dozen times since then, but
the only real change was that there were more smokers. The air
in the bar was 70 percent cigarette smoke, 28 percent alcohol and
slightly strained coolness, and 2 percent the smoke of something
that wasn't cigarettes. It was also dark, and Anna wasn't sure
whether this was because of the absence of light or the presence of
smoke, which prevented the light from passing through.

Gitta leafed through the drink menu, happily taking a drag,
when Anna joined her and the others. The list of cocktails seemed
endless.

"Sex on the beach," Gitta said.

"In this weather?" Hennes asked.

"That's the drink I'm gonna order, stupid."

Bertil was sitting with a beer, trying to look relaxed, which he
wasn't; Frauke threw Anna a glance, cursing her for inviting him.
Anna shrugged and ordered a glass of vodka.

"You don't even like vodka," Gitta said. "Have a cocktail with us, little lamb. They have the weirdest things—I'll find something pretty for you, something nice and colorful, with a lot of fruit . . . we're celebrating math after all . . ."

"Why don't you let her have what she wants," Bertil said.

"I get it." Gitta looked over at Frauke and winked. "I know why she brought him. He's her bodyguard. Come on, Bertil, don't look so stricken; it was a joke, all right? Relax. So, what I wanted to say was . . . once these final exams are over, we'll . . ."

Anna leaned back and watched Gitta, who was, simultaneously, planning their futures, gesturing wildly, smoking, drinking something that looked like a cross between a palm tree and a swimming pool, and trying to move closer to Hennes. Anna thought about how much she liked Gitta and about how little Gitta actually knew of the world, even though she always acted like she knew everything. She felt a strange disconnect from her old friend, and from Frauke and Hennes and Bertil, too. She sat there and heard them talking but didn't listen; she watched them but looked through them, like she was watching a movie. She was sitting on the other side of the screen with her vodka, and she was a thousand years old. None of them had ever seen an island sink into the sea; none of them had ever removed as many splinters from a wound as she had—the splinters from what seemed like half a cupboard full of plates. None of them had ever been in the stairwell of 18 Amundsen Street. And then it came to her, all of a sudden, like the crack of a shotgun: they're the ones inside a soap bubble. Not me.

She talked to them without even listening to herself, talked to them about unimportant things; she saw that glasses were emptied and refilled with more brightly colored liquids, with different flower-shaped fruits; she passed the joint that Hennes gave her without touching it; she saw the time go by but wasn't there. She was on a ship; she was out on the ocean; she was walking with Abel between the winter chestnuts, his hand in hers. At one point, she realized that Bertil was no longer drinking a beer but instead sharing a cocktail with Frauke—the two of them drinking out of the same glass with two straws. Anna thought this was cruel of Frauke because she knew that Frauke didn't take him seriously. No one took Bertil seriously. And she wondered if Bertil had shared Hennes's joint. Probably. Just to be cool. But she was too far away to give it more thought.

"Anna," Gitta said, "you're dreaming. And you haven't smoked anything . . . are you dreaming of your university student?"

"Which stu—ah, my student," Anna said. "Yeah. Yeah, I am. I think I'm gonna go out for a minute, I need a bit of fresh air, a few double Os."

"What?" Gitta asked, leaning against Hennes. "What are you talking about, little lamb?"

"O_2, Gitta," Anna replied. "Oxygen."

She got up and elbowed her way through the crowd; by now, too many people were squeezed in the spaces between tables.

"Wait," someone behind her said. Bertil. "Anna! I'll come with you."

She shook her head. "Thanks, Bertil," she said, "but I want to be alone for a minute. Not long, okay? I . . ." I want to see if the stars here form a dog and a wolf, too, she thought. If Perseus looks like a hunter, and how many hunters there are. "I'll . . . I'll be back in a minute," she said.

Walking into the cold outside was like walking into an icy wall. She chided herself for not taking her coat. She pulled her hands into the sleeves of her sweater and saw that she wasn't the only person who'd come out for fresh air. To the left of the entrance, there was a small aluminum table and a bench that was used more in summer; a few guys—guys Anna didn't like—were standing there in the darkness, holding beers. Two of them had extremely short hair and necks like bulls. She took a step back, instinctively, and then heard a voice she knew. The voice named a price, and Anna looked again. It was a voice that usually said very different words, melodious words, fairy-tale words. Abel. Of course. Abel on his nightly round through the bars. Somehow she hadn't thought . . . she hadn't expected to meet him here. She figured he'd be working the Seaside District. Stupid of her, she thought. There weren't many bars out there. By comparison, the city was packed with them. She felt warmth rise inside her, a nice and friendly warmth, like the warmth of a fireplace. It was strange: she heard him talking to guys who made her afraid; she met him while he was dealing; and still she felt warm inside.

"Hi ya, darlin'!" one of the two guys said, noticing her. "Can I get a light?" He came over to where she stood, followed by his friend, who had a cigarette between his fingers. "My lighter's fucked up," he said, looking at her in a way that she definitely didn't like. She thought that it might be a good idea to go back inside now, but the two guys were standing between her and the door to the bar. She wasn't sure how sober they were. "Sorry," she said. "I don't smoke."

"See, Kevin, she don't smoke," the guy with the cigarette said. "Very reasonable. Gotta think of a better pick-up line than that if you want to take this sweet thing home!" They were standing much too close; she could smell the booze on their breath. Shit, shit, shit, Anna thought, why did I have to come outside alone? Abel wouldn't help her. Abel wouldn't know her here, like he didn't know her at school.

Kevin put his hand out to touch her hair. At that moment, someone laid a hand on his shoulder and yanked him back with a jerk. It was Abel's hand. "Leave her alone," he said.

"Hi . . . Abel," Anna said. That was all she could think to say.

"That your fuckin' first name, Tannatek?" Kevin said. "Abel? I can't believe it. What kind of a name is that? And who's the chick?"

"Her name's Anna," Abel answered, putting his arm around her. "And keep your hands off her if you don't want things to get messy, got it?"

"Whoa. Steady . . . steady!" Kevin said. "Relax, dude."

Abel was probably ten or twenty pounds lighter than Kevin-with-the-bull-neck. But for some inexplicable reason, Kevin seemed to respect him. "That means . . . Don't tell me she's with you, Tannatek?" the other guy asked in disbelief. "I thought you . . ."

"Don't think too much," Abel said. "It'll make you grow ulcers on your head, Marcel."

Kevin laughed, and Abel pulled Anna to the side. "What are you doing here?"

"Gitta and the others are inside. I just wanted to get some air . . ."

Abel put his hands on her shoulders. "You're cold. You're shivering."

She nodded. "It's not important . . ."

"Sure it is," and then, in a very low voice, with a private kind of a smile, he said, "Rose girl, I told you the branches would wither and you would freeze. You wanted to stay on board . . ."

Anna nodded. "I'm staying."

He took off his parka, slid out of the black sweatshirt, and gave it to her before putting the parka back on. "Take this."

Marcel whistled through his teeth. "Striptease!" he said. "Just go on, Tannatek, strip! She can join you . . ."

"Shut your fuckin' trap, Marcel," Abel said, taking a step toward him. Marcel didn't move. He narrowed his eyes and looked Abel over, almost pleased. "Aw . . . whatsa matter?" he said. "You really want trouble? You can have it." Kevin laughed again, but more uncomfortably now.

Anna hurried up and put on Abel's sweatshirt. She had the thought that it would be better to have her hands free if it came to a fight, but of course that was silly . . .

"Come on," Abel said. He took her hand and pulled her away.

They headed down the street next to the Mittendrin, the dome towering behind them, piercing the winter sky like a strange, glowing plant. The street lay empty and quiet. Nobody followed them. On the walls of the old houses, the snow stuck to the frozen ivy leaves.

"I can beat up the two of them if I have to," Abel said. "Kevin knows that. But I won't have to. Don't worry."

"But I do worry," Anna said. "It's about all I ever do these days. I'm afraid."

He stopped and looked at her. He'd let go of her hand. "Me, too," he said. "But not of those guys. They're dumb. They're so dumb. They live out there, you know, where we live, too. Everyone there . . . well, almost everyone . . . is dumb. Ignorant. It's not their fault. They inherit the ignorance of their parents and hand it onto their children like a tradition, like a craft. They drink in the ignorance with their powdered milk, with each bottle of beer, and in the end they make their coffins of ignorance."

"And . . . you?"

"Me?" He understood and laughed. "I don't know. I'm a slipup. A mistake. An accident. I guess Michelle managed to bed some intellectual. I've always been different. And maybe back then . . . when I was very small . . . maybe she was different, too. I don't remember. Maybe she was a mother . . . before she gave up being anything at all. We . . . we got a letter from that social services office, the one with the shells and sisters, you know. It says Michelle needs to show up there and asks why she hadn't checked in lately. They plan to stop by again to ask questions . . ."

Anna put her arms, in the black sleeves, around him and hugged him, holding him tight for a minute. "Somehow, everything will turn out all right," she whispered. "Somehow . . . I don't know how . . . not yet, anyway . . . Let's walk in the snow for a while. It's so beautiful . . . they said it wouldn't snow again this winter, but now . . ."

"What about the others? The bar?" Abel asked as he walked along beside her. "Don't you want to go back?"

"Later," Anna said. "Though, to be honest, I don't even know why. I don't feel like sitting there, celebrating with them. They're celebrating that math is over, but really they're celebrating their own ignorance. They're just as ignorant as the people in your apartment building . . . just in another way, you know what I mean? I want something different . . . I want . . . I want to go to the U.S. on a cargo ship. I want to cross the Himalayas. I want . . . to fly . . . far away . . . somewhere. To some . . . desert. To the end of the world." She held out her arms and turned in the snow like a plane, like a child pretending to be a plane.

"Yeah," Abel said. "Maybe I'll come with you . . . to the U.S. and the Himalayas and the desert."

She stood, out of breath, and realized that she was beaming. "Let's do it," she whispered. "Let's go ahead and do it. After finals. Let's go away, really far away."

"And Micha?"

"We'll take her with us. It can't be bad for her to get to know the world a bit . . . we can do everything, Abel . . . get anywhere . . . together . . ."

He smiled. "Everything?" he said. "Together. With me? Anna Leemann, you don't even know me."

He took her hand and led her back to the Mittendrin. She wished he would kiss her again; she wished it so much it hurt, but she didn't dare to initiate it. She didn't know what he thought or what he wanted. He was right. She didn't know him.

Kevin and Marcel weren't standing in front of the Mittendrin anymore.

"So . . ." Abel said, "the others are waiting for you."

"Come in with me," she said suddenly. "Have a glass of vodka with us. I'm inviting you. You've taken the math exam . . ."

"I don't think I fit in with those people you're with," Abel said.

"Neither do I. Come anyway. They're harmless." Reluctantly, Abel let her pull him through the door. "Wait," he said. "Anna, what's this supposed to be? An introduction to refined society? Think about what you're doing . . ."

Anna laughed. "We're not living in the Middle Ages. Or in India—there are no castes here. Come on . . . Frauke will be excited to see you for sure. She once considered falling in love with you 'experimentally.'"

"Oh my God." He rolled his eyes.

And for a moment, Anna thought everything would be all right.

Abel would sit at the table with them and laugh with them and cease being the Polish peddler and change into a fellow student . . . a fellow fighter in the fight against finals, a human being with a first name.

The smoke-filled air surrounded them like a strange kind of ocean, an ocean very different from the one on which the little queen was sailing. Anna made her way through the crowd, to the table where the others were sitting. Abel followed her. She saw him greet some people with a nod, people she didn't know . . . and didn't want to know. He swam in the thick bar air like a fish in water, and still he hesitated to come to her table. Gitta was on the black leather sofa with her head on Hennes's knees. She looked sleepy in a comfortable sort of way, not really tired; she looked as if she had very definite plans for the night.

"Anna," she said, "where've *you* been hiding?"

"I met someone outside," Anna said and stepped aside to make a vague gesture in Abel's direction. Everyone at the table looked at her. Gitta sat up. She seemed to awaken from her sleepiness—or pretended sleepiness—with a start. "Oh, Tannatek," she said. "Hi."

The others didn't say anything. They just stared. And suddenly, Anna remembered that she was still wearing Abel's black sweatshirt. So what? She straightened up.

"Is there an extra chair somewhere?" she said. "I think I saw one before. We . . ."

She didn't get any further. For just then, Bertil stood up, made his way past Frauke, and came toward her. He was unsteady on his feet.

"So this is how things are," he said, very loudly, at least for Bertil. "I get it. I understand. I understand everything now. I'm good enough for math. For helping you study. But that's the only time.

I . . . you . . . so you, Anna Leemann. I've been . . . I . . . suspected this all along . . . I should have known . . . It was clear . . . absolutely fucking clear . . . It . . ." He held onto Frauke's chair. His glasses were sliding down his nose again, and then, with a sudden movement, he tore them from his face and threw them on the table.

"Bertil," Anna said, "you're drunk!"

"I'm . . . I'm not," Bertil said, but his words were heavy and slow. "I'm . . . I'm abso . . . absolutely . . . so . . . so-sober. F . . . f-f-for the first time perf . . . ectly . . . sober. You . . . it must be you . . . who is drunk. Look at your . . . yourself, how you're running around, in that disgus . . . disgusting sweatshirt . . . you're joining the club of anti . . . antisosh . . . antisocial elements now?"

He came closer, still unsteadily, awkwardly, almost blind, but his eyes were burning with an unexpected and dangerous rage. Anna stepped back; she saw Abel take a step backward, too. He hadn't backed off from the guys outside the bar, she thought.

"Bertil, sit down," Frauke said.

"Don't . . . don't order me around," Bertil said with his heavy tongue. And with a sudden, flailing movement of his arm, he pushed Anna aside and stood face-to-face with Abel. Anna lost her balance, grabbed onto the bar behind her, and knocked over a glass; she heard it crash, and felt a lot of faces turn toward her.

Staring at her and Abel and Bertil.

Abel stood motionless, as if he were made of stone. Even his face had turned to stone. Bertil took another step forward and flicked some snow off Abel's jacket, like he was attempting to clean it, a strange gesture.

"Sure, I'll never . . . never be as cool as T . . . Tannatek in his military jacket," he slurred. "But listen here . . . you're missing a button . . . a button on your jacket and . . . don't you wanna cut your hair again? Your Nazi friends surely don't . . . like you having it so l . . . long . . ." He reached out and plucked the black woolen hat from Abel's head. Abel took it back from him. That was all he did. His face was stoney. They were extremely close now; Bertil was a little taller than Abel but not half as broad-shouldered. They stared at each other. The bar was silent.

Then Bertil noticed the silence. He looked around, seeming to enjoy the fact that everyone was listening to him for once, and turned back to Abel. "If I had a . . . a weapon," he said, "I'd just . . . I'd just shoot you. L . . . like my fa . . . father did with that dog. One shot, poof, and that . . . that would be the end of you."

When he said that, Abel suddenly came to life. He grabbed Bertil's arm with his left, uninjured hand. Anna saw how tight the grip was, she heard Bertil gasp.

"If you want to fight with me, Bertil Hagemann, we'll go outside," he said in a low voice.

"Yeah. B-b-beating people up, that's some . . . something you're good at," Bertil hissed. "Just words . . . words are not your spesh . . . speciality, are they? But maybe the girls l-l-like that . . . if a guy doesn't talk much . . . but instead does oth-other things to them . . . maybe he's good in bed, right, Anna? Why don't you tell . . . tell us about it. We want all . . . all the details . . ."

At that moment Abel's right hand slammed into Bertil's face. His left hand was still gripping Bertil's arm, and Anna saw him flinch as pain shot through his right hand.

"So," Abel said, his voice still very low, "are you coming out with me or do I have to carry you?"

"Hennes," Gitta said, "do something." Anna actually heard

something like fear in Gitta's voice. Or was it her own fear? "If someone doesn't bring him to his senses," Gitta went on, "Bertil will let the Pole beat him to a pulp."

Hennes got up from the sofa and stood next to Bertil. Hennes's red hair shone, even in the darkness of the bar, even through the smoke; he stood as upright as always, in spite of the many colorful drinks, in spite of the joint. He put a hand on Bertil's shoulder.

"Let go of him, Tannatek," he said, very calmly. "We'll look after him. He's had too much to drink. He doesn't know what he's talking about."

Abel released Bertil and folded his arms across his chest. "I think he knows perfectly well what he's talking about," he said. "He's more honest than you, Hennes."

"Of . . . of course, I know . . ." Bertil began.

"Shut up, Bertil," Hennes said. And then, in a very loud and clear voice, continued, "Tannatek wants to leave now."

Anna saw Abel's eyes as he looked at Hennes. The blue in them had frozen, turned again into a solid block of ice.

"That's what I think, too," the bartender called out to Abel, whom he seemed to know. "Do me a favor, will you? I don't feel like throwing you out."

Abel took a deep breath, as if he wanted to say something, but then he turned around silently and left.

"Okay, and when he's far enough away, you see to it that your friend gets home," the bartender said to Hennes. "And when he's slept off his hangover, tell him I don't ever wanna see him in here again, understand?" Hennes took his hand from Bertil's shoulder, and Bertil slumped into a chair. "Shit," he mumbled. "Holy fucking shit."

"That's the first sensible thing you've said tonight," Anna said. Seconds later, she was running down the street, the same street she had just walked along with Abel. She caught up with him at the end of it, a few yards from the market square.

"Abel!" she cried, reaching out. He swung round, and lifting up his hands, said defensively, "Don't you dare touch me!"

"I . . . I didn't want that to happen!" Anna despaired. "I didn't know Bertil was . . . that he was so drunk and . . . I'm sorry! I'm so sorry! I didn't want things to end like that!"

"We're not living in the Dark Ages," Abel said. "Yeah, right. And not in India either. There're no castes here. Ha."

"But the bartender threw Bertil out, too, same as you! And he told us he doesn't want to see him there again! Of course, there are no castes! All men are equal!"

"Do you ever listen to yourself when you're talking such nonsense?" Abel asked.

"No," Anna said. "Abel. Can't we go somewhere, away from the others? Where there is nothing and no one? No people, no bars, no schoolyards, no tower blocks . . ."

He hesitated. Finally, he said: "The Elisenhain. The woods behind the village of Eldena. I promised Micha I'd take her there one day. She loves the woods when there is snow. We could go tomorrow."

"When tomorrow? Where can I meet you?"

"The Russian store at the corner of the last street before the woods. At four." He turned to go, and she heard him murmur, "I have to be fuckin' out of my mind. Crazy."

"Wait!" Anna called. "Where are you going now? Can't I come with you?"

He turned back, and the look in his eyes was strange. "No, Anna," he said. "Where I'm going now, you can't come with me."

Linda was sitting in the dark living room, pretending she wasn't waiting up, when Anna got home.

"You can go to bed now," Anna said and kissed her. "Sorry. I probably smell like a tobacco factory."

"You're shivering," Linda said. "Didn't you wear warm enough clothes?"

"I did," Anna replied. "Even a borrowed sweatshirt. It's not the cold. I think it's rage."

"At what?" Linda asked, but Anna just shrugged.

"Myself," she said.

The questions came the next day, all the questions that hadn't been asked the night before. A billion questions that pierced her like tiny sharp needles. Frauke shot most of them at her, but rumors are quick to spread, and the looks of classmates started to get under Anna's skin. Anna Leemann, at night, in the Polish peddler's sweatshirt? Is it true she's dating him?

"Oh, how exciting," Frauke said. "Tell us, Anna, what's he like? I mean, deep down inside, under the military parka and the black sweatshirt and . . ." She giggled. "Underneath everything?"

Anna didn't answer. She didn't answer anybody. Strangely, Gitta didn't say anything.

Abel was standing in the yard as always, in the freezing cold, his hands dug deep into his pockets. There was no fresh white snow today to cover the dirty old snow that wouldn't melt.

During lunch break, Bertil approached Anna, obviously unsure of himself. "I wanted to apologize," he said. "For last night. I mean, I can't really remember what I said . . . but judging from what the others told me, it can't have been too nice. I should have drunk less."

"Children and drunk people always tell the truth," Anna said.

"I'm . . . I'm sorry!" Bertil repeated, in despair. "Can't you forgive me?"

"Not now," Anna said. "And anyway, you're asking the wrong person for forgiveness. You need to walk across the schoolyard to the bike stands to find the person you should apologize to."

"No way." Bertil shook his head. "No, Anna . . . you're not really dating him, are you? Tell me it's not true."

Anna walked away without another word and went across the schoolyard herself; she was fed up with the talk—she was fed up with everyone, all of them. She didn't give a shit what they thought, and she couldn't do anything about the wall that Abel was building around himself out here. She stood next to him and asked, "White noise?"

He nodded.

"Please," she said, "can I have one of your earplugs? The others are making me ill. I can't listen to their questions anymore. Their stupid comments."

He didn't look at her. He handed her an earplug in silence. He seemed to have decided that it no longer made sense to pretend he didn't know her. The white noise from the old Walkman enveloped them both; like a blanket of new snow, it draped itself over them, shutting out all the curious looks.

And the world under the blanket was—surprisingly, wonderfully—absolutely quiet.

◆ ◆ ◆

At four o'clock in the afternoon, the sign in front of the Russian store at the corner of Hain Street swung to and fro in the wind, like it always did, alternately revealing its Russian name one side and the German translation on the other. Russian candies in their gold paper boxes were fading in the window, as were the Russian Matryoshka dolls, piled high behind the window blind. Farther along the street, three figures walked next to each other, toward the woods.

The beech trees towered against the winter sky in silence, their snow-covered branches like the work of fairies who had decorated the forest with a thousand tiny songbirds. The Elisenhain at four o'clock on a February afternoon seemed the most wonderful place in the world. A fairy-tale forest full of invisible stories, a storybook forest full of untold fairy tales, a forest full of fairylike tales . . .

"Bertil apologized," Anna said. They turned onto the old street, the one with the uneven cobblestones, on which you could still see the hollow tracks made by horse carriages in olden times. But now the cobblestones were buried deep in the snow. Micha was running ahead, like she usually did, counting the footprints of rabbits and deer.

"Bertil," Abel repeated. "Do me a favor, will you, and don't mention that name for a while."

"He's a sad person in his own way," Anna said. "He . . ."

"Is that it?" Abel asked bitterly. "Is that the reason you're walking next to me? You're collecting 'sad' people you feel sorry for and want to help?"

"You know very well why I'm here," Anna said, stopping to look at him. And she thought that maybe she should be the one to initiate a second kiss, if only to be sure there'd actually be one.

She was afraid he'd back away after everything that had happened last night, afraid he'd had a change of heart. She looked up at the beeches, hoping for a sign, but the towering trees remained silent.

So she threw her fear overboard and kissed him in spite of everything. And he didn't back away, and she wondered if he had been waiting for her to make a move.

"Hey," he asked after quite a while, a little out of breath, looking at the top button of her coat, which had come loose, "are you still wearing my sweatshirt? I didn't notice at school."

"I . . . I'll give it back . . ."

"Not now," he said. "We should catch up with Micha."

He took her hand in his, and they started to run, along the old street, sliding on the ice-covered cobblestones that lay beneath the snow. It was like they were children, two children about to enter a fairy-tale forest. It could have been Christmas, Anna thought. She wouldn't have been surprised to see tiny silver bells hanging from the branches and maybe polished red apples, too; to hear music coming from the treetops, very quiet music; or to find Gitta's old sled with the red stripe waiting behind one of the trunks . . .

"Catch me!" the third child called out, the child in the pink down jacket, as she fled into the woods, along a narrow path, through the giant columns of trees. A frozen rivulet wound its way along the path, meandering through the kitschy winter postcard scene; Micha jumped over the ice, giggling and carefree, running farther into the trees on the other side. Anna had fallen behind Abel after they'd let go of each other's hands on the narrow path, but now he slipped and landed on the frozen brook, and she laughed and ran past him. She caught up with Micha at a fork in the path. But she didn't stop.

Instead, she ran past Micha, calling back over her shoulder, "Now you catch *me*!"

A short way ahead, the path disappeared into a dense thicket of hazelnut bushes, covered with snow. Maybe this wasn't the path after all but a deer trail . . . Anna looked behind her as she ran. But Micha hadn't followed; she was still standing at the fork, strangely undecided. But now, Abel was coming. Anna ran on, toward the hazelnut thicket. She could dive into it and try to hide, she thought—though of course he would find her instantly. It was all a game, a children's game . . . he caught up with her just before the thicket and pulled her to the ground; they lay in the snow, panting. Anna tried to get up, to slip through his fingers, and, giggling, to run on; but he wouldn't allow it, and his grip was so firm it hurt. She looked up at him. His eyes were golden. No, she had imagined that, they were blue, like always. "Hey!" she said, "let go!"

"This is the wrong path," Abel said. "The woods are too dense in this direction."

"But it's beautiful here! In spring, it's filled with anemones. I often come to this part . . ."

Abel pulled her back onto her feet. His grip was still iron. It was his right hand that held her; in his hurry to hold her back, he probably hadn't remembered it was hurt. She could tell he was clenching his teeth with pain, but he didn't let go. "In winter, there aren't any anemones blossoming here," he said. "Micha is afraid of the dark. Let's go back; we'll take the other path at the fork." He was right. Micha was still there waiting for them. She hadn't moved even a step in their direction.

When they were back with her, Abel released Anna's arm and took Micha by the hand. Her eyes were big and frightened. "I thought Anna would go in there," she whispered, barely audible. "Into that part of the woods. You're not allowed to go there, Anna. Did you know that? There are fallen trees back there; the trunks are hollow, and the invisible live inside. They've got sharp teeth that glow like hot iron. And they can bite you."

Anna followed them along the other path, which led back to the old street, and only when they had reached it did the fear in Micha's eyes dissolve. "It's much better here," she said. "I shouldn't ever have run down that path, I forgot . . . the invisibles . . . they bit Abel once . . . there was blood; his whole sleeve was covered in blood . . ."

"Sometimes Micha tells fairy tales, too," Abel said, tousling her pale, snow-blond hair. "But, today, I'm not going to tell you anything about the invisibles in the woods. Instead, I'll tell you about the island of the beggar woman."

"The island of the beggar woman?" Micha asked.

"Yes," he said. Then he linked arms with Anna, and, still holding Micha by the other hand—the left one this time— started wandering back through the Elisenhain as Anna tried to forget the invisibles. She didn't feel like thinking about their sharp teeth, which could bite your arms, and make them all bloody. Not now. She just wanted to walk through the forest with Abel and Micha and listen to a story and stop worrying for a little while.

"The island of the beggar woman was the next island the ship came to," Abel said. "There was just a single building on it: a tiny gray house that looked strangely ragged. The wind whistled through the crevices in the walls, and you could hear it far out at sea:

"'Don't you have some coins for me?' it whistled. 'This house is all I own, you see, the curtains made of waves and foam, this is the beggar woman's home.'

"Next to the little house there was a bare tree, and the wind was whistling through its leafless branches, singing: 'Don't you have some bread for me? This tree is all I own, you see. It has no apples, has no pears; instead it grows a thousand cares.'

"The wind whistled in the cold chimney: 'Don't you have some warmth for me? This hearth is all I own, you see. There's no coal, no flames in it, my dreams are all I've ever lit.'

"'Let's go ashore!' the little queen exclaimed. 'We have to bring that tree back to life and light a fire in the cold fireplace! Maybe my diamond heart can help the beggar woman! It has to be good for something, a heart of diamond!'

"So they went ashore, and the beggar woman came running out of her gray house. She couldn't believe that anyone was visiting her. Clad in rags, thin and gray and torn, she looked ancient, though she may have still been young.

"'Oh!' she exclaimed, 'I've always wanted a queen to visit my island! I can offer you nothing, though, for nothing is all I own . . . Do you see the island out there, on the horizon? That's the island of the rich man. On clear days, you can see his palace. I've been writing letters to him for years, putting them into the bottles that wash ashore here. I've thrown a hundred bottles with letters into the sea, hoping the waves would carry them over to his island . . . In each and every letter, I have asked him for help, but I've never got an answer . . .'

"The little queen laid her hand on the dead tree, and she asked her diamond heart to give it back its life. But the tree stayed cold. 'It's me,' the beggar woman said sadly. 'Whatever I touch turns gray and cold . . . I just don't have the right touch for things.'

"'Come aboard with us,' the little queen said. 'We'll take you to the island of the rich man.'

"The beggar woman gave a deep sigh, for it is not easy to leave one's home, even if it is only a cold hearth and dead tree.

"But finally she allowed the rose girl to help her over the rail, and the green ship cast off. The rose girl saw the sea lion shake his head as he swam along next to them. 'We don't have time,' he said in a low voice. 'Don't you see that the black sails are much closer again?'

"He dove down into the waves, which were full of ice splinters; through the clear water, before he disappeared, the rose girl saw a circular wound on his right flipper.

"On the island of the rich man, there was a palace made of blue glass, blue like the ice on a frozen rivulet in a winter wood. And in the windowpanes the wind was singing:

"'What do you think this island can give? Love, joy, and light, a reason to live? Surely, there is no island that can give you more than that of the rich man.'

"Inside, in the warmth behind the thick glass of a greenhouse, orange and lemon trees were growing, along with high date palms and banana trees, in huge, delicately decorated pots. A nice warm fire danced in the fireplace, and there was a letter on the sofa, pinned down with a golden paperweight.

"'Dear travelers,' the lighthouse keeper read aloud. 'Please go ahead and take some of the fruit in my greenhouse. I'll be gone for a while. I got a message in a bottle this morning saying that there is a beggar woman living on that nearby island. I had never realized it was inhabited. Now I'm on my way there. I'll fix the island of the beggar woman. Everything I touch becomes fertile and beautiful. I don't know why; I just seem to have the right touch . . .'

"'Oh!' the little queen sighed. 'He's gone. He's sailed away on his own ship to visit the island of the beggar woman! He must have passed us on the way, but we didn't see him.'

"'The beggar woman could just stay and live in the palace from now on,' the rose girl said.

"'The beggar woman sat down between the orange and lemon trees. She looked a little lost.

"'Don't forget to water the trees,' the little queen said.

"'Yes . . .' the beggar woman replied distractedly.

"'And don't forget to clean the windows from time to time, so the light can get in and make the trees grow!'

"'Yes . . .'

"'They took a basketful of fruits with them and went back aboard their green ship.

"'Now she is happy,' the little queen whispered, pressing Mrs. Margaret so hard she became a little flat and grumpy. 'We helped her.'

"But the rose girl and the lighthouse keeper stood at the stern and looked back toward the island of the rich man. So the little queen looked back, too. And she saw that the palace appeared a little gray all of a sudden, as if it were losing its colors. The orange trees were already losing their oranges and had started to wither. On the island of the beggar woman, though, the dead tree seemed to have fresh green leaves now.

"'That's the rich man with his lucky hands,' the lighthouse keeper said.

"'And the beggar woman with her unlucky ones,' the rose girl added.

"'Oh no!' the little queen cried out. 'Maybe they have to meet so that everything turns out all right?'

"'Now will you all stop shouting?' the blind white cat said. 'I want to sleep. You can't change things. That's life. Poor stays poor and rich stays rich, and *those* two, they will *never* meet.'

"And that was when the little queen saw the black ship. It was sailing between them and the islands, so they couldn't see the palace or the gray house anymore. The black ship shut out the daylight, towering over them like a mountain range made of dark masts and sails and ropes, very close. They heard the wind in its rigging, the ever-singing wind:

> *Rail black and black the planks,*
> *Black the stern, the bow, the flanks*
> *We're the ones who never fail*
> *Black our mast and black our sail*
> *We don't fear a storm or rain,*
> *Who's not slaying will be slain,*
> *We are never hesitating,*
> *Lying in the shadows, waiting*
> *For the perfect time to strike*
> *And destroy what we don't like.*
> *You will soon be in our grip,*
> *This is the hunter's ship.'*

"'Will they kill us?' the asking man asked at the bow.

"'In the Elisenhain, between the hazelnut bushes,' the answering man answered from the stern, without any context, as usual. The little queen clung to the rose girl's sleeve. The shadow of the black ship was touching the rail. Two black figures—an overweight woman in a tracksuit and a man who seemed younger than she— were standing there, looking over at them. Behind them, the little queen could see two more people, an elderly couple.

"Suddenly, the silver-gray dog landed beside them.

"'Listen,' he said very quickly. 'If there is no other way, you must use the airship. It's under the polar bear skins in the cabin. If you take it out and bring it on deck, the wind will inflate the balloon. The cabin can be turned into a gondola—you've just got to fasten it to the balloon with the hooks you'll find there . . . but use the airship only in the case of an emergency. It will drift with the wind. And the wind has been blowing away from the mainland ever since we set out. If you use the airship, you might be safe from the hunters, but you may never reach the mainland.'

"When she heard this, the little queen kneeled down and put her arms around the dog.

"'Why do you say YOU?' she asked. 'What about you? Are you leaving us?'

"'Yes,' the silver-gray dog replied. 'I'll try to detain them for a while.'

"He struggled free of the little queen's embrace, and, with a great leap, he jumped—no, he flew—through the air toward the black ship."

10

Sisters of Mercy
࿔

"WHAT HAPPENED NEXT?" MICHA ASKED BREATH-lessly.

"I don't know what happened next," Abel said. "Maybe it hasn't happened yet. We've got to wait. And now, we're there."

They had left the snow-covered beeches behind and were standing at the end of Hain Street again, in front of the little Russian store at the corner. Abel unlocked his bike. "The lock has nearly frozen," he said. "It's really damn cold."

"Let's go home and have hot apple juice with cinnamon," Micha said. "And make pancakes. The weather's just right for pancakes. And you still have to show Anna how to make them. How to flip them in the air . . . and everything."

"Maybe Anna would rather go home now," Abel said. "Maybe she has to study for her next exam or practice the flute or . . ."

"Should Anna go home?" Anna asked.

Abel shook his head slowly. "Come with us." And then a grin

crept onto his face. "It's probably high time you learn some important things, like how to flip a pancake in the air."

The gray staircase was almost familiar now, the beer bottles piled in front of a door, the sharp teeth of the steps, the uneven banister. They hadn't gotten any farther than the first floor when the door downstairs opened.

"Abel!" Mrs. Ketow called. "Wait!"

"Go ahead," Abel said to Micha as he bent over the banister. Below, Mrs. Ketow's plump figure stood, tracksuited as always, holding onto the banister with one hand, trying to bend her head so she could look up at Abel.

"I just wanted to say . . . about Michelle . . . I know she ain't comin' back, right? I know she ain't comin' back."

Abel narrowed his eyes and looked at her. "How do you know?" he asked and started to walk back down the stairs very slowly. Anna followed him.

"I could tell the authorities. But I don't," Mrs. Ketow said in a lower voice. "I know a lot, I do."

Abel stood in front of her now. She was a lot smaller than he was. Her tracksuit was stained; her stringy hair was pulled back in a tight ponytail, which exposed her broad and somehow featureless face. One strand of hair, above her temple, was dyed bright red. Anna wondered what Mrs. Ketow would look like twenty pounds lighter. If she would be pretty. If she had been pretty, way back. From the apartment behind her, Anna heard children shouting.

"I know why the social worker keeps coming to your door," Mrs. Ketow went on. "Want to take the little one from you, don't they? You can't keep her, Abel, you know that. I just wanted to say, no worries. I have three foster children already, but that's okay, I could take a fourth one; there's room enough here. The little one, she could stay here, in this house. It'd be better for you—you could always see her; I'd let you—she'd just live with me. She's older than the others, so it'd work out pretty well. I'd tell those social workers . . . I don't have problems with them people . . ."

Abel took another step forward, and Mrs. Ketow stepped back.

"Give your friends from the social services office my best," he said coldly. "And tell them Michelle will be back." He looked dangerous again, a huge gray wolf in the stairwell, baring its teeth, and even though they were invisible teeth, Mrs. Ketow saw them.

"Michelle . . . I mean, she was okay," she said, stepping back farther. "We got along well, smoked a cigarette together from time to time . . ."

"I'm not Michelle," Abel said. "Why don't you take care of the foster children you already have—that's what social services is paying you to do." With these words, he turned and went up the stairs, this time without stopping. On the fourth floor, he unlocked the door to the apartment, slipped off his shoes, and covered his face with his hands for a moment, standing there in the hallway, just breathing. Anna stood beside him, helpless. She wanted to do something, to say something, something helpful, but nothing came to mind. The only thing that did come to mind was that she had seen Mrs. Ketow already today. Aboard the black ship. Abel lowered his hands and looked at her.

"Pancakes?" he asked.

She nodded.

And then she was sitting next to Micha on the narrow windowsill in the kitchen, while Abel mixed the batter for the pancakes. The kitchen was filled with the smell of sugar and batter and hot oil; the window fogged up. Anna drew a ship on it with her finger, and Micha drew a dog at the bow. From the old cassette player on the kitchen table, Leonard Cohen was singing:

> Oh the sisters of mercy they are not departed or gone
> They were waiting for me when I thought that I just can't go on . . .
> And they brought me their comfort and later they brought me their song
> Oh I hope you run into them you who've been waiting so long . . .

Mrs. Ketow was far away.

"See, when they start coming loose at the edges, then you shake the pan a little and throw the pancake in the air," Abel explained. "Look, like this . . ." Anna slid down from the windowsill. She stood behind him to get a closer look and, for a moment, placed her chin on his shoulder. She would have liked to have stood like this a little longer, but Abel stepped back and flipped the pancake, which turned over in the air. When he caught it in the pan again, Micha clapped her hands.

"Abel," she said, "can do everything in the world."

And Anna thought, if you could just flip your way through finals!

"Wait," Micha said. "I think I heard something. Maybe . . ."

Anna followed her to the hallway. The doorbell was ringing, obviously for the second time now. "Maybe it's her," Micha whispered.

"Who?" Anna asked.

"Michelle," Micha said. "She always loved Abel's pancakes. Maybe she smelled them and came home." She ran to the door and opened it wide before Anna could say or do anything. Anna wanted to believe that Michelle really would be standing in the doorway and everything would be okay. If only she could believe hard enough . . .

The person standing in the door was not Michelle, of course. It was a man whom Anna had never seen before. He wore a suede jacket lined with sheepskin, a knitted sweater with a brown pattern, and jeans. A silver ring shone in his left ear, and a broad smile brightened his three-day stubble. Under his arm he was carrying a black leather folder.

"How nice you finally got around to opening the door," he said, putting his foot against it so that Micha couldn't close it again. He took hold of her hand to shake it, then he shook Anna's hand, and then he came in and closed the door behind him.

"I don't know who you are," he said to Anna, "but my name is Sören Marinke. I'm from the social services office. I've been here before, but no one would ever let me in. I think it's high time we talk."

Now, sinking into it, Anna noticed that the sofa in the living room was too soft, as if it could suffocate you. It was silent now in the kitchen. She knew Abel was listening.

Marinke sat in one of the armchairs, opposite Anna and Micha.

"Well," he began, leaning forward in the armchair and putting his hands on his knees like someone who plans to discuss something in a very direct way and then immediately enact it.

"You're Micha, aren't you? Micha Tannatek? I'm Sören Marinke. You can just call me Sören . . ."

Micha shook her head. "Why would I do that?" she asked, and

Anna had to bite her lip not to laugh. Marinke looked somewhat irritated. "Micha . . . I'm here about your mother."

"She's on a trip," Micha said. "Her name is Michelle. She'll be back soon."

Marinke nodded. "We were wondering whether it might be a good idea if you lived somewhere else in the meantime. Till she's back from her, uh . . . trip." He threw a glance at Anna. "Are you related somehow?"

Anna shook her head. "I'm just a . . . a friend."

"She's Abel's girlfriend," Micha explained, and although this was not the time for it, something inside Anna jumped up and down with childish joy. She was . . . really, she was? She was Abel's girlfriend?

"Abel," Marinke said, taking a paper out of a folder to check something. "That would be Abel Tannatek . . . Micha's half-brother, is that correct?"

Anna nodded. Marinke obviously noticed another note because he quickly added, "I'm very sorry about . . . about Micha's father. But we have to find a solution. Micha's mother . . . do you know her? Do you know where she is?"

"No," Anna said. "Nobody seems to be sure." She wondered if she should have lied. If she should have said, sure, I know her, she's just gone for a while, she does this from time to time . . .

"This . . . Abel . . . it says here that he's seventeen . . . if Ms. Tannatek is really coming back in a few days, well . . . when you're seventeen, you should be able to live by yourself for a few days. It would be silly to try to find a placement for him, too . . . we would . . . I mean, I would turn a blind eye to that . . . but the little one definitely needs someone to look after her."

"That's what Abel does," Anna said. She wondered why Marinke hadn't asked where Abel was. He probably knew perfectly well that Abel was home and that he could have asked him these questions directly. Did he hope to get information out of her first, maybe information that Abel wouldn't have given him?

"If these notes are correct, he's taking finals and graduating in a few weeks. He can't look after a little girl all day long at the same time."

"Yes he can!" Micha exclaimed, jumping up from the sofa. "Sure he can! I don't wanna go anywhere else! I never ever want to live with anyone else anywhere!"

"Please sit down," Marinke said. "Let's work this out together. Don't you have any other relatives?"

"We do have Uncle Rico and Aunt Evelyn," Micha replied, her voice hollow when she said it. "But I don't like them. I don't go there unless I have to. We stayed there once, at Christmastime. They don't like kids. They hate it if you're too loud and stuff. Uncle Rico got really angry about something. Sometimes he smacks people across the face and shouts. They live as far away as the moon, and I won't go there. They wouldn't want me anyway."

"There's the possibility of a foster family," Marinke said. "See, Micha, if your mother's not coming back soon, then you could just . . . I mean—until she does come back—you could live with another nice family. But that is not the most important thing at the moment. What is most important is that we find out who is responsible for you, I mean, legally . . ." He realized that both Anna and Micha were staring at him, and he started to fidget in his chair uneasily. He glanced toward the kitchen. "The thing is," he went on in a low voice to Anna, "you see . . . I understand that the brother is not interested in our help. Like many people. I could go so far as to have the police pick Micha up from school, but I don't want to do that. For me, personally, this job is much more than just a job, I . . . I'd like to find the best solution for everyone . . . and to me, the best solution seems to be that we find out where the mother is. Maybe you want to think again about whether you know where she is . . ."

"Why are you here?" Anna asked.

"To help," Marinke replied, astonished. His eyes were green like the forest in summer, and they looked as if he meant what he said. She wondered if it was possible to explain things to him. No. He wouldn't understand. Nobody would.

"We don't need anyone's help," Micha said. "I've got Abel and Abel's got me, and we've both got Anna, and we don't need anyone else besides that."

Heavens, Anna thought, please don't let me start crying now.

"You need money to live on," Marinke said.

"We've got enough money," Micha said. "Sometimes we even go· out for hot chocolate. And we bought a book, to celebrate."

"And where do you get the money from?" Marinke asked.

"How do you know that Michelle Tannatek's on a . . . trip?" Anna asked quickly.

"Someone called us," Marinke replied. "A neighbor who's been worried. And Michelle hasn't picked up her social services check for a while." He sighed. "I guess it would be better to talk to . . ." He nodded toward the kitchen . . . Finally.

The kitchen door opened, and Abel walked in, carrying a plate stacked high with pancakes. Anna was confused. Did he want to prove that Micha wasn't starving? It was strange to see him standing there in the doorway, like a big brother from a fairy tale, holding a mountain of pancakes, when, except for the fact that he was carrying pancakes, he didn't really look like a fairy-tale brother at all. He had rolled up his sleeves, as if to make clear that he could throw Sören Marinke out of the apartment if he wanted to. The red scar on his left upper arm was shining, and he was having difficulty controlling his emotions. Threatening . . . that was the word. He looked threatening—like he'd looked in the student lounge, or in the Mittendrin, when he had stood face-to-face with Bertil. The plate with the pancakes was a ridiculous stage prop in his hand.

"Abel . . . Tannatek." Marinke stood up. "I am . . ."

"I know. You're from the social services office," Abel said. "I got that. But this is a totally unnecessary discussion. I just talked to Michelle. She called a few minutes ago. She'll be home soon. I'll send her over to you as soon as she gets here. Tomorrow."

"She . . . she called just now?" Marinke wrinkled his forehead. "Forgive me if I don't believe you."

"I can't force you to believe me," Abel said with that icy voice he sometimes had, "but tomorrow, you'll hear from our mother. I guess you have a phone number . . ."

Marinke leafed through his notes, then searched through his jacket pockets, and finally found a card, which he gave to Abel. "The telephone number's on there, too," he said. "Call me. I mean, in case your mother . . . is, uh, unable to make it for some reason. We can talk. We can talk about everything."

Abel put down the card on the table and set the plate next to it.

"What would we talk about?" he asked. "About Micha, and about how she's suffering here, without her mother . . . going hungry and all?"

"No, I just . . ."

"You'll want to see the apartment, of course," Abel said politely, his tone as sharp as a knife. "You want to know if we live in squalor. You just want to make sure that there aren't forgotten children, starving in their beds, like in other places . . . the newspapers are full of those kinds of stories, aren't they? The interesting thing is that the mothers of those kids are usually there." He gestured toward the hallway. "Please. Look around. Poke your nose into our cupboards. Search for any evidence you want."

"Abel . . ." Anna began. But the look he gave her made her stop.

"Okay," Marinke said. "If you insist I conform to the stereotype, I'll give you what you want to hear . . . naturally, I'm the bad guy from social services, who tears apart families for a living and puts children into unheated orphanages, where they're forced to live on nothing but bread and water." He shook his head, his voice still friendly. "I'm here to help," he repeated. As he reached out to put a hand on Abel's shoulder, Abel took a step back.

"Have a look around the apartment," he said. It was almost a command.

"Okay, okay." Marinke went into the hallway; Abel, Micha, and Anna followed him.

"What's the point of this?" Anna whispered. "Abel, this won't help . . ."

Marinke opened every door a few inches. It was obvious he didn't want to snoop. The situation was uncomfortable enough. Micha opened the door to her room. "This is my room. Please look around . . . I'm sure you don't have a loft bed like this," she said. Anna saw a smile glide across Marinke's face. "Abel built it," Micha added quickly. The smile on Marinke's face faded. Maybe, Anna thought, this is the same sadness I feel. Maybe Sören Marinke walks through his own apartment from time to time and feels sad because it's so beautiful. Marinke turned and left Micha's room, walked back through the hall, back to the front door. Now, Anna thought, now he will leave, and we'll be by ourselves again, and Abel can stop looking so threatening, and I can ask him about that call from Michelle . . . Suddenly, her cell phone rang. It was a reflex to reach into her pocket and take the call. A stupid reflex. She should have let it ring.

"Anna," Magnus said. "Where are you?"

She saw Abel looking at her, but she couldn't read his eyes. "Why?" she asked.

"Flute lesson," Magnus answered shortly. He didn't ask any questions.

"Shit," Anna said.

"Just tell me where you are. I can come and get you. If we take the car, we can still make it in time."

Abel's eyes were still on her. "No," she said. "I'll come home. Now. Could you drive me from there? I'm going to be late, I know, but could you?"

"Hurry up," Magnus said. "I'll wait."

Anna put her phone back in her pocket. "I totally forgot that I've got a flute lesson today," she said. "My teacher will be waiting for me. I've gotta . . . I've gotta go . . ." She turned to Abel, helpless. "I don't want to, I'd rather . . ."

"If you have to go, go," Abel said. Marinke held the door open for her. Why didn't he leave? Take his stupid folder and his smile . . . Why couldn't he leave them alone, for just a minute?

Fuck off! She wanted to shout, very loudly, and use words she didn't normally use. Fuck off, are you blind, blind like the white cat on the green ship? Don't you see you're interfering where you shouldn't? Don't you understand anything at all?

She reached out for Abel, but he stepped back like he had stepped back from Sören Marinke. "Go," he said. "Your lesson's more important."

He didn't shove her out the door exactly, but he drove her out, with the look in his eyes . . . and then, when Marinke had joined her in the hallway, he shut the door behind them. The last thing she saw was Micha shyly waving from behind him.

She climbed down the stairs, behind Marinke, without saying a word. It was as if they were one entity all of a sudden, an enemy entity that wasn't welcome in Abel's world. Her leaving was a betrayal, and she had seen it in Abel's eyes: she'd spent half the day with him and Micha, then gotten a one-minute call and left them instantly. A plate of fresh pancakes was standing on a table somewhere, slowly turning cold.

On the ground floor, Mrs. Ketow's door was slightly ajar. Anna ignored that and stepped outside behind Marinke. She had to hurry. She didn't have time to talk. But she talked to him anyway.

"Do you really want to help?" she asked. "I mean . . . if you do . . . why don't you just forget that Michelle Tannatek has disappeared?"

"Because that's not an acceptable solution," Marinke said. "You don't believe that story about the call either, do you?"

Anna shrugged. "It's not important what I believe," she replied. "What's important is that those two stay together, Micha and her brother."

"I'll try my best," Marinke said seriously. "But to do that, I have to find out a few things." He dug another card out of the pocket of his leather jacket and gave it to Anna. "Maybe you'll feel like calling me. After you've thought about things for a while. Maybe there are some things you could explain to me."

"Sounds like lines you picked from a cheap detective story," Anna said as she got onto her bike.

Marinke laughed. "Unfortunately, it's quite an expensive detective story. My job, I mean. Considering the workload. And . . . tell your friend that I'm not so easily intimidated. In my job, I'm often in contact with people who are much more dangerous. The bar where they shot Rainer Lierski . . . you know, the Admiral . . . I know all the regulars there . . . unfortunately."

"Wait," Anna said. "You knew Rainer Lierski?"

Marinke nodded. "Another client of ours. He disappeared into thin air for a while, but then reappeared, and there were problems right away. I can't say I'm sad he's gone." For the first time, his smile was grim, not friendly. And for the first time, it seemed genuine. He brushed a snowflake from the sleeve of his suede jacket. "In the end, he probably picked a fight with the wrong person."

"Or with the right one," Anna said. She thought about Marinke's remark while she pedaled as fast as she could down Wolgaster Street. She wondered whether she should help him. Whether she should call. Whether he might be helpful in spite of his too-friendly smile and his you-can-call-me-Sören attitude. If Abel had money, she thought, if he didn't have to work nights, if he didn't have to miss all those classes to be with Micha . . . wouldn't everything be better? No, Abel said in her head. Keep out of this. All of you, keep out. We don't want charity. Leave us alone. That's final.

When she got home, Magnus was waiting in the car with the engine running and her flute and music on the passenger seat. She was late for her lesson. She couldn't concentrate. She made a lot of mistakes. She fell asleep in the car on the way back, her head on her arms. She dreamed of Sören Marinke.

In her dream, he was sitting at a table in the Mittendrin, playing cards with Hennes and Bertil. Of course, this dream was utter nonsense. The minute Anna stepped through the doorway into it, she knew it was nonsense. Knaake stood behind the bar, watching the three players; at the very back of the room, on a long table, a coffin was open. Anna saw that it was filled with flowers, tiny white springtime stars. Anemones nestled between beech-tree leaves. It was like a scene in a kitschy Italian Mafia movie. Micha stood next to the coffin in her pink down jacket, hugging Mrs. Margaret. Anna craned her neck but couldn't see the body. Rainer Lierski, she thought. Or was it someone else? Was it the body of a woman under the flowers and leaves? In a dream, anything is possible . . . She looked around. If everybody who played a role in this story was here . . . Wait, where was Abel?

"We're back," Magnus said, stroking her hair, and she jumped. "Anna, we're home." She blinked. He was still sitting behind the steering wheel; he didn't move to get out of the car.

"Shouldn't we go in?" Anna asked uneasily.

"No," Magnus said. "I mean, yes, but in a minute. I'd like to know some things first." He didn't look at her; he was staring ahead. "Where were you? Were you where you've been spending more time lately? I've decided to ask as not asking gets me nowhere . . ."

"And if I don't say anything now?"

"Anna, your mother's worried."

They sat quietly for a while. A long while. Then Anna got out. Magnus could have locked the car from the inside, forced her to answer, but he wouldn't do that. She felt his eyes on her as she opened the door. "I'm going to bed," she mumbled. "I had a late night last night. I'm too tired for supper."

As she lay in bed, she remembered that her last history test was on Friday. She should have spent today studying. She searched for her notebook and took it back to bed with her. But the words kept running into each other . . . like wet ink, like water in an icy winter ocean, like the blueness of eyes that could be very cold if they wanted to be. *If you have to go, go. Your lesson is more important. Go.*

She gave up. She found Knaake's number and called him. It was eight thirty; it should be okay to call a teacher at eight thirty, shouldn't it? And definitely a lighthouse keeper . . .

"This is Anna," she said. "I'm sorry I'm calling so late . . . I just wanted to . . . you have the telephone numbers of everyone in your intensive class, don't you?"

"I should," Knaake answered. He sounded tired, as if he'd had enough of his students for the day and had just sunk into an armchair. She heard music in the background. She knew the tune . . . she wondered from where. "I need Abel Tannatek's number."

"Excuse me?"

"His cell phone number. Do you have it?"

"I do, but . . . hold on . . . I'll look . . . but I have to go upstairs." The music grew more distant. "Why don't you have his number? I mean, he's your boyfriend, isn't . . ."

"Jeez," Anna said, sounding almost angry. "It seems like as of today I'm officially married to him or something. I mean, I don't live in his pocket . . ."

"Anna . . . why 'as of today'?"

"Because today everyone was talking about the fight he almost had with Bertil last night." How good it felt to tell someone!

"Was there a fight?"

"Don't you listen to the rumors?"

"No," Knaake said. "I guess I don't. I just thought that the two of you . . . that it's been quite some time that you've been . . . forget it. It's none of my business. I have his number here. Do you have a pen?" As she took down the number, she realized that she was smiling.

"Okay, Anna . . . keep an eye on him, will you? I'm worried."

"Me too," Anna said.

"If he carries on like this, he won't make it through finals. And I think it's important that he pass them. Or am I wrong?"

"No," Anna said. "It's important. How well do you know him?"

"Not well at all," Knaake answered. "He asked me to help him find a job . . . something for after seven . . . I mentioned I'd worked as a research assistant when I was at the university . . . maybe he imagined he could do the same thing. But for something like that, you've really got to be a student at the university . . . I don't know . . . sometimes he seems to be dreaming up things that just aren't practical. It's more important that he studies for his exams."

"How's he doing in your class?" Anna asked. "I mean . . . are there any problems?"

"I'm not allowed to tell you. Don't you guys talk about grades?"

"No."

Knaake sighed. "Well, I'm not worried about my class. It's his other classes. He won't get credit if he's never there; that's the bottom line. In literature, he'll get the highest grade I give, and it's rare that anyone does."

Anna nodded. She'd known that, of course. "He wants to be a writer. Later. Books, I think."

"Later . . ." Knaake said. "Well, for now he's got to pass his finals."

"I know," she said.

There wasn't anything more to say.

She took a deep breath and dialed Abel's number. She wanted to say so many things . . . I didn't plan to run away like I did today. It was bad timing. And . . . did Michelle really call? And . . . are you going to act like you don't know me again tomorrow at school? And . . . what should I tell my parents? And . . . what was the point of the scene today with the social worker? And . . . I dreamed of Marinke and of a coffin full of anemones . . . but actually . . . maybe she didn't want to say any of this. Maybe she just wanted to hear his voice and to know that everything was all right.

She let the phone ring fifty-seven times.

He didn't pick up.

It was strange, but only after Anna had given up and turned off the lights, only when it was absolutely quiet and she was lying between the sheets alone, only then did the tune come back to her. The tune she'd heard through the lighthouse keeper's telephone line. And suddenly, she remembered the words to that melody; she knew them from one of Linda's old LPs.

Yes you who must leave everything that you cannot control
It begins with your family but soon it comes round to your soul
Well I've been where you're hanging I think I can see how you're pinned
When you're not feeling holy your loneliness says that you've sinned.

"Sisters of Mercy," she whispered, nearly sleeping. "Leonard Cohen."

The question of whether or not Abel would acknowledge her presence didn't come up since Abel didn't show up at school. She looked out the window every five minutes, waiting for a dark figure to appear at the bike rack, his hands dug deep into his pockets, his black hat pulled down low over his face, white noise in his ears. There was no one. A few other students also seemed to be looking for Abel during the break, hovering by the bike stands, trying to look inconspicuous. Clients, Anna thought, and she felt like smiling for a moment. She didn't smile.

Abel had said that he would send Michelle to Sören Marinke's office today. Had Michelle really come back? And if so, where had she been? She tried to call him twice. When she tried to call a third time, the line was dead.

"What's the matter?" Gitta asked at lunch. "You look as if you're nauseous." She put her hands on Anna's shoulders and looked at her closely. "Little lamb," she said, "tell me what happened. You've hardly said a word since yesterday morning. Let's skip class this afternoon and have a cup of coffee at the bakery instead."

Anna let Gitta lead the way. And, actually, it calmed her down a bit to drink hot coffee, even if it tasted like lemon with artificial coloring.

"So," Gitta began. "Everybody is talking. I say, let 'em talk. Let 'em fill their dirty mouths and minds with rumors."

"I've been wondering why you, of all people, didn't talk," Anna said, not sarcastically but frankly. "Why you didn't help to spread the rumors?"

"Little lamb, it might astonish you to hear this, but I am actually your friend, remember?"

"Hmm . . . ," Anna said.

"Now," Gitta leaned across the table and lowered her voice, "what happened?"

"He's gone," Anna replied and heard how miserable she sounded. "Abel's gone."

"But you're together, aren't you? I mean, did the two of you . . . ?"

"That's not the issue! This isn't a matter of passing a do-you-want-to-go-out-with-me-mark-with-an-x-yes-no-maybe note. And it isn't a question of who did what with whom. Doesn't anyone understand that? It's the other things that matter! Abel has disappeared!"

"Nonsense," Gitta said matter-of-factly. "Just because he wasn't at school today, that doesn't mean he's disappeared. He's gotta be somewhere."

"He doesn't answer his phone."

"Maybe he wants to be alone."

"Gitta, his mother has been gone for a while—nobody seems to know where she is—and yesterday he said she'd called, that she'd come back, and now he's gone. And somebody has . . ." She stopped herself. No, she thought, Rainer Lierski was really none of Gitta's business.

"Again, and in the right order," Gitta said. "Is there a little sister or not? Or has she disappeared, too?"

Anna nearly knocked over her coffee cup. Of course. Micha. Something must have happened to Micha.

"That," she whispered. "That just might be it." She stood up and slid into her coat. "Gitta, I'm sorry. We'll talk another time. I've gotta go."

✦ ✦ ✦

She pushed the buzzer for their apartment three times, waited for a while, then pushed again—three more times. Nobody answered. Anna covered her face with her hands, took several deep breaths, and tried to think. Then she noticed that she was doing what Abel usually did. And it helped. She knew now what she would do. She lowered her hands and tried the apartment on the ground floor. Someone buzzed Anna into the hall; Mrs. Ketow stood in her doorway, in the same tracksuit she'd had on the last time. She was carrying a child in her arms, a screaming and overfed baby with a dull look in his eyes. When she saw Anna, Mrs. Ketow stuffed a pacifier in the child's mouth, and he was quiet.

"What a sweet child," Anna said, though she didn't think so at all.

Mrs. Ketow nodded. "I look after my children well. The oldest is three—they're all foster children." She rocked the baby in her arms and looked Anna over. "Why are you here?"

"Do you know where Abel and Micha are?"

"Those two? Gone," Mrs. Ketow said. "Not that I'm surprised. I've always known that things couldn't possibly end well for those Tannateks. It's not the little girl's fault—she's a sweet child, that one—but the brother, he's a different story. Do you go to school with him? If I were you, I'd keep away from him . . . but now they're gone anyway . . ."

"What do you mean by *gone?*" Anna asked.

"I mean *gone* . . . done a moonlight skedaddle, the both of them," Mrs. Ketow said, and for a moment Anna was relieved, for wherever Abel and Micha were, they had gone there together. Nobody from the office for shells and sisters had taken Micha away. The baby spat out the pacifier and started screaming again, an unnerving, high-pitched wail. Anna picked up the pacifier and Mrs. Ketow wiped it pretend-clean on her tracksuit trousers, but this time the baby didn't want to be pacified.

"Needs his milk," Mrs. Ketow said. "You want to come in?"

Anna stepped into the narrow hallway behind her. The apartment was almost identical to Abel and Micha's, the wallpaper almost the same. The dark cupboards looked newer than the ones on the fourth floor, but they were equally ugly. And yet, everything felt different here. This apartment didn't breathe. It was dead. Maybe, Anna thought, it was that way because there weren't any children's drawings taped to the walls; maybe it was because of the broken plastic toys lying on a dresser in the hallway. There wasn't disorder in Mrs. Ketow's apartment, but there was something else . . . Anna searched for the word. Indifference, she thought. That was it. Nobody cared. The apartment was a lot sadder than the apartment upstairs. It was so sad, Anna wasn't able to breathe for a moment. The office for shells and sisters would probably not have found anything wrong with this apartment; everything was as it should be if a social worker chanced to come by. In the back part of the apartment, the other two children were shouting. Mrs. Ketow found the bottle and stuffed it into the mouth of the screaming baby, like she'd done with the pacifier before; it was like pressing buttons to make a machine work properly. Then she lit a cigarette and opened the kitchen window. "Smoke isn't good for the kids," she said. "The social worker told me that. I do what they say in general, I mean, they're paying for these kids. I look after them well."

"I'm not a social worker," Anna said. "I don't care what you do. I just want to know where Abel and Micha went."

"If you ask me, you won't see them again," Mrs. Ketow replied and took a drag. "I saw them, him with a big backpack like he's going on a trip and the little one, too. That was this morning . . . five or so . . . I get up early 'cause of these damn kids. They're a lot of work, three kids. I'll tell you . . . with three of them, I work a whole fuckin' day . . . what about you? You're young. You want kids? What do you want from life?"

"I want to find Abel and Micha," Anna said and turned to go.

But she couldn't find Abel and Micha. There was no trace of them anywhere. She wasn't a detective, and besides, those who don't want to be found won't be found . . .

At home, she avoided Linda's questioning looks, mumbled something about studying, and went straight to her room. She knew that Magnus was angry that she'd refused to explain anything to her mother. But wouldn't Linda have been more worried if she'd explained? Anyway, this was not about Linda.

Anna felt like she was drowning in the blue air of home. She almost longed for the ugly gray staircase at 18 Amundsen Street. She took out Sören Marinke's card and laid it on her desk.

Had it been a lie? Had Michelle really called? Were Abel and Micha with Michelle now? Or had Abel just run away with Micha because he knew that Marinke would take her from him sooner or later? If Marinke found out they'd fled, he'd send the police after them. Wherever they were heading, they would need a good head start. Anna mustn't call the number on Marinke's card . . . but then she picked up the phone and dialed it anyway.

She had to call. She had to find out what he knew. She invented a complicated introductory sentence, saying she wanted to talk to him and to find out whether he'd returned to the Tannatek's place or not . . . she knew she'd feel tongue-tied. Her heart raced.

But the voice that finally came through the telephone line belonged to a woman.

"I . . . I'd like to talk to Sören Marinke," Anna said.

"I'm sorry but that's not possible at the moment," the woman answered.

"Would it be better if I tried again later?" Anna asked. "I can do that. It's just that he had asked me to call him . . ."

"You won't be able to talk to him today," the woman said. "He's not in the office."

"So . . . do you know when he'll be back?" Anna asked.

"I can't tell you. I'm sorry."

"Is he ill?" Anna asked. "This is an important call; it's about one of his . . . what do you say . . . cases? Maybe I can talk to someone else?"

"I'm afraid not. There isn't anyone else. I'm sure he'll get back to you once he's in the office again. We're hoping that will be tomorrow."

"On his card his cell phone number is also listed," Anna said. "Do you think it would be rude to call him on it?"

The woman at the other end of the line sighed. "You can try, of course," she said. "But you won't have any luck. We tried the same thing."

"I . . . I don't understand . . ."

"Neither do I," the woman replied. "Listen, honey, Mr. Marinke hasn't come into the office today and he isn't answering his phone, and I think he's probably sick, but no one knows for sure where he is. So please be patient. Hopefully we'll know more tomorrow."

Anna dialed the second number on the card. The nameless woman was right. She got his voicemail.

Had the whole world decided to disappear? Michelle, Abel, Micha, Sören Marinke? Had they all disappeared? Would she be the only one left in the end? With the blue light and the robins in the garden?

When she woke up the next morning, the first thing she did was dial Abel's number. She knew it by heart now. Nobody answered. She left for school without eating breakfast. Maybe he was there. Maybe he was standing by the bike rack, his hands in his pockets, Walkman plugs in his ears . . . but he wasn't there. It wasn't just that there was no one at the bike rack. It was that there seemed to be a hole in the shape of a person. Abel's absence was almost visible.

The others were talking about history. Dates of events buzzed above their heads like strange, shapeless winter bees. Anna stood next to Gitta, and Gitta said, "Let's talk later, little lamb. Old Gitta has to stuff her face with facts till third period today." Anna had managed to hammer those same facts into her brain the day before—everything would be okay. She had to count on remembering everything she had learned before this week. Nothing could be less important than a history test. The silver-gray dog in the fairy tale had made a leap for the hunter's black ship—had he leaped out of Anna's world for good? In her head, a sentence kept coming up like an old-fashioned screen saver: What if I never see him again? What if I never see him again? What if I nev . . .

When the sheets of white paper, with the official school stamp— the only paper you were allowed to write on—were set in front of her at the beginning of third period, she had to pull herself together not to write this sentence into the upper-right corner instead of her name. They were taking the test in the gym, as a sort of dry run for their finals, which would take place there.

Final exams, Anna thought . . . and she heard Knaake's words again: Keep an eye on him, will you? If he carries on like this, he won't pass . . . and in the background, Cohen's ancient, Old World voice . . . Then she heard the gym door open; somebody walked in late but just in time to take the test. She looked up. It was Abel.

Gitta looked from Anna to Abel and back again. Of course he hadn't vanished. She'd told Anna that. Someone like Tannatek didn't just vanish; he was gone for a while, but then he turned up again. Or was she wrong? Could someone like Tannatek vanish? One day? Forever?

She tried to catch Anna's eye, but Anna didn't look at her. In a strange way, Anna had vanished, too. She had drifted away from Gitta, from everybody . . . so far away that she might never be able to find her way back, and Gitta wouldn't be able to reach her anymore.

She wasn't God after all; it wasn't her job to save Anna. She wasn't cut out to save anyone, and you couldn't save someone from herself anyway. Shit.

She looked over at Hennes, saw his red-gold hair glowing in a sun ray, saw him smile and wink at her before he bent over his test again. Tonight (and why wait till night fell, by the way?) she would forget about Anna. She wondered if she was the only one here who hung out in the streets enough to know the truth about Tannatek. And if he knew that she knew. She'd keep her mouth shut as she'd promised herself she would, and everything would take its course. Shit. Shit. Oh, what the hell.

11

Sören
❧

ANNA CLENCHED HER FISTS SO SHE WOULDN'T JUMP
up from her chair. Never had she been so happy to see someone. She
lowered her eyes, trying to hide her smile behind her hair. She heard
the history teacher say something to Abel, tell him to take the last
free desk at the far end of the room, and when she looked up again,
Abel was walking back there, passing her desk. For a moment she
looked into his eyes. And she got a fright.

The ice in his eyes had changed; it seemed to have become
darker, like the dark, clear ice on a frozen lake whose depth suddenly
becomes visible when the wind brushes the snow from the surface.
It was an endless depth, bottomless, and almost totally black. She
didn't know which thoughts and creatures were swimming down
there. They scared her. It was as if she were watching Abel drown
in the waters of himself. She shook her head, trying to rid it of these
thoughts. What had happened? Where had he been?

She turned to Gitta and Gitta shrugged. Their history teacher was distributing the tests now, densely printed with threatening instructions and questions. Concentrate, Anna thought. Read the text. Function.

And she did function. The facts were stored inside her head, reliable and secure—despite everything, she was still Anna Leemann, a good student. Her brain was complying, letting her fill it with things and then spitting them out as it was supposed to. She hurried, her pen gliding over the white paper, almost of its own accord. She felt strangely detached as she watched her small, tidy letters form on the paper in front of her. She didn't look up again until after she finished the first set of questions—half the test. The others were bent over their desks, writing frantically. The history teacher was standing at the podium in front of them. There was a second teacher in the room as well, a proctor. It was a Latin teacher whom Anna knew only by sight. Now he consulted his watch and left the gym. He was replaced by another teacher, who entered through the same door. Knaake. Anna saw him search the room for something, someone, scanning the rows of desks. She knew whom he was searching for. She saw when he found him, saw him nod and start to walk past the desks thoughtfully, his hands folded behind his back. And now, finally, she dared to turn around, too.

Abel wasn't writing. He was holding a pen; he had been writing, but now he looked at her and she read his eyes. This time they were easy to read. The message in them was not about the dark depth beneath the ice or about whatever had happened. It was about the history test. HELP ME, Anna read in those eyes. I HAVE NO IDEA WHAT TO WRITE. And she nodded, barely perceptibly, or so she hoped. She put her hand into her pocket, found something that felt like a piece of paper. She slid a pen into her pocket as inconspicuously as possible, stood up, and went to the front of the room. The history teacher noted the time on a list and nodded at her; she had official permission to go to the ladies' room. Her heart was racing. Of course, the history teacher couldn't read her mind. Anna hadn't done anything forbidden, not yet anyway.

A few minutes later, she was sitting on the lid of a white toilet, writing. The paper in her pocket had turned out to be a ten-euro note. Whatever. She was writing. She was writing tiny letters; she covered the bill with them, her fingers flying. She wrote down the answers for the first section in short keywords, noting dates and giving brief historical background. The thinking, the "Interpret this text in a historical context. Discuss the questions" part he had to do himself. She had already read the second set of questions on the test; she made notes for this part, too, giving more dates, jotting down half-finished sentences, which hopefully would help him to remember. At some point, he surely must have learned all this, too . . . She wasn't writing fast enough. She didn't have enough space on the bill. She thought about using toilet paper. She looked at her watch. She had to go back.

She folded the bill and fastened it under the lid of the toilet paper holder. Then she tore off a piece of toilet paper and stuck it into the door of the stall in which she'd been sitting. It was visible from outside if you were searching for it—a tiny white flag, a white flag made of snow . . .

She had to force herself not to run back to the gym; she tried hard to look as if she was sick and that was why she had spent so much time in the bathroom. She *was* feeling sick. She didn't know what would happen if someone figured out she'd cheated. She'd fail the test—she was sure of that—but what else would happen?

When she returned to the gym, thirteen minutes had passed. Thirteen minutes on the toilet. Of course, they would realize something was wrong . . . of course, of course, damn, Knaake was sitting at the desk now. She didn't see the history teacher anywhere.

"Mrs. Meyer's gone for a cup of coffee," Knaake said in a very low voice, looking up at her. Then he looked at his watch and noted the time on a sheet. "I just hope this watch is correct," he mumbled. "Gotta reset it one of these days . . ."

She wanted to hug him. She just nodded. According to what he'd jotted down, she'd been gone for only five minutes.

She threw Abel a short glance before she sat down again. Seven minutes later, he got up. Possibly it was more than seven minutes later—at least by Knaake's watch. She tried to concentrate on the second set of questions and to remember the answers she'd already written down in keywords on a ten-euro note. Abel had to find the right toilet now. He had to memorize the dates and facts, or to remember them if he'd already learned them once. He couldn't take that bill with him; he'd have to destroy it. What would he do with it? Tear it up and flush it down the toilet? She'd never thought this could work . . . Abel returned a few minutes after the history teacher, who came back with a cup of coffee. Knaake noted the time before handing the sheet back to his colleague. Abel sat down without looking at Anna. She didn't dare turn around to see if he was writing.

After the test, Anna stood outside in the cold schoolyard with Gitta and the others, watching them smoke. It would have been too conspicuous to walk over to Abel now. The others seemed to have forgotten Wednesday's gossip; they were talking about the test.

Hennes had his arm around Gitta's leather-jacketed waist, Frauke was talking to Gitta, and Bertil came and stood with them.

"So how was it?" he asked.

Anna looked at him. She didn't want to talk to him. But his question was honest, and it seemed like ages ago that he'd said the things in the Mittendrin that he shouldn't have said. She searched for her anger but couldn't find it anymore.

"It was all right," she replied. "But I'm not feeling so well . . . I got sick in the middle of it . . ."

"Poor lamb," Gitta said. "That's why you were gone for so long. You're pale, too."

Anna hoped that Bertil didn't see her wink. He didn't. He put a hand on her arm, worried. "Maybe you should go home."

"It's okay," she said. "Probably it was just nervousness."

"Sometimes it helps to get fresh air," Bertil went on. "To clear your head, I mean. The sea has frozen totally now. I was thinking about going out to Eldena later . . . we could go together. If you want to."

"The sea's frozen?" Frauke asked. "Do you think it's possible to walk to the other side of the bay, to Ludwigsburg?"

Bertil nodded. "Sure. I was at the beach yesterday, took our dog. He likes running over the ice. It's nice to be at the beach alone, in winter, at dusk . . ."

"I thought your dog died," Frauke said, giving a little shudder. "I thought your father shot him."

"That was a long time ago," Bertil replied, looking into the distance. "We have a new dog. Things are replaceable: dogs, friends, people . . . what do you think, Anna? Are you coming with me? I know you sometimes go for walks out there."

"Not today," Anna said quickly. "It's too cold for me out there today."

She thought of the black depth in Abel's eyes. He was standing in his usual place. She saw him shake his head ever so slightly. Don't come over here. Not now. Later, when the test isn't floating around in the air like this anymore. He was right.

"Now that the last history test is history," Hennes said, "we should keep our Polish peddler in business, don't you think? I mean . . . seeing as how he's bothering to hang around . . . Gitta, what are we doing Saturday night?"

"If you're talking about you and me, we're house-sitting," Gitta answered. "My mother's got the night shift. Someone has to make sure the leather sofa isn't stolen, and I can't possibly do that alone. Stop giggling, Frauke." She lit another cigarette. "We don't need the peddler for house-sitting," she added.

"We don't?" Hennes blew a strand of red hair from his forehead. "That's too bad, actually."

"I've got a stash somewhere," Gitta said. "Leave Abel alone."

Hennes whistled through his teeth. "Lately, the most astonishing people have first names. Listen, I just wanted to . . . you know . . . increase his salary, so to speak."

Gitta nodded. "We applaud your social conscience, Herr von Biederitz, but at certain times, certain people don't want to talk to certain other people. I'll explain it to you later. And now, accompany me inside, please, to enjoy two more unbelievably boring lessons to prepare your lordship for graduation."

Inside, Anna found herself next to Knaake in the crowd on the stairs. "Thanks," she said in a low voice.

"For what?" he asked.

"For . . . nothing," she said and understood that she'd better keep her mouth shut if she didn't want to get the lighthouse keeper in trouble. There were too many ears here. She thought of their conversation on the phone, and suddenly something came into her head, just before they reached the top of the stairs.

"Do you know Michelle Tannatek?" she asked, without any preamble.

He lifted his graying eyebrows. "Who?"

"Abel's mother."

He stood at the top of the stairs and let the crowd move past. He shook his head slowly. "She's never come to a parent conference, if that's what you're talking about."

"That's not what I'm talking about," Anna said, looking into his eyes. "Do you know her? Maybe from . . . a long time ago?"

"No," said Knaake, and he began to search his pockets for something that probably wasn't there. A memory, perhaps. She left him standing there alone, alone with his "No." She wondered what it meant.

After sixth period, there was a figure standing in the schoolyard who wasn't Abel . . . and who was obviously cold—a small figure in a pink down jacket. When she saw Anna, she started running toward her, and Anna caught her in her arms. The pink down jacket smelled of the wind and sea, and a little of cheap Polish tobacco, too.

"Micha," Anna said. "Micha, where have you been, the two of you? I was at your place, looking for you . . . I tried to call . . . what happened?"

"We were on an outing," Micha replied, but she seemed to know that it wasn't normal to go on an outing on a weekday. "Abel made us leave really early; we were on a bus and then on a train. We went to that island, you know the one . . . Rügen. I didn't have to go to school, because when you're on an outing, you don't have to go to school, do you . . . well . . . we had hot chocolate, and I hiked very far, with a backpack and everything . . . and a picnic . . . Where is Abel?"

"Here," Abel said from behind Anna, pushing her aside very gently and putting an arm around Micha. "What are you doing here?"

"Oh, they let us go early today," she explained eagerly. "But I didn't want to wait for you. Mrs. Milowitch always asks me questions . . . I like her, but she asks the same things that Mr. . . . that Mr. Matinke did. Things about Mama. So I came here, instead, even though it's really far to walk. I'm a good hiker."

"I think," Abel said, "that today we won't go to the student dining hall. We had our outing yesterday, and that was enough for a while. The train and everything . . . it was expensive. We'll just go home and think about yesterday, okay?"

"Okay," Micha said, looking down at her feet. "But . . . but couldn't we go somewhere else? I don't like being at home. I'm afraid Mr. Matinke will be at the door, and that he'll take me away with him. Yesterday, I couldn't sleep because I kept thinking about it. I dreamed that he had a net, like the kind you use to catch butterflies, except that it wasn't to catch butterflies—it was to catch me. Like in our fairy tale. He was hunting for a diamond heart—that's why he wanted to catch me."

Abel kneeled in the snow in front of her and looked into her eyes. "He'll never do that," he whispered. "I promise you that he'll never do that. You'll see. We'll invent something in the fairy tale to make him disappear."

"You could come with me," Anna said, hesitating. "Home, I mean. If you want to. Micha, you look cold. We have a fireplace to warm you. And I'll be able to find something for lunch, I'm sure."

"No," said Abel.

"My parents aren't there," Anna explained. "Not during the day. My mom comes home in the evening. You could . . ."

"No," said Abel.

"A fireplace!" Micha looked at him. "That must be really nice, don't you think? If there's snow outside and a fire inside, like in that book we read, and we could make hot chocolate . . ."

"No," Abel said.

"That's so unfair!" Micha stamped her little foot. "Yesterday, you wanted to go to Rügen, so we went; I've been hiking with you, in the cold, and I haven't complained, or not really that much . . . and today I want to see Anna's fireplace. Why can't we do something I want to do for a change!" She stamped her foot again, her eyes flashing so combatively that Anna nearly laughed out loud. "You go home and wait for the Matinke guy," she added, crossing her pink down-jacket arms. "And I'll go by myself with Anna."

Abel covered his face with both his hands, took a deep breath, and then looked at Anna. The dark, disturbing thing in his eyes had retreated a little, as if he had pushed it away with all his force. "Okay," he said. "Okay. Let's go."

Anna didn't look over her shoulder as they left the schoolyard. But she guessed at least a few people were watching them. Bertil, for example. She pictured him walking his family dog on the empty beach of Eldena, pushing up his slipping glasses from time to time, alone, like the day before and most days, in the ice-cold air, in the wind, next to the frozen sea.

◆ ◆ ◆

"You're right," Abel said in the hall. "The air is blue. I never really believed it." He smiled.

He hadn't said a word on the way here, but now he smiled.

"Yes," Anna said, "yesterday, I nearly drowned in it."

Micha was looking at the coatrack in the hallway, with its tiny wooden animal heads from some country they'd traveled to. Anna had forgotten which one it was. Finally, Micha found something that might have been a dog, stroked it gently with her forefinger, and hung her pink jacket on the hook next to it.

"You didn't choose the dog?" Anna asked.

"If I put my jacket over him, he won't be able to see anymore," Micha replied with great earnestness. "And he has to see, doesn't he . . . he's jumped aboard the black ship."

"Didn't Abel tell you more of the story on your outing?" Anna asked.

Abel shook his head.

"But we built a snowman," Micha said. "Oh, Anna, is that your living room? It's so beautiful."

"Yes," Anna said. She watched as Micha pulled off her socks and walked over the Turkish kilim in bare feet, following the patterns, to and fro, through an endless labyrinth. Then she gave up on that game and ran to the glass door leading out to the little garden. "There are robins!" she exclaimed. "Loads of them! And two real rose blossoms! Like on the rose island in our story! But there weren't any robins there. The robins have come to look at the roses, haven't they? Oh, Abel, aren't they pretty?"

Anna looked at Abel. He was still smiling.

"It's very different . . . from your place," she said. "Is that bad?"

Abel took her hand in his. "Thank you," he said. "For history. For everything. You saved me. I had . . . I couldn't remember anything, but I remembered when I read what you wrote." He searched his pocket and took out the ten-euro note that she had filled with tiny writing from top to bottom.

"Are you crazy?" Anna whispered. "You didn't destroy that thing?"

He shrugged. "I almost did, but then I couldn't. I think I'll keep it. It's the only thing I . . ." He stopped. "Micha, I'm not sure you should be jumping on that sofa."

"It's okay," Anna said. "I used to jump on it a lot when I was little. And I still do sometimes. That's what sofas are for."

"And your parents?"

"They only jump very rarely," Anna said, grinning, as she kneeled in front of the fireplace. "I promised you a fire, I think. And something for lunch . . ."

"Those logs in the basket look quite tasty," Abel said. "I guess they're not totally done, though."

When the flames were crackling in the open fireplace, it was as if all the worries and fears of the last twenty-four hours were burning to ashes, too. They sat in front of the fire, talking about how to prepare the logs for lunch, and Micha marveled at the sparks flying up from the pinewood. Everything was good. Anna wanted to ask Abel why he had gone to Rügen with Micha, why he hadn't answered his phone, why he hadn't told her anything before he left, but she didn't. Instead, she went to the kitchen and warmed up leftover quiche, which Linda had made the day before. She whistled as she got out the plates. When she came back to the living room, Abel and Micha were sitting on the floor together. They were both bent over a book Magnus had given Linda for Christmas, a picture book full of photos of the desert.

"I . . . we . . ." Abel closed the book carefully.

"Don't worry, you can look at it," Anna said. "This isn't a museum. My mother loves deserts. When I go to England, after finals, she said she's going to compensate by visiting the desert."

"Can I come, too?" Micha asked instantly. "I want to see a desert, too. I like sand, especially when it's warm. You can let it run through your fingers. Maybe there's a desert island in our fairy tale. What do you think, Abel? Why haven't we ever gone to see a desert?"

"You'd have to go very, very far by plane for that," Abel said. "I'm sure you don't want to have to sit still in a plane for so many hours."

"Of course, I do! I absolutely want to sit in a plane!" Micha exclaimed. "I've never been in a plane! Can we fly in one, Abel?"

"When we've finished this quiche, we'll fly upstairs on foot, and you can look at my room," Anna said quickly. "If you want, you can try to get a note out of my flute. It's not easy, though."

Micha didn't get a note out of the flute, but she held its slim silver body in her hands for a long time. Then she lay in the hammock in Anna's room and looked up at the ceiling and said she'd like to move in here, but, of course, she would miss her loft bed . . . and Anna and Abel just stood there and watched her.

"It will never be like this," Abel said in a low voice. "It will never be this nice at our place."

Anna put her arms around him and whispered, "It already is. Just not at first glance. Do you know that I sometimes feel better at your place? I thought about it yesterday . . . but, Abel . . . what happened to the silver-gray dog, after he jumped aboard the black ship? Is he okay?"

He ran his fingers through her hair, thoughtfully, and let his hand rest on her head for a moment, a strand of hair wrapped around his fingers. He had never touched her hair before. There were many parts of her body, she thought, that he had never touched. Suddenly she was very warm.

"The silver-gray dog," he said, "crept along the rail, on soundless paws . . ."

Micha looked up from the old picture book that she was holding on her knees. "Is the fairy tale going on?" she asked, obviously forgetting all the picture books and all the hammocks in the world . . .

"Let's go back downstairs, to the fireplace. You've gotta tell a fairy tale by the fire; that's where fairy tales should be told."

"The silver-gray dog crept along the rail, on soundless paws," Abel repeated while Anna fed the fire more logs, "till he reached the stern of the black ship. Then the little queen couldn't see him anymore. 'I hope he takes care of himself,' the lighthouse keeper grumbled.

"'Who are those people?' the little queen asked fearfully. 'Those people on the black ship?'

"'I recognized a few of them,' the lighthouse keeper answered. 'There is the jewel trader, for one. He collects all the jewels he can find, but he doesn't lock them away like the red hunter. He resells them, scattering them all over the world, over the oceans . . . then, there are the haters. You saw that elderly couple, little queen? That's them. The haters hate everything that is beautiful. They want to destroy the diamond. And last . . . there's the big woman in the tracksuit. Do you know why she's so fat?'

"'No,' the little queen replied, and her whole body shivered when she said that.

"'She eats the jewels the jewel trader brings to her,' the lighthouse keeper said.

"'Then . . . then, she'll eat my heart if he gets hold of it,' the little queen whispered.

"At that moment, a blast of wind whipped over the ocean, blew the waves into towers, and made the little pieces of ice clink against one another. The shipmates lost their balance and fell onto the deck in a heap. The blind white cat complained that someone had landed on top of her.

"'Sails down!' the lighthouse keeper shouted. 'There's a storm!'

"The asking man and the answering man clung to each other fearfully and shouted senseless questions and answers into the howl of the wind: 'Where is Michelle?' 'Maybe the lighthouse keeper!' 'Where does he come from?' 'In the box on top of the bathroom cupboard!' 'Who is his father?'

"The rose girl helped the lighthouse keeper lower the white sails—all but one. The black ship didn't take down its black sails. Instead, a strange mechanism on its masts started moving, amid storm and waves: one of the black masts rotated, and the travelers could see that there was a huge net fastened to it. A wooden arm extended, and now the net hung exactly above the little green ship. And then someone working some gears or cranks began to lower it—and it became a deadly butterfly net.

"'No!' the little queen screamed and covered her eyes with her hands. But she looked through her fingers.

"It was the jewel trader who worked the gears, steered the net. He had rolled up the sleeves of his leather jacket so they could see the white sheepskin lining inside. The diamond eater in her tracksuit stood beside him. There was one blood-red, dyed strand of hair on her forehead. Behind her, the two haters held onto each other, their eyes aglow with destructive frenzy. And behind the haters, the silver-gray dog pressed his body against the rail. He was nothing but a secret shadow.

"'The airship!' the rose girl said. 'We can still make it!'

"The little queen lowered her hands. Her eyes were big and dark with fear. 'But the storm will blow us in the wrong direction!'

"The net was sinking, lower and lower. And then, something unexpected happened. There was a scream, a piercing, horrible, eardrum-tearing scream that made the waves stop waving for a second, as if the whole ocean had suddenly frozen. At the same time, the net was lifted up again, the wooden apparatus turned its arm, and the huge trap dropped onto the dark sails. The black ship had caught itself. It seemed to fight with itself now: it buckled and heaved—the waves weren't still anymore; they pushed the ship around—ropes ripped, and sails fell down from masts like withered leaves from dead trees. One of them covered the fat diamond eater, and another one covered the two haters, who tried to free themselves with angry shouts. But where was the cutter?

"The green ship sailed on through the storm with its one remaining white sail, and the black ship stayed behind, tied up like a big beetle in a spider's web.

"'The silver-gray dog!' the little queen shouted against the wind. 'He's still on the black ship! We have to help him!'

"She wanted to turn the yellow rudder, to turn the ship, but on her way to the rudder, she stumbled over the white cat, who had fallen asleep on the floor again, and fell. The rose girl helped her up. Now the ship swayed to and fro gently, for the storm was dying down.

"The last high wave carried something in its glittering embrace. It was a body. For a moment, they saw it clearly, before the sea pulled it down into its bottomless depths.

"'The jewel trader!' the rose girl whispered. 'He's dead!'

"'Like the red hunter,' said the little queen. She put her arms around the rose girl and began to cry, and her diamond heart hurt inside her. 'So does everybody have to die?' she sobbed.

"When the water was perfectly still again, something else floated toward them in the light of the setting winter sun. Another body. The body of the sea lion. The asking man and the answering man fished it out of the sea with their long arms. They carefully laid it on the planks, where it turned into the body of a dog, and the little queen dropped down next to him. He was breathing, but he didn't open his eyes.

"'My poor dog!' the little queen whispered. 'What happened on the black ship?'

"'Let him sleep,' the rose girl said. 'He needs rest.' She carried the dog in her arms down into the cabin and put him to bed on the polar bear skins. On his left foreleg, the fur was missing in two shiny, circular patches, like burns."

"Two?" Anna asked. Micha had fallen asleep once more, lying on the sofa next to them.

Anna gently pushed up Abel's left sleeve. It was true. There was a second round scar next to the first one. "What is it?" she asked. "Is it what I think it is?"

He nodded. "Cigarette burns. Cigarettes get pretty hot at the tips." He pulled the sleeve back down.

"But who . . . who did that?"

"Is that important?" She looked at him. He sighed. "I did . . . Content now?"

"No," she said. "Why? Why do you do it?"

"Has Micha been sleeping for long?"

"You didn't answer my question."

"I'm not answering any questions," he said, smiling. "I'm not one of the answering people. I'm the storyteller."

She got up and walked over to the old record player to put on one of the LPs she'd found in Linda's Leonard Cohen collection. She turned the volume very low so as not to wake Micha, returned to the sofa, and leaned against Abel.

Travelling lady, stay a while until the night is over
I'm just a station on your way I know I'm not your lover.
Well I lived with a child of snow when I was a soldier
And I fought every man for her until the nights grew colder
She used to wear her hair like you except when she was sleeping
And then she'd weave it on a loom of smoke and gold and breathing . . .

"What does that mean?" Anna whispered. "What does all that mean?"

Abel ran his fingers through her hair again, and his hand wandered down and stayed on her throat. "It means everything," he whispered back. "And nothing."

And why are you so quiet now standing there in the doorway?
You chose your journey long before you came upon this highway . . .
Travelling lady, stay a while until the night is over
I'm just a station on your way I know I'm not your lover . . .

"I thought about not coming back," Abel said suddenly. "Of disappearing. Somewhere."

Anna nodded. "It wasn't an outing. You ran away. From Marinke. Michelle never called. Of course she didn't."

"Are you sure?"

"Well, did she?"

"I told you I'm not answering any questions."

She took his hand in hers and made it glide lower, under her T-shirt. It was a surprisingly hesitant hand; it very nearly fought against hers. Then the hand lay on her left breast, and she wondered if she could somehow manage to get rid of her bra without destroying the moment. In movies, these things happened so naturally; people were never wearing impractical clothing; there were never any hooks and eyes or buttons to get in the way.

"Anna," whispered Abel. "I'm not sure . . ."

"Isn't it enough if I'm sure?"

"But Micha . . ." He gave up and kept his hand where it was. And then he kissed her. And she thought, this is our third kiss, and wondered if it would be possible to count all the kisses in a lifetime or if there would be too many after a while. Though, with Abel, there wouldn't be much danger of losing track. She tasted blood in his mouth—her lips must have cracked with the cold—or was she just imagining that? She tasted the sea, in which he had been floating unconscious, as a sea lion, inside a fairy tale. She tasted the picture of a black net and of the sails that fell down like withered leaves . . . she wondered if she would ever meet him alone, without Micha.

With that guy, you'll only have a relationship based on fucking, she heard Gitta say. Anything but, she thought. Oh, Gitta, anything but . . .

And then she heard the door—and voices in the hall. Never had a kiss ended so abruptly. Anna opened her eyes, looked at Abel, and smiled. He didn't smile. He jumped up. She stood up, too, more slowly, and took his hand. "Wait," she said quietly. "Don't run away. Please. They don't bite, you know."

"I shouldn't be here."

"Of course you should," she said.

Micha woke up and yawned. "What's going on?" she asked sleepily.

"We gotta go," Abel said.

He looked around, in a panic, as if he wanted to run out into the yard and flee over the roofs. He pulled his hand from Anna's. He seemed totally lost in the big living room, in the blue air, lost in an ocean full of clinking pieces of ice.

The living room door opened, and Magnus and Linda came in at almost the same time. Linda stopped, surprised. Then she smiled.

"I see," she said, and now, she wasn't smiling anymore; she was laughing, a gentle, blue laugh. "Does that explain it?"

"What?" Anna asked.

"Your secretiveness," Magnus answered, shaking his head, setting his bag onto an armchair. "Yep, looks like that explains it."

Abel didn't say anything; he looked from Linda to Magnus and back again, like an animal in a trap, his eyes flickering nervously.

"This is Abel," Anna said. "And that's his sister, Micha."

"Hello, Micha," Linda said.

Magnus put out a hand, and Abel understood, with minimal delay, what was expected, and shook it. He still hadn't said a word.

"Nice to meet you," Magnus said in his low bass voice. "Are you at school with Anna?"

Abel nodded.

"I need some coffee urgently," Magnus declared and turned toward the kitchen. "Anyone care to join me?"

"Micha probably doesn't drink coffee," Linda said. "Maybe hot chocolate would be the better choice?"

"Hot chocolate is a very good choice," Micha said. "You have an awfully nice house. And so many books! I have been swinging in Anna's hammock . . ."

"Micha," Abel said and took her hand. "We have to go now."

"Why do we have to go?" Micha asked. "Is it that late? We don't have an appointment, do we? We could just . . ."

"Come on." Abel pulled her in the direction of the door.

"Abel . . ." Anna said.

"Thank you for the offer of coffee," Abel said putting on his parka. "But we actually do have an appointment. We totally forgot about the time."

He helped Micha into her pink down jacket with the artificial fur collar, and before she could say any more, he shoved her out the door. Then he shut the door behind them.

Anna opened it again. "What the hell are you doing?" she called. "Come back, you idiot!"

But Abel had already lifted Micha onto the carrier of his bike.

"No," he said. "Try to understand. There are too many thorns on the island of the rose people."

"There weren't any thorns until now!" Anna said in despair. "Until *right* now . . ."

"Think of what happened in the Mittendrin," Abel said, and now his voice was sharp like the edges of ice floes in an ocean. "Come on. You said that they will be happy to see you, all these fine friends of yours, and then? What happened then? It will be the same with your parents." He shook his head and got onto his bike.

"What's he talking about?" Micha asked.

"I don't think he knows," Anna replied and went back in. She slammed the door shut behind her and tried to breathe steadily. Magnus came from the kitchen, carrying a cup.

"Heavens," he said and put the cup down onto the dresser in the hall. He pulled a handkerchief from his pocket and gave it to Anna.

"What am I supposed to do with that?"

"Wipe your tears away, I thought," Magnus said.

"Strange." Anna stared at the handkerchief in her hand. "This seems to happen to me a lot lately . . . that I'm crying and don't even realize."

"Come into the living room with me," Magnus said in a commanding tone that he very rarely used. "And have a cup of coffee with us or a glass of whiskey, or whatever. But now, you'll tell us what this is all about."

"Okay," said Anna.

They talked late into the night—or, rather, she talked. She was a traitor. She knew she was a traitor. It was none of Magnus and Linda's business how Abel and Micha lived. But suddenly, it was as if a dam had broken, a dam behind which more tears lay, a flood of tears, a flood of stammered, drowned words and half descriptions.

Linda made sandwiches so the tears had something on which to fall. Magnus put the whiskey aside and opened a bottle of white wine instead.

And in the end, he said, "Anna?"

"Yes?" Anna asked.

"What do you want us to do?" He looked at her, earnestly; it was an important question. "Tell us what you want us to do . . . to help. I am a very critical person. I'm not sure if I approve of this, but in love . . . you might think this is a stupid remark . . . but in love, there is no criticism. In love, there is no rationality. I'll give you money if you need it. I will make calls on his behalf. Tell me what we should do."

"I don't know," Anna said. "If I knew, everything would be easy. He won't take money—he says he doesn't want charity. He doesn't want anyone to interfere. On some days, he acts like he doesn't even know me. And after today . . . I . . ."

"Please, don't start crying again," Linda said gently, gently rubbing Anna's back. "Everything will turn out all right."

On Saturday, the body of a man was found under the sand and snow on the beach in Eldena. In the pocket of his leather jacket, there was a wallet with a driver's license identifying him as Sören Marinke. He had been forty-four years old. His woolen sweater and the sheepskin lining of his jacket were stiff with frozen blood. Shot in the neck, the radio announcer reported.

12

Three Days of Sunshine
ॐ

"ANNA?"

She blinked, opening her eyes slowly. The rays of sunlight coming in through the window were reflected by the flute sitting on the music stand and fell to the floor like glass splinters. The hands of the old-fashioned clock on the edge of the bookshelf showed ten to four.

She had lifted her cell phone to her ear . . . still half-asleep . . . she must have nodded off reading.

The radio was talking to itself in a low voice. If one subtracted the half hour she'd been sleeping with her head on the desk, and if one assumed she'd gotten up at about seven o'clock, then she'd heard the news of Sören Marinke's death eight times at this point. The story had grown details, like blossoms, since then, but only a few: a man walking his dog had found Marinke in the morning, or rather the dog had found him, and Anna had instantly wondered the color of the dog. Was it silver-gray? With golden eyes? Surely not . . .

Later, the announcer said that the body had been there for quite some time, maybe a day, covered by sand and snow. It was completely frozen by the time it was found . . . obviously, it was impossible for a body to freeze totally in just a few hours . . .

"Anna?"

Eight times, she had calculated; eight times, she'd held her breath; and eight times, she'd breathed again, relieved. For eight times, she'd come to the conclusion that Abel couldn't possibly have had anything to do with Marinke's death. His alibi for all of yesterday was Anna herself. And the day before, Thursday, he had been to the island of Rügen with Micha. If they had really been there, that is. If . . .

"Anna, are you there?"

"Yeah, yeah, I think I am," she said, but her voice sounded far away. "I was . . . thinking . . . must have fallen asleep over my books. I've spent the whole day working out a stupid study schedule . . ."

No, she thought. No, that's not true. I spent the whole day not calling you. For, of course, it was him. Abel.

"Anna," he said, for the fourth time, as if there was nothing more to say, now that she'd finally answered. Nothing but her name. As if he'd just called to make sure she existed. She got up from her chair and went over to the window with the cell phone, her name ringing in her ears like an echo.

"Abel," she said, "I'm going to mark this day in my calendar with a red pen."

He was silent, sending something like a question mark through the line. "You never call me," she said. "Usually it's me who calls you."

"Did you hear the news?" Abel asked, ignoring her remark.

He was right, she thought, this was no time for flirting.

"Yes," she answered. "Your social worker is dead. A wolf bit him to death and buried him under the sand on the beach in Eldena."

"No," Abel said, with a pained tone in his voice. "No, he didn't. The wolf wasn't there. They've been here, Anna. Police. They . . . they visited . . . everyone whose cases . . . whose cases were on Marinke's desk. It seems there were quite a few people not happy with his interference . . . Thursday. Looks like he died on Thursday, but they weren't sure, or else they didn't want to tell me they were sure. It's all a mess . . . about the time of death . . . because of the cold . . ."

"You've got an alibi," Anna said. "For Thursday. You were on Rügen."

"An alibi, oh yeah," Abel murmured. "That's right. A wonderful alibi. A six-year-old girl. They will be back, believe me. They need a culprit. And I'm . . . I'm connected to both Rainer and Marinke. Everything fits."

"But you didn't shoot Marinke . . ."

"Do you think it was me?"

She hesitated; then she said, "The bus drivers, Abel! Didn't you go by bus to Rügen? And the conductor in the train, too . . . I mean, they're older than six."

"I hope so." He laughed.

"Can't you find out how to contact these people?"

"Yes," he said. "Yes, maybe. Maybe it's possible. It'll take a lot of calls, though. Tomorrow is Monday."

And now, he'll put the phone down, Anna thought, and I'll sit here alone, again, with my books and my radio and the slightly varying radio news reports of Marinke's death.

"Actually I called because . . ." Abel said and stopped. Anna heard Micha say something in the background, impatiently, as if she wanted to have the phone.

"Because we thought it might be nice to meet for a cup of hot chocolate again, in that café near the beach," Abel said. "I mean, if you're free."

No, she thought. No, I'm not free. I don't have time. I have finals in front of me, and a discussion with Linda behind me. A discussion in which she asked me—absolutely rightly—if it is smart to pursue a relationship in which one of the parties just has to open his mouth for the other party to come running.

"Give it to me!" Micha said breathlessly. "Anna, listen! I had this idea . . . it works like this: you bring your flute . . . for, you see, Abel told me the rest of the story—I mean, the part I missed because I was asleep—and we tried to wake up the dog after those two policemen had left . . . we tried all day long, but the dog just won't wake up. He's breathing, lying on the deck and breathing, and that's all . . . and so, I thought, you know, if you play the flute, really nicely and everything, isn't it possible that it will wake him up? In a fairy tale, that could happen, don't you think? And we could cook dinner together . . . we have spaghetti, you know, and . . ."

"One thing at a time," Anna said, smiling. "I'm on my way."

"Are you calling it a day, study-wise?" Linda asked, peeling onions, wiping her hands on a blue apron. Anna nodded and hugged her. "I might be out late," she said.

Linda took a corner of the apron and wiped away a tear that might have come from peeling onions. "Okay, honey, I hope not too late."

"Wait," Magnus said. She was half out the door already. "Here. If you stay for dinner . . . one usually brings something if one's invited to dinner at someone else's place."

He held a bottle of red wine in his outstretched hand, a bottle of good wine, wine so old it was about to turn to vinegar. Valuable wine. Anna shook her head. Magnus stuffed the bottle into her backpack and nodded.

"Talk to him," he said. "Maybe it's easier with a good bottle of wine. Talk to him about my offer. At least try."

And Anna hugged her father, too, because he believed that a bottle of good wine could solve most problems. Or, who knows? maybe he didn't really believe that. She got onto her bike.

For some reason, she'd thought that everything would be the way it was the first time: that Abel and Micha would be sitting in the back of the café, in the stern of the glass ship; that there would be exactly one empty chair at their table; and that she would walk toward it, a vague, light happiness filling her body. But, of course, nothing is ever as it was the first time. The café was packed. There were even people seated at tables on the terrace, outside in the cold wind, with the collars of their jackets turned up and their hands around cups of tea and coffee in search of a little warmth. And when Anna saw Abel and Micha waiting next to the stairs, amid people coming and going, she didn't feel light and happy. Instead, she felt a pang of sorrow.

She'd heard shreds of sentences as she'd passed people on her bike—bloody, raw shreds of words that were full of pleasant shivers. She knew why these people were here: to be near the place it had happened. All these people had heard the news. One group came in from the beach across the way, from the other side of the mouth of the little river, and Anna heard: "police tape . . . dogs . . . traces . . . snow dug up . . . did you see where he was lying?" Others were on their way to the beach: "have a closer look . . . maybe draw a conclusion . . . creepy . . . just imagine that . . . maybe during the night . . . and then that shot from behind."

Anna followed Abel and Micha out onto the pier in silence. The pier was quiet and free of people. "Why are we meeting here?" Anna asked. It was the first thing any of them had said. "Why here, with all these people?"

"Because we always come here, that's why," Micha said, but Abel shook his head. "That's not the only reason," he said in a low voice. "There's something else. You . . . you might think it's stupid, but . . . but I wanted to see who'd be here. This is the place where all rumors converge . . . I bet he's here, too, because he's also interested in the rumors."

"Who?" Anna asked.

"The murderer," Abel said, looking out over the sea. They had arrived at the very end of the pier, where a green light attached to a post was guiding the ships home, a light with neither a lighthouse nor a lighthouse keeper attached to it. "They will blame me for this, I'm sure," Abel said. "And there's only one way to convince them that it wasn't me . . . a better way than phoning bus drivers and train conductors. If I find the real murderer, if I present that murderer to them on a silver tray . . . understand? Then they will have to believe me. Then they will have to let me go."

"But nobody's holding you," Anna said. "Did they say that they believe that you . . . ?"

He shook his head. "Not yet." Damocles, she thought, had returned.

He put both arms onto the white metal rail and looked down onto the ice, where countless traces of life had marked the thin layer of snow: footprints of bald coots and ducks, swans and mergansers. And somewhere on the ice, Anna wondered, were there also traces of death—footprints of a murderer?

"It must be someone who's somehow connected to me," Abel whispered. "That only makes sense. I mean, why would anybody shoot Rainer Lierski and then Sören Marinke? And . . . who will be next?"

Anna shook her head. "Nobody. Because we'll figure this out before that. We'll find out who . . . or what . . . is going on here. I'm going to help you. I can keep my eyes and ears open . . . if you just tell me, where and when . . ."

He turned to her abruptly. The ice in his eyes gleamed in the sunshine. "No," he said. "Don't do that. Promise me you'll keep out of this mess. This isn't a game or a history test. I don't want anything to happen to you."

"Thanks," Anna replied angrily. "I just turned five last week."

Abel put his hands on her shoulders and looked at her even more intensely, as if he wanted to burn a hole into her. "They're dead, Anna," he whispered. "They're both dead. Dead as stone. Don't you get that?"

"I do." She looked down at her feet.

"If you two could stop fighting," Micha said, "it would be good, because right now we're supposed to wake the dog with the flute, remember?" She had been busy climbing on the railing but now stood next to them, her cheeks reddened, her pigtails half-undone. Nothing about her suggested the word *death*.

So Anna pushed her thoughts about Marinke aside and took out her flute. It was cold, of course, and it was out of tune, but a dog probably wouldn't hear the difference. "What do you want me to play?"

"I dunno," Micha said. "Something nice."

Abel nodded; leaned against the green, painted post, on which the light for the ships was attached like a traffic light; and started to roll a cigarette. "We should see if we can do something about that dog," he said. "He isn't well. His wounds are deep, and his sleep is even deeper. He had almost given up when they pulled him out of the water . . ."

Anna made a list in her head of all the pieces of music she could play by heart, from the easiest to the most difficult. She thought of all sorts of complicated melodies, but none seemed good enough to wake a wounded dog living inside a fairy tale. In the end, she closed her eyes and imagined that she was standing on the deck of the green ship. On the horizon, she saw the black sails of their persecutors, who hadn't yet given up. The little queen was standing there with her, and before them, in the cabin, lay the motionless body of the dog. Next to him, a blind white cat gave a bored yawn. And then she knew what to play.

She put the cool silver to her lips and asked the flute for a simple melody, one without ornamentation, a melody whose text you could read in the air . . . if you knew it:

> There's a concert hall in Vienna
> Where your mouth had a thousand reviews
> There's a bar where the boys have stopped talking
> They've been sentenced to death by the blues

She heard Abel humming next to her, and she was pretty sure she'd heard the words before; it was a song from one of Linda's old LPs, and it was probably on one of Michelle's cassettes, too . . . the cryptic, dark poetry of an old Canadian.

Ah, but who is it climbs to your picture
With a garland of freshly cut tears
Take this waltz, take this waltz,
Take this waltz, it's been dying for years . . .

"The little queen bent down to pet the silver-gray dog," Abel said. "And in this very moment, the dog blinked. He lifted his head ever so slowly, looked at her with his golden eyes, and wagged his tail. Then he rose, crept out of the cabin, and jumped into the water. A little later, a sea lion was swimming in the waves, next to the green ship. But the waves had almost stopped moving, and the lighthouse keeper scratched his ear with the arm of his glasses. "Soon, soon the sea will freeze," he said, "and we won't be able to sail on any longer. And what will we do then?"

Anna put down the flute. For a moment, she thought she'd seen something out there, in the water, something in the middle of the mouth of the river, which was kept free of ice so the fishing boats could pass. It was a round, dark head with glittering black eyes. Nonsense. Later, she would think that it hadn't been a sea lion's head at all but, instead, the head of a man—and a vision of something that would happen much later, but, of course, that was even more nonsense.

Abel took her free hand and led her off the pier, back to the café. Micha ran along beside them like a little dog.

"'The sea hasn't frozen yet, has it?' the little queen said. 'But what's that over there? Another island? Shouldn't we go there and have a look?'

"'No, we shouldn't,' the lighthouse keeper replied. 'For that, my little queen, is the island of the murderer.'

"'I don't believe that,' the little queen said, shaking Mrs. Margaret so hard that her blue flowered dress flew up and down. 'Mrs. Margaret is shaking her head, do you see? I want to go there and find out for myself who lives on that island.'

"The lighthouse keeper heaved a deep sigh and steered the ship toward the island. It was a tiny island, tinier than all the islands they had visited so far. On one side, somebody had erected a sign that read: ISLAND OF THE MURDERER.

"'Huh!' the little queen exclaimed. 'Who writes signs like that? Stop! I want to go ashore!'

"'Ashore?' the lighthouse keeper, the rose girl, the blind white cat, and the asking man asked in a neat choir. Only the answering man answered, murmuring something about 'seven times daily.'

"'You can't go ashore on an island where a murderer lives,' the rose girl said.

"'Oh yes, I can,' the little queen said. 'A queen with a diamond heart can go ashore on any island. Maybe the murderer doesn't want to be a murderer anymore but, instead, someone else, something opposite, like . . . a savior, for example. He needs someone to tell him how he can change.'

"And with these words, she climbed over the rail and jumped onto the cliffs of the tiny island.

"'Wait!' the rose girl called and jumped after her. The lighthouse keeper, the asking man, and the answering man followed her. Only the blind white cat, licking her paws, stayed on deck, and the sea lion was nowhere to be found . . . in any of his forms.

"The little group began to wander over the tiny island. It wasn't just the tiniest, it was also the barest island they had seen. There were no trees, no bushes, no grass—not even a house. But the murderer who lived there . . . where was the murderer? Where was he lurking?

"'He is here,' the little queen whispered after a while. 'Very near. He can see us. I can feel his eyes on me. But he doesn't want to talk to us. How can I help him turn into something different if he doesn't show himself?'

"'Let's go,' said the lighthouse keeper. 'Let's leave this creepy island before one of us is murdered.'

"'No,' the rose girl said. 'No, I don't think the murderer is here anymore. He must have left a long time ago. Or swam away.'

"'But where is he then?' the little queen whispered uncomfortably. 'Maybe . . . maybe he is on board? Maybe he has been on board for a long time?'

"'Where—on board what?' the asking man asked.

"'On the thirteenth of March,' the answering man answered, though this answer didn't fit the question, of course.

"'The black ship,' the little queen said doubtfully. 'He's already turned into someone else. We just don't recognize him. Or . . . is he on board our own ship?'

"When she said this, everybody looked at each other: the lighthouse keeper looked at the rose girl, the rose girl looked at the asking man, and the asking man looked at the answering man. The answering man looked back to the ship, where the white cat was still grooming.

"When the green ship cast off a little later, distrust was creeping over the deck like an unwanted passenger who had come aboard at the tiny island. Maybe, each of them thought, one of them was a murderer. Maybe someone they had previously trusted was someone who murdered because he or she was born on an island with a sign saying 'Island of the Murderer.'

"The waves looked like dark green honey. It must be the distrust. They were stuck in a sea of suspicion, hardly moving anymore. If things stayed like this, they would never reach the mainland."

Abel fell silent, and Anna had to force herself to resurface from the honey ocean so that she could see where they were. They were standing in front of the café. But that wasn't the reason Abel had brought the story to a halt. The reason was a figure approaching them along the harbor: a figure with his hands deep in the pockets of his jacket, now scratching his ear with the arm of his glasses.

"Knaake," Abel said in a low voice. Anna nodded.

"Let's go in," Abel said.

"Why? You don't want to see him?"

"I want to see what he does," Abel answered. "Where he goes and how he behaves. Just . . . so . . . Come on."

"Will you tell the fairy tale inside, and will there be hot chocolate, and can I have a piece of cake with it?" Micha asked as she raced up the stairs without waiting for answers. She was a little queen. Of course there would be hot chocolate and cake.

Anna didn't think they would find a table, but they were lucky— there was a couple just leaving one next to the window overlooking the mouth of the river, and Micha snatched their spot like a cat would a mouse. The young man helped the young woman into a long black leather coat, and then he slipped on his own coat, which made the words *cashmere* and *smooth* pop into Anna's head. He was wearing a gray silk scarf and his hair was red, nearly golden . . . then he turned and, of course . . . of course, it was Hennes. And, of course, the young woman in the black leather coat was Gitta.

"Seems like everyone's here today," Abel said in a low voice.

It was a weird situation: They looked at each other, two versus two, here versus there, this side versus the other.

"So, little lamb," Gitta said finally, "here you go, have our table. Have you been over there? At the beach? You heard what happened, right? It was all over the news . . ."

Anna nodded slowly. "We haven't been there . . . no. Have you?"

"Yeah," Gitta said. "It was kinda creepy. I mean, that guy found the dead body, just this morning, and it had been there for a day or so . . . in our neighborhood, all hell's broken loose, police driving by regularly . . . I actually started wondering if it might be a good idea to open up a snack bar, you know, for anyone who's coming by to look . . . Hennes insisted on going down to the beach—he thought he'd find footprints that haven't been trampled . . . the great bloodhound . . ."

She pressed her body, in a black leather coat, against him, and he tried to pull her away. "Come on, didn't we want to . . ."

"He's also good at finding footprints in the woods," Gitta went on, winking at Anna. "I guess I'll have to learn sooner or later . . . how to track. Maybe I'll even take up hunting. Those blinds you hide in look pretty cozy to me . . ."

"Wait a sec," Anna said. "That sounds like Bertil, not like Hennes. Hennes, do you hunt, too?"

Hennes rolled his eyes. He even looked charming when he was rolling his eyes. Hell.

"Come on, Gitta," he repeated. "Let's get going. Now."

"The family von Biederitz has a hunting lodge out at Hanshagen, didn't you know that?" Abel said. "They probably own the town, too."

"No," Anna said. "I didn't know that." She watched as Hennes pulled Gitta away by her arm, a little too possessively. Gitta in her black biker gear; Gitta, who despite her clothes could only afford an old scooter; Gitta with her hated, overly hygienic mother didn't fit in with Hennes's family any better than Abel did with Anna's. Anna imagined Gitta sitting in a hunting blind in her leather coat, trying not to move . . . a majestic stag on the clearing in front of her . . . as she raises her gun, the leather jacket rustles, and the stag flees. Or maybe it chokes while laughing. Or Gitta sidles up to it instead, and propositions it . . .

"What are you laughing at?" Abel asked.

Anna shook her head. "Weird thoughts," she answered. "It's good to laugh."

"I ordered three hot chocolates and a piece of cake, all by myself, without any help," Micha said proudly. "I'm just telling you because you didn't see me do it. And look! In here, it's already springtime."

She was right. On each of the tables in the café, a single red tulip stood in a narrow white vase. "Yeah, it's spring in here," Abel said. "I wonder if it'll ever be spring out there."

Outside, in the eternal winter, Knaake was walking out onto the pier with thoughtful steps. He stood at the green pole with the light on top, and it looked as if he were listening to some long-forgotten melody still hanging in the air at the end of the pier. Then he reached into his pocket and took something out, which he held to his eyes—a small pair of binoculars.

"Didn't you say that's the lighthouse keeper?" Micha asked. "He's looking for the ship. The black one. He's looking for the last person on it, I mean, apart from Mrs. Ketow and the haters, Uncle Rico and Aunt Evelyn. For, you know, I don't think those three are really dangerous. Uncle Rico—definitely not—he doesn't even want to have me. He might have to take me in because he's my only close relative. If another guy from shells and sisters comes and says . . ."

Micha kept on talking about the ship and about "shells and sisters," which by now sounded like the name of a grocery-store chain to Anna, but she wasn't listening very carefully. She saw Knaake turn around with his binoculars. He wasn't scanning the horizon anymore. Instead, he was looking at the beach of Eldena, opposite the pier, on the other side of the mouth of the river. Was he able to see the police tape from where he was standing? Could he make out the faces of the curious people who were prowling around like stray cats on the lookout for food? Next, Knaake aimed his binoculars at the café. Maybe he saw them. What else did he see? What else did he expect to see?

Anna followed his gaze to the café terrace, where people were giving up and starting to leave—it was just too cold out there. Someone with a big gray dog walked past. Anna put a hand on Abel's arm and pointed.

The person with the dog stopped at the beginning of the pier, looked out over the frozen sea for a few moments, turned, and walked his dog back along the river. He was pushing a bicycle, too, with one hand.

"Bertil," Anna said. Abel nodded. Had he seen them? He'd seen Knaake, who was still standing out there at the end of the pier . . . that much was sure—he had seen him and turned the other way.

"So did the sea stay thick?" Micha asked, gently stroking the red tulip on their table with her index finger. "Or did it turn more liquidy again? Did they find out which one of them was the murderer?"

Abel sipped a little of his hot chocolate, covered his face with his hands, and took a deep breath. "That sea . . . ," he said after lowering his hands, ". . . that sea stayed thick and green. Worse, it became thicker and thicker. And, finally, it stood still. The waves weren't moving anymore. The ship had stopped.

"Then, there was a cracking sound right in front of the green ship. One of the motionless waves broke like glass, and, in a rain of splinters, the sea lion heaved himself out of the ocean, onto its rigid, shining green surface.

"'The sea,' he declared—and the tone of his voice had something very final to it—'the sea has frozen.'

"'But how . . . how can we go on?' the little queen asked in despair.

"'On foot,' the rose girl answered. 'We'll have to walk.'

"So they all climbed over the rail, one after the other: the asking man, the answering man, the lighthouse keeper, the rose girl, the little queen with Mrs. Margaret in her arms, and the blind white cat. They walked a little ways away from the ship; then they stood, hesitating, a pitiful cluster of figures in the middle of shining, dark green endlessness.

"'What will we do if we get lost in this eternal winter?' the little queen asked timidly. 'If we lose each other? Where will we find each other again?'

"'We'll meet wherever spring is,' the rose girl replied.

"And then they started wandering over the ice. Just once, they turned to look back at their green ship with the yellow rudder; the lighthouse keeper got out a small pair of binoculars, the existence of which he had forgotten until that moment, and he looked through them.

"'Now I can see it!' he exclaimed. 'I can see the ship's name! It's painted on her bow, right above the waterline; we just didn't realize it was there!'

"He gave the binoculars to the little queen, and she, too, saw the blue letters on the green hull of the ship.

"'What's she called, then?' the asking man asked.

"'Thanks, same to you,' the answering man answered.

"'She's called *Hope*,' the little queen said. 'Our ship is called *Hope*.'

"The rose girl sighed. 'And now we're leaving her behind,' she whispered."

Abel took hold of his cup and leaned back in his chair.

"Is that all?" Micha asked.

"For today, yes. Before I can go on telling you what happens, the little queen's crew has to continue on foot for a while over the ice."

"But look! Out there, they are walking over the ice, too, just like in the story!" Micha called out. "See? Over there? I want to do that, too! There's even a woman with a stroller!"

At that very moment, the woman Micha had spotted seemed to notice that she was getting dangerously close to the shipping canal, where dark water was coming through the thin layer of ice. She stood there for a moment, as if undecided, then turned and went back toward the beach, the way she'd come, pushing the stroller in front of her. Two children, about two and three years old, were running around her in circles, like young dogs, pushing and shoving each other. The woman herself was wearing a coat and a head scarf; she looked a little like people in those photographs from 1945, fleeing from the Russians, walking over the ice. But probably, she was just part of the curious crowd that had gathered by the police tape on the beach.

"I think," Abel said as he looked into his empty cup, "it's time to go home. Anybody need to go to the bathroom before we head out?"

Micha nodded, and, when she'd left, Abel leaned forward, closer to Anna.

"Mrs. Ketow," he whispered. "Micha didn't recognize her, but I'm pretty sure it was her."

"Now we've got everyone gathered here," Anna said. "Everyone who's got anything to do with the fairy tale. Apart from the haters, but they don't live anywhere near, do they? Apart from them, everyone's here."

"No," Abel said in a low voice. Then he took something from his pocket and put it on the table in front of her. It was a bank statement. "You were right."

Anna's eyes scanned the paper. The amounts of money going in and out of the account were ridiculously low, not much more than a child's pocket money. Only at the very end, there was a bigger amount. One hundred euros, drawn from a cash machine in Eldena.

"That wasn't me. I didn't take that out," Abel said. "That was her. Now she's starting to take our money."

"Michelle," Anna said.

Abel nodded. "She's the only other person who can use this account. I wonder if I should close it. Or change the password. But I probably can't even do that because I'm still not eighteen. She's the only one who can do that. In any case . . . she hasn't gone off to God-knows-where to start a new life." He looked around, looked over the heads in the café and outside at the people walking over the ice, at the harbor, at the beach of Eldena. "She's here. Somewhere close. I just haven't spotted her yet."

Anna went home with Abel and Micha. It just happened. Or maybe the little queen had decided that she should; maybe she had scratched words into the dirt on some invisible windowpane: TAK HER HOM WITH YOU, like K IS EacH Oth ER.

Abel made spaghetti. And that night, Anna almost believed that Linda was right. That everything would turn out okay. Abel was standing in the tiny kitchen, humming a melody to himself, wearing a makeshift apron like some backyard chef; Micha was painting a picture for school in the living room, a "what I did this weekend" picture; and Anna was cutting up tomatoes. From time to time, she went into the living room to look at Micha's artwork. First, a flute appeared; then, a piece of cake seemed to grow out of the flute; then, a red tulip was growing out of the cake; then, red police tape was slung around the tulip . . . and then Anna discovered someone who Micha said was Abel and someone she said was Anna—the two of them discernible only by the color of their hair—and, in the end, a green square filled the rest of the paper. On the square, she'd written "Hop" and drawn a yellow triangle: a green ship with a yellow rudder. A gray animal was flying in the middle of the picture—it might have been a dog, but it might just as well have been an elephant. Abel and Anna kissed in the kitchen for too long, forgetting the boiling tomato sauce, which spilled over the rim of the saucepan and onto the stove. They wiped it away and laughed. How absolutely, wonderfully all right everything was!

"How can I be so happy," she whispered, "when there's a murderer walking free somewhere out there?"

"Go on being happy," Abel said as he painted a circle on her cheek with some tomato sauce. "Maybe it's contagious. I hope so."

They ate the spaghetti at the small living room table, and Abel didn't say anything when Micha decided that it was easier to eat it with her fingers. "Now there's only one last thing to do before you go off to bed," Abel finally said. "Remember what we wanted to do today?"

Micha twirled a blond strand of hair around her finger. "Cut my hair." She produced a tragic sigh.

"Yep," Abel said. "Today is hair-cutting day. If there weren't any hair-cutting days, we'd all end up running around like wild people and nobody would recognize us anymore. Just imagine, you come to school one day and your teacher asks, 'And who might this wild child be?'"

"She wouldn't ask that," Micha giggled. "Mrs. Milowicz only asks when she can talk to Mama, but she asks that all the time."

"Soon," Abel said. "Tell her, soon, Micha."

Then he fetched sharp scissors and a comb from the little bathroom, and Anna watched as he combed Micha's blond hair. "Snow hair," he said. "Polar bear hair. When she runs around in the sun in summer, it turns even lighter . . . nearly white."

Anna saw his hands slide through that snow hair, saw them handle the scissors. She imagined those hands in her own hair, imagined those hands doing things that had nothing to do with hair cutting. Tonight, she thought, tonight when everything's all right, maybe . . . maybe I won't go home tonight. Will he leave after Micha's gone to bed? Does he have to meet someone in town? Or will he stay? Does he want what I want?

"Hold still," Abel said. "You know these scissors are sharp. So sharp you could cut someone's neck with them and kill him." The scissor blades reflected the light of the ancient living room lamp hanging from the ceiling. Micha was fidgeting on the sofa, fed up with holding still. "Stop it!" she demanded. "You're tickling me, and you've cut off enough! It's my turn! Give the scissors to me . . ." She half-turned to snatch them from Abel, and that was when it happened: Abel's hand slipped. He cried out; Micha screamed; Anna saw the glittering metal of the blades sail through the air and land on the floor. She looked at Abel's fingers. There was blood on them.

"Fucking hell!" he shouted. "Micha, are you crazy? What was that about?"

"You cut my neck!" Micha cried out. "Now I'll die and it's your fault!"

Abel found a handkerchief and pressed it to the place where the blood came from. It was just a tiny cut on Micha's neck, a scratch made by the scissor tip when it grazed her skin. It was nothing really, but Micha kept on crying, and Abel pulled her into his arms and hugged her while pressing the handkerchief against her neck.

Anna breathed again. Suddenly dizzy, she had to sit down in one of the armchairs. Nothing had happened, and still the whole scene seemed symbolic—blood on a person's neck, blood like the blood from a bullet wound—and she thought of Rainer and of Sören Marinke in his ice-cold grave beneath the sand and snow.

"Just a tiny little pain," he sang softly, "three days of heavy rain . . . three days of sunlight . . . everything will be all right . . ." He held her like a much smaller child, the child she'd once been.

She stopped crying and finally freed herself from his arms. "Am I still bleeding?"

"No," Abel said. "The singing's done the trick. It always does. You know that."

Micha nodded. "When I was small," she explained to Anna, trying to sound very grown-up, "and I fell and hurt my knees, we always sang that song." She wiped the last tears from her face. "And it always, always stopped the bleeding, didn't it? Can I get one of those teddy-bear Band-Aids?"

Abel lifted her up—another gesture from former times, from when she'd been smaller—and carried her to the bathroom to find the Band-Aid. Suddenly, Anna thought: she's growing up. One day, she'll be too big to be carried around like that. One day, he won't be able to hold onto her, she'll move on, and he'll be left all alone. Maybe the responsibility for Micha is more of an anchor than a burden. A lifeboat. A wooden plank to hold onto so you don't drown. She shook her head to rid it of these thoughts. She could hear Abel and Micha laughing in the bathroom; she heard water running, the accident with the scissors already forgotten, and everything was all right again, just as the song said. When Micha came back to the living room to say good night, she was wearing turquoise pajamas, stamped with a lopsided Mickey Mouse, who obviously had trouble focusing his eyes. She proudly showed Anna the green Band-Aid with the teddy bear, which was stuck to her neck. A trophy. And then the door of her room shut behind her, and Abel flopped down onto the sofa.

Anna put Magnus's bottle of wine on the table. "Let's drink away that scare."

He nodded his head, went to the kitchen, and came back with a corkscrew and two water glasses. "Looks like we don't have wineglasses."

"I'd drink it from the bottle with straws," she said. "But I do need some of it now." She sat cross-legged in the armchair and held out her glass. The wine hadn't turned to vinegar yet. Fortunately.

"Bad luck seems to really feel at home here lately," Abel murmured. "Since Michelle left, it's settled in like it wants to stay forever. It follows us out the door, sticks behind us like a dog. You can run as quickly as you want to, but it's always quicker." He picked something up that had fallen under the table and looked at it, a small thing resembling a shaver.

"Is that a . . . hair trimmer?" Anna asked doubtfully.

Abel nodded. "Hair-cutting day. I'm wondering what will happen when I switch this thing on."

"Buzz cut," Anna said.

He nodded again. And then Anna stood up and took the trimmer from his hands and set it aside. "If I promise not to stab and kill you with them, and to stop drinking till I'm done," she began, "would you give me those scissors? I don't want you to look like someone you're not. Ever again."

"Tell me . . . where's that sweatshirt of mine?"

She reached into her backpack, grinning. "Linda washed it. I only realized when it was hanging on the line."

He shook his head. "Just be careful, Anna Leemann," he said seriously, "that you don't try to change me into someone I'm not." But he gave her the scissors anyway, and she stepped behind the sofa, took the comb, and started pulling it through his hair, like he'd done to Micha's before. Snow hair, ice hair, was it white in summer, too? She couldn't remember—she hadn't looked at him once last summer. He'd been there, at school, but not existing. The sound of the cutting blades made her shiver.

"Magnus asked me to tell you something . . . from him," she said. It was just as well he had to keep still now, she thought, because then he also had to listen to her. "My father . . . We've been talking about a few things. Not about everything, not about Sören Marinke, for example. But about the fact that your mother left . . . and that money isn't exactly raining down from the sky. I know you don't want charity. Don't move, I'm dangerous with these scissors. But he said he'd like to offer you something. He'd lend you the money, and later, when you've finished school, when you have a job . . . you can pay him back. He'd be in no hurry to get the money. You could pay it back, slowly, no matter how long it took. It would be a loan without interest, not like a bank . . . that would be the advantage . . ."

Abel didn't say anything. For a while, there was only the sound of the scissors. Outside, cars were racing by. Anna heard her own breath. She heard the pounding of her heart. Finally, she put scissors and comb on the table. "That's it. Done. Not a buzz cut but still shorter than before."

"Thanks," he said. She followed him into the bathroom and looked into the mirror from behind him. He was smiling. "You should think about becoming a barber. I mean . . . I *know* that's why you're taking finals. Ha! Look, I'm not sure about your father's offer. I mean, I don't know him."

"No," Anna said. "Me neither, to be honest. I just know that he likes feeding the birds in our yard and that he loves my mother. That's all."

"More than I'll ever know about my father," Abel said. "I don't even know his name. About university . . . I told you we only have that one account. Well, that's not quite true. We do have another one. One that was opened a long time ago. For school. I don't work only so that we have something to live on. I also work to be able to put money into that account, so that, later, everything can be different . . . for Micha . . . that's what matters most, that things will be different for her than from how they've been for me. It's not enough, of course, the money in that account, not yet. I'll think about your father's offer. Give me some time."

"Okay." She put her arms around him and kept looking into the mirror, looking at the two of them. "Do you have to go out tonight?"

"No." He looked down at her arms slung around him. She thought he'd remove them, but he didn't. "The only thing is . . . I'd like to go out to the beach," he said. "People say they come back, don't they?"

"Who?"

"Murderers. They come back to the site of the murder. Now, at night, when nobody else is at the beach . . . maybe we'll meet someone there. Maybe not . . . maybe it's crazy. Probably it is."

"It is," Anna said. "But I'll go with you. And you know what else we'll take along? That bottle of wine. If we don't meet a murderer, we can sit in the snow and drink wine. I feel like doing something stupid tonight."

The beach lay in the light of a vague half-moon, long and gray. Up in the night sky, clouds chased each other. It was windy and ice-cold. Anna wore one of Abel's sweaters under her coat. They walked along the beach side by side. Abel had stuffed his hands deep into the pockets of his military parka. Anna knew that she wasn't allowed to touch him now. There were too many unwritten rules. She carried the wine bottle in her backpack. She would try to change these unwritten rules, to rewrite them, to loosen their hold . . .

The police tape, senseless in the night, was singing in the wind like a violin out of tune, a strange, unreal sound. The square separated from the rest of the beach by the tape was like a grave. They stood there for a while, at the rim of the pit that no longer held a body. How long would they leave the tape there? What was it good for now? The snow had long since covered old footprints, and now there were new ones—dozens, hundreds of new ones. Maybe the police were hesitant to remove the tape out of respect, respect for the dead, as if his death would become a fact only when this last reminder of him had vanished—the senseless tape between the senseless metal poles stuck in the sand. The taped-off grave was at the far end of the beach, near the little hut where the university surfing program kept its boards in the summer. One of the two official entrances to the beach was behind it. In the summer, you had to buy a ticket to enter. Right behind the entrance gate, the woods—the Elisenhain—used to begin, its high beech trees towering over the farthest sand dunes. Now there weren't many beeches left, and instead a tarred driveway led through tidy yards to a new housing development, the one where Gitta lived. The woods had receded and now began behind the development, on the far side of Wolgaster Street.

Anna wondered if the murderer had come from the woods. If he had walked through the neighborhood, past the sterile, modern block in which Gitta lived, past its huge glass windows, past the few trees leftover from former times . . . if he had walked through the gate in the fence that was open to everyone in winter, had hidden behind the surfers' hut to wait for his victim . . . "At night," she said. "I imagine it happened at night. Or someone would have seen it."

She let her eyes wander along the beach, and, for a moment, she thought she saw someone at the other end. But there was no one.

She must have been mistaken. And if there was someone lurking behind the surfers' hut right now, someone with a weapon . . . ? And if someone was waiting in the dark shade under the trees, behind the fence . . . ? If someone was standing near the houses closest to the beach, holding a pair of binoculars, looking their way . . . ? The island of the murderer was empty. He was close, very close. It was as if she could feel his eyes on her.

"Abel," she whispered. "What are you thinking about?"

He had clenched his fist around the police tape and was staring down into the pit from which they'd pulled Sören Marinke's body. "I'm wondering if he had children," Abel said. "Strange. I didn't think about that before."

"They didn't say anything about children on the news. So I think probably not."

"Or a wife. A girlfriend. Anybody. Anybody who cared about him. I wonder who's crying for him." He shook his head. "Let's go. There's nobody here. It was a stupid idea to come."

Black shadows filled their footprints in the beach like puddles, the blackness grabbing their ankles as they walked. At the other entrance, closer to the mouth of the river, Abel took Anna's hand. Their bicycles stood next to the lonely little ticket counter, but they left them there and walked on, over to the small fishing harbor off the bank of the river. In summer, a few sailing boats were docked near the fishing boats, and it was here that Anna had met Rainer when he'd lured Micha onto a boat that wasn't his. Now there were only a few stray cats tiptoeing along the docks; maybe some of them were blind. Where the wind had cleared the dark ice of snow, the half-moonlight was reflected in the frozen river.

"Sometimes I can't tell the difference anymore," Anna whispered, "between beauty and desolation. Isn't that weird? Sometimes I don't even know if I'm extremely happy or extremely sad. It happens a lot when I think of you."

They sat on one of the benches along the shore and drank Magnus's wine from the bottle. It was too cold not to be close to each other, so the unwritten rules were softened. They sat, huddled together like winter birds on a branch. The wine warmed them a little, from inside.

"When these final exams are over, I'm going to write," Abel whispered. "About everything. Not just a fairy tale for Micha. About the beauty and the desolation. About the cold of these nights. There are words for everything . . . you just have to find them. I want to sit at a writing desk that is so big I could sleep on it, and I want to see the sea from there. I'll have it one day . . . it's going to be so big that Micha can sit on it and watch me write. Or she could draw a picture to go with the words."

"And me?" Anna asked. "Is there a place on that desk reserved for me, too?"

"You've got your own place in the world," Abel answered. "You'll go away and forget us. Aren't you planning to go to England as an au pair? You don't need us. You've got your music and . . . everything . . . there isn't any room for us."

"Crap," Anna said. "I don't even know if I want to go to England anymore. Maybe I'll stay here. Will you build a drawer in your writing desk so that I have somewhere to sleep when it's raining?"

She put the bottle down and kissed him; she pushed the unwritten rules far, far away; she undid the buttons of her coat, the zip on his sweater she was wearing; she wanted to take his hand in hers, again, as she'd done on her parents' sofa.

He freed himself and stood up. "Let's go back to the bikes. It's getting late."

But they walked arm in arm. They walked slowly, taking a detour around the huge boathouse where the university sailing-club boats were dry-docked in winter. Anna let her fingers glide along the fence. And then she stopped. "The door," she whispered. "The door is open. The door of the boathouse. See that? Do you think someone's in there right now?"

They stood in the darkness, listening intently. There was nothing.

"Somebody forgot to lock it up," Abel said. Anna pulled him with her. "Come on!" she whispered. "We can have a look at the boats! Maybe there's a green one with a yellow rudder . . ."

"There are just small boats in there," Abel said. "Why do you want to go in? We . . ."

"Come on," Anna begged. "Let's do something stupid! It's not every day you find an open boathouse full of sailboats!" She let go of him, took a few steps toward the entrance, and spun around once, twice, three times—her open coat flying, whirling around her like a dress. She spun and spun, her face turned up to the night sky, until she felt dizzy. She laughed. She felt reckless, wild. When she stumbled, Abel caught her in his arms and laughed, too, a little hesitantly. "You're drunk."

"And what if I am?" She led him to the open door, pulling him into the boathouse.

"We can't . . ." he began, but she put a finger on his lips.

"Nobody's watching us. I want to see the boats. Maybe I'll learn how to sail one day . . . do you know how?"

"No."

"There must be a light switch somewhere . . ."

"Oh, great . . . switch on the light, and everybody will know for sure that we're here. I don't need any more trouble than I've already got. Please, forget about the switch. If you insist on looking at these boats . . . I've got a flashlight . . ."

The white light appeared in the darkness. Abel had been wrong. There weren't just small boats; there were yachts as well, one obviously being worked on. There was a short ladder beside it, a mess of cables on the floor, and next to them, a portable sander. Maybe it was this boat's owner who'd forgotten to lock up. They wandered among the sleeping boats for a while, Anna touching the curves of plastic and wood with her hand.

"I'd like to sail on this one once," she said, "or on that one over there . . . but none of them are like the little queen's ship . . . am I right?"

Abel shook his head. Then he put a finger to his mouth and switched off the flashlight. Anna listened. Had there been a noise? The noise of running feet? She felt cold all of a sudden. The island of the murderer was empty. She had forgotten all about him. He was close, very close . . . She stepped closer to Abel, holding onto him like a child, as if she had changed into Micha, a panicky, six-year-old Micha. She felt her heartbeat mixing with his.

"Abel, we're not alone in here," she whispered, "are we?"

"I don't know," he whispered back. The running feet were coming closer now, someone was running behind the boats. There was a loud clattering noise . . . Anna held Abel even tighter. And Abel switched the light on again. Anna closed her eyes.

A second later, she heard him laugh, relieved. "You can open your eyes," he said. "It's not our murderer. It's a rat." Anna saw it now, too, a big brown rat sitting under one of the boats next to the bucket it had knocked over, blinking into the light, confused.

But Anna still felt Abel's heart beating rapidly in time with her own. She didn't let go of him, not this time. Instead, she put down her backpack and unzipped his parka. Maybe this was the opportunity she'd needed. The one opportunity she'd get. She wished it was summer. Summer is generous with opportunities, with warm evenings, with beautiful starry nights . . . with places like beaches or park benches and soft grass on pastures full of flowers. But in this story, all there seemed to be was winter, eternal ice-cold winter. And a boathouse full of sailboats, she thought, was at least free of snow . . .

She kissed him again and saw him put the flashlight on the boat next to them. Her hand crept under his sweater, under his T-shirt, and lay on his warm, bare skin—innocent at first—over his heart. She felt its rhythm, and she felt his hand, too; his hand had caught hers and held it captive, but she pulled it free. She had closed her eyes . . . it was easier to feel with closed eyes . . .

Now, she thought, a little dizzy, maybe from the wine. Yes. *Now.* I've got to do it now before courage leaves me. Right now, I'm not Anna Leeman but someone else, someone much more daring . . .

They were still locked in a kiss, and Anna's hand made its way, as if on its own . . . it found a belt, opened it, found more and livelier body warmth . . . her coat had fallen from her shoulders. She thought about practical things . . . that they could use her coat to lie on, that this concrete floor was damned hard, but then, not only the floor . . . Her other hand discovered one of his hands, somewhere, and pulled it under her own clothes—and then the kiss ended abruptly. She realized that Abel was whispering her name.

"Anna, please," he whispered. "Please, don't do this. It's not gonna work out . . . you want to have an adventure . . . a little girl who wants to have an adventure, but it won't end well . . ."

"Sure it will." Her lips were so close to his that she brushed them while speaking. "Don't worry . . ."

She let go, but just to get rid of her sweater, the T-shirt . . . it was a single smooth movement, easier than she'd thought it would be. She unfastened her bra, and then stood there, naked down to her waist. She wasn't cold. She'd never been warmer. Heavens, she really was drunk. Somewhere in her head a tiny voice said, what are you doing here? This is so not Anna Leemann—what has gotten into you? She ignored the voice.

She saw that the light of the flashlight painted strange patterns on her breasts—she was a work of art, art of the night. Look, she wanted to say, look, this is all part of the fairy tale. But he averted his eyes.

"Why are you worried?" she whispered. "Don't you know more about this than I do?"

"No," he whispered, and there was despair in his voice. But she ignored it. He was still looking away.

"Stop it. I don't want this, I . . ."

Stop it? I'm just starting, she thought with a smile. I'm just starting to live. I'm just starting out in this world. She released his fingers and her hands returned to his body, to depths not yet fully explored, where she found proof that his body did want what hers did. It was obvious. His breathing, close to her ear, was strangely irregular. She smiled at that, too. His breathing was out of rhythm, strained, as if he was holding something back, something violent. He was talking to her again, through clenched teeth, words she

didn't grasp the meaning of. "This . . . for me . . . This has nothing
to do with . . . with tenderness, only with . . . violence . . . don't force
me . . ."

She wasn't forcing him, was she? Her fingers closed around his
erection very gently, as if around something new that only belonged
to her, something she was taking possession of. She didn't know
anything, she was just learning, she wasn't forcing him, no . . .

And then, there was something like a click. Like the flick of a
switch. All of a sudden. Abel's passivity left. His hands tore her
hands away, he freed himself, and she thought he'd push her away.
But instead, he grabbed her by the shoulders and turned her so fast
she couldn't react.

"Wait!" she said. His warm body was very close to hers, almost
too close now, and his hands weren't gentle, weren't careful. She still
wanted what he wanted, but it was happening too fast . . . or did it
have to be like this? She wasn't sure; she didn't know much about
this. He knew better, of course, but . . . "Wait!" she begged again.
"Can't we . . . please . . . you've gotta show me, how . . ."

It was as if he didn't hear her. Not anymore. He pushed her
down to the floor; she fell onto her knees, painfully, landing on the
concrete. She didn't understand what was happening. But she knew
it was wrong. Later, in her memory, she would relive the scene again
and again: she tries to get to her feet, but his whole weight is on top
of her, and his hands, his hands hold her tight. He is too strong for
her. "No!" she whispers, struggling to get free. "Stop it! Not like
this . . . it wasn't meant to be like this . . . if it has to be like this, I
don't . . . please . . . forget about the whole thing . . . Stop it! *Stop it!*
I'll scream . . ."

She doesn't scream. She can't. He is pressing one hand over her mouth. And that is the moment she knows, there is no going back. That she has lost. All sense of romance is gone. The only thing left is fear, fear of something she doesn't have any control of. All human glands stop their secretion . . . this can't work. Too much raw, dry skin. No liquids to make things slippery, to glide into.

She thrashes like a trapped animal, trying to hurt him with her fists, but they don't even touch him. She is helpless, a bundle of stupid, helpless fear, kneeling on the concrete floor of an empty boathouse like in absurd prayer. Everything has happened so quickly, much too quickly. She presses her legs together; he forces them apart with his knee; and then, the sharp pain, the penetration of a foreign body. Violence also works without secretion. That thing behind her, it is not Abel; it is no one she knows; it is something that only makes her afraid, something that hurts her, and, worse, something that wants to hurt her. An animal. The pain tears her apart in the middle. It is everywhere. It was turning her inside out. The light of the flashlight is pale and unearthly. She sees the vague shapes of the boats; she watches the shadows to distract herself from the pain. It doesn't work. She feels the animal deep, deep inside her. It moves. It pushes her down onto the cold floor, again and again, and the worst thing about it all is its hand, covering her mouth, keeping her from screaming. She closes her eyes so she doesn't have to see the concrete floor anymore. That doesn't help either. The pain grows when she can't see anything anymore; it is grinding her up like the stones in a mill. She won't survive this; she will give up; she will just give up, she thinks, and die. She only wants it to be over.

And then it is. It only took seconds. The hand isn't covering her mouth anymore; the weight on her back is gone. She doesn't move. She crouches on the floor, on her knees, bent over, with her head on her arms. There is a noise like the breaking of dishes in a kitchen. Glass breaking.

When she lifts her head, everything is dark. The flashlight. It must have been the flashlight that broke. She hears footsteps running, running away, fleeing. Then everything is quiet.

She wasn't sure how long she'd been cowering on the floor. A long time. She'd heard the rat again. Apart from that, she'd heard nothing. There was nobody in the hall. She was alone. No hidden murderer. Just herself . . . and the memory of what had happened.

She was bleeding. The blood trickled out of her, together with time. Of course, it wasn't only blood—it wasn't only time. There was something else she didn't want to think about now, a part of an animal—a person—that she didn't know. She tried to think "Abel," but the name wouldn't form inside her head, the letters refusing to get into any order that made sense or was even pronounceable.

She didn't cry. Not this time. And finally, she got up, found a tissue, and wiped away the blood between her legs. There wasn't as much as she'd thought. She put her clothes back on. She realized she was shivering. Her fingers were ice-cold, and she could barely button up her pants. When she walked over to the door of the boathouse, the pain came back. She was limping.

On the way to her bike, she tried to think the pain away. By sheer willpower. To walk normally so that no one would notice anything was wrong. There was no one around, of course, but there would be tomorrow . . . Magnus . . . Linda . . . people at school. When she thought about school, she felt sick. She would never, ever tell anyone about this. Not even—especially not—Magnus and Linda. And because she couldn't tell anyone, she told herself.

"Stupid little girl," she said to herself, spitting out the words, disgusted. "Stupid little girl; you wanted to have an adventure. There you go. You've had your adventure now."

And then, as she unlocked her bike, she started humming, a ridiculous old children's song.

Just a tiny little pain,
Three days of heavy rain,
Three days of sunlight,
And everything will be all right . . .

He'd lost her!

Damn, he'd lost her. He knew she'd been here, on the beach. He'd seen her with him; they hadn't seen him of course. The shadows behind the surfers' hut were deep and dark. But now he didn't know where to look for her. And he would creep home, sneak past his parents' room, secretly, like a thief in his own house—something he'd gotten used to doing the last few weeks. The dog wouldn't give him away. The dog was sleeping deeply. He'd seen to that.

He'd lost her.

Somewhere between the beach and the place where the sailboats were docked in summer. He'd been too timid, too bent on not being discovered. The white snow made the nights too bright; it had become more and more difficult to follow her without being seen. He'd given them too much of a lead, and they'd grabbed it like a present and disappeared.

He returned to the beach, saw the rectangle of the police tape in the distance, heard it crackle in the night breeze. He realized he was shivering. He didn't want to think of that police tape now, didn't want to think of the dead body that had lain there, didn't want to think of the blood slowly trickling down from the wound, dyeing the snow red. He didn't want to wonder what Sören Marinke's last thought had been. Of whom he'd been thinking. Maybe Sören Marinke had loved, too.

He found himself standing on the ice. He walked out, far out. It didn't matter when he got home—either they would realize he'd been gone or they wouldn't—and if they did, he could still tell them a story about bar-hopping with friends. He could try to look guilty and hungover. Bar-hopping with friends? He didn't have friends.

Not even she wanted to be his friend. Not even Anna.

He took off his gloves, kneeled down, and burrowed his bare hands into the snow that covered the frozen bay. The snow was very cold. Sometimes he couldn't fight the thought that it would feel good to lie down in it and to never have to move again. Just to lie there, in the whiteness. Forever.

13

Snow
ॐ

ON MONDAY MORNING, THE BLUENESS OF THE LIGHT
in the Leemanns' house had changed. Something had cracked, and
a dirty color had seeped through, the color of dried blood.

"It is my fault," Anna whispered, sitting on the side of her bed. "I
have destroyed the blue light."

But there was another voice, a tiny little voice of reason, whispering to her. Your fault? asked this voice. Oh no. It wasn't you who
has destroyed anything. It was . . .

Please, said Anna, don't say that name.

She took a long, hot shower and washed her hair several times.
She hadn't taken a shower the night before. If she had, Linda would
have known that something had happened.

She'd been afraid she'd find Linda waiting up for her, in the
living room, which would have been the end of her; Anna would
have dissolved in tears in her arms. For a moment, she'd longed for
that. But Linda hadn't been there. Anna had heard her tossing in

bed, next to Magnus; she knew that her mother would sleep only when she was home safe and sound. What was Linda afraid of? Was she afraid of exactly what had happened?

Anna hadn't slept. She had lain in her bed silently, staring at the ceiling, waiting for morning to come. Now she sat at breakfast very quietly. She didn't eat.

"Is something the matter?" Magnus asked.

She shook her head. She nodded. She shrugged.

"Did the two of you fight about something?" Linda asked.

"Yes," Anna said, relieved at this chance to explain things. "Yes, I guess you could say we did. I need a little time to think about it."

On the floor in the hall, beneath the mail slot in the door, she found a white envelope with her name on it. Abel's writing. When she touched the envelope, it burned hot in her hands, like the glowing, smoldering tip of a cigarette. She tore it up into very tiny pieces and threw them into the trashcan outside.

She got onto her bike and rode to school like she did every day: there were two more weeks of classes before the reading period before finals. She still was in pain. On the bicycle seat, it came back, tearing at her insides. She rode past the turnoff to school. She couldn't go there. She couldn't bear the thought of seeing Abel. She didn't want to see his ice-blue eyes. His eyes would be her undoing. She wondered what she could have read in them last night, in the boathouse. She rode to the city, got off her bike, and wandered the streets aimlessly. She'd lost her hold on reality.

It had happened once before, after she'd been in Abel and Micha's apartment the first time, but this time was different. Now it was really gone, and it felt as if it was gone for good. What was reality good for, anyway?

At some point, she found herself on the pedestrian bridge that led over the river. In summer, this part of the river, the city harbor, was full of big ancient ships. Now it was frozen, too; only the narrow path in the middle, which they kept open for the ships, was glistening like a trickle of unidentified body fluid. She rested her arms on the railing of the bridge and looked over at the restaurant-ship.

"If I could get my thoughts in order," she said aloud, "if only I could get my thoughts in order . . . Maybe I have to talk so I can think. What happened? And what does it mean?"

She looked around; there was no one who could hear her.

"I'm afraid," she said to herself. "I'm afraid again. I have to bring the right questions and answers together. It's a puzzle. And the first question is, who is Abel Tannatek?"

A swan waddled over the ice. Dirty and white, swans aren't beautiful, Anna thought; they've never been beautiful, and I wonder who first used that adjective to describe them. It's the same with the putrid, slimy sunsets over the sea. "If I could flick a switch and turn on a light," she went on, "then what happened yesterday might be clearer. Then again, maybe it already is clear. Maybe the light was already turned on, on the beach, in the snow . . . the murderer always returns to the place of the murder. So who went to the beach last night? Who was standing there, right beside me? The wolf in the fairy tale killed his victims by creeping up from behind and cracking their necks. He never looked into their eyes. For had he seen their eyes, he might have pitied them, and he knew that. The wolf knows himself very well."

She still felt that warm, heavy weight on her. She felt the crea-ture's breath on her neck and the pain, and suddenly she felt sick.

She crouched down, holding onto the railing of the pedestrian bridge, but her stomach was too empty. The wolf knew himself very well; he had warned her . . . it had been her fault. It had been her fault. But had it?

No, said the reasonable part of her. Of course not. Don't you remember—you have heard men say this about girls, read it in cheap newspapers, and always thought, how stupid and how wrong: *she asked for it, wearing those things, drinking too much, flirting . . . she asked for it, she wanted it.* Don't you remember how you talked about these things with Gitta once and how you both agreed . . .

But I did want it, said unreasonable Anna to reasonable Anna.

Not this, said reasonable Anna. You wanted to have sex with him, that's all. It would have been the perfect place, a dry place, no snow, no Micha around . . . a perfect night, too. How could you have known what would happen? You couldn't. All you saw and felt was your love for him. You were wearing this love like a cloak, safe and warm, you thought . . . and he tore it apart.

But he did try to warn me, interrupted unreasonable Anna, realizing how much she sounded like a hardheaded child, trying to change the truth by the sheer force of her will.

There's no talking away what happened, said reasonable Anna. Don't even try it. It happened and it is horrible and you remember what Gitta said, way back when on the leather sofa.

She remembered, of course. *And you'd probably catch something nasty, too.* And if she was right? Anna wondered if she should have a blood test or something done, somewhere, anonymously, but she couldn't come up with the right thing to say. For even if the test was anonymous, a nonanonymous person would draw the blood.

What happened, Miss Leemann? Was this a . . . "No," she said, aloud. "No. What you want to say is the wrong word. I know what you're thinking. You're thinking *rape*."

"And that's what it was," whispered reasonable Anna.

"Who, Miss Leemann?" the person drawing blood would ask. "Who did this to you? Do you know the guy?"

"He is . . . he was my . . ."

"He's your boyfriend?"

"No," she answered. "Not anymore, and maybe he's a murderer, and it's all over anyway. It's over."

She noticed that she was kneeling in the snow on the bridge. She was kneeling again.

"And I wonder," she whispered, still caught up in conversation with a nonexistent person taking her blood in a nonexistent clinic, "I wonder . . . thinking about it now . . . he's got a little sister, and I wonder how much he loves her really and in what way."

When she heard her own words, the air became colder by a few degrees. "Maybe that," she continued, "is why he doesn't let anybody come near Micha. What if Sören Marinke suspected the same thing? And what if that was the reason he had to die?"

She thought of Micha in her pink down jacket with the artificial fur collar, of her pale blond braids, of Abel's fingers running through her hair. She thought of Micha's bed. There's room on it for the two of us, Micha had said to her, or something like that. There's room for Abel and me. Was Abel doing what he had said Rainer Lierski would do?

Was he . . . another hard word . . . hurting . . . horrible . . . was he abusing Micha?

She stood up. "I have to do something," she said, but she said it in such a very low voice that she could barely hear the words herself.

"I have to find the truth. I have to talk to somebody about all of this, somebody who exists, somebody real. Possibly the police, the ones who are trying to find Marinke's murderer . . ."

Before she left the bridge, she closed her eyes for a moment and saw the picture of Micha's schoolyard again: how Abel flew across that yard, meeting Micha in the middle, swirling her around in the clear winter air. And she felt again how he'd hugged her tight in their literature class, in the tower made of newspaper pages. No. She couldn't talk to anyone. And least of all to the police.

She just couldn't. Part of her—unreasonable Anna—still loved him. Maybe she would never stop loving him.

Anna hadn't only lost her hold on reality, she'd lost her flute as well. She'd had the flute with her that night, in her backpack. Stupid enough in the cold. The flute had borne silent witness to what had happened in the boathouse. After, she'd wrapped it in Abel's dark-blue knitted sweater and stashed it in her closet. She'd called her teacher and told her she couldn't make it to this week's lesson.

It had been a long time since she'd played the piano in the living room. She had stopped piano lessons a while back, deciding to concentrate on the flute instead. The final music exam only required you to play one instrument, but on that instrument you had to be pretty perfect. Now she went back to the piano. The piano seemed safer somehow, something neither Abel nor Micha had touched with their presence. She practiced her flute pieces on the piano. That was crazy, of course; she couldn't hide the flute in her closet forever.

She no longer felt a part of the small, domestic scenes in her everyday life. She saw Magnus feed the robins. She saw Linda cut vegetables in the kitchen. She contemplated them from the outside, like painted scenes. She, Anna Leemann, was on the other side of these pictures, with no real connection to any of the things happening within.

On Tuesday morning, there was another white envelope on the floor in the hall that someone had pushed through the mail slot. White as snow, white like white noise . . . with her name on it. She tore it up into tiny white flakes and let it snow into the trash. She returned to school. She saw Abel walk through the schoolyard outside. He looked up—maybe he sensed her there—she looked away. She felt dizzy all of a sudden.

In her head, Gitta, who wasn't there, whispered . . . words, angry words: *Don't you start thinking that rubbish again, blaming yourself, little lamb. You know what they ought to do with guys like that? I'll tell you. I've got some disgusting ideas for how to punish them . . .*

Anna tried to avoid the student lounge during break time, but Frauke, whom she'd met in the corridor, pulled her inside. She was afraid Abel would be there. And he was. He was sitting on the radiator, at the back of the room, rolling a cigarette he would have to smoke outside. He looked up when she came in, just for a second, and then turned away. He couldn't run away—he was trapped in that corner by the amorphous mass of other students—and Anna couldn't turn on her heels and leave either, without Frauke asking her what was the matter. It was an impossible situation.

Anna managed to hold herself together. She managed to drink a cup of horrible coffee from the broken coffee machine with Frauke and to talk about nothing for five whole minutes, or rather, to let Frauke talk and pretend she was listening. She'd turned her back on Abel but felt his presence.

At lunchtime, he was standing at his usual place near the bike racks. Anna saw him from the window—black hat down over his ears, hands in pockets, earplugs in his ears. He'd shut out the world. At one point he talked to two guys—maybe he sold them something; she didn't see.

He wasn't Abel anymore. He'd turned back into Tannatek, the Polish peddler, whose presence at school was a riddle to everybody and whom most people were a little afraid of.

She wondered if that was it. If things had turned back to an earlier point, if everything was now as it had been before, and if she could just act as if she'd never known him.

No. Things weren't how they'd been before. Rainer Lierski was dead. Sören Marinke was dead. And a small girl with pale blond braids and a pink down jacket was wandering over the ice, in a fairy tale, helpless in wind and weather. The weather forecast said there would be a snowstorm.

"Little lamb," Gitta said, turning up at Anna's door in the afternoon, very real now, not just a voice in her head. "Little lamb, what's wrong?"

"I'm poring over my books," Anna replied, standing in the doorway, refusing to let Gitta in. "Why should anything be wrong?"

"Oh, come on," Gitta said. "Something's happened. Between you and Abel. You're not talking anymore. Do you think we're all blind? We're worried about you."

"Who is 'we'?" Anna asked.

Gitta brushed the question aside with her hand and searched for her cigarettes. "If you won't let me in, then I'm going to smoke," she said. "And the smoke will get into the house through the door."

Anna shrugged.

"But you won't get rid of me so easily. So things didn't work out, did they? With Abel? The whole thing has run up against a brick wall."

"So what?"

Gitta blew a smoke ring into the cold air. "What do you know about him?"

Anna narrowed her eyes. "What do you mean, what do I know about him?"

"I mean it just as I said it. What do you know about Abel Tannatek?"

"Maybe," Anna said, "the question is what do *you* know about Abel Tannatek? Is there something you want to tell me? Is that the reason you came?"

Gitta smoked in silence for a moment. "No," she said finally. And then, "Sometimes I find myself thinking about that police tape on the beach. It pops into my head that . . ."

"Oh, does it," Anna said, suddenly defensive, "and do you know what sometimes pops into my head? Hennes von Biederitz. And Bertil Hagemann. One of them bragging about what a good shot he is, the other trying not to talk about the fact that he's probably a good shot, too. Hunting. Bertil was out there on the beach both days before Marinke's death. He said so himself. As to where Hennes was . . . I guess you'd know better than I would. Or maybe you wouldn't?"

Gitta stared at her, perplexed. "What do these two have to do with anything?"

"That," Anna said, "is exactly what I'm wondering." And she closed the door.

◆ ◆ ◆

On Wednesday, there was a third white envelope in the hall. When she touched it, it wasn't glowing like the first one. She would tear it up like the two other envelopes. She would . . . she saw her fingers opening the envelope, knowing these were the fingers of unreasonable Anna. The paper was filled with tiny haunted letters. There was her name.

Anna. Anna, are you reading this? I'm not going to stop writing to you. I have nothing, only words. I am a storyteller.

I want to explain something to you. But I can't. Later, maybe later.

The words that I will have to find for that explanation will be sharp and they will hurt, much worse than the thorns of roses. There is a reason for what happened. I can't be forgiven so I am not asking you for forgiveness. We lost each other, and we will never find each other again. Rose girl, the sea is cold and . . .

She put the letter back into the envelope and tore it up, into even smaller pieces than the other envelopes. The icy wind took the scraps from her fingers and carried them away with it, high up into the sky like snowflakes falling up instead of down. There were tears burning in her eyes. We will never find each other again. No, she thought, we won't. Ever.

The situation at school grew even more impossible. Anna forced herself to go to her literature intensive class. Abel seemed to have forced himself, too. He was even on time and was already sitting at his desk when she came in. Who'd had the bright idea to shape the desks into a U? They sat opposite each other but didn't look at each other; they looked everywhere else. There were three yards between them, three yards of glass splinters, fleeing footsteps, pain, blood, a hand covering someone's mouth, the weight of a body, the breathing of an animal. There were two dead bodies between them.

Once, she looked at him. He'd taken off his sweater. He was sitting there in his T-shirt, and she saw the two circular scars on his upper arm. But now there weren't just two. There were three. The third one was bigger, or actually longer—a broad line. She looked away, looked again. The line was not a line. It was a row of single, circular wounds so close to each other that they melted into one. She tried to count them, but Abel turned his head, and she lowered her eyes.

The pain, she thought. The pain is the same as mine, just in a different place.

After the unbearable double lesson, she waited until everybody had left. Abel was the first to go. Knaake still sat at his desk. Then he looked at Anna, stood up, closed the door, and sat down again. He didn't say anything. He took a thermos full of tea from his bag and poured tea into a cup. He was in no hurry.

"I have to talk to someone," Anna said. He nodded.

"Let's just assume something happened," Anna began. "Something . . . bad, between Abel and me. Something that has to do with . . . trust . . ." She put her hands to her cheeks and felt a feverish heat there. She hated herself for the fact that she blushed. "Something I can't talk about . . . let's assume it was my fault, in a roundabout way."

"Let's not assume that," he said softly. Did he know what she was talking about? No, he couldn't.

"Okay, let's assume it was *not* my fault . . . I mean, I *did* trust him," Anna said in a low voice, without looking at Knaake. "But I don't know what to think anymore. You know . . . about the two murders . . . Lierski . . . he was Abel's little sister's father. Abel hated him. He was afraid that he would . . . that he would do something to Micha. I think he was kind of known as . . . for being a pedophile. Maybe it wasn't true, but Abel was sure. They've arrested someone for Lierski's murder, someone who owned the right kind of weapon and who knew him, but I don't know if it really was him after all . . . and then Sören Marinke, at the beach . . . you heard it on the radio. He was the social worker who'd turned up at Abel and Micha's apartment . . . Abel isn't eighteen yet—you know that—so in theory, he shouldn't have custody of Micha. She should go live with relatives or a foster family, but Abel refuses to let that happen . . . their mother, Michelle . . . whom you don't know . . ."

She looked up. He was shaking his head. "No, Anna. I don't know her."

Yeah, right, Anna thought. And where did Michelle get those old Leonard Cohen cassettes . . . How many people in town listened to stuff like that? She knew of only three: Michelle, Linda . . . and Knaake.

"Michelle disappeared," Anna said, "a few weeks ago. She just up and left. But she can't be far. She's drawn money from the household account. From an ATM in Eldena."

Knaake was staring into his cup, as if he could find Michelle Tannatek in there, if he only looked hard enough. Like he knew exactly what the woman whom he was searching for looked like.

"There is this fairy tale," Anna whispered. "A fairy tale Abel is telling his little sister. Sometimes there are people in it who really exist. Sometimes I recognize them too late. I recognized Sören Marinke too late. He also died in the fairy tale. The bad guys all die. But who decides that they're bad? I'm . . . I'm afraid . . . afraid that someone else will be found dead beneath the snow. Someone else who's been shot in the neck."

"But you haven't gone to the police."

"No. I . . ." She didn't say, I love him. It would have sounded so trite.

Knaake got up and went over to the window, cup in hand. "There are many possibilities," he said. "An infinite number of possibilities. I'm no detective. But maybe there are more possibilities than you're seeing."

She lifted her head. "Yes?"

"Possibility number one is the simplest," Knaake said. "Abel Tannatek shot both men, the first because he hated him and the second because . . . tell me, why would he have shot the second one? Does it make sense to kill a social worker? A social worker is just a government agent . . . if you shoot one, another will take his place." He laughed grimly. "It's like a computer game."

"And the second possibility?"

"Possibility number two: Somebody else shot them. And here we have two possibilities again. Somebody did it to help Abel. Or . . . somebody did it to make people think that Abel did it. But that all sounds a bit too much like an old black-and-white Mafia movie."

"But are there other possibilities?"

"Sure. Dozens. For example, why do we think that it was the same murderer? Because of the shot in the neck? A nasty way to kill someone, by the way. The Nazis were known for this practice. Executions."

Anna caught her breath. "You think . . . you think it might have been two different people?"

"It's possible, isn't it? The second murderer copied the handwriting of the first."

"You *are* a detective." Anna smiled. She stood up and went over to the window to stand next to him. Knaake smiled, too.

"A bad one. I hold this literature intensive class, but I read my share of crime thrillers too, you know. So let's assume . . . assume Abel did kill Rainer Lierski. If things are as you said they are, he had a reason."

"And somebody else killed Marinke? To make it look like Abel did?"

"Maybe. Or else . . . maybe the truth lies elsewhere. Maybe there's someone out there acting absolutely irrationally. Someone who actually thinks she can solve a problem by killing a social worker. Who wants to protect Abel and Micha but doesn't understand anything. A person who's messed up her life completely and thinks she can only help from the shadows, a person who also hates Lierski for something he did . . . a person who drowned her intellect and her charm in alcohol a long time ago . . ."

Anna pressed her nose against the cold windowpane. Down there, in the yard, a dark figure was standing near the bike rack, hands dug deep in his pockets as always.

"Somebody acting absolutely irrationally," Anna repeated in a whisper. She looked at Knaake. "Who?"

"Michelle," he said.

The thought was new and strange, and Knaake shook his head right after he'd spoken the name. "Of course, these are only wild speculations." He went back to his desk and screwed the lid back onto his thermos. "Like I said before, I don't know Abel's mother. But if you want . . . I could try to find out some things. It would be like a game . . . a change from gathering dust between high literature and stupid detective stories." He shook his head again, as if to shake the dust out of his nearly gray beard.

"A dangerous game," Anna said.

"I'd prefer to play it myself, however . . . instead of your playing it." And then Knaake put a hand on her arm, all of a sudden. "Anna, you're not the only one I'm worried about. There's someone in the schoolyard, someone suffering in a horrible way. I'm sorry . . . how stupid . . . I don't know what happened between the two of you. I don't know if it can be forgiven. The hardest thing always is to forgive yourself."

Knaake tucked his leather briefcase under his arm and opened the door. "Take care," he said. "I'm not sure we'll be having school tomorrow. They said there'll be a big storm tonight. Get home safely."

"I can't go home yet," Anna murmured. "I may ride out to the bay before the storm comes. I need to think."

"Don't stay out too long," Knaake said as she left.

A big storm? Actually, a thaw had set in. Outside, drops were quietly falling from the trees and the sun shone warm and bright.

The hardest thing always is to forgive yourself . . .

He doesn't mean me. He means Abel. But Abel already told me that that's not possible, he said so in that letter, and maybe in every letter he wrote.

Abel wasn't standing by the bike racks anymore. It was as if he, too, had melted away. Anna got onto her bike, still feeling the pain between her legs, a hurt that might never leave her, but she didn't ride home. The wind was refreshing and warm; it blew her out of town, down the bike path along Wolgaster Street, past the Seaside District, past the turn leading to Wieck and the harbor, past the woods of the Elisenhain, past the new housing development—around the bay to Ludwigsburg. In summer, the beach near the village was crowded, but not as crowded as Eldena. There was no entrance fee and no fence. The beach out here was much narrower, wilder, and longer—a beach full of mysterious corners and secret hiding places in the tall beach grass. Anna left her bike near the long building housing the old café. There was snow on its thatched roof now.

She walked between the wind-bent pines down to the beach. Out on the ice, white swans and black bald coots were huddled in weird lumps. You could walk across the bay to Wieck—the café lay exactly opposite. Today, there was no one on the ice.

She wandered along the beach, the wind at her back. She stepped over ice floes the sea had stacked, one on top of another, into strange works of art. She realized she'd stuffed her hands into the pockets of her coat and pulled her hat down low on her face. As if she was him, she thought. All she lacked now were the earplugs of the old Walkman, full of white noise. But no, she didn't need those—the wind produced its own white noise, and she was at the very center of it.

The coastline turned to the right, away from the bay, leading out toward the open sea, and she followed it until the sand became too narrow. When she could walk no farther, she forced herself to climb up the short slope through the trees. There was a path up there, a path that led back through the pine forest. But she didn't want to go back, not yet. She found a bench between the trees, a cold, snow-covered bench. She sat and looked out over the ice.

She had come to think, but her head felt empty.

When she closed her eyes, summer crept out of the trees around her. She could feel it enveloping her, feel the sunlight on her skin. The snow long gone, a thin line of beach lay beneath her, golden yellow. The pines waved fresh green needles, the beach grass swayed in the summer wind. And there someone was building a sandcastle, a castle with towers decorated with shells and sea grass, with flags made of colored paper, with pinecones for inhabitants—the builder was a small girl with blond braids, dark and wet from swimming, a girl in a pink bikini bottom and a large knitted dark-blue sweater with the sleeves rolled up on top. Anna heard her laugh—there must be other people down there she couldn't see from here—she heard a woman's voice . . . Michelle, she thought, Michelle is here; she's come back; everything's all right; this is next summer; and everything has turned out all right in a secret way. There must have been some other explanation for everything. Neither Abel nor Michelle had had anything to do with the murders; otherwise they wouldn't be here now, would they? And Abel had always loved Micha just the way you're supposed to love a little sister, or the way a father loves his daughter, no less. And me, I'm down there at the beach, too, she thought, together with them. Didn't I just hear my own voice? She opened her eyes and the vision was gone.

The beach lay silent under the snow.

But all this, she thought, this summer scene . . . if it happened, it would mean I've forgiven him. That I've forgiven what happened in the boathouse. The hand. The pain. The sound of running feet, fleeing.

No, thought reasonable Anna. It is not possible. Not this. That cloak of love you were wearing—he's torn it to shreds, undoing the seams of trust that held it together. How can you ever wear those shreds?

I could mend it, said unreasonable Anna, with impossibilities; with the impossibility of forgiveness itself, use that as a thread. You would always see how torn the cloak is, of course. It would never look new again. A love in pieces. And I would never be warm in a cloak like that, of course.

Abel knew that, *Rose girl, the sea is cold.*

She realized that the temperature had dropped suddenly. The thaw had stopped; the wind was icy, and it was bringing new snowflakes, only a few at first, but there was a dense white wall closing in, slowly consuming the sky. For a moment, she still felt the sun of the daydream on her skin, and then she noticed she didn't feel anything at all. It had been an illusion. The cold had rendered the skin on her cheeks numb. There was no feeling in them anymore, and her fingers in the gloves seemed to belong to someone else. How long had she been sitting here? How long had she been dreaming of summer? She'd thought it was only seconds, but now she wasn't sure. Evening was creeping in, the sky was darkening. Stiff with cold, she had trouble standing up. She had to go back, back to her bike, back home, back to where it was warm.

The moment she stepped onto the path leading back through the pines, the snowstorm reached Ludwigsburg. The wind threw handfuls of snow into her face; she ducked down, crouching low; she heard the pines creak and moan; and somewhere, a big branch broke with a loud crack. It sounded like a shot. She hunkered down deeper, trudging as best she could, but she wasn't really getting anywhere. The storm was filling the path with snow, making it disappear. Snow found its way into Anna's boots, her clothes; she cursed under her breath, bracing herself against the wind, her head lowered. By now, she could no longer feel her feet. The way back had become endless.

And then she saw that someone was following her. Someone was there, a dark figure in the swirling snow between the dark tree trunks. She could only see it out of the corner of her eye. She turned around. There was no one. She must have imagined it. It must have been something else—a bent tree, a thicket, a shadow. She fought her way on, step by step, and the shadow returned to the edge of her field of vision, a flexible shadow, hunched like herself. Again she turned, and again there was no one.

She knew, though, that the figure would reappear once she turned her back to it.

And suddenly, fear gripped her with icy claws. Absolute, sheer terror.

Fear of the storm that was too strong for her, fear of the shadow behind her, fear of the cold and the dark that would inevitably come, fear of being alone. Was the figure behind her just something bred and born of this fear? A creature sprung from her own imagination? What if it wasn't? She stood, holding onto the trunk of a pine, her breath unsteady; she was freezing, shivering. She could almost feel the metal at her neck, the metal of a weapon pressed against her skin. It was only her wet scarf, of course. I'm afraid, she'd told Knaake, afraid that another dead body might be found in the snow.

But never, not even for the blink of an eye, had she thought this body might be hers. She forced herself to walk on, but she still didn't seem to be moving forward; she looked back, far too often, in vain; the figure following her melted into the forest every time she turned her head. She thought of Linda and her insane fear that something might happen to her only daughter.

How sensible Linda's worries seemed now!

All the worst things, the things at the mention of which you would just shake your head and laugh, all those things were coming true. Stop worrying, I'll be home on time, I'm not gonna get raped. Stop worrying, I'm not gonna get myself killed. Stop worrying. Stop worrying.

She felt the person following her coming closer; she felt it clearly. And something in her longed to drop in the snow and wait. Her breath became more ragged; it felt as if she were breathing snowflakes, in and out, along with the sharp and icy wind.

"Abel," she whispered. "If that's you, hurry. Come here. End all this. I've had enough."

But suddenly, she knew it wasn't Abel. It was someone else. She didn't know how she could tell—she just could. That wasn't much use, she thought.

And she understood that she wasn't only fighting the snowstorm, she was also fighting herself and her capacity to forgive. If the absolutely impossible was possible . . . the snowflakes the wind hurled at her were wet with the blood of the night in the boathouse, the icy storm that took her breath away felt like a hand covering her mouth. Could she leave this behind? Find something beyond?

She moved through a snowstorm made from the tiny white pieces of torn envelopes. And she was alone in this storm. She realized she longed for Abel's presence, the Abel he had been before the night in the boathouse, the Abel she had kissed on a sunny day in town. If that Abel had been here, she would not be so afraid, even of death.

"I will die," she whispered, almost soundlessly, as she stumbled on. "I will die, and I know what will happen. They will make him responsible for my death. They'll think it was him, that he killed me out here . . . the real killer will make them believe that. It all makes sense. But who . . ." Who knew that she'd come out to Ludwigsburg? Only Knaake. She began to feel colder. What if she'd confided in the wrong person? The murderer's island, she thought, is empty; the murderer is among us . . . what about the lighthouse keeper's glasses, the glasses he'd supposedly forgotten on the ship? The little queen had returned to search for them, and she'd run directly into the arms of the red hunter . . . and why had the lighthouse keeper made them take down the sails in the storm? It had sounded sensible, but still, the little queen's green ship lost speed, allowing the black ship to close in . . . but wasn't that just a fairy tale?

She could see the figure clearly now; she whirled around—nothing. It was a broken tree. And then, she made out the long silhouette of the café. Soon, she was struggling to unlock her bicycle. The lock was covered in ice . . . finally, thankfully, it gave way. But the storm was too strong for her to ride. So she just pushed the bike along the road, against the storm.

There were three cars in the parking lot next to the café, all three of them covered with snow. She didn't remember if there'd been any cars when she'd arrived. Maybe. Maybe their owners were out walking like she was, or maybe they'd left their cars here weeks ago. She pushed her bike on against the storm, along an endless, narrow lane; at some point, the path would lead onto Wolgaster Street, but that wouldn't be for another mile. A mile more of white, icy nothingness—a mile along which no one could help her. A grave a mile long.

She lowered her head again and clutched the bike. Could she

use it to defend herself somehow? To push it toward the person following her—to shove it in his face and run? It's no use, she told herself. Where would you run to? But she didn't let go of the bike.

It was her last comfort.

She didn't turn around again. She knew her pursuer was still there. Turning around wouldn't help; he could choose any moment to catch her. Maybe he liked chasing her, making her afraid; maybe he liked it when she turned; maybe he was secretly laughing. She wouldn't do him any more favors.

She tried to recall her dream of the warm summer day. If this snowstorm was to be the last thing she saw, she wanted to picture something pleasant in the meantime. But the cold wind blew the nice pictures and thoughts right out of her head; all it let stay was the fear.

It was beginning to get dark now; she was barely moving forward anymore because the snowdrifts on the lane were too high—then, behind her, she heard the sound of a car engine. She stopped. It was him. It had to be him. Him or her. Her pursuer. When the car stopped beside her, she realized that tears where streaming down her face. It was a miracle she actually felt those tears; she'd thought she couldn't feel anything anymore.

She let the bike drop into the snow. She let herself drop into the snow. Somebody jumped out of the car, came toward her, grabbed her, and pulled her up.

"My God, are you mad?" said Bertil. "What are you doing here?"

Ten minutes later, she was sitting in the passenger seat of an old Volvo, still crying. She couldn't stop. Bertil had put her bike in the backseat next to his dog. The car had gotten stuck in a snowdrift when he'd stopped, and he had to drive backward and forward several times before it pulled free. Warm air from the heater was starting to fill the car.

"It's going to get warmer in a minute," Bertil said. "I've been looking for you. I just had to find a place where I could turn the car . . ."

"A place . . . to turn the car?"

"Yes. I passed you once already, a few minutes ago. But I could only turn in front of the café. Don't say you didn't see the car. I flashed the lights at you so you'd see me and know I was coming back for you . . ."

"I was walking with my head down," Anna said. "I didn't see you. You've . . . you've been looking for me? How come you knew . . . ?"

When she said this, he stopped the car, reached over, and pulled her into his arms; and she didn't fight it. He smelled different from Abel. He smelled of snow and peppermints and dog.

He was warm and alive. He was there. He'd been looking for her.

"Gitta saw you ride out here," he explained. "She told me. She said that if you were going in this direction, you were probably heading out to Ludwigsburg . . . she knows you . . . I waited for a while. In case you came back. But then I thought it might be a good idea to go and have a look just in case."

"Yeah," she replied between the sobs she still wasn't able to control. "Yeah, that was a good idea. Bertil, I . . . I thought someone . . ." She stopped.

"You're ice-cold," he said and turned the heat up. "Why did you come out here? Didn't you hear the storm warning? Or have you just gone crazy? I don't even know if we can make it back in the car. The roads are a mess."

"Yeah," was all she said. "Yeah." She held onto him, onto the warmth of a living being. She didn't want to go anywhere; she just wanted to sit here in the car and hold onto someone. No matter who it was. At some point, he let go of her and started driving again. In the back, the silver greyhound was panting. Anna turned around. He had golden eyes. How strange.

The windshield wipers were racing. Bertil drove along in second gear, avoiding the snowdrifts. In some places, he had to pick up speed to get over one, and then he'd stretch out his arm in front of Anna as if to keep her from flying through the windshield. He was swearing through clenched teeth. Then, between the curses, he asked, "What happened, anyway? With Tannatek and you?"

She swallowed the last sobs. "Nothing."

"Are you kidding me? Of course something happened. And that's the reason you rode out here in spite of the storm warning, isn't it? Did he harm you?"

She looked away. More than I could find the words for, she thought. But I am not going to tell you. The pain is mine alone.

"If he did," said Bertil as he maneuvered the Volvo around another snowdrift, "if he harmed you, I'll kill him. I'll kill him."

Anna held onto the door handle and noticed that she hadn't fastened her seat belt. "Better watch the road," she said, "or you'll kill us instead." But inwardly, she thought that she'd heard almost exactly the same sentence before. Abel had said that about Micha's father. If he touches Micha, I'll kill him.

The wheels slipped and spun for a moment, but Bertil managed to right the car again. "Snow chains," he said, "what you need now are snow chains. Damn. I can't see a thing." The wind blew snowflakes against the windshield, the flakes like mad dancers seeking the spotlight; it was hypnotizing, the to and fro of the wipers and the steady appearance of new flakes, coming nearer, growing bigger, and disappearing.

"How can you drive in this weather?"

"I can't," said Bertil. "I have to. You would have frozen to death out there . . . There's the big road."

The turn was so treacherous that the Volvo skidded again. On the big road, there were other cars, and at first, Anna felt safer, but then a car in front of them skidded and stopped. Bertil cursed, loudly this time. The Volvo came to a halt a few inches from the other car's bumper.

"Somebody was following me," said Anna. "Out there, in Ludwigsburg, between the pines. Maybe the person who killed those two men—Lierski and Marinke. You know who I'm talking about."

"Do I?" Bertil asked as he waited for the other car to drive on and then stepped on the accelerator again. Somewhere ahead of them, the orange lights of a snowplow and a tow truck were blinking. One side of the road was completely filled with snow, and only one lane was open. Bertil stopped again to let a car coming from the other direction pass them.

"Aren't you afraid?" Anna asked.

He shook his head. "The worst that can happen is . . . what? That we get stuck? That we have an accident?" He looked at her. "The worst is always death. I don't mind that. Then I'll die in this car with you. That would be okay."

"Bertil, please . . . watch the road." The dog was whining behind Anna. He had crouched down, his head beneath the front tire of Anna's bike.

"The road!" Bertil laughed. "What does the road matter. I love you."

"I know," Anna said. "But watch the *damn road!*"

"You know? You don't know anything, Anna," Bertil murmured, turning his attention back to the road. "I'm the one who's always there, who'll always be there for you. But I'm always second best. I'm the freak with the thick glasses, the too-tall freak who's too cautious, the freak who'll never be cool. The teachers say that I'm intelligent! Intelligent? Fuck intelligent. I've always wanted to be something else. If I had a choice, I'd choose to look like Tannatek. You can bet I would. I don't, though. I don't have a choice."

"Bertil . . ."

"People like you always end up with guys like him, and later, they're surprised by what happens . . . Do what you want, Anna Leemann. Do what you think you have to do, but whatever that is, I'll be there, in case of emergency . . . I hate being the safety net, nothing more than the safety net. But if I can't be anything else, I will be that."

There was another snowdrift. He braked too hard, the dog howled, and the Volvo lost its grip on the road. When Anna opened her eyes again this time, the car was turned around. "Shit," Bertil said, for the umpteenth time. "The wheels are spinning again. We gotta put something under the front tires . . . I've got a blanket in the back . . ."

He jumped out, and Anna stayed behind, alone in the car, in the tiny capsule of warmth. She turned to the silver-gray dog. "He's mad," she whispered. "He's absolutely mad, you know that? I should love him for this, for getting me out of the storm, for wanting to take care of me, for the very fact that he loves *me* . . . but you can't force yourself to love somebody. And it's true, everything he says about himself. The world is so unjust. We . . ."

Bertil opened the driver's door, and an icy gust of wind blew a handful of snowflakes into the car. "Move over!" he shouted against the storm. "Into the driver's seat! I'll push. You drive!"

"I can't drive a car!" Anna shouted back, but she slid over anyway.

He bent into the car, put her right hand onto the clutch. "Foot onto the left pedal, first gear, gas is on the right side!" he shouted. "You've never done this?"

"I did once, with Magnus . . ."

"If we wait any longer, it's going to get worse, and we might never get the car going again. Come on! I'll push!"

He slammed the door shut, and Anna started the engine, but the tires still didn't have a grip on the road, and outside, the snow was turning the world into a whirling chaos.

"Abel," whispered Anna. "Abel, I don't want to freeze out here with Bertil! Where are you? *Where are you?*"

And all of a sudden, she knew what she wanted. Very clearly. She wanted to be with him. If she made it out of this, she would go and find him . . . walk, run, pedal, let the wind blow her toward him . . . whatever. She couldn't forgive him, for that was impossible. The cloak of love would be forever torn, never new and beautiful again, allowing the wind to blow through the holes, making her freeze in the cold. But she would live on wearing it for she couldn't do anything else. And he couldn't go back to being the Abel he was before the night in the boathouse, for that wasn't possible either. He'd have to live on wearing the memory of what he did. And still . . . and still.

Magnus had been right: in love there wasn't rationality.

But where would she find Abel? At school, sure, tomorrow, but it was impossible to talk to him at school, where the others were watching. She accelerated again, the car seemed to want to move and didn't. The wheels were spinning. The dog behind her was whining, a high, desperate sound.

If we lose each other in this endless icy winter, where will we find each other? she heard the little queen ask. And she heard the answer: *Where it's spring.*

The tulips. Red tulips in white vases in the café at the beginning of the pier in Wieck. "Here, spring has already arrived," Micha had said.

Anna pushed the accelerator once more, and this time, the car leaped forward. She let it roll, braked, and disengaged the clutch; I can do it, she thought, I can drive; if I have to, I can do anything. She slid back into the passenger seat, and the storm blew Bertil back into the car. His dark hair was full of white snowflakes, his glasses instantly fogged up in the warmth.

"Cheers," he said. "That driver's license is all yours."

He leaned over, and Anna knew he was hoping for a kiss. For a moment, he seemed so full of hope, so happy—she kissed him on the mouth with closed lips, quickly. "Come on," she said, "let's get out of this."

When they saw the lights of Eldena, the neon advertising of the supermarket there, the street lamps of the new housing development, Anna felt a great relief. The snowdrifts in the fields were behind them. Here, the road was a road once more.

Anna looked at the clock on the dashboard. Five thirty. It was as dark as midnight. "Can you let me out at the bridge in Wieck?" she asked. "Linda . . . my mother . . . she meets friends at the restaurant there every Wednesday. I can go home with her."

"Don't you want me to take you home?"

"You really don't have to," Anna said. "Just drive me to the bridge. That way you won't have to go into the city. You can just go around it and avoid the traffic. You live on the other side of the city, don't you?"

He nodded. "Okay . . . you're sure your mother's there?"

"Absolutely sure," Anna replied. And she was sure that her mother was there. It just depended on what was meant by "there." In Linda's case, "there" was a house full of blue air in Greifswald. She would never do something as weird as meet her friends in a restaurant in Wieck every Wednesday. Bertil helped her get the bike out of the back.

"You're soaking wet," he said. "You should get home fast."

"Yes," she said. For a moment they stood there, facing each other through the snow, freezing. The wind had subsided a little, but the snowflakes were still falling steadily, as if they wanted to cover the whole world.

"You said someone's been following you," Bertil said. "Are you sure about that? Did you see anyone?"

"Yes. No. When I turned around, there was no one . . . What do you think? That I imagined the whole thing?"

"I don't know. I think I should stay close. The safety net."

"Thanks," said Anna. "Thanks for getting me out of that storm. But I don't need a safety net."

"Ha," Bertil said.

She flung her arms around him and hugged him very tight for

a very short second, thinking, I am sorry, I am sorry, I am sorry, Bertil, but it will never be the way you want it to be. And she turned around quickly, walked toward the door of the restaurant, and leaned her bike against some patio chairs. She lingered in the waiting area of the restaurant until she heard the Volvo leave. She counted to a hundred. The warmth in that tiny room was seductive— a part of her wanted to stay, wanted to sit down, wanted to order hot tea, wanted to call Magnus and ask him to come pick her up. She didn't stay. She stepped out into the cold again, out into the snow. She ran the whole way over the bridge, skidding, slipping, nearly losing her balance twice. She ran along the river, to its mouth, ran till she reached the café, her wet pants sticking to her legs. She saw the lights inside as she approached it—pale, white lights—it wasn't open anymore, probably they had closed at six, maybe they'd just locked the doors now. She ran even faster.

The chairs on the terrace, chained together, were hardly perceptible under the snow. The glass window was towering over them like a glacier. And there, on the lee side of this glacier, someone was cowering. She saw the tiny orange glow of a cigarette. A single bike stood in front of the stairs that led up to the café. Anna stumbled over her own feet, rushing up the slippery metal steps; she fell, got up again, and saw the cowering figure get up as well. For a moment she was afraid it was someone else.

It was no one else.

It was Abel.

He didn't say anything. He ground out his cigarette and stood there, waiting until she caught her breath. He looked away, out over the ice lit by the floodlight on the side wall of the café.

"If we lose each other, we'll meet where it's spring," she said, finally. "How long have you been waiting for me out here?"

"Since Monday," he replied. "I've been waiting every afternoon since Monday."

"Since . . . Monday," she repeated. "Every single afternoon?"

He nodded. "It was cold."

"And . . . Micha?"

"She was with me the first two days. Sliding over the ice, watching other people ice-skating. Now she's got this idea in her head that she needs ice skates, too. Today, she's visiting a friend she knows from school. I . . . I didn't let her go anywhere for a long time, because I was afraid somebody else would come for her and take her away . . . but first graders do have to visit their friends, don't they? You can't forbid it forever . . . I'm going to pick her up now. It's just about time."

He hadn't looked at her while he spoke. His voice said, I'm talking about other things so that I don't have to talk about this one thing. But to find each other again, Anna thought, they had to talk about it. They had to try at least.

"What happened . . ." she began.

"What happened can never be undone," he said. "I wrote that to you. I don't know if you've read the letters . . ."

She shook her head.

He nodded. "That's good. They were stupid letters. Stupid words. Useless." And at last he did look at her. There was snow in his eyebrows. He must have been waiting a very long time, here in the cold, where spring existed only behind the glass window of the café. "I don't ask you to forgive me. What happened is unforgivable.

It's the worst . . . the worst of all things. It's exactly what I didn't want to happen."

She found his hands and for a moment she pulled back from the touch, her body remembering the danger of touches. But then she took them in hers. He wasn't wearing gloves. How many hours had he been here, waiting? How many ice-cold, endless hours?

"So let's not forgive," she whispered. "Nor forget. The night will remain there. Behind us."

"But still you're here."

"But still I'm here."

She opened her arms to him, but he shrank back. "I'd rather not," he said. "You shouldn't touch me."

But she took his hands in hers again and held them for a long time, and the wind blew through the cloak of torn love and she was cold, very cold. They were cold together, inside all the impossibilities of the world. Behind the window of the café, the tulips were blooming in the dark.

"I didn't tell anybody about that . . . night," she said and felt how he nodded.

"I kind of concluded that from the fact that I'm still alive. Your father hasn't killed me."

Together, they wandered back. He pushed his bike along with one hand. She said nothing about Bertil, nothing about her insane walk in Ludwigsburg, nothing about the talk she'd had with Knaake, nothing about being followed. What she said, after a long time of silence, was, "Let's go skating. Tomorrow, after school. With Micha."

And then they got onto the bus, with their bikes, because it was still impossible to ride them. The bus moved so slowly that they could have walked. It didn't matter. They stood there, holding their bikes, without talking, and Anna leaned against Abel very lightly. He didn't draw back this time.

When he got out, she stayed in the bus, singing to herself silently. There was no pain in her any longer, nowhere. The cloak she had put back on had covered everything like snow.

"My God," Linda said when Anna came in through the door, just in time for dinner. "You're all wet. What happened?"

"Everything," Anna answered, shaking her hair like a dog. "The worst and the best. I need to take a hot shower. And I need to practice the flute after dinner, and . . . Linda . . . can I ask you something? Something important?"

"Yes." Linda sighed. "Whatever you want."

"Okay," Anna said. "Are my old ice skates still in the basement?"

14

No Saint
ক৩

THE ICE WAS SMOOTH AND WIDE, AND IT LAY HIDDEN
under the snow like a secret thought.

Where the sea met the beach, the waves had piled the ice floes
on top of each other, exactly as they had been piled on the opposite
side of the bay, in Ludwigsburg, forming strange figures you couldn't
take apart, like a puzzle or a riddle. The three of them had climbed
over the piles of ice floes to reach the plain, smooth ice behind them,
but somehow Anna felt as if she were still standing between those
surrealistic figures, in an inexplicable, multilayered chaos . . .

"Anna? Anna!" Micha said and pulled her sleeve. "Are you
dreaming?"

"Yeah," Anna replied, "I am . . . a dream about finding out how
everything fits together."

"But can we start now? You've got the skates with you, haven't
you? The ones I can wear?"

She nodded and kneeled down to open her backpack. Abel had

walked ahead of them and was standing near the orange buoy, a relic from summer. He was looking out at the horizon. Maybe he had to be alone for a moment.

Anna thought about school while she helped Micha put on two pairs of socks and her old skates. She thought of the others' faces. Of Bertil's when he'd come into the student lounge and seen them sitting on the radiator in the corner, she and Abel, silent and together. He'd nodded and said, "Of course. Of course." Then he'd turned on his heels and left. But in the doorway, he'd turned back and said, "Take good care of yourself, Anna Leemann. Think of the snowstorm and the shadow out in the woods. And don't believe everything you hear . . ."

And Abel had looked at her, questioning, but she'd just shaken her head. She would tell him later. Maybe.

The strange thing was that Gitta had said something similar after Abel had disappeared into class. "Good to see the two of you together again," she said. "Though it's weird. Neither of you seems happy about it. Bertil told me he plucked you out of that snowstorm yesterday."

"He found me because you told him that you'd seen me head out. That's what he said anyway."

Gitta had nodded. "Take care of yourself, Anna. And don't believe everything you hear . . ."

There wasn't literature class that day, but she'd passed Knaake in the corridor. "I'm on it," he said walking by her, winking. "But I don't know what I think yet. One shouldn't believe everything one hears . . ."

Had they all gotten together to confuse her? Whom and what shouldn't she believe?

"Now," Micha said, closing the last plastic clasp. "With these skates, I'll be so fast I'll arrive at the mainland before the thirteenth of March. In the fairy tale, you know." She held onto Anna's arm, stood up, and started marching over the ice. Then she took bigger steps, and then she started to glide. Anna watched her glide away. She hadn't known that Micha could skate; she'd figured she'd have to teach her. But the pink down jacket was all but flying now. Micha threw her arms up into the air and gave a scream of joy and made a pirouette without losing balance, like a true little queen.

"We don't give children enough credit," Anna murmured. "They can take perfect care of themselves. But what . . . what will happen on the thirteenth of March?"

She slowly walked over to Abel, and he looked surprised, too. "I didn't know Micha knew how to skate."

"What about you?" Anna asked. "Can you skate?" She bent down and got her own skates out of the backpack. And another pair that belonged to Magnus.

Abel shook his head. "I've never tried. I'm just gonna stand here and watch you two."

"Oh no," Anna said. "We're not doing this without you."

A little later Abel stood next to her on the ice, unsteady on his legs, helpless like a newborn foal, and she laughed. Neither of you seems happy, Gitta had said. But on that day, happiness came creeping back, it was an in-spite-of-everything-happiness, a childish, stubborn happiness, and Anna welcomed it with open arms. She took Abel's hands and skated backward, pulling him along through the snow, far, far out onto the ice. "You just have to move along!" she shouted. "Your knees! You've gotta bend your knees! You've got joints there, haven't you? It's easy!"

"No!" he shouted back. "I don't have knee joints . . . I'm sure I don't! I . . ." And they ended up in a heap on the ice, and Micha came flying and landed on top, because she couldn't resist, and, somehow, they sorted out their arms and legs and got up again. They each took one of Abel's hands; they tried to push him, tried to pull him, tried to leave him alone and tell him from a distance what he had to do—it was impossible to teach Abel to skate. It was a disaster . . . It was the most wonderful thing in the world.

Anna's stomach hurt from laughing so hard. She had snow in her hair, snow in her mouth, snow in her shoes . . . what did it matter? In her head, the sun was shining so brightly she could barely see. Later, she would think that these days—this one and the next—had been their best. She would always remember the light playing in Abel's and Micha's pale blond hair. She'd always hear their laughter. It was such happy and unburdened laughter, laughter from a world without dead bodies or social services, a world in which no one ever disappeared.

And then they were lying on the ice next to each other, flat on their backs, the three of them, and Abel said, "In summer, you know . . . in summer, I want to swim with you, right here. We'll lie in the water just like this, only the sky will be a different color then. And the water will be warm and blue, and the sailors will pass us on their way out to the island of Rügen."

"And we'll eat loads of ice cream," Micha added.

"Definitely." Abel rolled onto his stomach. "And then we'll lounge around on the beach all lazy, and we'll build sandcastles . . ."

"With sea grass for decoration and pinecones for inhabitants," Anna said.

Abel nodded. "When summer comes, there'll be no more black

ship. And no problems. When summer comes, I'll be eighteen."

"The thirteenth of March . . ." Anna began.

"That's the day we're going to reach the mainland," Abel said, smiling.

"And we're gonna celebrate," Micha said. "We're gonna celebrate Abel's birthday. On that day, he'll be a grown-up. Just like that, bang . . . and then he can be my father for real. It won't be long now, Anna. Next Wednesday."

Anna wanted to say that she wasn't at all sure about the laws and that it was probably a lot more complicated than Abel and Micha imagined. But she didn't say so. She said instead, "There's hot chocolate in the thermos in my backpack."

"Oh yeah, and we brought cookies!" Micha jumped up, and they started pushing and pulling and shoving Abel back toward the beach. And then they got rid of their skates and had a picnic between the piled-up ice-floe puzzles.

"Be a bit careful with that hot chocolate," Abel said to Micha. "Better close that jacket again. We don't want to wash another sweater. Remember, the washing machine is broken . . ."

"You said we can still wash things by hand," Micha said.

"Yeah, we can." He sighed. "Tomorrow is washing day, like in the olden days, in the days of real fairy tales. But washing takes time, Micha. It takes time. And we've already got enough washing."

"Can't you get someone by to . . . repair your machine?" Anna asked.

Abel shook his head. "The thing is old enough for a museum. We'll have to buy a new one. And I will, some day . . . but for that, I'd have to use our savings for school, and it'll take me a while to bring myself to do that."

Anna thought about the house full of blue air and the washing machine in the basement, which would just be replaced if it broke. When you were ironing shirts on the big old wooden table down there, you could hear the robins at the window.

"While you're waiting to buy a new machine," she said, "you could just do your laundry at my house. It won't take long. We've got a dryer, too. You could come by tomorrow afternoon and bring your clothes; we'll put them in the machine; and in the evening, you can take everything home with you, clean and folded. It would save a lot of time . . . time that you could use to get some studying done."

"Oh, please, let's do that!" Micha exclaimed. "I can look at Anna's books again and blow into her flute and watch the fire in the fireplace and . . ."

"And your parents?" Abel asked.

"They might be home," Anna answered. "And will bite no one."

She looked at him, and he avoided her eyes. Finally, he covered his face with his hands, breathed in heavily, and then lowered his hands again. "Okay," he said. "Okay, we'll come." He stood up and shook the snow off of his jeans. "I'm doing a thousand new things in spite of myself," he said. "It's not easy, you know, to jump over your own shadow."

"As long as you're better at it than skating . . . ," Anna said and stood up too. She wanted to say more, but that wasn't possible because he was kissing her. Reasonable Anna wanted to draw back: the danger of touch. But unreasonable Anna welcomed the kiss like happiness. Maybe, she thought, it's better to take these moments when you get them—there might not be too many in life.

◆ ◆ ◆

The most wonderful days. There were only two of them. The day on which Abel didn't learn to ice-skate and the day on which the laundry didn't dry.

They went to pick up Micha from school together that Friday. The teacher Anna had talked to before was standing in the yard with Micha when Abel and Anna came skidding through the snow on their bikes. It was still snowing, and the streets were as bad as they'd been the day before. "Abel Tannatek," the teacher said to Abel. "My name is Milowicz. I'm Micha's teacher. And you're her brother, aren't you?"

"Yes, that's me," Abel answered, "and we've got something we've got to do."

"Wait." She reached out for him but didn't dare detain him physically. "I'd really like to talk to your mother. I've been trying to reach her for a long time . . ."

"Are there problems?" Abel asked. He'd taken Micha's little hand. "Problems in class?"

"No, that's not it, it's just . . . Micha told me her mother has gone on a trip, and it seems to be such a long trip . . . is it true she's away, traveling?"

"Yes," Abel said. "Yes, that's true."

"And who looks after Micha?"

"Santa Claus," Abel growled and helped Micha onto the carrier of his bike. Mrs. Milowicz was still staring after them when they left the schoolyard, her face puzzled.

"How can she understand?" Anna asked. "You're being unreasonable. I mean, it's not her fault, is it? She hasn't done anything wrong . . . she's just a teacher and she's worried."

"She's too curious," said Abel. "Maybe she put the social worker onto us. Maybe it wasn't Mrs. Ketow after all. By the way, we're still waiting for the next social worker to turn up. It looks like no one's taken over Marinke's cases yet . . . who knows, we might get lucky and they won't remember us until after the thirteenth of March."

Anna had hoped that Magnus and Linda would be late, like they were last Friday, but Fridays weren't regular days in the house of blue air, and both of them were already home. She had warned them, of course, because of the laundry. She wondered if that was the reason they were there. They both said they'd just happened to finish work early. Naturally.

Anna saw Abel flinch as he hung his jacket on the coatrack in the hall and heard Magnus's voice from the first floor. He flinched like a frightened dog. Anna put a hand on his arm. "Stay," she said, as she would to a dog, and felt stupid. She thought of the dog that belonged to Bertil's family, in the backseat of the Volvo, the dog that bore an uncanny resemblance to the animal in the fairy tale. She could still hear his whining in the snowstorm.

"How nice to have visitors," Linda said. "I thought we could have lunch together . . ."

Abel was sitting at the table like an animal ready to jump up and run. Everything he said was distilled, ice-cold politeness, and Anna was close to kicking him under the table, but she didn't. Micha had no trouble with the situation. She told Linda everything about her school and the friend she'd visited on Wednesday . . . that they'd built an igloo together . . . that she wanted a dog when she got older, or actually, a dog and a white horse. The horse had to stand in the middle of a garden full of apple trees, of course.

"Yes, I agree," Linda said. "That's where white horses belong."

Toward the end of their lunch, Abel was sitting in his chair, a little calmer, and his eyes had stopped darting around the living room as if it were a trap he had to escape.

"And now it's probably best if you just throw your clothes into the machine," Linda said, "and I'll see to it that they get cleaned and folded. I think I've already been introduced to one of your sweatshirts . . ."

"Then Linda has a lot to do for her university classes," Magnus said, throwing a glance at Linda. "And I'm very busy with a mountain of patient files."

Anna had to keep herself from grinning. But listen you will, she thought, oh, you will, despite all your efforts to melt into the background. Well, go ahead and listen . . .

"We got something important, too," Micha said. "We're going to hear the next part of a certain fairy tale . . ."

Anna led the two of them up to her room. All you could see from the window now was a strange and distant memory of the garden. The roses had completely disappeared under the snow, and a single lonely robin was waiting for Magnus on top of the birdhouse.

They sat on the floor with their backs against the big bookshelf, watching the snowflakes gently floating down from the sky outside, and Abel said, "Let's see . . . the fairy tale . . . In the fairy tale, the little queen and her crew are just now starting to walk over the ice. The ice is smooth and wide, lying beneath the snow like a secret thought. But at the shore of the murderer's island, the waves have piled the ice floes on top of each other. The secret thought had broken into big splinters, interlinking with each other and forming strange figures you couldn't take apart, couldn't sort, like a puzzle or a riddle."

He put one arm around Micha and then, after a moment's

hesitation, one around Anna, and, although it was quite un-comfortable, Anna left the arm there. "It was difficult to walk over the ice. They kept slipping, losing their balance, falling, standing up again, walking on. When the ship had shrunk to the size of a child's toy behind them and then become nothing more than a tiny green spot, they stopped again and looked through the binoculars, one after another. It had started to snow.

"'Aren't those our pursuers over there?' the asking man asked.

"'Under the beeches, where the anemones bloom in spring,' the answering man answered, and the rose girl had the distinct feeling she'd heard that answer before. Possibly, she thought, the pool of answers was limited. There are fewer answers in the world than questions, and if you ask me now why that is so, I must tell you that there is no answer to that question.'

"The little queen saw their pursuers had reached the green ship. The black ship was also stuck in the ice, and now the fat diamond eater and the two haters were on foot as well. But there was another person with them, a young woman who had pulled her blond hair back in a very serious, grave way . . . like a teacher. She was wearing teacher's glasses.

"'Who's that?' the little queen wanted to know and held the binoculars down to the golden eyes of the dog.

"'That's the gem cutter,' the dog answered. 'Do you see the tools sticking out of her coat pocket? Take good care, little queen; the gem cutter, too, wants to own your diamond heart. She wants to grind and polish and form it after her own ideas. But if she manages to do that, you won't recognize your own heart . . .'

"'Look! There!' the little queen exclaimed. 'They are climbing aboard our ship! Do they think we're still there?'

"But shortly after that, from the deck of the green ship, a colorful balloon drifted up into the cold air. A gondola hung beneath it, a gondola designed only for emergencies, and in the gondola, sat the two haters and the diamond eater.

" 'They're fleeing!' the little queen said and started to dance in the snow, jumping up and down happily. 'They're afraid of the endless ice! Look, the wind is blowing them away from us! They gave up! I guess they will return to their own islands!'

" 'They will,' the lighthouse keeper said gravely, 'and I can tell you why. They don't think we'll make it. They think the diamond is lost anyway, lost in the eternal ice of this story. There's only one person who believes that the diamond will survive. One single person who is not aboard the gondola.'

" 'The cutter,' whispered the rose girl.

"The silver-gray dog nodded. 'She will keep following us,' he said. 'We should hurry.'

"That was when the rose girl remembered something. She reached into her backpack and took out a pair of skates. And then another pair and another pair . . . the whole backpack had been full of skates.

"Only there weren't any skates for the blind white cat. 'And all the better,' said the cat. 'Cats are not made for ice-skating. It's much too undignified. Who's going to carry me?'

"The asking man asked the answering man if he would like to take turns carrying the cat, and the answering man answered: 'In the box on top of the bathroom cupboard.' Another answer, the rose girl thought, that she had heard already.

"So they started skating, and the gently falling snow covered their traces. The silver-gray dog was running next to them, on foot.

When he had tried to skate, his four legs had gotten into such confusion that he almost couldn't sort them out again. And any way, he preferred being a tragic character as opposed to a comic one.

"They skated over the ice for a long time; they skated a long way; they skated through a snowstorm, holding onto each other so as not to get separated. They skated through clear weather and drank hot chocolate from a thermos the rose girl had found in her backpack. After that, the backpack was empty and she wanted to leave it behind, but the silver-gray dog shook his head. 'An empty backpack would be a trace,' he said. 'And all our traces must be wiped out so the cutter can't find us.'

"And so when the snow had stopped falling and covering their traces, they wiped them out very thoroughly themselves. Still, every time they looked back through the lighthouse keeper's binoculars, there was a tiny, stubborn figure following them with jewel-cutting tools sticking out of her coat pockets. The cutter. She didn't seem to have binoculars of her own. So how did she know the right way?

"'Let's wait for her!' the little queen begged. 'Maybe she's cold. Maybe she's afraid of being on the ice all by herself. She is only one, and we are many . . .'

"'If she finds us, she will be more than one,' the silver-gray dog said. 'Little queen, haven't I told you about the ocean riders?'

"'Never,' answered the little queen. 'Mrs. Margaret, do you know about the ocean riders?'

"Mrs. Margaret shook her head and lifted her arms, patterned with white and blue flowers, helplessly.

"'But me, I know about them,' the lighthouse keeper said. 'I saw them race by from my window up there in the lighthouse once; I saw them on their horses. Their horses are green like sea grass and white like shells and as fast as the night. They gallop over the water; they fly over the ice. The ocean riders guard the seven seas and see to it that everything is in order there. They never sleep, and when they're called for, they follow the call . . . over the waves, through the white foam, through the storm . . .'

"'Yes,' the silver-gray dog said, and he bared his teeth when he said this. 'Yes, they see to it that everything is in order on the seven seas. But what order means, what the rules are, what is right and what is wrong . . . that is decided by the ones paying the ocean riders. The red hunter has been paying them, the diamond trader has been paying them, and the gem cutter is paying them as well. But us, little queen, we have never paid them. What could we have paid them with? An apple from the garden on your island?'

"'A splinter of the diamond,' the white cat remarked, stifling a yawn, and the little queen started, frightened.

"'But if we had paid them with a splinter of my heart, my heart would have a missing piece!' she exclaimed. 'And I . . .'

"'Don't worry, little queen,' said the silver-gray dog. 'Nobody's going to break a splinter off your heart. For the ocean riders, traveling over the ice is forbidden, and fleeing is against their law. As long as the cutter doesn't call them, you have nothing to fear. And she will only call them when she is absolutely sure that she's following the right wanderers. When she's caught up with us.'

"They skated on all day long. When evening came, the distance between the cutter and them had grown smaller. She wasn't near enough yet, but just the same, she was much too near.

"'Could I borrow the binoculars again, please?' the rose girl asked, but the lighthouse keeper said that he had misplaced them somewhere and couldn't find them.

"'I've got pretty good eyes,' the silver-gray dog growled. 'I don't need binoculars.' He narrowed his golden eyes and stared a hole into the thickening dark. 'All day long . . . I wasn't sure whether I was only imagining it, but now I'm sure . . . red threads. We're all wearing red coats. One of us has left red threads in the white snow to show the cutter the way. One of us is a traitor.'"

Abel fell silent.

"And? Who is it?" Micha asked, out of breath. He shrugged. "I don't know."

"It can't be the cat," Micha said. "She doesn't have a red coat, only her fur. Or do you think . . . she might have pulled some threads out of someone else's coat? She's probably got sharp claws . . . The silver-gray dog can't be the traitor either, for the same reason. And he was the one to discover the thing . . ."

"The asking man and the answering man are too dumb," Anna said. "And apart from that, they're just made up."

Abel lifted his arms. "But it's all made up!"

"No," said Anna. "No. That's not true. There are only two people who could be the traitor. The lighthouse keeper . . . and the rose girl."

Abel stood up. "We'll see," he said. "We'll see what happens and how the story goes on. I can't tell you yet. I guess it's going to be sometime till our laundry is dry, even with the dryer . . . tell me, what would you be doing now . . . if we weren't here?"

She thought. "I'm afraid I'd be studying. What would you be doing if you were at home?"

He smiled. "Studying, I'm afraid."

"You can have my desk," Anna said. "I'll sit on the bed with my books. I do that a lot because it's more comfortable . . . we should really be doing something to prepare for final exams. They won't just take themselves. Not really anyway."

"I'm really lucky that I don't have finals," said Micha. "I'll go downstairs and see what Linda's doing."

"Linda," Abel repeated when Micha had left to hop down the wooden stairs. "Linda. So she's already on a first-name basis with your mother. Like she's known her for years."

"I think," Anna said, "I think . . . Linda always wanted a second child, you know. Another child she'd watch grow up and keep safe . . ."

Piano notes drifted up from the living room, single notes without a real tune; someone was just seeing what happened if she touched the keys. And between the notes, you could hear Micha's and Linda's voices.

"Damn finals." Anna gathered her books on her bed. For a moment she thought that there were a hundred things she'd prefer to be doing right now, but then, when she looked up from her book, she thought that, actually, everything was as it should be: Abel was sitting at her desk, his head bent over a different book, lost in what he was reading, and it looked as if he belonged there. They had slipped into a surreal kind of everyday life: Anna was on her bed, and he was at the desk; they were studying for exams, like a thousand other people in Germany were doing. She smiled and read on, marked lines, words, passages of text; she tried to build rooms in her brain, create drawers, file facts. A safe and absolutely normal occupation . . . miles away from a dark boathouse.

The piano downstairs had fallen silent; she heard the clatter of baking trays, and the smell of fresh cookies crept to her nose. Linda and Micha were working together in the kitchen.

At some point, Anna got up and walked over to the desk, stood behind Abel, put her hand on his back. He looked up and smiled.

"When I say to the moment flying . . ." she whispered the words from *Faust*, putting her arms around him, ". . . linger a while—thou art so fair."

"Yeah."

"Are you still stuck on *Faust*? I've made my way to Herta Müller . . ."

"Everything I own," Anna said, quoting, "I carry with me . . ." She looked at her arms still wrapped around him. "But it's true, you know," she added.

He understood, but he laughed away the romance of the moment. "You better not try to carry me," he said. "I might be a bit heavy . . ."

"You could take a one-minute break from Herta and kiss me."

"I could. But after that I've got to read on. Final exams . . ."

"Sure. Final exams . . ."

Later, Abel took another break, a longer one, but not to kiss Anna. He went outside to help Magnus shovel the driveway. She stood at the bathroom window, watching. It was odd to see them together: Magnus's broad back in his ski jacket, Abel in his worn, old military parka, which was not made for this weather. They were shoveling equally fast, but not too fast. They weren't in a hurry; this was not a competition. For the first time in days, Anna thought of Abel's right hand. He was using it in a normal way again. So Rainer hadn't broken the joint after all. Anna saw that they were talking. She wondered what about. Maybe about Magnus's offer of a loan. Maybe about the snow.

"Linger a while," she repeated, whispering, "thou art so fair . . ."

And she imagined how things could be later. It was stupid, but the picture just appeared in her mind: she saw Abel and Magnus shoveling snow together . . . in twenty years, in thirty. Magnus had grown old, his broad back still strong but bent from time, his hair nearly white at the temples. And Abel . . . Abel was a different Abel, an adult one, one who was absolutely self-confident and didn't let his eyes dart around the dining room at lunch, as if he were caught in a trap.

"Nonsense," she whispered. "Thirty years? You don't stay with the person you meet at seventeen . . . What kind of fairy tale are you living in, Anna Leemann?"

And still the picture seemed right.

"Look at that," Linda said, stepping up behind her. "They do get along, after all."

"There are fresh cookies!" Micha said and held a plate out to Anna. "And we have to stay. Linda just realized that the dryer is broken! Totally broken! We've already hung the clothes on the line in the basement . . . I've been standing on a chair helping . . . and tomorrow, everything will be dry for sure, but tonight we're allowed to sleep here. What do you think of that?"

"I don't know," Anna said slowly as she turned toward Linda, "what Abel will think of that. Is the dryer really broken?"

Linda shrugged and nodded. Anna went down to the basement and tried to turn it on herself, but Linda and Micha were right. The machine was silent; it didn't work. Anna unplugged the cord and plugged it in again—without success.

When she came back from the basement, Abel was brushing the snow off his parka while Micha was dancing around him, still balancing the plate of cookies, singing, "We're staying, we're staying, we're staying overnight! We're drying! We're drying! We're drying on the line!"

Abel lifted his arms defensively. "Will you stand still for a second?" he said. "Micha. We can't stay overnight. We have our own home, and it's not here. We can come back tomorrow and pick up the damn laundry then."

"Damn is a word you're not allowed to say," Micha declared, folding her arms. "And did you look outside? It's snowing again, and I'm sure there will be another storm! Please, Abel! Please!" She put down the plate on the floor and clung to his leg. "Please, please, please! Only this one night! I still want to play the piano a little bit and decorate the cookies and everything!"

"Do you have to go out tonight?" Anna asked in a low voice.

Abel covered his face in his hands. This time, he left them there longer, and she saw him try hard to make a decision. She actually thought she saw him curse silently behind his hands.

"I'll just end up saying yes again," he whispered. "I'll end up saying yes to so many things, I'll forget the difference between yes and no—and I'll lose my mind." He looked at Anna. "Keep my mind for me. See to it that nobody steals it. I might have to go out tonight. I don't know yet."

Was he waiting for a call? She didn't ask. He was not an answerer after all. He was everything else. A seller of white cats' fur. A storyteller. A stranger, still.

"You can sleep in the guest room," she said. "The two of you. There are two beds." And, in a much lower voice, "The key is in the door at night, inside. Take it with you so you can get back in. You're not a prisoner. This is not a trap . . . just a broken dryer."

✦ ✦ ✦

And then they sat at dinner like one big family. The lamplight was warm, and the kitchen smelled of potato casserole. And Micha talked with her mouth full about how she had baked cookies and how she could almost play the piano already.

And Linda smiled. And Abel wasn't fidgeting in his chair like he had been at lunch. Once, Anna took his hand under the table and pressed it very quickly, and he pressed back.

"Abel can make potato casserole, too," Micha said and put her fork down. "He can do anything . . . pancakes and pasta and cake. Even birthday cake. With candles on top. We'll have one pretty soon and maybe with strawberries because it's nearly spring. Or we can have frozen strawberries. Abel can make strawberry cake!"

"He seems to be a real saint, that brother of yours," Magnus said drily.

The conversation stopped.

"What's that supposed to mean?" Anna hissed. "Why the sarcasm?"

"What's sarcasm?" asked Micha.

"Sarcasm is when someone says the opposite of what he means," Abel said in a low voice. "So, in other words, I'm no saint. I'm the opposite of a saint. He's right. And the opposite of a saint doesn't belong here, I guess . . ." He pushed back his chair, his hands on the edge of the table, and Anna put her hand on his.

"Stay," she said. "Please. Please. Magnus is just joking. You see, Micha, that father of mine is really good at shoveling snow and feeding birds and curing sick people, but he can't even scramble an egg, and, compared to that, anyone who can make potato casserole is definitely a saint. To be honest, Magnus couldn't even tell the *difference* between a snow shovel and a potato."

Micha laughed; and Magnus laughed, too; and Linda tried to laugh with them. Only Abel didn't laugh. But he didn't leave either.

"I've already made up the beds in the guest room for you," Linda said.

"Do you want us to help with the dishes?" Micha asked. "I'm really good at washing dishes . . ."

Linda shook her head. "Our dishwasher is also really good at washing dishes. Sleep tight."

And Anna watched Abel and Micha go up the stairs, hand in hand, like a picture on an old-fashioned postcard—as if everything was still all right, still perfect. But nothing was all right anymore, she could feel it. And later, she wondered if it was at that very moment that Abel decided he had to go out. If maybe it didn't have anything to do with a call. Maybe he wouldn't have left the house that night if Magnus hadn't made that stupid remark. And maybe things would have turned out differently as a result . . .

She lay in her bed reading for a long time, not able to sleep. The cell phone on her desk rang, but she didn't answer it. Gitta, she thought. Who else.

They'd said good night to each other, she and Abel, good night and no more . . . a little like strangers. She'd heard him whispering with Micha for a while, but now everything was quiet. Finally, she tiptoed over to the guest room and opened the door. Light from the streetlight outside dripped into the room like rain. One of the beds was empty. They were lying on the other one, together, Micha rolled up like a kitten in Abel's arms, fast asleep. And Abel? Was he sleeping as well or was he just pretending?

She stood there for a moment, looking at Abel. His face was so close yet infinitely far away. The shadow of the bed and the figures on it fell on the wall like a weird, distorted creature. An animal crouched low, waiting to strike. A wolf. She closed the door without a sound, crept back to her room, and crawled under her own covers.

He stood on the pedestrian bridge, looking out over the ice. The flakes had ceased to fall, but the river was covered with snow; even that thin layer of ice in the middle, where the fishermen had broken holes for their hooks, had frozen again—a network of invisible traps cloaked in snow, deceiving, dangerous. He knew where the frozen-over holes were; he knew where the ice was thin—he didn't need to see it.

He pulled his scarf tighter. How cold it was! This winter was colder than any winter he could remember, and he'd seen many winters. To be precise: sixty-three of them.

The lights of the restaurant-ship were groping their way onto the ice, timid, as if they were afraid of the cold. He looked at his watch. Nine thirty. He was too early. She wouldn't be here till ten. She had this unpronounceable name . . . Milowicz? Mirkolicz? He'd been surprised when she'd called him. Maybe she didn't know anything. Maybe this meeting would be good-for-nothing. But maybe it wouldn't. Maybe together, they could find out something.

Save something. He had the feeling that the whole situation was getting too much for the boy. Someone had to help.

He still wasn't sure what had happened. There was Michelle, for example. He had the feeling that Anna was right, that she was really close, so close they couldn't see her. But where was she? He'd found out some things, of course. He had his suspicions. But he wasn't sure. He would have preferred not to know one thing that he did know now. That made him sad. Incredibly sad. He walked over the bridge, to the other side of the river, where the restaurant-ship lay. He went down the stairs and stepped onto the ice. It was solid, solid like stone. It felt good to walk on it.

And then he heard steps behind him. The sound was almost hushed by the snow, but it was there. Probably it was just someone who'd come from the restaurant-ship, someone taking a walk between drinks. Or it was a person also waiting for a date. He turned. He saw a silhouette, its outline not very clear against the pale lights of the ship. It was too dark out here on the river. He didn't feel like meeting anyone; he'd meet her in half an hour—that would be enough.

He turned back and walked farther down the frozen river, a little farther downstream, and then he would climb the stairs again and be back on shore. It would be time by then . . . the steps behind him were catching up with his. Maybe they were hers? Maybe she'd come early as well and seen him? He'd ventured so far from the lights now that it was absolutely dark around him. He'd thought the streetlights at the other side of the river would light the ice here, but the chunky bodies of the old vessels hibernating here, those antique monsters of sailing ships, shut out the lights.

He felt fear creeping up inside him. He didn't really think it was her. For the last few days, he'd been the follower, the pursuer, the spy—unseen, he hoped, unheard, unnoticed. Now somebody had turned the tables. The vague figure behind him came closer. It was blocking his way back to shore, and he realized that he was walking toward the middle of the river. He reached the place where the ice was thin, or where he believed it to be thin. He stopped.

It didn't make any sense to run away. He wanted to know now, to know who was following him. He wanted to talk to that person. He was still afraid, but he was sixty-three years old—it wasn't as if he'd never been afraid before, and up to now he'd always overcome his fear. This wasn't a deserted beach, after all; this was the city harbor, in the middle of town; the restaurant-ship was only a few hundred meters away, the street even less.

He turned again, wanting to wait for the figure to reach him, but it already had . . . it was standing directly in front of him. He wasn't met by a face. It was the barrel of a pistol. Of course, he knew the face behind it, even in the dark . . . it wasn't as dark as he'd thought. He heard himself breathe in sharply, in an onset of panic—and of surprise.

"You?"

"Of course," the figure answered. "Didn't you know? Haven't you known for a long time?"

"I . . ." He took a step backward, and the thin ice creaked beneath his feet. Directly behind him, there must have been a frozen-over hole.

"You started snooping around," the figure said. "Like a mediocre detective. It's not good to want to know too much."

"I . . ." He tried to think. What if he screamed? What if he slapped the weapon out of that hand and ran toward the shore? He wasn't fast—he knew that—and he felt paralyzed, his legs frozen stiff, like the ice on the river. He couldn't run. He couldn't scream, either. His vocal cords were ice-cold.

"Why?" he heard himself whisper. "Why all this?"

"Did you ever love?"

He nodded. "I think I did . . ."

"Not like this maybe. If you really love, nothing and no one is allowed to get in the way. Do you understand that? I won't allow anything to happen to her. This is not about me. It has never been about me. Turn around."

"No," he said. "And why?"

"Because I can't look someone I shoot in the eye."

He heard something like a suppressed sob, and at first he thought it was himself. But then he realized it was his opponent. And he understood one thing: he must not turn around. No matter what happened. There had to be a solution. A way to get out of this, unharmed. He didn't feel hatred for the figure holding the pistol, only pity. Maybe this was somehow his fault . . . he should have understood sooner . . . he should have intervened . . .

"Turn around."

He didn't. He took a step back. He felt the thin ice give way beneath him. It happened quickly. One second he was standing on the river, and the next, there wasn't anything beneath his feet. He didn't feel the cold. The world just disappeared.

And somewhere in the city, someone was wandering the streets aimlessly, hands deep in the pockets of a jacket, white noise in his ears. Somewhere, far away from the river and much later. Somewhere and sometime. No saint.

And somewhere else—and we know where, don't we?—someone was waiting on a restaurant-ship . . . in vain.

And somewhere, a silver-gray dog with golden eyes barked in his kennel. Maybe a boy with glasses heard him when he opened the gate. Perhaps, unable to sleep, he'd just gone for a walk.

And somewhere, on a leather sofa, two bodies were moving,

entwined like a puzzle, like ice floes, and the light fell on dyed-black hair and on red hair, while in the ashtray, the butt of a joint slowly turned to ashes. How late was it? They hadn't looked at the clock when they'd gotten back . . .

And somewhere, somewhere very close by, a vanished person lay in deep, exhausted sleep.

In the middle of the night, Anna woke up because an ice-cold body was pressing against her. She wasn't sure if she was really awake or if she was dreaming. The body smelled of winter air and cigarettes and of something familiar, and for a moment she was stiff with fear. The body was much too close, and a memory of it being even closer flashed through her like lightning, painful and red.

"Abel?" she whispered. He didn't answer. He was fully dressed and he was cold as snow.

She pushed the memory aside with all her force, rolled over on her side and put her arms around him. She tried to warm him, but she couldn't. It was as if he would never, ever become warm again. The shutters shut out the night and created a new, denser night in the room, a kind of absolute night without up and down, right or left. She couldn't see a thing, all she could do was feel. And she felt the torn cloak of love, the one she had made up to explain things to herself. It was real in that night; she could feel its fabric brush against her skin. She lifted the cloak and put it around the two of them to shut out the world and all reason. She buried her fingers in his hair, laid her hands on his ice-cold cheeks.

And then she heard a strange and frightening sound, like the whimpering of a dog, very low . . . it lasted only seconds, but it was such a desperate sound, such an infinitely helpless sound, that she shuddered. "Abel," she said again. She wanted to ask him something, but she didn't know what. She just held him tight, and, finally, she fell asleep, still holding him in her arms.

When she awoke in the morning, she was in bed alone. She walked over to the guest room barefoot. Abel and Micha were still asleep, together in one of the beds. She must have dreamed that encounter in the night. He'd never been outside.

15

Thaw
৵৲

"THE SNOW IS MELTING," MAGNUS SAID AT BREAK-fast and pointed outside, where thick round drops were falling from the roof. "My robins will come back."

The sun was shining on the snow. It would take some time for the snow to go, but it was a beginning.

Nobody said much at breakfast. It was a good kind of Saturday-morning sleepiness, Anna told herself. The silence didn't mean anything. She went to the basement with Abel to take the dry clothes down from the line. Upstairs, they heard Micha trying to play the piano again.

"She'd stay if I'd let her," Abel said, smiling. "She's already forgotten me, hasn't she?"

"Bullshit," Anna said. "You're a saint, remember?" And she hugged him with a shirt in her hand, which led to a weird kind of entanglement.

"Last night," she whispered. "Did you leave the house?"

He hesitated. "Yes," he answered finally. "Not for long, though. I had to . . . deliver something."

"And did you come to me afterward . . . or did I dream that?"

He stroked her hair. "You dreamed that," he said.

"It wasn't a nice dream," Anna whispered. "In my dream you were unhappy . . ."

"Come on," he said. "Let's take the laundry upstairs. We should get going, or Micha will start to think that we live here."

"Wait," she said on the stairs. "Did you actually think about it? About Magnus's offer? The loan?"

"Magnus . . ." Abel murmured. "He's the only reasonable person here. Do you realize that? He would rather see me gone for good. I wonder what conditions are attached to his offer. He'll name them sooner or later. Maybe one is that I go really far away to study . . ."

"Nonsense," Anna said, but she had a bad taste in her mouth as she said it.

When she gathered Abel's books from her desk, her fingers felt heavy as lead. Stay, she wanted to say. Stay here, with Micha. Don't ever leave again. Don't ever go out at night again. Stay. You don't have to work nights. Forget those calls, those contacts, those deliveries. Forget the white cat's magic fur. Throw away this world of the night; fling it into the river . . . Her cell phone was still lying on her desk. She remembered the call she hadn't taken yesterday and checked the mailbox, without really listening, while Abel was packing his backpack.

And then she did listen. It hadn't been Gitta. It was Knaake's voice.

"Anna," he said. "I might be on my way to finding out something. Call me as soon as you can."

She shook her head and pressed the send key to call him back. It would be better, she thought, to walk out of the room. Abel was still standing behind her . . . actually, it would be better not to call back at all. Maybe she didn't want to know what he'd found out. Her heart was racing all of a sudden.

"Fischer?" a female voice barked into the phone. She flinched.

"I . . . I thought . . . I guess I have the wrong number."

"Or you don't," the voice said, a no-nonsense voice without an ounce of friendliness to it. "This is Heinrich Knaake's phone."

"I . . . but . . . is he there?" Anna asked, confused. "Can I talk to him? I'm one of his students, and he left a message that I should call him . . ."

"He's here all right. But you can't talk to him. He's in a coma. In the ICU. I'm the doctor."

Anna closed her eyes and reopened them. "Excuse me?"

"The cell phone was in his jacket pocket. It's a miracle it's still working. Tell me, do you know who should be informed? Is there family?"

"No," Anna answered and tried to swallow her confusion. "I . . . don't know him that well. Not at all, to be honest. What . . . what happened?"

"He fell through the ice," the no-nonsense doctor said. "They pulled him out of the river last night, in the city harbor. We don't know how long he was in the water. He was lucky someone came along and saw him. The person who did, though, didn't pull him out. He called the fire department from a pay phone. The fire department! Now that was a bright idea! And then he hightailed it, our anonymous caller." She laughed a hard, rough laugh—it was really more of a cough than a laugh. If you worked in the ICU, Anna guessed, you got that kind of a laugh—about these kinds of things, anyway.

She was dizzy. She sat down in the chair at her desk.

"Can we see him?"

"If you don't expect him to talk to you, then sure. We're on Löffler Street. We'll be here." The doctor hung up. Probably she had a dozen other things to do.

Anna stared at the cell phone. She should have taken the call last night, she thought. Could she have somehow stopped him from falling through the ice? What on earth had he been doing on the ice in the city harbor anyway?

"Anna?" Abel asked. "What . . . ?"

She looked at him. The room was still spinning around her. "The lighthouse keeper," she said. "Something has happened to the lighthouse keeper."

The room was white like the snow outside, much too white. The beeping of the machines made it unreal. Micha groped for Anna's hand. With her other hand, she held on to Abel. They hadn't wanted to take her, but she'd insisted.

"I'm on the ice with him, don't you remember?" she'd said. "With the lighthouse keeper! In the fairy tale!" Now, seeing him, in his white-snow bed, Micha shook her head in astonishment. "He's not wearing skates," she said. "We were skating, weren't we?"

The no-nonsense doctor left them alone. She was busy with other patients. There was a mind-numbing smell of disinfectant and plastic.

They found three chairs, pulled them up to the bed, and sat down. The monitor above Knaake's still form showed the narrow green line of his heartbeat. The face on the pillows was nearly as white as the pillows themselves. His eyes were closed. The sailor's beard, which had turned him into a lighthouse keeper, seemed withered in a strange way. They sat there for a long time, silently.

"He liked Leonard Cohen," Anna said finally. "Like Michelle. Did you know that?"

"Yes," Abel said. "And I know that Michelle had a fling with a teacher a long time ago. A long, long time ago. And that he was a lot older than she was."

"He told me he didn't know her."

Abel nodded. "Easy for him to say. Maybe he doesn't remember her." He leaned forward and touched the limp hand from which an IV emerged—or, rather, into which it disappeared. He touched the hand very gently. "I wanted to ask him. Point-blank. I should have done it. Now . . ."

"Ask him when he wakes up."

Abel nodded. But in his eyes, the ice was melting. Anna saw the water in them, and she knew that he was thinking the same thing she was: Knaake might never wake up again. The doctor had shrugged. "What do you want from me? Percentages? Chances? It's darn cold in the water out there. *Darn* cold."

"The story," Anna whispered. "Tell us how the story goes on. It's important. The thirteenth of March is next Wednesday, and we've got to reach the mainland. I guess none of the crew slept well that night, bedded on the cold ice, with a traitor in their midst . . ."

"None of them slept well that night," Abel repeated. "For they slept on the cold ice, with a traitor in their midst. A traitor, thought the rose girl, and a murderer—was it one and the same person?

Once, in the middle of the night, she'd thought she'd heard the silver-gray dog whimper . . . very close.

But in the morning, the silver-gray dog was nowhere to be found. The lighthouse keeper wasn't there either. And a thaw had set in. There were fissures, crevices, and deep clefts in the ice now—holes, through which you could make out the water, like dark, lurking eyes.

"'Oh no!' whispered the little queen. 'They haven't fallen into one of these holes, have they?' That was when they heard the cry of a bird, and a moment later a big gray seagull landed next to them. She started pecking the ice with her beak, over and over, as if she wanted to destroy it all by herself. No, the little queen thought, the gull is *writing*.

"'I found him,' the little queen read aloud. 'The lighthouse keeper. He must have gone away, alone at night. Come. Hurry.'

"The seagull inclined her head and nodded, and only when she rose up into the air again did the little queen realize that her eyes were golden. They followed her over the ice till they reached one of the holes full of black water. In it, the lifeless body of the lighthouse keeper was floating. The rose girl helped the little queen pull him up onto the ice. But he still didn't move. One of his fists was closed around something: a red thread.

"'It was him!' the little queen whispered. 'He showed the cutter the way!'

"She looked up, and then she saw the dark figure standing at the top of the next snowdrift. The sharp ends of tools were sticking out of her coat pocket.

"The little queen looked back at the lighthouse keeper. A tear fell on his breast, a royal tear, and, all of a sudden, he started breathing again.

"'But we can't stay here!' the rose girl urged. 'We've got to go! Quick!'

"A short while later, they were racing away on their skates, faster than ever, around crevices and more holes. Behind them, the cutter was gliding through the torn white desert on her own skates. She had worked on them all night. She had made them from pure gold, and at their tips she had left some space to put the pieces of diamond. The cutter didn't stop when she passed the body of the lighthouse keeper.

"Only the gray seagull hovered over him for a while before she stretched her wings and followed the small group of runaways.

"In the distance, a narrow green line had appeared. The mainland. It was close. But not yet close enough."

Abel fell silent.

"So the lighthouse keeper was our traitor," Anna said in a low voice.

Abel nodded. "He's been following me. He thought I wouldn't notice. It's none of his business what I do at night . . . but I didn't want anything to happen to him. Anna, I don't know how he managed to fall through the ice. I . . . I wish he'd followed me last night. If he'd been where I was, he couldn't have fallen through the ice . . . and if I'd been where he was, I could have pulled him out . . ."

"It's okay," she said and put an arm around him. "It's okay."

"I wonder," Micha said, "what kind of creature this gull-wolf-sea lion-dog will turn into at the end. Possibly a prince who marries me?"

"Definitely," someone whispered, and Anna jumped. She nudged Abel and pointed to the pale face on the pillows. Knaake was still lying there with his eyes closed. But now he was moving his lips. "A prince," he repeated.

Anna bent over him, as close as she could, and laid a hand on his forehead.

"Mr. Knaake!" she whispered—why was she whispering? "It's me, Anna. Can you hear me? What happened? What were you doing in the city harbor, on the ice? Why did you go out there all alone?"

He shook his head, very slowly. "I wasn't alone," he answered, barely audible. "There was someone else there, too. Someone with . . . a weapon. I took a step back . . . into the shipping channel . . . to avoid the bullet."

He opened his eyes now, carefully, as if his eyelids weighed tons; he looked at Anna, then at Micha, and then at Abel. And then he closed his eyes again.

"Who?" Anna asked. "Who was there on the ice with you?"

"I . . . can't remember," Knaake answered. "I really can't remember."

He groped for Anna's hand on the bed. She felt his cold fingers, felt that he wanted to tell her something, but she couldn't tell what. She bent even lower.

"Anna, Anna," he whispered, "take care of yourself." There it was again—that sentence so many people seemed to be saying to her lately.

"You're sure you don't remember who it was?" she asked. "Please, you have to try . . ."

But Knaake said no more. She wondered whether he'd fallen asleep or lost consciousness—or whether he just didn't want to answer. The green line of his heartbeat shivered across the monitor, revealing nothing, and left her alone with her fear. She rose from her chair and turned to Abel, who'd risen as well. When he pulled her into his arms, she felt his cheek against hers, and it was wet. The water of the thaw.

"He's gonna make it," he whispered, his voice soft with relief. "He's not going to die. Someone who talks doesn't die. He's gonna make it. Anna, I . . . is it possible he thought he was following me last night but it was someone else? Someone who was even angrier about it than I was?"

Micha pushed her way into their hug and looked up at them. "He's gonna make it, and we will, too, won't we?" she asked. "Reach the mainland? In time?"

Anna visited the lighthouse keeper again on Sunday morning—without Abel. He didn't talk to her this time.

The no-nonsense doctor looked at her strangely when she told her he had spoken the day before. "Sometimes, if someone wants something badly enough," she murmured, "one sees it happen for real."

"But he did open his eyes!" Anna insisted. "He did talk to us."

"Hmm," said the doctor. "Well, he hasn't spoken to *us*, that's for sure. And to be honest, I don't know if he'll ever talk to anybody again."

Anna tried to concentrate on schoolwork all of Sunday, but her thoughts were elsewhere—wandering about the ICU; on the beach, where by now the police tape had probably been removed; and on to the Admiral, in front of which Rainer Lierski had been found on the street. Wandering to Abel. More than anything in the world she wished she could be with him now, that they could find out the truth together.

Her cell phone rang twice, and she recognized Bertil's number. Bertil of all people. She didn't answer. In the evening, Abel called. They didn't talk about Bertil; they didn't talk about police tape; they didn't talk about people falling through the ice. They talked about summer. About what they would do when it finally arrived. Maybe they would sail somewhere. Swim far out to sea. Forget the winter.

"Tomorrow," Anna said, "tomorrow, we'll begin the last week of regular . . . mostly useless . . . classes . . . I wonder what will happen with Knaake's class. Tomorrow . . . tomorrow we'll see each other."

"Yes," Abel said. "Micha said I should say hi, and tell Linda hi from her, too."

"Abel. It's your birthday this week."

"Yes."

"On Wednesday they're going to reach the mainland."

"It's not Wednesday yet."

"No," she said, smiling. "See you tomorrow."

"See you tomorrow," Abel said.

That night, Anna dreamed of blossoming red flames, of an inferno, of a burning house. No, it was a boathouse full of boats. The flames were everywhere, the heat was unbearable, and she was right in the middle of it. She saw herself from the outside. Or *was* the figure she was watching even herself? Was it Abel? In her dreams, the boundaries were blurred.

And then Monday came. And she understood, too late, what the dream had meant.

16

Truth
ॐ

SHE WAS SITTING IN MATH CLASS WHEN THE AN-
nouncement came on, over the loudspeaker.

Math would be her third exam, required if you'd chosen music
and arts as your intensive classes. One more week of lectures she
didn't understand and that she wasn't interested in, and after that
there'd be no more classes, just sitting at home, cramming formulas
into her head . . . she knew she should listen, but the information
just drifted by her. Abel was sitting in the back of the room; he'd
been late again and looked tired, like he so often did. She bore the
tedium for the sake of being able to talk to him afterward. She didn't
even know about what. She just wanted to talk to him.

And then the announcement came on.

"The students' drama group," the disinterested voice of the
secretary said, "asks for a moment of your attention."

Anna put her pen down and leaned back. Every year there was
an announcement like this at the end of the term. It was usually a

short scene from the play they were doing, a friendly advertisement for their production. A welcome interruption to the lesson. Strange, that was Bertil's voice. She hadn't known Bertil was in the drama group. She glanced over at Gitta. Gitta shrugged and started to doodle things on the side of a folder. And suddenly, before Bertil's words got through to her, Anna thought with surprising clarity: *I have lost Gitta. Gitta was once my friend, no matter how different we were. But I've lost her.*

Only after she'd thought this did she hear what Bertil was actually saying. There was some noise in the background, people talking, music—it sounded like a club. What was playing had been prerecorded, and it wasn't a good recording. The Bertil on the recording seemed to be repeating a question he'd already asked. "I said, 'If I asked you, would you come with me as well?'"

"Where to?" somebody else asked. And this other person was Abel. Anna sat up.

"You know exactly what I'm talking about," Bertil said, "and it doesn't have anything to do with where. To my place, to your place … I don't know where. Or do you already have an appointment with somebody here?"

"Bertil," Abel said and laughed a strange kind of laugh, "I don't get what this is all about. You hate me."

"No," Bertil said. It all sounded amazingly honest, but was it? When had this conversation been recorded? Where? And what were they talking about? "Hatred and love lie close to each other," Bertil said, and that was the one sentence that did sound like a school drama production.

"This is bullshit," Abel said. "Go away."

"I thought it was a matter of price," Bertil said in a very low voice.

"What do they usually pay you? I've got money, you know. Enough. You'd be my chance to find out something about myself. If I . . . until now, I thought I was . . . you understand . . ."

"Yeah," Abel said. "I understand. But I'm not interested."

"But you do go home with guys, don't you?"

For a moment there was nothing but the broadband noise of the recording and the background music.

"It is," Abel said finally, "a matter of price."

At this, Gitta got up and ran out. Anna sat there completely motionless. She'd turned to stone; she couldn't move. She didn't understand, yet she understood everything.

Gitta knew she should have reacted more quickly. The sheer surprise had paralyzed her. Paralyzed her like Anna, or like Abel, who'd still been sitting, frozen, at his desk when she'd raced out. Never had Gitta run down the school corridors so fast, but she knew she wasn't fast enough. Where was the damn secretary? Had she left Bertil alone with the microphone and walked out to do something else? That was the only possible explanation . . . Bertil was insane . . . insane . . . he was insane! Gitta forced herself to run even faster. Why didn't anybody else do anything? Why was she the only one running? Why had no one tried to stop this announcement? It was reverberating from all the speakers in the school, and by this point everyone knew it had nothing whatsoever to do with the school play. She stumbled, recovered her balance, and raced up another flight of stairs, along another corridor . . .

"Bertil," Abel's voice said through the speakers, blurred by the bad recording. Cell phone, Gitta thought. Bertil recorded this with a cell phone. Inconspicuously, secretly. He's not stupid.

"Bertil, I don't know what it is you expect. I don't do this on a daily basis. I'm not a . . . how do you call it? Not a professional. To find someone like that, someone who can . . . help you find out about yourself . . . show you stuff . . . for that, you'd have to go to Berlin or, I dunno, Rostock. Some bigger city. What I do is something that just . . . it happens when the opportunity arises. When someone asks me. And it's usually older guys."

"What are you?" Bertil asked. "Bi?"

"That's none of your business," Abel said. "But no. I'm one hundred percent straight."

"I don't get it . . . you only go with guys."

"It's a market. And it's a matter of price. It's not so hard to clench one's teeth if it means money. Even though you probably wouldn't understand that." Abel's voice was bitter like bile.

"So, okay, thanks," Bertil said. "I'm as one hundred percent straight as you. What I just said was . . . not totally honest, I'm afraid. It was more of a test. I just wanted to know. I mean, I did know—I've been watching you, but I wanted to hear it from you."

"So you're happy now?" Abel asked. "You know, I almost felt sorry for you. Do we understand each other? You're not gonna tell anybody about this conversation, right?"

"Of course not," Bertil answered. "I'm not suicidal."

But he obviously was, Gitta thought. Even though he'd kept his promise. Technically, he hadn't spoken to anyone about this conversation. He'd just played the recording . . .

When Gitta flung open the door, he was standing next to the secretary's desk, alone, the cell phone in one hand, leaning forward and speaking one last sentence into the microphone, "I just thought," he said, "that somebody should tell Anna."

Then Gitta's fist landed in his face.

But it was too late. She knew it was much too late.

Anna turned. She was the last to turn. Everyone else had turned during Bertil's announcement—they were all looking at Abel, every single one of them. The math teacher was standing at the blackboard and looking at him, too. She seemed absolutely helpless, as if she knew she had to say something. But what could she say?

Abel stood up and left. Without a word. He walked through the aisle between the desks, his eyes lowered to the floor. He closed the door behind him very quietly, and somewhere a second door closed behind him, the school door, possibly forever. He walked across the schoolyard. They saw him walk away, leave a world he'd never really been part of. They saw him pull his hat down low and get onto his bike. He forgot the Walkman's earplugs. Maybe, Anna thought, he didn't need them anymore; maybe the white noise had finally made it into his head.

She stuffed her books into her backpack and stood up. She felt that she was now the one the others were staring at. Some of them were whispering. Frauke threw her a glance so full of pity she could have thrown up. She covered her face with her hands, just for a moment, and took a deep breath. Then she walked down the aisle like Abel had, but she didn't look down at the floor. She made herself look at the others, even at the teacher, at every single person in the room. Some of them averted their eyes. She walked upright, her head held high.

She walked through the corridors of the school with her head still held high, she left the building with her head held high, she pushed her bike through the slush in the schoolyard with her head held high. She rode out to Wieck, rode over the old bridge, rode along the harbor till she reached the mouth of the river. Near the café, she got off her bike and walked out to the pier with her head held high.

She saw that the ice was melting away. She saw that the bald coots were swimming in open water again, in the shipping channel, where the ice had first disappeared. She saw the dirty white swans. And suddenly, her legs gave way. She grabbed onto the white painted railing in order not to fall. She didn't hold her head high anymore. She doubled up with something that wasn't pain but was. Crouched down, she waited for the tears to come, but there weren't any. She cried without tears.

She understood now. She understood so much.

She remembered how Abel had opened the door of the apartment, wearing a T-shirt, his hair tousled, and how he hadn't let her in. She remembered the words he'd said. Can I come with you? No, Anna. Where I'm going now, you can't come. I still have to go out . . . what I do is something that just . . . it happens when the opportunity arises. How often had the opportunity arisen since she'd known him? Which nights had he been standing in front of a bar, selling the fairy-tale fur of the white cats—and which nights had he been selling himself? Which mornings had he slept through literature class, with his head on his arms, because he'd gone with someone in the night, someone who'd paid the right price? She'd never thought that these things actually happened, not here, not in this tiny city. Maybe in Chicago, she heard Magnus say.

"Of all the ways to earn money," she whispered. "Abel, why did it have to be that one? Because the opportunity arose? When? When did you start to clench your teeth and is it . . . ? Is it a symbol? A symbol of how far you'd go for the little queen? How far you'd go across the ice? You know, there'll come a point . . . a point at which the ice will break . . ."

She thought of the darkness in the boathouse. Of the broken flashlight. She started to understand what had happened that night. It had been a kind of revenge, revenge for all the clenching of teeth he'd had to do. Revenge taken on the wrong person.

Maybe she'd really been the first woman . . . that was an amazing idea.

When she closed her eyes now she saw images she didn't want to see, images of cheap pornography. It's usually older guys. Usually. Could you get used to anything? Did everything become a kind of routine in the end? She opened her eyes.

Gitta, she thought. Gitta had known, right from the beginning. Gitta had kept her mouth shut. But now . . . now the whole school knew. And when he'd left, it looked as if he'd left for good.

She had to find him.

Bertil landed on the floor between the big desk and the wall, trapped, and Gitta stood over him for a moment, looking down on him. There was something like a delicate smile on his face. Behind them, the door opened. Gitta looked up. The secretary, who should never have left in the first place, came back in and stood there, confused and a little frightened.

Gitta turned back to Bertil. "My God, you're sick," she said. "Absolutely sick . . . insane. The only person you've exposed and unmasked with this is yourself."

"I have seen to it that the truth is brought to light," Bertil answered.

"Yeah, that's what you did all right," Gitta said. "And the truth is that you're sick." He was still lying on the floor below her—like an injured insect, fallen on its back—and rage boiled up inside her. She lifted her foot—and stopped. "No," she said, "oh no. You're not even worth kicking. I hope they throw you out of this school."

She slammed the door behind her and found herself standing in front of the headmaster and a couple of teachers. "Do it," she said to them. "Throw him out. Expel him. Save the expense of the paper on which you'd have printed his diploma."

The headmaster grabbed her arm before she could walk away. "What's really going on here?" he asked. "Is that story true? And whom are you talking about? Tannatek?"

"Abel?" Gitta asked and snorted. "Abel has expelled himself from school today. You'll never see him again. Me? I'm talking about Bertil Hagemann."

On the fourth floor of 18 Amundsen Street, nobody opened the door. Not even Mrs. Ketow came out when Anna passed her door. She'd heard her voice, amid the screaming and shouting of fighting children somewhere in her apartment. Mrs. Ketow had given up on Micha, Anna thought. She'd sailed back to her own island in a gondola beneath a balloon, that faded and worn-out island with its forest of too-orderly shelves and its pastures of colorless, cheerless, and comfortless wall-to-wall carpeting.

Behind the door with Tannatek on the nameplate, everything was very quiet.

Abel didn't answer his cell phone. She rode back to the city, rode up and down the cobblestone streets, searching without a lead to follow. She didn't find him. For a moment, she thought he would be sitting on a chair next to Knaake's bed in the ICU, but nobody was sitting there. Knaake lay still, with his eyes closed, beneath the silent green line of his heartbeat.

"Did you know?" Anna whispered. "About Abel? Was that what you'd found out and wanted to tell me?" And what if something else had happened between the two of them . . . between Abel and his teacher? No. Oh no, surely not. She refused to imagine it. She left the hospital to get rid of the thought.

She rode out to the Seaside District again, this time to Micha's elementary school. The schoolyard was empty. Idiot, she scolded herself. She should have come here right away. Now, it was twelve thirty, much too late; he'd picked up Micha long ago. He still didn't answer the phone.

"They're on an outing," she whispered into the thaw, into the air in the abandoned schoolyard. "On the island of Rügen. Or anywhere. They'll be back. When they were gone last time, they came back. They'll turn up somewhere, of course they will."

What had also turned up back then was Marinke's dead body. What was it Bertil had said? I'm not that suicidal.

She'd kept his number—why? She hesitated. But then she finally called him. The phone rang for a long time, and her knees went all wobbly . . . she reached his mailbox. She didn't leave a message. She got back onto her bike and rode home, slowly.

When she parked her bike near the front door, her phone rang. She grabbed it without looking at the display. "Yes?"

"Anna," said Bertil. "You called me; I saw your number . . ."

"Yeah," she said, relieved, and inhaled the warm air deeply. "I just wanted to know if you, if . . ." What should she say? If you're still alive?

"I'm sorry," Bertil said, "for what I've done. Maybe it wasn't the right way to . . . I just wanted the truth to be known."

"I want the truth, too," Anna said, and suddenly, she felt light, weightless even. "And I know the truth now. I know who didn't shoot Lierski and Marinke."

"Excuse me?"

"Was it you?"

"Me? Have you lost your mind completely?"

"That description better suits someone else in this conversation," she said. "Just tell me if you shot them."

"Sure, I run around at night shooting people I don't even know," Bertil replied with a weird laugh. "Now, that's logical."

"How did you know that Marinke was shot at night?"

"I just assumed he was. In daylight, it would have been too hard to shoot someone at the beach of Eldena without a witness, wouldn't it? But, Anna. I have nothing at all to do with this mess. The only person I know who's connected to all three of them is Tannatek."

"Three," said Anna. "So you know it's three . . ."

"Knaake's accident . . . it's all over school. Everyone's talking about it."

"He fell through the ice."

"He did?"

"Bertil." She nearly laughed. "Isn't it strange? Everything you do achieves the exact opposite of what you intend. That car ride in the snow, for instance . . . you wanted to prove to me that I need you to save me, but you made me afraid of you. And now . . . now I know that Abel hasn't shot anybody. I wasn't sure until now, but now I am."

"Why?"

"Because you're talking to me at this very moment. Because you're still alive after what you've done."

She hung up on him and unlocked the front door.

There were voices coming from the living room. She stood there, listening. One of the voices was Linda's, but the other one didn't belong. It was the high-pitched voice of a young woman . . . Anna recognized it, but she couldn't remember where from. She put away her coat and shoes and followed the voices.

Micha's teacher with the unpronounceable name was sitting on the sofa, next to Linda.

"Anna," Linda said. "This is my daughter."

"I know." Mrs. Milowicz managed a strained smile. "We've already met."

The hand she reached out to Anna was smooth and cool. "What happened?" Anna asked.

"Why don't you sit down?" Linda said.

"No!" Anna felt panicked. "I want to know what happened!"

Then she sat down, or rather dropped down into one of the armchairs, and stared at Micha's teacher. She was so young, so blond, her light green blouse so springlike, and, all of sudden, Anna wondered what Michelle had looked like. She'd never seen a picture of her.

"Why don't you say something?" Anna asked. "Say something! Please! Where . . . where are they?"

"Where are who . . . what?" Mrs. Milowicz asked.

"Micha told her she lives here," Linda explained. "It sounds like a white lie. Mrs. Milowicz has been asking her for her address so she could speak with Micha's mother, and this is where she's ended up."

"That's . . . all?" Anna asked.

Mrs. Milowicz nodded and blew a crumb from her spring-green blouse. "I'm worried about her. Her brother, who seems to take care of her, well he's . . . well, he's a little scary, to be honest. I find him a bit threatening. And the way he shields his little sister from . . . everyone . . . from me, for instance . . . in private, I mean . . . that is . . . I don't know. It's strange. But you'd know more. You know him. Your mother told me that . . . he might just make a bad impression . . . and that my worries are unnecessary."

Anna looked at Linda. Thank you, she thought. Thank you, thank you, thank you.

The light-green spring blouse wriggled into a light-green spring coat in the front hall. There was even a light-green spring hat made of felt and adorned with a blue flower. Micha's teacher was pretty in her spring clothes. Anna would've liked to have had such a teacher, back then, when she'd been six years old. Not anymore, though, she thought.

"I also planned to talk to Abel's teacher," Mrs. Milowicz said. "We had an appointment. But he didn't show up."

"No," said Anna.

And then the door shut behind her, behind the burst of light-green spring.

"Thank you," Anna said to Linda, aloud now. "Thank you, thank you, thank you."

"And what," Linda asked, "is going on now?"

It took her all afternoon to explain. The words were too hard to say. She almost wished that Gitta were there so that she could tell Linda; Gitta had no problem with hard words.

"Gitta would say . . ." she whispered in the end, "that he's a hustler."

"I'd use another word," Linda offered. "In the movies, he'd be known as a gigolo . . ."

"No," Anna said and looked down at the floor. "A gigolo is someone you call if you're a woman, someone who provides a service in a professional way and doesn't have a problem doing it . . . someone who may even have fun with you . . . especially in the movies. It's not so negative, is it? This is different. It's only guys, older guys. And we're talking about someone who's not gay. And I don't know when he started the whole thing. It's possible that he's been doing it for a long time . . . He's seventeen, Linda, like me . . . it's all so wrong. It's not so difficult to clench your teeth, he said, it's not so difficult . . ."

Linda tried to pull her into her arms, but Anna got up and stepped back. "I'm sorry," she whispered. "But please, don't touch me. Not now. I have to find him, Linda. I have to find him, but I don't know where to look anymore."

She stood at the window of her room for a long time and watched the drops fall outside. Right now, in the forest, she thought, the first anemones would be blossoming in the melting snow. She hadn't told Linda anything about the boathouse, and she never would. She'd never tell anybody.

When it was dark, Linda came in, silently as always, nearly invisible. "Anna," she said. "Just one thing. Your father . . . I'm not going to tell him anything about this. And maybe it's better if you don't either."

"Okay," Anna said. "Okay. Thanks. Linda, I . . . I'll go now. I don't know how many bars there are in the city, but I have to at least try to find him. He must be somewhere . . ."

"Do you want me to come with you?" Linda asked. She was serious.

Anna shook her head. "Tell Magnus that I've gone out with Gitta."

Strange, she thought, when she left the house. Hadn't it always been the other way around? Tell Linda that I'm fine . . . tell Linda that she doesn't have to worry . . . let's not tell Linda about it, she'll just be alarmed. Nothing seemed to stay the way it had been since she had met Abel. He still didn't answer the phone.

He wasn't there. He was nowhere. He'd vanished, dissolved, disappeared into thin air, melted away like the snow in the thaw. She'd never been in so many bars in a single night. She hadn't known that there were so many. Students' town, she thought. She wouldn't study here; she hadn't ever planned to, but today it had become an impossibility. She had to leave this place as soon as possible. She had to leave it and go far, far away.

After a while, she got better at walking into a bar and looking over the heads in the crowd as if searching for someone. Well, she was . . . she was searching for someone. She forced herself to ask. People knew him, of course. Some of them gave her a smile of pity. *Poor little girl*, was written in their faces, *you're searching for that guy? You don't think he's waiting for you, do you? What kind of adventure do you think you're having?* She wondered how many of them knew. Did the whole city know more than she did? The part of the city that existed beyond well-lit school desks . . . beyond the blue air and the robins in nice little backyard gardens . . . far away from the freshly painted, sleek fronts of old, renovated houses?

It was after two when she reached the student dining hall. The student dining hall offered music on Thursday and Saturday nights, but today was Monday . . . still, she heard music spilling out onto the street. Obviously, there was some kind of party going on down there, some kind of unscheduled event. She was tired. She wanted to go home. She would have just walked past the dining hall, but somebody called her name. Gitta. And suddenly, she was thankful for Gitta's presence. She drifted through the darkness toward her, as if she were a safety buoy.

Gitta was standing in the black night in her black clothes, smoking. Next to her were a group of other smokers whom Anna didn't know. Gitta said something to them, put an arm around Anna's shoulders, and walked her a couple of paces away.

"Little lamb," she said. "I fucked up. I was too late. I'm sorry."

Hadn't she lost Gitta? Or had Gitta forgiven her for not letting her in, for shutting the door in her face, for hardly talking to her anymore . . . ?

"I should have been faster," Gitta went on. "He'd just said his last insane sentence when I got to the secretary's office. I was so mad, I knocked him down. Don't you ever get mad?"

"Yes," Anna said. "Often. Much too often. You knew about it already, didn't you?"

"About Abel?" She drew on her cigarette. "Possibly. Is that important?"

"Yes," Anna said. "It's important because you didn't tell me.

Gitta . . . thank you. But it doesn't change anything. I'm here because I'm looking for him. To tell him it doesn't change anything."

"Don't you go and say 'I love him' now or I'll start crying," Gitta said. Then she hugged Anna, her cigarette in her outstretched hand, and her face seemed indeed to be wet.

"You haven't found him, have you?" she asked, her voice a little hoarser than usual.

"No."

Gitta pointed to the black hulk of the student dining hall with her cigarette. "Try in there, my little lamb."

At first, they didn't want to let her in. The bouncers wanted to see her ID. Anna didn't have it with her, of course, but she was eighteen . . . This was ridiculous . . . She was looking for someone, damn it . . . Could she just take a look to see if he was there? No, she didn't have any beverages in her bag that she planned to consume inside the club. What was all the fuss about? She covered her face with her hands for a moment, took a deep breath, went up to one of the bouncers, stood on her toes, and kissed him . . . on the cheek, but still. "Thank you so much," she whispered. "Thanks for letting me in."

She felt his eyes following her. He hadn't planned to let her in. She disappeared into the crowd of sweating bodies trying to get rid of—or get into—jackets and coats near the door. There was a single room in which you could dance; chaos ruled the long bar; the old tables and benches along the wall were filled with sweaters, glasses, beer bottles, and more bodies. It took her a while to get used to the darkness, which was pierced and flecked by the shimmering light of a disco ball. The music was as loud as a construction site. She felt the bass in the soles of her feet, in the tips of her fingers, in the roots of her hair. The outlines of the bodies around her melted into one another; black light interrupted, broke, shattered the images into a thousand tiny pieces of a puzzle she would never complete. On one bench, she saw a couple kissing, but she couldn't find them again moments later. Had it just been two jackets? It was impossible to find anyone in this confusion. Why had Gitta told her to look in here? Was he here? Had she seen him? Why hadn't Gitta joined her?

Because, she thought, if I find him, I have to find him on my own. And then she did. She found him.

He was sitting in the far corner, on a bench behind a table stacked with jackets and sweaters. It was stupid, but the thing that caught her eye was his black woolen hat. First, she hadn't thought it was him. There were dozens of people with black woolen hats like his. But when she squeezed her way through people and chairs around the table and sat down next to him, she could see that it was him. He was sitting there, leaning against the wall behind him. For a moment, she thought he was asleep. He wasn't. His eyes were open, staring at the blob of bodies on the dance floor. It looked as if the earplugs of his Walkman had just slid out of his ears, as if he'd tried to listen to white noise even in here—or maybe to the incomprehensible words of the old Canadian—but then given up. He was still wearing his military parka, despite the unbearable heat, and holding a half-empty bottle of beer.

She put her hand on his, and only then did he take note of her and turn his head, with unnatural slowness. Something like a smile appeared on his face. It was a bitter smile, bitter like his voice on Bertil's recording.

"So?" he said, and she leaned over to hear him through the noise. "So, did you come to talk to the outlaw?" Something was wrong with his voice . . . it wasn't just bitter. "That's what it is, right?" he went on. "A . . . a beautiful story. The princess and the outlaw. The underdog. The pariah." He spat the words into her face, and now he was laughing. "How come the best . . . the best descriptions come from India, country of castes?"

"It's you who knows about words, not me," Anna answered. "And right now, you're talking nonsense! Abel! I've been searching for you! I've been searching for you all day!"

"Search . . . for someone else," Abel said. His voice was still strangely slow, and then Anna saw that there was something wrong with his eyes as well. The ice in them had eaten up the pupils; the thaw had set in everywhere, she thought; the hole in the ice had grown bigger and bigger, but here, in Abel's eyes, the opposite seemed to have occurred. The dark windows of his pupils were nearly frozen over.

"Shit," she said. "What did you take?"

His hand moved through the air, a gesture meaning nothing and everything. He put his beer bottle on the table, an exercise that seemed to require maximum concentration. "Is that . . . important?"

Anna grabbed his shoulders and started to shake him, and he just let her. There was no tension under her hands; he was a bundle of clothes. "You said you don't take the stuff you're selling!" she shouted against the noise of the music. "You said . . ."

"Let go of me, princess," he said with a weird smile that she didn't like. "Said, said. Did you actually believe me?"

"Yes!" Anna shouted. "I did! I did believe you, you idiot!"

"It was true, too," he said, and suddenly, he found enough strength to slap away her hands. He knocked the beer bottle over in the process, and the beer leaked out onto the table. He seemed not to realize, and he put his arms in the puddle on the table and his head on top of them as he'd done on the mornings he'd slept through literature class. Finally, he turned his head to face her, his changed eyes meeting hers. "True," he repeated. "It was true. I told you . . . I can't afford to lose my head . . . with Micha . . . but now it doesn't matter anymore. Not one bit."

He put his face back onto his arms, as if to leave her, to walk away, but she wouldn't let him, she was shaking him again. "Where is she?" she shouted. "Where's Micha?"

"At home," he answered. "In bed. We were . . . we went on an outing . . . and now she's in bed, sleeping. What did you think? Did you think I stopped looking after her?"

"If nothing matters anymore?"

He tried to focus on her but didn't quite manage. "Go away," he said. "Leave me alone. What do you want?"

"To bring you home."

"Forget it," he said and got up. He was unsteady . . . holding onto the table. "Leave me alone." He pointed to a collection of empty bottles, letting himself fall back onto the bench. "See, I've got company. Ha."

She moved closer, so close their shoulders touched. She didn't want to shout anymore to be heard. He smelled like beer. She still didn't know what he'd taken, but he was right, of course. It didn't matter. He'd given up.

"I don't know if this will get through to you," she said. "Probably not. But in the event you've forgotten it tomorrow, I'll just say it again then. I've been searching for you, because I wanted to tell you that Bertil didn't achieve anything with his announcement. He could have saved himself the trouble of recording your conversation. I know something now that I didn't know before. So what?"

"But everybody . . . everybody knows everything," Abel murmured. "Now. No, everybody knows nothing. Nobody knows anything. Nobody knows everything . . ."

"Can you hear yourself talking? Does it make sense?"

"What does make sense in life, anyway?" he asked. "Go away, princess. Leave your outlaw alone. You won't . . . you won't change him."

"I'm not going anywhere without you," Anna said decisively.

"God, look how they're dancing!" he said, as if he hadn't heard her. "How they're dancing! Isn't it insane? The world is turning the wrong way around, and they don't notice . . . they're just dancing! Do you want to know how the fairy tale continues?"

"Yes," she said, "please." And she leaned her head on his shoulder, where his jacket was wet with spilled beer, and watched the dancing . . . they were dancing . . . it was insane, true enough.

"The little queen and her crew saw the mainland . . . that evening," Abel began, haltingly, stumbling over the words, tripping, falling, like a child learning to walk. But he got up each time he fell, and then the words came quicker. "And they cheered and hugged each other. 'It won't be long now!' the rose girl said. 'Maybe we'll reach it tonight!' the little queen exclaimed. 'Where is the weapon?' the asking man asked; 'soon,' the answering man answered, but this time it was obviously the wrong question and the right answer. High above them the silver-gray seagull shrieked, her shriek a shrill warning, and at first they didn't understand. They raced on their skates, toward the dark mass of land. And then the gull shrieked again, louder, and they came to a halt quite abruptly. One step ahead of them, the ice ended. They saw now how strong the ice was. It was nearly three inches thick, but then it suddenly stopped. Between the mainland and the edge, there was a wide stream, a roaring river of water that had been snow not long ago, an insurmountable monster of ice-cold water.

"They took off the skates and stood there at the edge of the ice silently. The silver-gray seagull landed in front of them, inclined her head, and squinted at them. The pupils in her golden eyes had nearly vanished, as if she were turning blind like the white cat. Maybe the wind up there above the sea had been too cold. The little queen bent down to pet the gull's feather coat, but it was the silver-gray dog again, and her hand touched fur. He pressed against her legs, as if he was trying to find shelter from the cold, and then he barked loud and bared his teeth. He had sharp teeth, teeth like a wolf. The little queen followed his gaze, and the rose girl turned, too.

" 'Here she comes,' she whispered. 'The cutter with her sparkling tools. We have to swim.'

"But the raging current was too strong, too powerful.

" 'We will swim,' said the little queen. 'But if we swim, we will die. And I still don't know what death is like. Our journey was so long, and I've met so many people, and nobody, not a single soul, has explained death to me.' "

"And?" Anna asked. "What happened then?"

"There's no *then*," Abel said, turning the beer bottle upside down, and a last drop fell down onto the table.

"But that's not the end of the story," Anna said. "The end takes place the day after tomorrow. Till then, we'll find a way to get across the water. The sea lion can swim. He's a strong swimmer. Come on."

She took his arm and pulled him up, wanting to pull him with her, get him out of that corner, pull him around the table—and that was the moment he found his strength a second time. This time, he really did find it. He pushed her away . . . she staggered back and held onto a chair so as not to fall; she saw how he lifted his right arm as if to hit her. She ducked. There was no blow. He stood there looking at her for a second, arms hanging limply by his side, then he sank back onto the bench and closed his eyes. "Go away, Anna," he said once more, in a voice too low to hear. She read the words on his lips, "Go away now. Far away. And don't ever come back. The fairy tale doesn't have a happy ending."

She left. She left him alone, alone with the dancing crowd, where you could be lonelier than anyplace else.

"Little lamb," Gitta said when she met her in the lobby of the dining hall, "didn't you find him?"

"No," Anna said. "I'll find him tomorrow. Tomorrow, when he's sober again and has had some sleep."

"Yes, do," Gitta said, and Anna saw that Hennes was standing behind her.

"Yes, do," he repeated and pushed the red hair out of his face with that unbearable gesture. He was holding a glass, and the color of the liquid in the glass was beautiful, and the glass was beautiful, and the hand was slender and beautiful. Look, she thought, how they're dancing. Insane. "Anna!" Hennes said. "Wait! What Bertil did today . . . that conversation he recorded . . . I . . . I'm really . . . if I say anything now . . ."

"Then it will only be wrong," Anna said. "Go, Hennes. Take Gitta inside and dance with her."

That night she did not dream of flames. She dreamed of Ludwigsburg. Of the pines creaking in the snowstorm. And she knew who'd followed her. Who'd scared her.

"I passed you already," Bertil had said. "I just had to find a place to turn the car . . ."

She hadn't seen him come toward her from the big road, hadn't seen him drive by, because he hadn't. In her dream, she saw the three snow-covered cars in the parking lot, behind the restaurant, near the beach, at the very end of the little lane. And suddenly, she was sure one of them had been a Volvo. And suddenly, she thought she remembered the panting of a dog between the pines. And suddenly, she heard Gitta say again, don't believe everything you hear. Gitta hadn't told Bertil that she'd seen Anna ride out to Ludwigsburg. Oh no. He'd followed her. He'd followed her to Abel's apartment back then—somebody has to look after you, he'd said, more than you think—and had kept following her, creeping after her. He'd scared her on purpose, out there, in the woods, so that he could save her.

He'd let her go ahead, let her push her bike through the storm, for a long, long time, until she was exhausted enough to let him rescue her. He'd been waiting, lurking . . . that was why the car hadn't been warm—he'd been driving for only a few minutes. Of course. Of course. Of course.

When she awoke, it was late morning, nearly noon. She must

have slept hard. Outside the window, in the yard, the snow had nearly melted. The sun was shining in a new and golden way. She dressed hurriedly.

She knew what she had to do. Right now.

She'd go out to the woods, to the Elisenhain, to see if the anemones were already there, their little blossoms peeking through the leftover snow. And she had the feeling she'd find some. The feeling they'd be waiting for her. The anemones . . . and spring itself. She'd pick a bunch of them, a bunch of tiny white flowers, and then she'd ring Abel and Micha's doorbell, and they would have breakfast together, a very late breakfast. And Abel and she would talk about everything. Since she'd known him, life had been a roller coaster, up and down. At one moment she was shouting in triumph, at another she was sunk in despair—even old Goethe had known the feeling—and this was a day for shouting in triumph. A day on which everything could and would be explained—and settled. A day made to talk about the future, a future in which he'd no longer have to do what he'd done to earn money. She'd tie him to a chair and slap him with Magnus's money if she had to.

She knew a good place for anemones, the best; it was near that place where Micha's invisibles lived, by the hazelnut bushes. She'd tell Micha that the invisibles had melted away with the snow.

That they didn't exist in spring.

It was high time spring came. It was the twelfth of March.

17

Michelle
ॐ

THE WOODS WERE IN FLOWER—THEY WERE BLOS-
soming!

There was still snow between the high gray trunks of the
beeches, silver-gray, Anna thought, but between the last patches of
cold, new patches of white had come into being, as well as a few
yellow and violet patches. Cowslips, liverworts, and of course her
anemones—such a difficult word for such a tiny flower.

The path was muddy and brown. In some places, she sank up to
her ankles, her boots getting caught in the marsh, and she laughed.
Winter was over.

She left the path. She walked into the mud, into where it was
the deepest, and spun around beneath the trees with her arms
outstretched. She saw the hem of her winter coat fly like the hem of
a dress . . . She had Linda's old Cohen LPs in her backpack. And the
flute. She had plans. She had great plans.

Micha could learn to play the flute if she wanted to. Or the

piano. The house of blue air was too big and the apartment at 18
Amundsen Street too small. They could move. And once Micha
was settled in . . . maybe Abel would leave town with Anna, go
somewhere, anywhere, to study. Someplace nobody knew him and
nobody knew her, and they could visit Micha, all the time. But now
that the snow was melting so fast, maybe he'd see certain things in
a different light. And tomorrow, he'd be eighteen. From tomorrow
on, he wouldn't have to fear that someone could take Micha away.
She hoped it would be as he thought. She could have asked Magnus.
Magnus knew about things like that, law-related things, but she
hadn't asked. She'd feared his answer. No, she told herself, Abel
is probably right. From tomorrow on, everything will be all right.
We'll reach the mainland. It's so close already.

She passed a hunting blind, its four wooden supports standing in
the mud like the legs of a giant creature stuck fast, and suddenly she
thought of Bertil. These were the grounds where his father hunted.
Maybe he'd been sitting in this blind not long ago, a gun propped
up next to him. Did his father allow him to shoot, even though he
didn't have his license yet? Now that the ground was thawing, the
deer were sure to come out of their hiding places. She saw their
footprints in the mud; here, the animals weren't shy. Gitta had told
her that sometimes the deer and wild boar crossed Wolgaster Street
and wandered into the yards in her housing development, where
they ate the young sprouts off the bushes.

Something was rustling behind her, and she turned around.
She didn't feel like meeting a wild boar out here or, worse, a sow—
when did they have their young? Now everything was quiet again.
Probably just a bird looking for worms among the dry leaves. She
could hear the first blackbirds and tomtits. It must have been a bird.

She returned to the path, the one she'd run along with Abel and Micha. She ducked and slipped through the still-bare branches of the hazelnut bushes, their buds almost green at the tips, about to open, to spill new life, new leaves into the world. Here . . . here was the fork in the path. Behind it, there weren't any invisibles now, in spring.

Last spring, she'd picked flowers with Gitta here, in this very spot. Really. With Gitta, who'd never admit now that she picked flowers in the forest like a little girl. This was the best place in the whole of the Elisenhain. Anna parted the thicket. The narrow path was covered in deer tracks: deer and wild boar. She came out on the other side and stood in front of a vandalized stretch of mud. There weren't any anemones left here, not this spring. The wild boars had really done a good job. She smiled. There would be enough anemones elsewhere in the forest.

But why, she wondered, why had they searched for food here, where there weren't even many beeches? Strange. She wanted to walk around the trampled earth . . . and then she saw that the wild boars had been trying to unearth something. Something was there, in the mud, something multicolored—red and blue, fabric. There was the rustling sound again, a ways off, but still uncomfortably close. She looked up. Hadn't the branches of that tree over there just moved? No. She was beginning to imagine things. Her imagination was still caught somewhere in Ludwigsburg, between the pines, in the middle of a blizzard. "But that was in the winter," she whispered, "that was ages ago. Because now . . . now, spring is here. Back then, I was scared . . . but now . . ."

Now, all of a sudden, she was scared again. She stepped toward the hole the wild boars had made. Clothes. There were clothes under the mud, clothes someone must have thrown away . . . a red shirt, a blue raincoat . . . she kneeled, close to the pit, too close. Hair, there was hair in the mud, long strands of tangled hair. A doll, she prayed . . . please, God, I haven't prayed since I was a child in church on Christmas, but please, please . . . listen to me . . . please, let it be a doll.

She realized that she was shivering. Her teeth shattered uncontrollably, as if she had a high fever. She forced herself to take a branch, to free the clothes of leaves and sticks with it, to scrape the earth away. Look, look . . . don't look away . . . you've got to look now. There weren't only clothes. Of course not. Not only. There, under the earth, lay the body of a woman. It might have been lying there a long time or might have been buried hours ago. She couldn't see it that clearly; everything was smeared with mud. And she was thankful for that, thankful that she couldn't see the face beneath the layers of mud. The woman lay on her back—she could see that. Long blond hair . . . she thought of Micha's teacher. Micha's teacher, Mrs. Milowicz, the cutter, who wanted to form and thereby destroy the diamond—or so Abel thought. Mrs. Milowicz, with her spring-green coat. Maybe she owned a blue coat as well, or had owned one—she was the only one who'd followed the little queen to the end. She was her last threat. Everybody else had either been killed or fled. Anna leaned forward. The branch she held found a hand, though it was barely recognizable as a hand. Even in the earth beneath the snow, there were insects at work, microorganisms, time. This body had been here for more than a day. Anna averted her eyes. She felt sick and cold. There'd been something, something that had attracted her attention . . . she looked again. And suddenly, she knew. It was the fact that the woman had been buried on her back, as if someone hadn't so much disposed of her as buried her. And then, she discovered something else. Something lay next to the body, something that might once have been placed on the dead woman's breast: two thin planks of plywood, like parts of a fruit crate, held together with a simple piece of cloth, now half-decayed. It looked as if it had been ripped off something else; had it once displayed a pattern of flowers? She knew this flower pattern, blue and white . . . she'd seen it before . . . but where? The cloth held the planks together in the shape of a cross.

Anna pulled the cross out of the hole without touching the body or the clothes. She wasn't cold anymore, she was sweating. Her heart racing, the forest spinning around her head. Someone had written big letters onto the planks, with a black marker. Letters, words, now nearly faded away into nothingness. But that wasn't true, of course. She could read the letters. The cold had conserved the neat block letters. They looked as if it had been very important to someone that they be readable.

MICHELLE TANNATEK

12.4.1975 – 14.2.2012

Anna's brain started calculating like a machine: nineteen. She hadn't yet celebrated her nineteenth birthday when she'd had Abel. She'd died at the age of thirty-six.

Anna closed her eyes, and what she saw among the leaves and the twigs and the mud wasn't a dead body but a white cat. She was blind and asleep, sound asleep. One of the answers the answering man had repeatedly given came to her mind: under the beeches, where the anemones grow in spring. The asking man must have asked the right question at least once, but not at the right time: where is Michelle?

She hadn't ever left on a trip.

Or maybe she had, on a very, very long one . . .

"Why?" Anna whispered. "Why did you do that? *Did* you do that?"

She opened her eyes, got up, realized that she was still dizzy, and staggered back. Then she doubled over and threw up. In her head, everything was tumbling into and onto each other—thoughts, words, sentences from the fairy tale. It had started with the doll, the doll she'd found under the sofa in the student lounge. Mrs. Margaret. Mrs. Margaret wore a white dress with a pattern of blue flowers. The hem of Mrs. Margaret's dress was frayed, as if someone had torn off a piece of it. What for? For some kind of souvenir? For a greeting? And had he then tried to lose Mrs. Margaret so that he wouldn't have to explain anything to Micha? Michelle couldn't see that souvenir anymore, couldn't ever understand the greeting. She was too fast asleep to ever wake up again.

What else had the answering man said? All these senseless answers he'd given, so a few of them hadn't been senseless. Remember, Anna, remember, that he's been telling you the truth all this time . . . without telling you the truth. There was another answer that was given again and again . . . in the box on the bathroom cupboard. Then she remembered the asking man's last question, also asked seemingly out of context: where is the weapon?

She saw Abel standing in the bathroom again, searching for a Band-Aid, the box in his hand, angry that she'd followed him there instead of waiting in the living room. "No," she whispered. "No, I . . . I don't want this. I don't want this to be true. I . . . I was so sure . . ."

And then she thought of Micha's teacher. The last pursuer of the little queen. She dialed Linda's number as she hurried back through the forest, stumbling, running.

"Hello."

"Linda, it's me. Have you got Micha's teacher's telephone number? Did she leave her number?"

"No, I . . ."

"Linda, you've gotta get it. Right now. It's important. Call her. Tell her she has to be careful. No. Tell her not to leave her apartment. Tell her . . ."

"Anna, what's the matter? Where are you? Weren't you going to visit Abel? Has something happened?"

"Yes. No. I'm on my way there now. Call the teacher, Linda. Please. Do it now."

Her hands were shaking so much she almost couldn't unlock her bike. You could open the lock anyway, without knowing the combination, Abel had said that. But she, she couldn't do that. She lived in a different world, and he'd been right about everything. *Go away, princess. Leave your outlaw alone. You won't change him . . . go away, Anna, far away, and don't ever come back. The fairy tale doesn't have a happy ending.* He'd warned her. He'd warned her the whole time, exactly as he'd done in the boathouse. And she hadn't listened to him. Why had he warned her? Had he loved her despite everything? And what did that even mean, despite everything? Was a murderer able to love? She wasn't certain. She wasn't 100 percent certain, and she had to be certain, or else she'd never believe it. She couldn't tell anyone if she wasn't certain. *You're crazy,* a small, reasonable voice said inside her. *You'll ride home now, little lamb . . . You'll call the police, and then you'll go home as quickly as you can. Heavens!*

Wasn't that Gitta? Gitta's voice of reason in her head. Gitta of all people! She nearly laughed.

So what're you gonna do, little lamb? Ask him? Just straight out?

No. No, I'm not that stupid, Gitta. I'm going to go to the bathroom and look through the contents of the box on top of the cupboard.

And then? When you've done that? When you've found out? What then?

Anna didn't answer Gitta's last question, and Gitta wasn't there anyway.

Her head was strangely light when she reached Amundsen Street; her feet weren't touching the ground, as if she were moving along in a dream. Not a nice dream.

The door to tower number 18 was open. She kicked one of the empty beer bottles in the stairwell, to make Mrs. Ketow come to the door and stick her head out and listen, so that someone would know that she was upstairs. But how much help could she expect from Mrs. Ketow? When she rang the doorbell on the fourth floor, she was ice-cold again, shivering, her body temperature seemed to be shifting rapidly between hot and cold . . . maybe she did have a fever after all.

The door opened. Anna's heart was beating with such force that the roar filled her head completely.

"Hi, Anna!" said Micha. "Abel isn't here."

Anna breathed in and breathed out again. "Can I come in anyway?"

"Sure," said Micha. "I'm just reading a book. I can read a book all by myself now, or almost. It's difficult, but it's exciting, too. There's this dog . . . Did he tell you that they're standing in front of a stream now? I mean, in the fairy tale? I wonder how they'll get over it. If there's a way."

"I don't know if there's a way," Anna replied and wrapped her arms around Micha and hugged her very tightly. "I really don't know."

"Hey, you're crushing me!" Micha said as she slipped out of Anna's arms, laughing. "I've gotta go read now. About the dog."

And then she disappeared into her room, disappeared into the story of a dog, a different dog, one that wasn't silver-gray. Anna remembered how Bertil had told them about a kind of silver-gray dog: a Weimaraner. It was a Weimaraner. He had become too sharp. Too dangerous. He'd attacked a jogger. He'd thought he was saving his family . . . Abel was that dog. If it was all true . . .

"Micha?" she called, taking off her shoes in the hall. "Where is he?"

"He went to buy something!" Micha called back. "He'll be back in a minute! I have to keep reading!"

Anna didn't take off her coat. She went to the bathroom and shut the door behind her. The box was sitting on top of the bathroom cupboard. It wouldn't mean anything, she thought, if she didn't find something. He could have stored the weapon somewhere else, or even be carrying it with him. She had to stand on her toes to reach the box. She put it on the dresser next to the sink, a dresser Abel had painted green and Micha had decorated with a yellow flower. She opened the lid of the box.

Packages of pills. Loads of packages. Not the ones he sold . . . Children's Tylenol. Dramamine. Rohypnol . . . maybe that was something he sold? Teddy-bear Band-Aids. A thermometer. Cotton balls. She took a deep breath. She pushed aside a few blister packs.

The box was deep. And beneath all the silvery foil of the blister packs, there was something black.

A gun.

Her heartbeat grew loud again. She felt it in her toes now, like she'd felt the bass in the dining hall the other night. She took the gun out of the box. She didn't know anything about guns. About weapons in general. She stood in front of the mirror and tried to hold it the right way. It looked ridiculous in her hands. She put it back in the box. And she would have pushed the blister packs over it again.

But at that very moment, the bathroom door opened.

The door of the apartment must have been opened first . . . there must have been footsteps in the hall. Her heartbeat had been too loud for her to hear them. She took a step back.

"Anna," said Abel.

Bertil hadn't ever climbed down from a hunting blind that fast before. With each rung of the ladder, his binoculars swung against his chest. In his head, there was only one word, and that was a name: Anna. Anna, Anna, Anna. He'd given up following her around. He'd been an idiot. What he'd done in that snowstorm had been stupid—stupid and dangerous. He should never have scared her on purpose. The announcement at school had been even more stupid.

And suddenly, he wondered why he was alive.

If what he'd suspected all along was true, then Tannatek had no problem shooting people. He couldn't imagine it. How it felt to shoot someone. He'd never told anyone, but whenever his father fired at an animal in the forest, he looked away. He was a coward. He knew it. The only thing he could shoot at was the bull's-eye on a target. Hennes was different. Hennes was perfect. Hennes went hunting with his father for real, and he had a hunting license. He didn't have glasses that slid down his nose. He could have any girl he wanted . . . any girl but Anna, that is. Not that Hennes had wanted Anna. But it was Tannatek, of all people, who'd got her in the end. Wasn't that strange? Bertil'd been following her for so long—and following Tannatek, too. He'd found out so many things but not enough.

He'd almost stopped. Now, he was glad that he hadn't, glad that he'd followed her out here as well. He felt nauseated when he kneeled next to the pit the wild boars had made. He'd never seen a dead body before. Anna probably hadn't either, he thought. His glasses were slipping again. He didn't need to read the name on the wooden cross to know whose body it was, but he read it anyway. Then he dialed the police. But where would he tell them to go? Here?

Where was Anna? Had she gone home? Had she gone to the police herself? He hadn't followed her out of the thicket. He'd let her leave on her own. A mistake, Bertil, he told himself, an unforgivable mistake.

So he'd tell them to come here first. They wouldn't believe him anyway if they didn't see this.

She couldn't say anything. She just stood there, in the middle of the tiny bathroom, motionless. She watched his blue eyes wander. Their pupils were back to their normal size, but he looked tired. Exhausted. He looked like someone finished up. He was carrying a plastic shopping bag. His eyes, his bleary ice-blue eyes, slid from Anna to the green dresser next to the sink to the open cardboard box to the shining black of the weapon inside. His movement was so fast she didn't even really see it. He let go of the bag. Then he was leaning against the doorframe, the gun in his hand. He was playing around with it—like people do in the movies.

He looked at the weapon. He looked at Anna.

"So," he said.

She was still mute with fear. Scream, Anna, she thought. Scream for your damn life. Downstairs, Mrs. Ketow is eavesdropping . . . She couldn't scream.

He nodded as if she'd asked him something. "Yes, Anna. Yes, I know how to shoot. Self-taught, I'd say. The guy they nicked for the first murder, do you remember? The guy who was trading weapons? He'd sold me this gun, a while back. He must have forgotten he did because he didn't tell anyone. But it explains why he had another like it." He'd been speaking in a low voice, low enough to keep Micha from hearing his words.

She realized that she'd kept her voice low, too. Where had she found her voice? And if she'd found it again, why didn't she speak louder?

"I found Michelle's grave, Abel. The grave in the forest."

He nodded. "The thaw."

"The wild boars have been digging there, in the mud." Why did she tell him? To gain time? Time to do what? "She never called. She never withdrew money. She's been lying in the earth out there the whole time."

"Of course. I told you. The white cat is sleeping."

He was still playing with the weapon. "Micha . . . ," she began.

"Is asleep, too, by the way," he answered. "I just looked in on her. She fell asleep reading. That book about the dog." He smiled, and it wasn't a mean smile. It was a smile that she still liked a lot. The lines of a song appeared in her head, a song from Linda's LP collection:

> ... *it's written in the scriptures, it's written there in blood*
> *I even heard the angels declare it from above*
> *There ain't no cure there ain't no cure*
> *There ain't no cure for love* ...
> *All the rocket ships go flying through the sky*
> *The doctor's working day and night*
> *But they never ever find a cure for love* ...

"Tell me," she said. "Tell me the whole story. If you're going to shoot me, I at least want to know the story first."

"Are you crazy?" he asked.

"Yes," she said.

"You think I'd shoot you?"

"I do. I haven't believed any of this for a long time ... but now I do."

He looked at the gun. "Aren't you afraid?"

"Of course I am," Anna said. "Of course I'm afraid. But that doesn't help."

He shook his head. "No," he said, "it doesn't help to be afraid. Bad things happen anyway. You're right." He took a step toward her, into the bathroom, and she wanted to step back, but there was nowhere to go. There was a single chair in the tiny room, next to the shower; they'd thrown towels and clothes over the back of it. He sat down, heavily, weapon still in hand, his eyes on its shiny black.

"Back then, when Lierski was living here with us, it was the same," he said. "I was ten when he moved in—that was before Micha was born. I always knew he'd get me one day when I was alone. I was afraid, but it didn't help to be afraid. Michelle didn't believe me. She'd finally met a man who wanted to stay . . . Strange, next to nothing has changed in the apartment since then. The first time anything happened was here, in the bathroom. In this exact spot. On some days I find it hard to believe that the bathroom just went on existing afterward. As if nothing had happened . . ."

"What he did to you, I mean, did he . . . ?"

"Of course. You don't have to say it. It doesn't help to call a spade a spade. She still didn't believe me afterward. She said I was making things up. It took her a long time to throw him out. When he left, I was twelve." He looked up, only for a second, and then averted his eyes. "Do you understand? Do you understand why I shot him? It wasn't revenge. It was because of Micha. I didn't want the same thing to happen to her. I don't think he cared whether he had boys or girls—as long as they were young. There were so many people who knew about him . . . there was a lot of talk . . . you can go and ask at the Admiral . . . but nobody had any proof, and nobody did anything. And maybe a few of those guys at the Admiral even know it was me who killed him, but they've kept their mouths shut. We know each other . . . out there."

She leaned back against the wall. The wall was colder than anything else had been this winter. The wall had been here back then, too. Tiles, she thought, easy to wipe clean, to sterilize. All the misery of the world focused in a tiny bathroom on the fourth floor. So that was what the night in the boathouse had been about.

"You said something about clenching your teeth, to Bertil . . ."

"Does that make sense to you? It's got something to do with the inhibition threshold, I think. If Rainer Lierski hadn't already done what he did to me, I'd never have said yes later . . . one night at a club, a guy propositioned me. It was a long time after Lierski. I don't know how old I was. Maybe fifteen? Don't ask me now what I was doing in a club at fifteen. I guess the ID wasn't mine. You might not believe it now, but I was quite a pretty boy then. Blue eyes . . . blond curls. My hair was longer then . . . that was before the buzz cut." He laughed. "That night, I suddenly understood that you could get money for doing it. That you didn't have to suffer without payment. It was a revelation. What happened to me had already happened—there was no way to undo it—and I'd survived. I'd survived two years in this apartment with Lierski. And I knew that I would survive anything else, too. I mean, I *did* survive. Later on, it wasn't clubs anymore. There are different places, places everybody knows about . . . they drive out to the parking lot at the B109, in the woods, when they want to hook up . . . damn far on a bike, but it's not such a bad job after all, doing this from time to time. It's . . ." He stopped. He did what he always did: he covered his face with his hands. But to do so, he had to put the gun down. It lay next to him now, on the chair he was sitting on.

That was Anna's chance. All she had to do was to step forward, to snatch the gun. She didn't. She stayed where she was.

"I hate them," Abel said, his face still behind his hands. "I hate all of them. Every single guy."

He looked at her again, picked up the gun. Chance squandered, Anna Leemann.

"I thought Marinke was someone I could offer a deal to," he said. "I followed him . . . Jesus. I mean, who goes for a walk on the beach in Eldena at night? It was as if he wanted something to happen. Maybe he was looking for adventure, something different from his life at the office. There he was, with his leather jacket and his I-understand-you, you-can-call-me-Sören look . . . he looked so gay. But I was mistaken. I offered to go with him, to do it for free, to do whatever he wanted, if he'd just forget about Micha and Michelle. I misjudged him. He gave me a look of contempt, spat out in front of me. So this is how it is, he said. Forget it, boy, and while we're talking about fucking . . . what about your sister? Am I wrong, or do you love her a little too much? That's when I decided he had to die. He really believed that. That I would do that to Micha. It was easier the second time. Like it was with the other thing. The inhibition threshold drops. If you shoot one person, the second one is a game. He was a coward, by the way. He turned voluntarily . . ." He shook his head. "No, that's not true. That's a lie. It wasn't easier."

He rolled up his left sleeve. Anna counted three circular scars next to the long one. One more than last time.

"One for each of them," Abel whispered. "These are scars of pity. I had to do something afterward. Something I'd feel . . . maybe not even out of pity but more for me, so I'd know I still exist in spite of everything . . . ridiculous, isn't it? Like a child pounding its head against a wall. This is Lierski. And Marinke. And that is Knaake."

"Knaake," Anna repeated, her voice flat. "Why, Abel? Why did you do that?"

"He was finding out stuff," he replied. "He was following me. I told you that. He took a step back, onto the ice in the shipping channel, to escape the bullet that I hadn't even shot. I saw him fall through the ice . . . I called the fire department from a pay phone—it was the only number I could think of to call. I suddenly felt I just couldn't do this anymore. I didn't want him to die. He was a traitor, but I liked him. I . . . I really hope he makes it . . . I wish . . ."

For a moment, it was silent, the silence echoing and reechoing from the tiled walls of the bathroom, like the pain and fear of a small boy a long time ago.

"Bertil?" Anna asked.

"What about Bertil?"

"Is he still alive?"

"Of course he's alive. Why would I do anything to Bertil?"

"After what he did yesterday . . ."

"You don't get it, Anna. This is not about me. It's about Micha. Bertil's a different story. He's never been any threat to Micha. If he'd started figuring out the truth about the murders . . . then, well . . . but he wasn't even interested. He was only interested in this other thing, and that he figured out—as the whole school knows. I was stupid to talk to him. But I'm tired, Anna. I've had it."

"And . . . Michelle?"

"Michelle. Michelle. Everything started with her."

"But there's no scar on your arm for Michelle. Or is she the long one? But that one came later, didn't it . . . ?"

"The long scar," Abel said and smiled again, "that's you, Anna. What happened in the boathouse was worse than anything else. I did to you what Lierski did to me. I didn't want to. I just . . . how do you say it? I just lost control. It happens. Some things are just too much. But I don't have a scar for Michelle because I didn't kill her. That's simple."

"You didn't? Then who did?"

He stood up without letting go of the gun. He stood in front of her and looked down at her . . . he was taller than she was. "There was so much blood," he said. "Blood everywhere. On my hands, on her hands, on my shirt, her face, on the tiles, smeared in streaks, on

the small round blue carpet . . . I threw it away later, that carpet . . .
I hadn't known that blood was that red, that light red: big, fallen,
burst droplets of blood . . . the color of poppies. A sea of blood,
a red endless sea, purple waves, carmine froth, splashing color . . .
I remember that I thought all of this back then. Micha was still
sleeping. I was the one who found Michelle.

"She'd slit her wrists . . . long, deep cuts in both arms . . .
she'd wanted to make sure. Blind white cat. Self-centered beast.
She never thought of us, not for one minute. She ran away from
her own problems, her fucked-up life . . . the wrong guys, booze,
unemployment, drugs. We have an old bike trailer in the basement . . .
we used it to transport furniture and stuff we found in the trash
. . . I put her into the bike trailer and took her to the Elisenhain. She
loved the anemones so much. We used to go for walks there when
I was little, before Rainer Lierski . . . I was sure someone would see
me, stop me. I almost wanted somebody to. But nobody did. That
was the day the island sank, and the sea was red."

He fell silent. He lifted the gun and put it in his pocket.

"You really thought that I did it, didn't you?" he whispered.
"That I shot my mother? That I'd shoot you?"

"What are we going to do now?" Anna whispered.

"I don't know. You tell me. Everything's ending."

"No!" she whispered. "No. Not for me. Everything's just
beginning. We're seventeen."

She put her arms around him and hugged him as tightly as she
could.

"Are you trying to tell me that you'll stay? In spite of everything?"
he whispered. "Anna, I'm a murderer. I'm a murderer and a hustler
and a dealer. I'm everything that's unthinkable in your world."

"I am not staying with the murderer," she said, her words muffled by his jacket. "I am not staying with the victim Abel Tannatek or the culprit Abel Tannatek. I am staying with the storyteller."

She pulled him out of the bathroom, into the living room. She pulled him down on the sofa. She realized that she was crying again. She couldn't help it. She didn't know who started to kiss whom, but it was a desperate kiss, a kiss in front of the sharp edge where the ice had broken and the water was rushing by in an unpassable stream, separating them from the mainland.

"We'll find a solution," Anna whispered. "There is one. There must be one."

But first, something else seemed more important, and it happened as if it had to happen. The most improbable of all the things that could have happened. Maybe it happened because there was nothing standing between them anymore—no more secrets, no more lies, no mistrust, nothing. The torn, invisible cloak of pain was enveloping them both as it had done in that night in the house where the air was too blue. Anna felt Abel's hands under her T-shirt, careful, timid, hesitating, and she didn't force these hands to do anything this time. She gave them time. She thought about the white sails on the deck of the green ship whose name they'd only found out late in the story.

Everything was different from the dream. Much more complicated. Much more real.

She tried to get out of her clothes, got all tangled up in them, and laughed. And that, she knew, was all unreasonable Anna, as reasonable Anna had never done any of this. Reasonable Anna had left for good. Finally, they were sitting on the sofa naked, the two of them. She was on his lap, and she really, really did hope that

Micha was sleeping. And this, she thought, was the moment to say something about a condom, but she didn't . . . the inhibition threshold had dropped. K IS EacH Oth ER, she thought . . . letters on a window . . . she let her hands wander down, and she guided him, and it was surprisingly easy now . . . it was a gliding movement like skating over the ice . . . everything was easy . . . there was no pain . . . there was a rhythm they both shared, and she was leading . . . it was different from dancing, when the man leads the woman. She led his fingers to the right spot. And with her eyes closed, she saw the color green, not blue like his frozen eyes, but green . . . green like the ocean beneath the ice. She hadn't known sex had a color. The color created waves . . . foaming, frothing, whirling up, and everything was good, everything was right, and maybe, Anna thought, this color would cover everything else—the not-good, not-right things that had happened. The pain held in the tiles of a bathroom. The running footsteps in a boathouse. Bertil's announcement and its contents, the frantic fear that the same could happen to Micha. The wave of green, ocean color would break . . . right now, she could feel it . . .

"Anna," said Abel. She opened her eyes and looked at him, frozen in her movement.

"If something . . . if I can't be here anymore," he whispered, and Anna thought of the cold walls of court buildings and penal institutions and didn't want to think further, not now. "If I can't be here anymore . . . what will happen to Micha? She seems to love your mother . . ."

"My parents would adopt her," Anna said. "On the spot."

He nodded and closed his eyes, and she closed her eyes again, too, and seconds later, the green wave broke and washed over them.

Not exactly at the same time—exactly at the same time is always a lie—but the waves of the ocean in which they swam together followed one after the other. They stayed like this for a long time, sitting there, breathing each other's breath, in and out. They kept each other warm in the last cold of the winter. There was a solution, Anna thought again, a way out . . . if this became possible, then everything else was, too.

"Of course," Abel whispered. "Of course, there's a way out. I know it now."

And she wondered if he could feel her thoughts through her skin.

I am completely happy, she thought, hoping that he would feel this thought, too. At this moment, I'm completely happy, isn't that strange? Actually, it isn't strange at all. Ah, linger on, thou art so fair.

A car stopped in front of the house; they heard the engine and then voices, those of Mrs. Ketow and several men . . . hurried voices. There was something sharp in their voices, something dangerous— the edge of the ice and a raging current.

They stood up and went over to the window, still naked.

"Shit," Abel said in a low voice, "I didn't think they'd be that quick."

Two cars were parked in front of the house. One belonged to Magnus, the other to the police . . . a green and white police car, Anna thought—the ocean riders. Everything in Abel's fairy tale made sense.

She'd never gotten into her clothes faster. Everything was happening too fast now.

Abel hugged her again, for a very short moment. "There is a way

out," he repeated, and she didn't understand . . . she understood
nothing. She ran after him, into the hall . . . Micha emerged from
her room with sleepy eyes, the book about the dog in her hand. She
saw Abel rush out of the apartment . . . he didn't turn back to look
at Micha. There were policemen on the stairs, she could hear their
steps . . . maybe someone shouted something, shouted for her to
stand still, stay where she was . . . for Abel to stand still.

She stood by the front door, pressing Micha against her with one
arm. Abel wasn't running down the stairs, he was running up the
stairs . . . the stairs leading to the door of the attic that no one ever
used. There was a narrow landing in front of the attic door, where
Abel came to a halt.

Out of the corner of her eyes, Anna registered other people on
the stairs behind the policemen: her parents . . . and Bertil. She
didn't look down at them, she looked up at Abel. The policemen
had stopped on the fourth-floor landing, where Anna and Micha
were standing. They were looking up as well.

"Abel Tannatek?" one of them called.

"Yes," said Abel very calmly. "Yes, that is me."

"Get down here," the policeman said. "We're here to arrest you
for murder. Everything you say from now on . . ."

"My God," Abel said with half smile, "you actually say that in
real life?"

He looked at Micha. And then he looked at Anna. She saw that
he was holding the gun. She heard the release of the safety catch.

"Anna," he said. And he lifted the weapon and took aim.

She was too surprised to react.

Or, maybe she wasn't surprised at all.

She didn't hear the shot. The world became strangely silent. That was how she saw the storyteller for the last time—in an absolutely silent world, in a staircase. He'd hit his target.

When she fell into darkness, she knew that she would never see him again.

She'd loved him to the very end.

18

The Storyteller
ॐ

"THEY STOOD AT THE EDGE OF THE ICE, YOU KNOW, and looked over at the mainland. It was so close and yet so far away that they could never reach it. And behind them, the cutter came closer and closer. They could hear her golden skates scratching over the ice.

"'So I will drown,' the little queen said. She jumped into the ice-cold water headfirst, and the blind white cat, whose absolute blindness several people had begun to doubt, shook her head. 'Tz-tz-tz,' the cat hissed, and then she rolled into a ball on the ice and fell asleep. The asking man and the answering man put their hands in front of each other's faces so as not to see the little queen drown.

"Only the rose girl acted. She jumped into the water after the little queen, without thinking twice.

"She found her hand in the roaring stream, a small, helpless, royal hand, and they clung to each other. But they couldn't swim against the current. It was much too strong, and the water was much too icy. And then they felt something pulling them; there was something pulling them against the current. The rose girl managed to lift her head out of the water and saw the sea lion's head next to them. He had sunk his teeth into the little queen's sleeve and was swimming against the stream. And suddenly, she could feel herself moving toward the shore. The rose girl saw the sea lion fighting the water. He needed all his strength to pull her and the little queen along. He was a strong swimmer, but the current was stronger. She tried to help him, tried to swim by herself, but he shook his head. 'Hold still,' his golden eyes begged. 'It's easier if you're still. You can't help me.'

"So she held still, and the little queen held still as well, and the cutter stood on the ice, watching them. She lifted her hand and made a barely perceptible movement, and the little queen and the rose girl both knew that the movement was a signal, that she was calling someone—the ocean riders. The ocean riders on their sea-grass-green and snow-white horses, who would come to restore the order they believed to be justified.

"The current tugged at the three, trying to drag them away. It hit them and bit them and drooled on them greedily, but in the end they reached the shore. With the last of his strength, the sea lion crept onto the beach, and there he lay, limp and motionless. The rose girl got up and started patting him, to bring life back into his body; and the little queen laid her hand on his neck, so that he knew she was there and that he'd managed to get her onto land safely.

"When she did this, he lifted his head.

"And on the other side of the stream, the ocean riders dashed over the ice. At its edge, they stopped their horses, who reared and whinnied. Maybe it wasn't true. Maybe it was only a rumor that the ocean riders could gallop over the water. Or maybe the current was just too strong here, even for them.

"The cutter pointed at the little group on the mainland. 'Do you see the sea lion?' they heard her say. 'He took them over there, the silver-gray sea lion with the blue eyes.'

"The rose girl looked into his eyes. They weren't golden anymore; they'd frozen to blue ice. At this moment, one of the ocean riders lifted his rifle—they all carried hunting rifles—and a shot rang out over the water. With the sound came a bullet, and that bullet hit the sea lion between the eyes.

"'No!' the little queen screamed, and she jumped up. Before the next shooter could fire his deadly rifle, tears sprang from her eyes and fell down into the stream, flooding it. And it became so warm that the rest of the ocean warmed up in milliseconds. For someone who has a diamond for a heart also has tears that are as warm as the sun. The ice melted in an instant, and the ocean riders sank into the sea, together with the cutter. Then the current carried them away, along with the asking man and the answering man and the sleeping white cat and the lighthouse keeper, who had still been lying somewhere on the ice.

"The little queen and the rose girl watched them drift away. They would never find out what happened to them in the end.

"Finally, they turned and started to walk away from the sea. The rose girl had lifted the sea lion up and was carrying him with her. But he wasn't a sea lion anymore.

"He had changed into a human being.

"'He saved me,' the little queen said.

"'He saved us,' the rose girl said.

"'But he lost himself in the process,' said the little queen. 'He will never know that he saved us. And I will cry. I don't cry now because all of my tears have fallen into the ocean. There will be more tears, though, growing inside me, and I will cry them all my life. I still don't know what death means, but my sea lion knows it now . . .'

"'Don't cry,' the rose girl begged. 'Don't cry all your life, little queen. He does know that he saved us. He will stay with us. As a memory. Do you see the house up there on the cliff?'

"The little queen swallowed the tears that had already started to grow back. 'Yes,' she replied. 'I see it. It's beautiful. There are roses in the garden, and someone is feeding the robins.'

"'Do you hear the music spilling from the windows as well?' the rose girl asked. 'Piano and flute. You could live there. You could live in that house and play music instead of crying.'

"And the little queen nodded."

"And that's the end of the fairy tale?" Micha asked.

"That's the end of the fairy tale."

"No," Micha said and stood up. "No, that's not the end. Because, you know, the little queen decided something else. She didn't want that diamond heart anymore. She exchanged it for a normal heart. The diamond heart she put on the sea lion's grave."

"That was a very good idea."

"So . . . did it end well, in some ways?"

"Yes, it did . . . in some ways. It was the sea lion's greatest wish that the little queen would reach the mainland. And his wish was fulfilled, and, I think, in the end he was happy."

She stood up, too. They'd been sitting on folding chairs in the yard, watching the robins, but when Micha had jumped up, all the robins had flown away.

"I can hear the piano," Micha said. "Linda's playing. I think I'll go in and help her. I have to think of something else now, quickly, otherwise . . ."

"Go ahead and help Linda with the piano," Anna replied. "I'm going to stay here a little longer."

She closed her eyes and saw the landing on the fifth floor again. She couldn't help it.

She saw Abel standing there. He smiled. She saw that he was holding the gun. She heard the release of the safety catch.

"Anna," he said. And he lifted the weapon. It was then that she understood his way out and why he'd asked her what would become of Micha. He hadn't wanted to leave like Michelle, not without taking care of everything first. He put the barrel of the gun into his mouth. He didn't hesitate, not for one second. She didn't hear the shot. The world became strangely silent, and she fell into a cold darkness, dark like the ocean deep . . . deep under the ice.

The darkness only lasted for seconds, maybe not even that long. She opened her eyes, and, up there on the landing, he wasn't standing anymore. She looked down the stairs and saw that Linda had buried her face in her hands. She saw that Bertil wanted to come up the stairs, saw Magnus grab his arm and hold him back, his grip as firm as steel. None of the policemen moved. She thought she should have run. But she didn't.

It was Micha who ran.

She freed herself from Anna's arms and ran up the stairs, and Anna followed her, climbing the steps very slowly. She saw him lying there, saw the blood in which he lay, so incomprehensibly red, light red—big, burst droplets of blood the color of poppies. A sea of blood, a red endless sea, crimson waves, carmine froth, splashing color . . . Micha was kneeling next to his legs and had laid her arms and her head on his knees, where there was no blood. And she was singing, very, very softly.

Just a tiny little pain,
Three days of heavy rain,
Three days of sunlight,
Everything will be all right.
Just a tiny little pain . . .

And Anna asked herself, were the words running out of Abel's head with the blood, all the words he'd wanted to weave into stories later . . . later, always later. Words that could have been written in summer by the sea . . . in Ludwigsburg, in a secret hiding place between the beach grass; or in a student apartment in some faraway city; or on a journey around the world. Shouldn't she be saving the words somehow, collecting them? All the words . . . the words of the storyteller. She stood there very still, next to Micha, and it broke her heart to hear Micha sing. The place in her, though, where her tears should have come from, was rough and dry. No, she didn't find any tears in herself to cry for the storyteller.

The storyteller didn't exist anymore.

They buried him a week after the thirteenth of March. After his eighteenth birthday. Anna put a bouquet of anemones on his grave, a bouquet of spring. Linda held Micha's hand the whole time, and Micha held Mrs. Margaret's hand . . . Mrs. Margaret, in her blue-and-white-flower-patterned dress. Anna didn't hold anybody's hand. She walked next to Magnus in silence, without looking at him.

Micha's uncle didn't care where she lived. He signed all the necessary papers with a resigned shrug. So she would be adopted. Micha Tannatek would change into Micha Leemann. She'd reached the mainland as Abel had wanted her to. She would never go through what he'd gone through.

And still, Anna searched for tears inside herself.

Abel's picture was on the wall above the chimney now, the one good photo Micha had found of him. She'd insisted they have it framed and hang it there, so Abel could see what she was doing all day long. So he would stay with them. And every time Anna passed that picture, she thought she'd find her tears. But they never came. She must have used them up while Abel was alive, for now that he was dead, there were none left. They had talked for the longest time, Magnus and Linda and her. Everybody knew everything now. Or did everybody know nothing? Nobody knew anything . . . Nobody could know everything.

Anna still played the flute, but she didn't practice the pieces she should have practiced. Instead, she played the simple melodies of Leonard Cohen. She still didn't know if she'd ever be able to ask Knaake about him. Or whether he would wake up again. Finals had become irrelevant. She'd decide later whether to take them . . . and when. Linda and Magnus didn't press her. Maybe, Anna thought, she wouldn't go to university. Maybe she'd do something different altogether. She just had to figure out what. She'd talk to Gitta about that when she felt ready.

Bertil called for a while, but Anna never answered, and finally she changed her number. She felt sorry for him, but she couldn't help him.

Leonard Cohen sang from one of the scratched LPs,

Baby I've been here before,
I know this room, I've walked this floor
I used to live alone before I knew you
I've seen your flag on the marble arch
But love is not some kind of victory march
No it's a cold and a very broken Hallelujah
Hallelujah, Hallelujah . . .

Somewhere in a parallel world, things were different.

Somewhere in a parallel world, Abel hadn't fired that last shot. Possibly, he hadn't fired the one before it either, the one that killed Sören Marinke. And Knaake had never fallen through the ice over the shipping channel. And if these two things hadn't happened . . . the last shot hadn't. Somewhere in a parallel world, Abel was in prison, maybe for a long time . . . maybe he was in therapy . . . therapy that didn't heal anything but brought some things in order. Time couldn't change the past, but it brought peace. And parallel Anna . . . she waited.

She was waiting for him when he took his first step back into the normal world. She watched him walk toward her, a smile in his winter-ice eyes. She had long since grown up. They married on a February morning as clear as crystal. Micha was their only witness. They sent her postcards from their journey around the world . . . from the desert and several remote islands. Later, Micha often visited them, an adult Micha with a husband and two children. And in the house where Anna and Abel lived, somewhere at the end of a quiet, green lane, there were children as well. Laughing kids, badly behaved kids, dirty and loud kids, who ran through the yard, lighthearted. There were a lot of flowers in the garden, but no roses, and the only songbird to never stray there was the robin.

She told him about the garden when she visited his grave. He lay there, in the slowly stirring March earth, a piece of dead matter. But in their parallel world, they lived on, side by side. She developed each part of their parallel world in meticulous detail . . . the sunflowers in a vase, the late afternoon light coming in through a window, glasses he wore when he was older, a shelf full of books, a faded leather armchair.

Nothing was perfect, but everything was all right. The light was never just blue.

And the snow that fell onto the roof in winter . . . it fell softly . . . softly . . . and it covered the house, the armchair, the books, the children's voices. It covered Anna and Abel, covered their parallel world, and everything was, finally, very, very quiet.

About the Author

ANTONIA MICHAELIS is the author of *Tiger Moon*, which was the winner of an ALA/ALSC Batchelder Honor Award and was named a *Kirkus Reviews* Best Book. In a starred review, *Booklist* said of her novel *Dragons of Darkness*, "Michaelis deftly interweaves magic and realism in an intricate, provocative story that explores the connections between people and events, the allure and dangers of uncompromising idealism, and the power of love." She lives with her family in Germany.

This book was designed by Maria T. Middleton. The text is set in 11-point Adobe Jenson, an old-style typeface designed by the fifteenth-century French printer Nicolas Jenson. Redrawn in the 1990s by type designer Robert Slimbach, Adobe Jenson remains a highly legible face with a distinct calligraphic character. The display typeface is Celestia Antique.

This book was printed and bound by R.R. Donnelley in Crawfordsville, Indiana. Its production was overseen by Erin Vandeveer.